Guillermo tried to clear away the mists that eddied through his head like early-morning ground fog. Where was he?

Intubation completed, the anesthesiologist slipped a mask in place and began to administer a mix of oxygen and nitrous oxide. In any hospital in America, the team would also have been hooking up an array of sensors: fingertip pulse detector, temple disks to monitor EKG, nasal-tracheal temperature probe, automated blood pressure cuff. This was not a hospital, though, nor was patient survival an issue.

Guillermo, deep in a narcolepsis from which there would be no return, never felt the incision that neatly split his skin from collarbone to groin. Nor the sharp bite of the knives and forceps that peeled the layers of muscles sheathing his rib cage. Nor did he hear the snarl of the air-driven saw as it began to cleave his sternum.

Twenty-eight minutes later, the surgeon peeled off his blood-smeared latex gloves. The anesthesiologist and the scrub nurse began wrestling what remained of Guillermo into a body bag.

The PDA was still uploading the worksheet when Marta heard a commotion at the back of the van. They were bringing the night's second patient. Darn, she thought; from the sound of it, the chloroform had worn off early on this one.

"A well-plotted and exciting medical thriller . . . top-notch"
—*The Knoxville News-Sentinel*

Books by Tony Chiu

FICTION
Port Arthur Chicken
Realm Seven
Bright Shark (with Robert Ballard)

NON-FICTION
Ross Perot: In His Own Words
PEOPLE Celebrates People
(edited by Richard B. Stolley)
CBS: The First 50 Years

POSITIVE MATCH

MATCH

TONY CHIU

BANTAM BOOKS
NEW YORK • TORONTO • LONDON
SYDNEY • AUCKLAND

This edition contains the complete text
of the original hardcover edition.
NOT ONE WORD HAS BEEN OMITTED.

POSITIVE MATCH
A Bantam Book

PUBLISHING HISTORY
Bantam hardcover edition published September 1997
Bantam paperback edition / July 1998

ISBN-0-553-57546-5

Published simultaneously in the United States and Canada

Bantam Books are published by Bantam Books, a division of Bantam
Doubleday Dell Publishing Group, Inc. Its trademark, consisting of the
words "Bantam Books" and the portrayal of a rooster, is Registered in
U.S. Patent and Trademark Office and in other countries. Marca
Registrada. Bantam Books, 1540 Broadway, New York, New York 10036.

PRINTED IN THE UNITED STATES OF AMERICA

OPM   10 9 8 7 6 5 4 3 2

Thanks, Mom

POSITIVE
MATCH

IT was a good night to cross. Or so the Mexican teenager told himself as he tried to quiet his runaway heart, tried to work up saliva to soothe his parched throat. An hour after sundown, the desert floor was still warm to the touch. The darkness, though, had grown deep and seamless enough to cloak an entire army of liver-eaters. Guillermo Chacon did not normally rattle easily, having reached the age of seventeen in the southernmost state of Chiapas, where the insurrection was in its fourth year. But tonight was not just another rally against the greedy *patrones* or another protest march against the corrupt *militares*. Tonight he would take the first steps toward a new life in America.

Was it too late to turn back?

Guillermo was flat on his belly atop a ridge less than one kilometer from the promised land. Yet he could only sense, rather than see, *el norte*, for the clouds that had begun to thicken in late afternoon now blotted out the moon and the stars. All to the good, the guide known as

El Zopilote had insisted, as was the fact that at this time of year the Rio Grande flowed no higher than a man's thigh. According to the guide, even tonight's wind was friendly. It blew from Texas, which meant that if the green-shirts of *la migra*—the U.S. Border Patrol—lay in ambush, Guillermo would hear them before they heard him.

The teenager felt a tap on his shoulder.

"Here, have a look." El Zopilote, a grizzled former military officer of perhaps fifty, held out a pair of monstrous goggles.

Guillermo was familiar with such a night-vision device from countless Schwarzenegger and Van Damme movies. He was not prepared for its great weight, though, and had to brace his neck to keep his head upright as the guide secured the nylon straps.

There was still nothing before his eyes but blackness.

Then El Zopilote toggled a switch and Guillermo gasped as a glowing green landscape sprang to life. Just like in those movies, he marveled; not only did the goggles pierce the darkness, but they also seemed to pull an empty Coca-Cola can on the far bank to almost within reach. He began feeling a bit more confident about the evening ahead.

"Twenty-five-power magnification," the guide said. "Nice, eh?"

Guillermo nodded. He was trying to make sense of a world where sand and clumps of dried cattails were the color of a pale green apple; where trees and boulders took on a deep emerald hue; where water and sky appeared darker than the rind of a ripe watermelon. The terrain across the river looked as forbidding as the surface of the moon.

"Tell me, my young friend, do you see *la migra*?"

Guillermo shook his head.

"What about the liver-eaters?" El Zopilote was referring with obvious amusement to the evil spirits that were said to stalk the border in search of young runners to snatch and gut.

"No," Guillermo conceded sheepishly. He felt a reassuring pat on the back from El Zopilote, surely the best frontier-crossing guide in northern Mexico. Fewer than one in ten of his clients was caught and sent back, truly a miracle in an era when the border was like a combat zone. It had not always been thus. For instance, Guillermo's father's cousins, who lived in Mexicali, still talked of how for generations they had been invited across the river to *el norte* each fall to help with the harvest. Until, that is, the early 1990s, when those north of the border started to say that for every *campesino* coming to work the fields, two more sneaked across to steal free schooling for their children or free doctoring for their sick. Mistrust had quickly hardened into hatred, especially in California. Who in Mexico did not know of their infamous Proposition 187, which encouraged *los gabachos* to treat Guillermo's people little better than stray dogs? Who did not know of the forty-kilometer-long wall that separated the two countries from Portero far out into the Pacific Ocean itself?

The ever-tighter security at the border had forced many guides to find other lines of work.

Not El Zopilote, who succeeded in part because he refused to guide those who were diseased or unable to comprehend simple English words—those without hope of escaping notice in America. Guillermo himself was accepted only after a physical examination and a blood test confirmed he was in good health, with no sign of AIDS or tuberculosis. And though the teenager's schooling had stopped at age twelve he had acquired many *gringo* phrases from the cartoons and cable movies and baseball games pirated by the satellite dish of Don Joaquin, the village elder.

The second reason for El Zopilote's success was that he used *la migra*'s own weapons against them. For instance, his computer could see inside those of the Border

Patrol. Thus, he had known that for the last few nights
the green-shirts were swarming over this stretch of the
Rio Grande like maggots on a carcass. Guillermo and the
others had passed the time in Nueva Cuenca, a village far
from the river, practicing a video game on which their
safety depended. Rather than try to teach his mostly illiterate clients the use of a compass, the guide had loaned
each something the size and shape of a Nintendo Game
Boy. The units were actually directional receivers tuned
to a short-range transmitter planted at the pickup site
just off Texas State Highway 170.

Tonight El Zopilote's computer finally brought good
news: *la migra* was shifting their cordon thirty kilometers upriver, where their helicopter patrols had spotted
large numbers of runners massing across the river from
Ruidoso. After a light dinner, Guillermo's group piled
into a van for the long drive to this desolate staging area.

"It is almost the hour," El Zopilote said softly. "Will
you use your young eyes to check the other side again?"

Guillermo swung his head to the left and started a
slow sweep. By this time tomorrow, he thought, I will be
in Denver, far from the killing fields of Chiapas. His el-
dest brother had been the first to fall, shot by *militares*
dispersing a protest march; then his mother, caught in a
crossfire on her way back from market; and finally his
fiancée, when Zapatistas tried to rob the store where she
clerked. It was at Luisa's funeral eight months earlier that
he had vowed to leave his village and head north.

Guillermo's decision won the support of Don Joaquin.
The village elder had used his connections to locate El
Zopilote, and to negotiate a fair fee with the guide. He
had taken up a collection for the young man's slow bus
journey up the length of Mexico and for the crossing itself. He had even arranged a farewell party. Guillermo's
eyes moistened as he thought of the presents he had received that night: Le Tigre polo shirt, Levi's, Nikes, and
best of all, the digital Timex now on his wrist.

Only one in the village had opposed the trip: the outsider who had come the previous year to treat those maimed by the *militares*. Nguyen-Anh Dupree might have been a *norteamericano*, but he had the face of a martial-arts star, which was why most called him Dr. Kung-fu. Guillermo sometimes did errands for him. The frontier is very dangerous, he had warned; those tales of liver-eaters are not mere superstition. Dr. Dupree himself had heard of runners swallowed by the desert night; of long trucks, like those that brought the meat to the *carniceria*, in whose refrigerated vans unspeakable acts occurred; of guides grown fat by betraying their clients. Well, thought Guillermo, Dr. Dupree has not met my guide, a man of honor as well as great skill.

Suddenly the hairs on Guillermo's nape bristled: something more powerful than the wind was rustling the bushes on the far bank.

"What is it?"

Guillermo adjusted the focus, then let out his breath and said, in a voice tinged with relief, "A fox. Going to the river for water."

"Proof that El Zopilote's computer does not lie." The guide reached over to unstrap the goggles. "If *la migra* is in the hills, they are upwind of the fox, no? If so, does the fox dare leave cover to drink? Of course not. Come."

Guillermo followed him down from the ridge to where the other runners waited. There would be a dozen men crossing tonight. A few were as old as thirty, but most were teenagers like himself.

El Zopilote began by having them double-check their gear. Back in Nueva Cuenca he had given each a well-worn gym bag that would help the runner blend into his new hometown; Guillermo's bore the purple-and-white insignia of the Colorado Rockies baseball team. Did everyone's gym bag contain water and three granola bars? A watertight Ziploc containing false identity papers, bus ticket, and a hundred dollars in U.S. currency? Good. Was the directional receiver working? And the flashlight? Good.

"Now, take off your clothing and shoes and place them in your bag," the guide said. "You wet them in the river on a night like this, and it will take many hours for them to dry."

The runners exchanged uneasy glances.

"No, I will not send you to *el norte* naked as the day you are born," El Zopilote said, unzipping a large duffel. He pulled out a black nylon two-piece jogging outfit. "Fast-drying. Plus, with these on, you will be like ninjas, like the night itself. Lucky for me we have only true *mexicanos* tonight—no yellow-hairs—or I must buy black caps too."

The joke broke the tension; the runners were still chuckling as he passed out the last of the garments.

El Zopilote waited until they finished changing before reviewing his instructions one final time.

It is four kilometers to the pickup site, he said. Not a long walk, nor a perilous one, as long as you stay alert.

We begin at 2230 hours, when I start sending you across singly in five-minute intervals. Once on the far side, look for my red marker. He held up a penlike instrument, aimed it into the night, and clicked. A thin red laser beam split the darkness and splashed a glowing dot onto a distant boulder.

The marker will direct you to one of three arroyos that climb into the foothills, El Zopilote continued. The arroyos reach almost halfway to the pickup site. They are treacherous with rocks and deep ruts, so be sure to use your flashlight, since this is not the night to turn an ankle. But the arroyos are the safest way from the river, because *la migra* does not like to take their expensive new Jeeps down into them.

Just this side of the highway, he said, you will see a navy blue panel truck—your ride to El Paso. It will wait until 0300 hours. Should anyone fail to arrive because he is lost or injured, the driver will inform me and I will remain here at the staging area until that runner makes it back. "*Amigos,* if you miss the rendezvous, do not despair," the guide concluded. "There will be many other nights to try again, eh?"

El Zopilote consulted his watch, then led the runners to the top of the ridge overlooking the river. He strapped on his night-vision goggles and studied the far bank. At last he said, "Guillermo, have you the strength to be the first tonight?"

"Yes," Guillermo replied, his body thrumming with fresh adrenaline.

"Good. Then I await your postcard from Denver. *Vaya con Dios.*"

The two men embraced and then Guillermo was scrambling down the slope toward America.

BENDING aside the microphone of his headset, a man wearing a Lone Star Beer T-shirt, faded jeans, and lug-soled trail boots popped a stick of chewing gum into his mouth. He hated the wait, especially on nights like this, when the wind blew toward Mexico and he couldn't smoke because it might betray his presence. It was bad enough just worrying about the Border Patrol. If those bastards stumbled across him they would demand to know what he was doing out here at this hour in an electric golf cart with a shitload of exotic equipment. What could he say—that he was a *National Geographic* photographer like the guy Clint Eastwood played a few years ago, the one who chased around Iowa after that broad from the rafting movie?

The man checked his watch again. It was finally 2230 hours.

Another day, another dollar, he thought, reaching for a cylindrical unit that looked like a radar gun. He climbed up on the seat of his golf cart, anchored his left elbow in a cleft in the rocks, and readjusted his headset into a more comfortable position. As he powered up the Starlight nightscope and squinted into the eyepiece, his lips tightened into a mirthless smile.

Right on schedule, the first runner was working his way down a ridge toward the river. The slim, barefooted figure was clad in black and would have been impossible to spot with ordinary binoculars. But through the scope, the large X on the front of the runner's nylon shell—made with an ink visible only through an infrared lens—shimmered like a pale-green neon sign.

He tilted the scope up a few degrees and locked on a cluster of figures standing atop the ridge. They were out to bag three runners tonight, the ones who had tested out as the healthiest and strongest. Confirming that two other shirts were also inked with Xs, he returned his attention to the river.

The first runner was just now wading out of the water and moving up to dry land. He knelt to kiss the Texas soil, then sat, opened his gym bag, and took out a pair of shoes. They look brand-new, thought the man; enjoy 'em while you can, my little wetback.

The runner knotted the laces and stood. He glanced around for a few moments, then started for the northernmost arroyo.

The man in the Lone Star T-shirt swung the headset microphone close to his mouth and keyed the unit. "Eagle One here," he whispered. "Our pal's done his usual outstanding job painting the targets."

"Amen," replied Eagle Two. "Whoever he is, we ought to hire him to prep our next turkey shoot."

Now Eagle Three keyed into the loop: "Looks like the first *cholo*'s coming your way, Eagle One. Good hunting."

"I roger that. Eagle One out."

The man powered down the scope and lowered himself onto the seat of the golf cart. He had forty-five minutes to kill. Damn, he could use a cigarette. Instead, he popped another stick of gum, released the vehicle's brake, and stepped on the accelerator. The cart glided away with a whine too faint to carry on the wind.

*   *   *

ONCE past the steep climb at river's edge, Guillermo found the trail less difficult than El Zopilote had described. The arroyo was indeed strewn with obstacles, but he could easily pick a path with the thin beam of his Mag flashlight. The young Mexican was sweating heavily. It was no longer nerves; the nylon jogging suit was simply too heavy for this hot, clammy night. Yet he didn't mind, because ten minutes earlier his ears had picked up the first faint drone of traffic on Texas State Highway 170.

How far had he come? Far enough for a drink of water. He dug out the bottle and treated himself to a long tug. Then he pulled the directional receiver from his back pocket. El Zopilote had warned them the devices might not work until they were clear of the arroyos, but Guillermo couldn't resist. The light-gray screen glowed to life to reveal a pulsing black triangle—just like in the practice sessions back in Nueva Cuenca.

Confidence renewed, Guillermo stowed his gear and resumed his trek. He allowed his mind to wander to the things he had to do in the days ahead. As soon as he arrived in Denver, he must find the post office. El Zopilote had asked to be sent a postcard. Then there was the letter of thanks to Don Joaquin, accompanied by a bag of sweets or several packs of Marlboros. Finally, he would write Dr. Dupree of how he had outwitted the liver-eaters. Or might that offend the *norteamericano*, who had meant well no matter how scary the stories he told? Perhaps the note to Dr. Dupree needed more thought.

Up ahead, the arroyo veered off to the left. Forty minutes earlier Guillermo would have anxiously probed the darkness with the flashlight before proceeding; now he did not even hesitate.

He was ten paces past the bend when he heard a soft click behind him, like a pebble bouncing off a rock.

He snapped off the flashlight and froze.

Guillermo had never been as numb with fear, not even when Luisa's father had caught them together, naked, in the grove beyond the fields. Be brave, he thought, struggling to control his bladder. Eight . . . nine . . . ten. If it was an animal, or *la migra*, surely something would have happened by now. He permitted himself a shallow breath.

There was the noise again.

Guillermo wanted to flee. Instead, moving with agonizing slowness to keep his nylon outfit from rustling, he turned and pointed the flashlight in the direction of the sounds.

He mouthed a prayer and flicked on the beam.

A split-second glimpse of a shiny metal pole tucked behind an outcrop of rock and then his eyes were assaulted by a flash of pure white energy that exploded not with the sharp crack of lightning but the soft pop of a soda bottle being uncapped. The young Mexican staggered backward and caught his left heel in a rut and then he was falling and thudding to the ground with enough force to drive the wind from his lungs.

Though blinded and dazed, Guillermo was dimly aware of a new sound: footsteps crunching ever nearer. Suddenly a strong arm was encircling his chest from behind and pulling him upward. A brief whiff of stale tobacco, cologne, and chewing gum but before he could scream his face was smothered by a cloth that carried a stench as vile as the devil's breath. No matter which way Guillermo twisted there was no escaping the pungent fumes that made him light-headed and sick to his stomach.

The man in the Lone Star T-shirt felt his prey surrender to the chloroform. He lowered the limp body to the ground and waited for his high to subside before raising one of the runner's lids and beaming a penlight onto the pupil. It remained dilated. Out cold, so there was no need to duct-tape the kid's mouth. Good. Gags had been discouraged ever since one runner reacted badly to the chloroform and choked to death on his own vomit.

Hoisting the young Mexican into a fireman's carry, he labored up a steep path to the rim of the arroyo, where he had parked the golf cart.

The cart's passenger seat featured several unusual custom accessories: a lap belt with two wrist cuffs and, anchored to the floorboard, a pair of ankle cuffs. The restraints were made of rip-resistant 400-denier Cordura fabric and fastened by way of a special noiseless Velcro developed by U.S. Army researchers in the late 1980s to improve battlefield security.

After strapping in the unconscious runner, he returned to the arroyo to retrieve the kid's gym bag and flashlight, as well as the tripod-mounted stroboscopic flash that he had fired to trigger the ambush.

With the aid of his scope, the man crept the cart away from the river. On reaching a narrow trail that paralleled the Rio Grande, he stopped, pulled on his headset, and keyed the unit: "Van, this is Eagle One. Bagged my quota for the night and am raring to come in. Any Smokies out and about?"

"That's a negative, Eagle One. You are good to go."

The man in the Lone Star T-shirt breathed easier; no Border Patrol bastards had entered this sector. "I roger that, Van. Eagle One out." He switched on a small spotlight mounted on the front of the cart, turned left onto the trail, and sped off to collect his bounty.

Two minutes short of his destination, he stopped and doused the spotlight. He lit a cigarette and inhaled deeply before opening the kid's gym bag. It contained clothing, a water bottle, a new Bible printed in Spanish, and a Ziploc bag that held papers, a bus ticket, and cash. The cash was off-limits—back at the van, Phil would be counting it to make sure all one hundred bucks was there—and who the hell needed a Trailways ticket to Denver? And damn, no Walkman or electric razor or designer sunglasses, like some of the runners carried. He rezipped the bag and played his penlight on the kid's wristwatch. A crappy Timex, but new enough to give one of the nephews for Christmas, so he pocketed it. He took a last drag from his cigarette, switched on the spotlight again, and floored the accelerator.

The hum of a massive compressor was audible before he rounded the final bend. He skirted several parked vehicles—a late-model minivan, two pickup trucks, his own 750cc Harley-Davidson—and approached the source of the hum, a long refrigeration van rigged to a Peterbilt cab. The van bore license plates from each of the four states along the U.S.–Mexican border. It was unmarked, as always. Each time, though, they painted a new sign on the door of the cab; tonight's read: ALAMO ICE CREAM FACTORY, SAN ANTONIO, TX.

He continued around to the rear of the van and parked at the base of a ramp that led up to the open back doors. The man had a pretty good idea of what went on in there but tried not to think about it too often.

Two men in polo shirts and Bermuda shorts emerged from the darkened interior and hurried down the ramp.

The baby-faced one got into the cart and drove it up the ramp.

Phil, who was stocky and in his late thirties, approached holding out an envelope.

"Thanks, Phil. Hey, any idea when you all are fixing to do this again?"

Phil shrugged.

The man in the Lone Star T-shirt tried to hide his disappointment; the kids needed stuff for the new school year, and another fast six hundred bucks would come in handy. "Well, see you around."

"Yeah. See you around." As Phil climbed back up the ramp he heard a motorcycle coughing to life and roaring away. He hurried through the darkened rear of the van, where they stored the golf carts, and pushed through a metal door.

He squinted while his eyes adjusted to the bright circular halogen light that was suspended over a full-scale operating table on which the young Mexican lay. The temperature in this room was a good thirty-five degrees cooler, thanks to the van's massive refrigeration unit.

Two men—the anesthesiologist and the baby-faced scrub nurse who had driven the cart up the ramp—were cutting away the runner's nylon jogging outfit.

The circulating nurse, a pleasant-looking woman in her late thirties named Marta, had already donned a surgical gown. She was standing before the built-in shelving that covered one wall of the van. On the shelves sat some two dozen aluminum-sided containers that looked like picnic coolers fitted with dials and gauges. Each bore a decal that read PROPERTY OF MEDEX. She finished checking one last gauge, then picked up a rather shopworn device the size of a paperback book. It was a personal digital assistant, or PDA, a handheld computer lacking a keyboard and mouse; the user operated it by touching the screen with a stylus.

Earlier Marta had started a file on each of tonight's patients, using the blood- and tissue-typing data furnished to MedEx by some Mexican border-crossing guide. "Phil," she said, "mind giving me a hand ID'ing this one?"

Phil opened the runner's gym bag and dug out the false identity papers: "Guillermo Echeverria, it says here."

Marta used the stylus to pop the Echeverria worksheet up on-screen.

"We about ready to go?" asked Phil.

"Two minutes," replied the anesthesiologist. He started to prep the patient for an IV needle. "Damn, I think the chloroform's wearing off."

"So get the drip started. I'll go fetch Lester." Phil opened the locker containing the disposable surgical gowns and the black neoprene body bags. He pulled on a gown, went to the front of the van and knocked lightly on a door, then continued to the sink to begin his scrub.

A tall, balding man in his mid-fifties emerged from his

makeshift office with a CD in his hand. Like many surgeons, Lester Haidak preferred to operate to music. "I thought we'd start the evening up-tempo," he said, adjusting his horn-rimmed glasses. "*The Big Chill* soundtrack. Any objections?" Hearing none, he slid the disc into a boom box and joined Phil at the sink.

It was the prick of the IV needle that brought Guillermo back to the cusp of consciousness—along with the opening chords of "I Heard It Through the Grapevine." Do they have parties at the offices of *la migra*? he wondered groggily. And how could it be so cold if the sun is shining brightly enough to burn through my closed lids? A mosquito was attacking the inside of his left elbow. Guillermo went to scratch it, but his right arm wouldn't move. He forced his eyes open, then quickly shut them against the merciless glare of the overhead halogen light.

"Not a problem," the anesthesiologist announced as the patient began to squirm. "The penny's kicking in."

Guillermo, unaware of the Pentothal now coursing through his veins, tried to clear away the mists that eddied through his head like early-morning ground fog. Where was he? Mindful of the painful light above him, he cautiously cracked open an eye. Slowly things swam into focus. Instead of the green-shirts of *la migra*, he saw *norteamericanos* in the kind of gowns and caps and masks they wore on the doctor shows that Don Joaquin so enjoyed watching. Instead of a mosquito biting his elbow, he saw a needle from which a thin clear plastic tube snaked. And just beyond his arm he saw a cart that held glistening instruments like the ones in Dr. Dupree's clinic, as well as a power drill fitted with a circular blade.

Not all *gringos* are cruel beasts, he thought gratefully. These kind doctors are going to repair the wounds caused by my attacker. A curiously euphoric lethargy was making his eyes heavy again, too heavy to keep open. His thoughts drifted to the panel truck filled with anxious runners waiting near the highway, to El Zopilote waiting back at the staging area. He was letting them all down, and his guilt made him weep. Suddenly his chest and belly felt cool and tingly, like when his mother would wipe his fever-racked body with a damp towel. Guillermo found the memory comforting and tried to hold on to it as the bright red glow that suffused his lids faded to dark gray and then to black.

In fact, the tingly sensation experienced by Guillermo was the surgical team beginning its pre-op scrub and drape. Normally they would wait until the anesthetics had taken, but on nights like this, speed had a higher priority than protocol.

The anesthesiologist injected the patient with suc-cinylcholine, then spritzed a weak cocaine solution inside his throat and fed a tube down his windpipe. Intubation completed, he slipped a mask in place and began to administer a mix of oxygen and nitrous oxide; halothane was also on hand should something stronger be needed. In any hospital in America, the team would also have been hooking up an array of sensors: fingertip pulse detector, temple disks to monitor EKG, nasal-tracheal temperature probe, automated blood pressure cuff. This was not a hospital, though, nor was patient survival an issue.

On the boom box, Marvin Gaye gave way to the Temptations.

The anesthesiologist picked up a battery-operated taser that was a miniature version of the stun guns that the Los Angeles police officers had wielded on Rodney King. He touched the prongs lightly to the patient's right cheek and fired a charge. No reaction. He switched the instrument to the left cheek and fired again. No reaction.

"He's all yours, Lester," the anesthesiologist announced.

Haidak held out his gloved right hand, palm up. The circulating nurse, Marta, passed him a scalpel.

Guillermo, deep in a narcolepsis from which there would be no return, never felt the incision that neatly split his skin from collarbone to groin. Nor the sharp bite of the knives and forceps that unpeeled the layers of muscle sheathing his rib cage. Nor did he hear the snarl of the air-driven saw as it began to cleave his sternum.

Twenty-eight minutes later, Haidak peeled off his blood-smeared latex gloves. "How much time before the next one?"

"They're probably outside now," Phil replied.

"Aw, Christ." From carriage-trade surgeon to foreman of an abattoir, he thought. Haidak ripped off his disposable gown, balled it along with the gloves and gauze mask into a bundle, and stalked off to his office.

The anesthesiologist and the scrub nurse began wrestling what remained of Guillermo into a body bag.

Phil quickly slipped out of his surgical gear, retrieved Haidak's bundle, and dropped both into the body bag. Then he grabbed another envelope containing six hundred-dollar bills and headed for the rear of the van.

The circulating nurse, Marta, reviewed the Echeverria worksheet on the screen of her PDA. Then she carefully cross-referenced the inventory she had compiled during the surgery against the contents of nine aluminum-sided containers: liver; kidneys (two); pancreas; lungs (two); bone marrow (650 cc's); corneas (two); heart. Given more time, she thought with regret, they could have harvested parts for homeostatic transplants as well: the intestines, bone, cartilage and connective tissue, and skin.

Marta hurried over to the briefcase that MedEx always placed aboard the van. It contained a battery-powered satellite uplink. Remote areas like this were great for performing harvests but terrible for telecommunications, since the low population density discouraged cell-phone providers from installing relays. She jacked the PDA into the Comsat Mobile Link, then used the stylus to pop the communications software up on-screen and tap SEND. It was always frustrating to wait for the built-in modem to initialize, for the auto-dialing, for the link to be established, for the host to answer and exchange handshakes. Minutes mattered. Though each organ had already been matched with a recipient of the same tissue type, it took time to solve the logistical nightmare of rapidly dispatching the many containers they would fill tonight from here on the border to Dallas and then to destinations all across America.

Finally, fresh words appeared on-screen:

> WELCOME TO MEDEX.
> ENTER PASSWORD:

She hand-printed her maiden name.

> NAME OF FILE TO SEND:

She hand-printed *ALAMO.1*.

The PDA was still uploading the Echeverria worksheet when Marta heard a commotion at the back of the van. They were bringing in the night's second patient. Darn, she thought; from the sound of it, the chloroform had worn off early on this one.

T U E S D A Y
S E P T E M B E R   2 2

THE swimmer had been grinding laps in an outdoor pool in downtown Phoenix for a half hour now. It was a gorgeous early autumn afternoon, but with school back in session and the tourist trade in Arizona slack until Thanksgiving, he had the pool of the Best Western to himself. Though in his late forties and on the burly side, the man was fit enough to wear racing Speedos without embarrassment. The lycra trunks, combined with the Barracuda anti-fog goggles and the Rolex Oyster on his right wrist, set him apart at a hotel whose idea of room service was telephones programmed to speed-dial the nearest Pizza Hut.

Nearing the deep end again, Leonard Reifsnyder angled downward and kick-turned off the wall into a crawl. Up and down the pool he dashed until his cardiovascular system was near collapse. Hard exercise helped him manage stress—and topping the evening's agenda was a meeting on which his company's fate hinged. Reifsnyder gathered his rubbery legs, grabbed the curved rails of the ladder, and hoisted himself out of the pool.

Up in his room he turned on CNN. The commercial that filled the screen was for Senior Depot, a new chain of superstores that offered deep discounts on products like bifocal glasses, aluminum walkers, Efferdent, and Depend adult diapers. He muted the sound and dug out the business card of the vice-president of a local health maintenance organization.

Reifsnyder was a cofounder and chief financial officer of a health-care corporation called Caduceus 21. Hillary and Bill Clinton's attempts to reform the industry had died the death of a thousand lobbyists, but his company was proving daily that quality medicine could be delivered at below-market prices. As a result, many faltering local hospitals and health plans were clamoring to affiliate with it. Among them: Valley of the Sun Wellness Alliance. Reifsnyder's interest in the HMO was nil, but he had needed an excuse to travel west this week and the Phoenix group had jumped at the chance to open its books to him.

He went to the telephone and punched in the number on the business card.

"Stan Krieger here."

"Stan? Len Reifsnyder. Glad I caught you. Look, sorry for the short notice, but I need to ask for a raincheck on dinner. My stomach's acting up a bit."

"You know, I told Bettina that I thought you looked a little pale. Why don't you come in and we'll do a quick workup."

"No need," Reifsnyder replied. "Just an occupational hazard for us road warriors. If God had meant us to eat airline food, He'd have given us Teflon stomachs. I'll be fine."

"Are you sure?"

"Stan, I'm staring at the biggest bottle of Kaopectate you've ever seen," Reifsnyder said. "Heck, if I didn't have your three-year projections to work through, I'd be in bed already. We still on for the morning? Good. See you on the practice tee at eight-thirty."

The next call was home, to Knoxville, Tennessee. His twin nieces, whom he and his wife were raising, were eager to report on their day in school. When he finally rang off, he instructed the front desk to hold all calls.

Reifsnyder stepped out of his trunks and quickly showered off the chlorine from the pool. He was pulling on a fresh shirt and slacks when CNN began its bottom-of-the-hour recap.

The White House was vowing that eighty percent of the American forces in Cuba would be home by Christmas. The Vatican confirmed that the new pope's first Asian tour would include Hong Kong, though the city had been under martial law since Beijing annexed it in 1997. An amateur videotaper had caught a Supreme Court justice outside a porn shop in Virginia, stowing a shopping bag full of cassettes in the trunk of his Corvette. The exiled queen of Jordan had arrived at a medical center in Portland, Oregon, to undergo sophisticated tests. And the Dow Jones, still unable to sustain a rally from its Wild Wednesday market crash earlier that year, was up less than a point.

The last two items struck Reifsnyder as particularly auspicious omens for his company.

The Jordanian queen had fled to Geneva in the first weeks of the Palestinian uprising that followed her husband's death. Her choice of hospital was a public-relations coup for Caduceus 21, which had been managing the Portland complex for less than four years. Before, its staff physicians included many FMGs, or foreign medical graduates of schools in places like Grenada and Guadalajara, and it ran annual deficits that generous government subsidies could not shrink. Today it was the city's most profitable medical center. And its facilities, which now included the premier organ-transplant program in the Pacific Northwest, had attracted several renowned specialists, including the endocrinologist whom the U.S. State Department had persuaded to treat the American-born queen.

Turnarounds like Portland had helped the privately held Caduceus 21 blossom into an $825-million-a-year firm since its founding in late 1989. That success was based on the innovative solutions it had devised to the industry's most pressing problem, runaway costs.

The conventional answer was consolidation, in order to achieve economies of scale. That is, a chain could better bargain for equipment and drugs than a single hospital negotiating for itself; an HMO could better control fees if its subscribers were treated by contract doctors who billed less per visit in return for a guaranteed number of visits. But a decade's worth of health-care mergers and takeovers had produced a consumer backlash. There was mounting anecdotal evidence of what critics called "bean-counter's disease": arbitrary limitations geared more to the bottom line than to patient welfare. Women recuperating from childbirth had told of being asked to vacate the maternity ward in just twenty-four hours. Accident victims told of being ambulanced not to the nearest ER but to the closest hospital affiliated with their health plan. Health-plan subscribers told of being denied reimbursement for consulting a specialist not under contract with their group—even when their group didn't have such specialists.

Caduceus 21 dared set a different compass. It was an inescapable fact that more than three quarters of America's annual medical budget went to treating less than ten percent of the population, the newly born and the nearly dead. Reifsnyder had few peers in axing waste. Yet he knew few savings were to be gained by nickel-and-diming the ninety percent whose maladies generally ran to fevers and broken bones and appendectomies.

True health-care reform rested on rethinking medical practices with high price tags but low success rates: the neonatology team battling to keep alive an incompletely developed baby born fifteen weeks prematurely, the intensive-care unit sustaining a comatose patient sure to flatline as soon as the plug was pulled. As a New York physician had written in an Op-Ed article several years ago, "Letting people die from serious, life-threatening diseases that cannot be cured or even reasonably treated without great expense is not necessarily a bad thing."

But though the medical profession accepted the concept of triage, the general public did not. In the early 1990s the Oregon legislature, seeking to stretch dwindling federal Medicare funds, had proposed rationing health care; the state would guarantee payments only for treatments that demonstrably extended—not just prolonged—lives. The measure was defeated.

What government was not allowed to try, the private sector could. Reifsnyder and the other cofounders had created Caduceus 21 as an experiment in shifting the lion's share of resources from staving off the deaths of a few to curing the sicknesses of many. That philosophy enabled the company to open its health plans even to those with preexisting conditions; after all, someone with cancer or AIDS might still need treatment for sinusitis or a fractured wrist.

On the other hand, candidates for high-cost procedures underwent a rigorous medical screening immune from favoritism and political clout. For instance, Caduceus 21 would have welcomed baseball great Mickey Mantle as a subscriber—but specifically excluded certain treatments for his alcohol-ravaged liver. When that liver turned cancerous, the doctors performing the transplant on Mantle conceded that his two-year survival rate was only fifty-five percent. In fact, he died ten weeks later. The cost of those final days: more than a quarter of a million dollars and, more tragic, the waste of a healthy liver that could have given a younger but less revered recipient two or three decades of life.

At the same time, no one in the industry worked harder than Caduceus 21 to encourage healthy subscribers to stay healthy. Members could enroll in low-cost exercise classes, stop-smoking programs, and counseling for alcohol and substance abuse. They could visit satellite clinics, conveniently located in neighborhoods and malls, for treatment of common aches and pains, prenatal care, and even free vaccinations for their children. And if they made time for annual checkups, they received a discount on their health-plan premiums.

The Caduceus 21 approach lacked glamour in a society that regarded maintenance as a nuisance; most Americans preferred buying a new VCR or refrigerator or car to repairing the old one. It was also out of step in an investment environment geared to quarterly earnings rather than long-term growth. The naysayers finally fell silent in late 1993, when the first several HMOs and hospitals under Caduceus 21 management broke into the black.

Data from these and subsequent turnarounds had allowed Reifsnyder and a fellow cofounder, Mary Osteen, to devise the Provider Efficiency Index, a unique formula to measure subscriber health, subscriber satisfaction as expressed by annual renewals, and provider costs. The PEI had withstood the analysis of skeptics to become an accepted industry yardstick, as well as Caduceus 21's most persuasive sales tool.

Predictably, the company was closely studied by rivals and by business schools. Nowhere did interest run higher than on Wall Street; a jackpot in fees awaited the firm that took Caduceus 21 public. Reifsnyder endured an average of fifteen calls per month from investment bankers insisting the time was ripe for an initial stock offering. His standard response: Your interest is gratifying but premature, a polite way of saying, Don't call us, we'll call you.

Reifsnyder was one of four people who knew that such a call was in fact imminent.

With the two largest health-care megachains acquiring ever more facilities, Caduceus 21 either had to keep pace or be relegated to bit-player status. Thus, a series of deals had been quietly lined up that, if consummated, would vault his company into the topmost tier of the industry.

Unfortunately, they could not finance the expansion by issuing stock; the Securities and Exchange Commission's filing requirements for companies going public were not something with which Caduceus 21 could easily comply. The alternative was to have an investment-banking firm arrange a long-term loan from an insurance company or pension fund. Such a private placement was easier to secure when the financial markets were unsettled, which was why Wall Street's current confusion heartened Reifsnyder.

Atop the hotel-room dresser sat five clear-plastic folders. Each was embossed with his company's logo: a stylized "21" on which rested a caduceus, the winged staff entwined by two serpents that was the traditional symbol for the medical profession. The folders held twenty-page analyses of the investment-banking firms still under consideration. All were reputable. Tonight he and his colleagues had to divine the firm most eager for a profitable new account—and therefore the least likely to dig for corporate skeletons. He slid the folders into his briefcase and was out the door when he remembered how cold it got up in the mountains; he went back to fetch a sweater.

Twenty-five minutes later Reifsnyder parked his rental car at Scottsdale Municipal Airport and strode through the private-aviation terminal.

The familiar adobe-colored Gulfstream IV sat on the tarmac. As he neared it the pilot, a dark young man with aquiline features, clambered down the boarding ladder. "Good to see you again, sir," he said with a lilting accent that Reifsnyder had never quite been able to place.

"Hello, Lino. I understand you've put in a long day."

"Yes, sir. Here, let me take your briefcase."

Reifsnyder followed him aboard.

"Care to join me up front tonight, Mr. Reifsnyder?"

"No thanks, I've got some paperwork to do. What's our flying time?"

"Approximately seventy-five minutes, sir," the pilot replied, heading forward.

Reifsnyder settled into a seat and strapped himself in. The interior of the corporate jet was undistinguished, yet it was the lap of luxury compared to the way he, Aurelia, Mary, and Carl had traveled during Caduceus 21's infancy. To pitch their visionary blueprint from coast to coast, they had taken out second mortgages and maxed their personal credit cards. That meant flying on advance-purchase tickets requiring the dreaded Saturday-night stay; renting cars from local agencies with depots thirty minutes from the airport; bunking at motels where most clients took rooms by the hour; and dining at the greasiest of spoons. The four of them had been close in those days, Reifsnyder reflected, in the manner of strangers thrown together in the same foxhole. Not anymore. Even before Carl's death, their social orbits had diverged. Now he, Aurelia, and Mary rarely saw each other outside the office except at holiday parties, kids' birthdays, and, of course, when the Gulfstream IV came calling.

Ironically this jet—or more precisely, the man who owned it—was the prime obstacle to taking Caduceus 21 public.

He insisted on remaining a silent partner, impossible under the SEC rule that mandated full disclosure of all who held a stake of ten percent or more. But his wish had to be honored, for the company owed its very existence to him. He had furnished encouragement, advice, and a vital cash infusion the moment they signed their first client in 1989.

Nor could Caduceus 21 have grown as quickly without the pivotal alliance suggested by its silent partner. In 1992, he had brought to the company's attention a start-up firm called Medical Expediting Systems Inc., which procured and shipped human organs. Such transfers were strictly regulated by a landmark 1984 congressional bill that divided the country into sixty-nine territories and forbade shipping an organ from one to another without the approval of the United Network for Organ Sharing, based in Richmond, Virginia. MedEx had somehow obtained a waiver from the act—a miracle Reifsnyder was sure had been orchestrated by their financial angel, not that he had ever been emboldened to ask.

In any event, Caduceus 21 and MedEx entered into an exclusive agreement that enabled the health-care company to establish a nationwide network of transplant centers that currently numbered seven. And MedEx had grown into a global enterprise. In the United States, where federal and state laws continued to prohibit the sale of organs, its agents worked with trauma centers to secure donations from the families of brain-dead accident victims. In countries where the sale of organs was legal, its agents were quick to the sites of disasters—be it an earthquake in Nicaragua, a train wreck in Zaire, a typhoon in Bangladesh, the shelling of a safe haven in Bosnia—with releases for the relatives of the terminally injured, cash, and medical teams to harvest the organs.

After the MedEx deal, their silent partner receded into the background—"Think of me as that crazy uncle in the attic," he had joked—and was now content to receive periodic reports by way of e-mail and teleconferences. Reifsnyder, Aurelia, and Mary had long since made their peace with their benefactor's eccentricities. Only when they had to go west for face-to-faces on critical strategic issues, like tonight's selection of an investment banker, did the need for cloak-and-dagger travel arrangements suggest that there might be a bit of Faust to their bargain.

Overhead, the twin jets whined into life. Reifsnyder glanced at the wet bar, decided against a drink, and reached for his briefcase. By takeoff, he was again immersed in the dossiers on the bankers.

THE plane touched down at the small municipal field south of Santa Fe, New Mexico, at 6:17 P.M.

Reifsnyder was gathering up the folders when the pilot

emerged from the cockpit. "You prefer to fly back tonight, sir?"

"Tomorrow morning's fine, Lino, if we can leave by six."

The young man consulted his clipboard. "If you don't mind, we better go tonight. Miss Osteen must be in Amarillo before nine tomorrow, and I am to return Dr. Wilkes to Denver by noon."

"That's a lot of solo flying, my friend."

"Not a problem, sir." The pilot unlatched the door and started to lower the boarding ladder.

The sun was still high in the western sky as Reifsnyder stepped from the cabin, but here, more than seven thousand feet above sea level, the temperature felt a good twenty-five degrees cooler than in Phoenix.

A charcoal-gray Range Rover with dark tinted windows angled across the apron and pulled up alongside the plane. The driver who hopped out was older and lighter-complexioned than the pilot of the Gulfstream IV, but otherwise Pedro bore a marked resemblance to Lino, down to the hard-to-place accent. Though Reifsnyder, Aurelia, and Mary each averaged a trip and a half per year to Santa Fe, they had never met any of their host's employees besides Lino and Pedro; the household staff was always given time off when the Caduceus 21 officers came to town.

"You have a good flight, Mr. Reifsnyder?"

"Yes, thank you, Pedro. How's Century?"

"In excellent health, sir, and *Tío* is happy that you make a safe arrival."

On leaving the airfield, the driver picked up U.S. 285 and looped west of downtown Santa Fe. Reifsnyder gazed idly at the postcard-pretty New Mexican capital. Supposed to be worth a stop, he thought; one day, he'd make the time.

Some distance north of the city, they exited the highway onto a state road that ran ruler-straight across the sere landscape. The driver followed it west for five minutes, then turned right onto a county two-lane that began to curve as the land rose.

The man whom Reifsnyder and the others had come to see was L. C. Chisholm, known to friend and foe alike as "Century." Of America's true billionaires, he was one of two who had never made *Forbes* magazine's annual roundup of the hyperwealthy. Unlike the other man, a real-estate developer who lived in remote northwestern Montana, Chisholm was thought by the IRS to be a mere multimillionaire.

It was therefore unsurprising that the entrance to his ranch was marked by only a battered, nameless mailbox at the foot of the driveway. A lost motorist proceeding past a metal gate long since rusted open, then up the dirt-and-gravel driveway, would eventually come to a farmhouse. Reifsnyder saw the family who occupied it eating dinner on the front porch. They waved at the Range Rover. The driver waved back and continued past onto a rutted track that led toward a distant line of trees.

Chisholm had already been a widower, with no children that Reifsnyder knew of, when he moved to Santa Fe back in the early 1970s. After purchasing enough land to feel safely buffered, he had built the house of his dreams on a three-acre preserve atop the highest ridge on the property, ensuring his privacy by way of a ten-yard-deep circle of piñon trees.

The Range Rover passed through the tree line and began climbing the remaining 150 yards to an austere, flat-roofed building of stone, adobe, and terra cotta. It looked like something out of the local historical society's photo archives, as did the string of low bungalows for staff and guests that sat off to the left. So insistent was Chisholm on maintaining the pioneer-days illusion that his commercial-strength satellite communications dish was a half-mile away and all but invisible from the grounds.

Reifsnyder hopped down from the Range Rover and headed up a stone path flanked by beds of cacti. He was nearing the house when the massive oaken front door swung open to reveal an elegant black woman wearing a boldly printed dress and sandals.

"Hi, Doc," Reifsnyder said.

"Thank God you're here," replied Dr. Aurelia Wilkes, the chief medical officer of Caduceus 21. Wilkes, who was in her early forties, saluted him with her martini glass. "Century's as antsy as a kid in a toy shop. Kept asking Mary and me for our thoughts on the bankers."

"So how did you guys make it through the afternoon?"

"Told him you were the financial whiz and sat around watching him make sushi. Did you know it takes more than an hour just to prepare the rice properly?"

Reifsnyder shook his head in bemusement. Chisholm, the son of a missionary couple, had been born in Japan; though interned during World War II in a camp his parents did not survive, he had never lost his affection for some of the hallmarks of Japanese culture. "Does he have a clue who we're recommending?"

Wilkes's eyes narrowed in thought. "I think not. But he's made a few sarcastic cracks about Joslyn."

"As we expected."

"As we expected," Wilkes sighed. "Come, he's waiting."

Reifsnyder trailed her through the vestibule into an immense space that deserved consideration in the *Guinness Book of Records*. On his second visit here, in 1988, he had surreptitiously paced it off and found it to measure almost four thousand square feet. Yet so pleasing were its proportions, so subtle the illumination from the large windows and skylights, and so unified its decor that the room seemed merely big rather than overwhelming.

Music was playing. It took Reifsnyder a moment to place it: *The Girl from Ipanema*, a Brazilian-tinged jazz album his first girlfriend had owned.

"That you, Reifsnyder?"

The reedy voice issued from the open kitchen in the far left corner of the room, where a diminutive man with snow-white hair was at work next to a big-framed woman who seemed to have wandered in from a dude ranch.

"Sure is, Century."

"About time."

Reifsnyder and Wilkes exchanged wry smiles and started across a burnished oak-plank floor scattered with exquisite Native American rugs.

Directly before them loomed a massive freestanding fireplace open on two sides. To their right, the long wall that partitioned off Chisholm's private quarters was hung with five oils by Georgia O'Keeffe. Chisholm reserved this part of the room for his hobbies. Directly in front of the hearth was a snug reading alcove consisting of a tan Eames wingchair and low bookshelves filled with biographies; farther back, under a skylight, stood his collection of miniature bonsai trees. The southern half of the room was lined with picture windows through which Santa Fe was visible. Grouped before the fireplace were Mission-style couches and armchairs; the dining area, just this side of the kitchen, featured a restored eighteenth-century refectory table large enough to seat twelve.

In contrast to the rest of the room, the kitchen was decidedly modern. Many a four-star restaurant would have coveted its appliances—except, perhaps, the squat, coin-fed soda chest, of the type once found in every rural gas station in America, that was decorated with a large Dr Pepper decal.

At the near end of the island counter that separated the kitchen from the dining area stood Century Chisholm, all five feet five inches of him. He was arranging his freshly molded morsels of raw fish and rice, which looked as artistic as a Ginza sushi master's, on a large, footed birch tray.

When Reifsnyder first met him, a decade earlier, Chisholm had probably been in his mid-sixties. He seemed to have aged little beyond a deepening of the web of fine lines on his pale face. This was most likely due to a series of deft tucks and collagen injections. He wore as always a faded chambray workshirt buttoned to the collar, chinos secured by a plaited leather belt, and moccasins.

Chisholm eyed his handiwork critically. "It'll do," he pronounced, then swiped his hand across his apron and extended it to Reifsnyder.

"Good to see you, Century." Reifsnyder turned to the woman beside Chisholm, a tall brunette in her midforties. She was scooping portions of green wasabi mustard onto four delicate saucers and then spooning in several tablespoons of soy sauce. "Hi, Mare."

"Hello, Len," replied Mary Gossman Osteen. The chief executive officer of Caduceus 21 had on a flame-red silk blouse, faded jeans, and hand-tooled Lucchesi boots of a hue that matched her blouse.

Reifsnyder looked her up and down before saying, "Good God. Two days in Amarillo and you go native."

"Amarillo." Osteen made a face. "Charming place if you're into restaurants that serve roadkill."

Chisholm's eyes brightened like a depraved department-store Santa Claus's, a telltale sign that he was about to slip into his cornpone mode. "Damn Yankees, none of you got an appreciation for white-trash cuisine. Next time y'all visit, I've a mind to cook up a mess of peccary-and-armadillo stew."

"What color Kool-Aid do I bring?" asked Osteen. "Purple or green?"

"Heathens, deliver me from these heathens." Chisholm, who clearly enjoyed being ribbed by Osteen, shook his head in mock sorrow. Then he gestured to a cluster of sushi made not with fish but with cucumbers and avocado and egg custard. "Lookee here. Had to do these up special for Dr. Wilkes. Gal here can take a scalpel, carve up a human body without batting an eye, but raw fish gives her the willies."

"I follow the toxicity reports, Century," Wilkes said. "If you want to ingest that much lead and mercury, it's cheaper to buy a battery."

"Horsefeathers. Same shop supplies the Japanese imperial family—they fly it in here from Tokyo once a week."

"Yeah. The flight that glows in the dark."

Chisholm chuckled, but the avuncular gleam was quickly fading from his eyes. He checked the kitchen clock, then retrieved a baking pan of quartered potatoes and slid it into the oven. "Reifsnyder, why don't you go pour while Dr. Wilkes and Ms. Osteen help me fetch the first course."

Reifsnyder glanced at the champagne flutes on the table and crossed to the soda chest. The lid wouldn't open. He began patting his pockets for change: "Damn it, you old skinflint, what if I don't have any nickels?"

"Machine takes quarters, too."

Reifsnyder found a coin and fed the slot. Under the lid, nestled on ice, were two bottles of Roederer Cristal Rose '85. He grabbed one and began peeling off the foil as he headed for the table.

Next to each plate were a pair of chopsticks and one of the saucers Osteen had prepared; in the center, on a lazy Susan, sat the tray of sushi and an assortment of *oshinko*, or Japanese pickles. Reifsnyder twisted the bottle to free the cork, waited until the rising vapors curled away, then filled the glasses and took his seat.

Chisholm grasped his flute. "I want to tell you again how proud I am to know you," he said. "Cruel fate brought you all together—and Carl as well, may he rest in peace. But something special came out of your griefs. You dreamed up a bunch of theories everybody said was poppycock and you didn't quit until you made 'em work. A lot of folks who're getting good doctoring have you to thank. So does this old man. Of all the ventures in my life, this has surely been the most pleasing and worthwhile. To our company and its future."

They lifted their glasses as one and sipped.

"Now then, business before pleasure," Chisholm said. "Who we going to let do our placement, and why?"

It's showtime, thought Reifsnyder. As the others helped themselves to pieces of sushi, he started with the candidates from the "bulge bracket," Wall Street's name for its bluest-chip investment bankers. The Caduceus 21 research department had run back-channel checks on all the bulge firms and found several to be fully booked with major deals, another riven by dissension, and one facing an SEC investigation. That left Merrill Lynch, First Boston, and Salomon Brothers, whose strengths and weaknesses he succinctly outlined.

"Them bulge firms charge more?" asked Chisholm.

"A little, yes, but that shouldn't be the deciding factor."

"What should be?"

"Who'll service us the best. I'm not suggesting these firms aren't first-rate, nor that they wouldn't kill to do our deal. But we need to nail it by spring, and the presidential election is the year after next."

"Explain."

"The political jockeying starts early these days, Century. You couldn't go to a state fair this past summer without bumping into one candidate or another, and the first primary's not for sixteen months. The point is, we hear the Merrill Lynch guy's going on unpaid leave this winter. Figures if he advises the Republican front-runner, it puts him at the head of the queue to run Treasury."

"Still leaves two of them bulge firms."

"Same problem, other party. The rainmaker at First Boston's backing the vice-president, the one from Salomon's supporting the senator from Nebraska."

Chisholm plucked at his upper lip, then nodded.

Reifsnyder moved on to the last two finalists.

The Everett-Joslyn Group of Baltimore, Maryland, specialized in health-care issues and had played a role in most of the industry's major consolidation deals of the 1990s. If selected, senior partner Thomas Joslyn would both prepare the report on Caduceus 21 and oversee the private placement.

"He's probably the shrewdest and most credible analyst around," Reifsnyder said. "And the most outspoken. Back in the Eighties, he was working for one of the insurance giants. Michael Milken wants to do a deal with him —this was when Milken was still Master of the Universe —so he flies Joslyn out to one of those fancy retreats Drexel Burnham used to stage. All weekend long, Milken's pitching the hell out of the guy. Finally it's Sunday afternoon and they're all playing croquet or something when he starts in again. Joslyn turns, leans on his mallet, and says, 'Mike, I admire what you've done and you're a great host. But I wouldn't use one of your junk bonds to wipe up dog shit.' "

"He the same feller that euchred us out of a deal a couple years back?" asked Chisholm.

"The same guy."

"Said something amusing about us at the time."

Reifsnyder nodded, his heart sinking as he reflexively glanced at Wilkes and Osteen. The three of them had debated whether to include that tart quote in the Everett-Joslyn dossier; in the end, they had left it out.

"Didn't spot it in the report you gave me," Chisholm said, with a quick smile that never reached his eyes. "Refresh my recollection."

Reifsnyder thought suddenly of the tooth-drilling scene from *Marathon Man*—the dentist played by Olivier was, like their host, a master of orchestrating discomfort and pain—and then regrouped: "Well, we were talking to Southeast Health Network about a possible affiliation. Joslyn repped a group that wanted to buy them outright. He told *The Wall Street Journal* that all C-Twenty-One really wanted of SHN was to strip its assets—that we were, and I quote, nothing more than a pack of Jack Kevorkians posing as Marcus Welbys."

"Clever line," Chisholm allowed. "But mean-spirited, wrongheaded, and just plain smart-ass."

"They're real good at what they do, Century."

"Who cares? Fuck 'em."

Reifsnyder quickly moved to the final contender, Marx Dillon & Neil, a relatively new company founded by two Goldman Sachs employees impatient with that firm's slow partnership process. If selected, senior partner Rob Dillon would handle the placement based on a report prepared by health-care specialist Marguerite Sepulveda.

"The Mexican gal," Chisholm said. "Look good to have another minority in on the deal besides Dr. Wilkes here."

Wilkes, who seemed unperturbed by the comment, said, "I don't believe she's Hispanic."

"No?"

"That's right," Reifsnyder said. "Her former husband is."

"The gal a partner?"

"As of July first," Reifsnyder replied. "Junior, of course, with a minor equity stake. The firm's so young there's still just three senior partners, the founders."

Chisholm reached for another piece of sushi, took a bite, and chewed on it for a bit. "July one, hunh? Where are we, late September? Time enough for her to learn that being a partner's not like being on salary—she's got to produce more than just good work. How old is she?"

Reifsnyder scratched his head and turned to Osteen. "Mare, you sat in with us last time. Mid-thirties?"

"Thirty-four, tops," Osteen agreed. "Real committed, too. She started out on the West Coast following the computer industry, but moved to New York and switched to health care after her brother, or maybe it was a half-brother, died a slow and nasty death."

"AIDS? Cancer?" asked Chisholm.

"Congenital heart defect. He spent almost two years on the wait list, but no donor. Which wouldn't happen today at one of our facilities. Anyway, Sepulveda's become one of the better analysts in our industry."

Chisholm studied Osteen with interest. Normally

stingy with compliments, she had praised this banker twice in the last minute. "Everybody's got flies on 'em, Ms. Osteen," he said quietly. "What kind're circling Ms. Sepulveda?"

"I think she'd be happier at a firm with deeper resources. Correct me if I'm wrong, Len, but isn't Marx Dillon more famous for gung-ho salesmanship than for its research department?"

"Well, their research staff's the youngest and most inexperienced of all our candidates," Reifsnyder said. Then he grinned. "As for Rob Dillon, they say he could sell hamburgers to Hindus."

"Nothing wrong with that," Chisholm observed. "So if Ms. Sepulveda's too good for her partners, how come she ain't with one of them bulge firms?"

"She used to be," Osteen said. "Goldman Sachs, but she found herself in an awkward position there. When Marx and Dillon left to start their own firm, they invited her to tag along."

Chisholm frowned. "Awkward position?"

"One of Goldman's corner-office guys developed a lech for her," Osteen said. "Sepulveda wasn't the least bit interested. We're not talking pubic hairs on the Coke can or M&Ms down the breast pocket, but I gather he made things pretty uncomfortable."

"This come from the gal?"

"No," said Reifsnyder, "sources at Goldman."

"Fair enough." Chisholm took another sip of champagne. "Okay, fine briefing, Reifsnyder. Can't fault any of your finalists, outside of those poor-mouthers from Baltimore. You get enough to eat? More sushi, anyone? Then let's wrap this up while I go make dinner."

OUTSIDE, the sun was setting behind the western range and the sky was deepening from russet to indigo.

The night's main course, four well-marbled steaks, lay

on a chopping board next to two uncorked bottles of Opus '82. While the others cleared the table, Chisholm checked the progress of the potatoes in the oven, then lifted off the griddle atop the Bonnet range to reveal a grill. He fired up the imitation-charcoal element and fanned his hands palms-down above the grill, flexing his fingers. The heat felt good. Lately he'd taken to keeping the air-conditioning at a lower setting, but he didn't want his guests to be uncomfortable.

"Dr. Wilkes, medium, right?" Chisholm said. "Reifsnyder, medium rare? And Ms. Osteen, you take yours the same as mine?" He coated a steak with an herb mustard and laid it on the grill. Suddenly he turned to the two women: "You think Ms. Sepulveda did the right thing?"

Wilkes, like the others long accustomed to the circularity of Chisholm's thought processes, cleared her throat. "You mean change jobs rather than file a sexual-harassment suit? I hate to admit it but, yes, I do."

Chisholm's eyebrows shot up. "She who fights and runs away lives to fight another day?"

"That's unfair," protested Osteen. "Who wants her life ripped apart on Court TV? Our culture treats whistle-blowers like dirt, I don't care how many laws are on the books."

"What would you have done, Century?" asked Wilkes.

The corners of Chisholm's mouth curled upward. "Same thing she did, Dr. Wilkes. Unless she knows up front the jury's awarding her several million dollars. If not, might as well start taking in wash because no one on Wall Street's going to give her the time of day. No, our Ms. Sepulveda sounds like a gal who knows how to look out for herself."

He slapped on a second steak, then queried Osteen about her progress in recruiting high-profile outside directors for the Caduceus 21 board. She named six who had expressed interest, including the retired CEO of a Detroit auto maker and a former First Lady.

"Speaking of which," he said, "what do you hear from Little Rock?"

"That we should check back after the first of the year, when they start planning the rest of their lives in earnest. I think we have a shot at getting her."

"Good," Chisholm said, unconsciously warming his hands over the grill again. "Can't stomach their politics but we're talking names here, not ideology. Now then, we got four bankers left. Any of 'em going to squawk about doing a private placement?"

"They'd all prefer to take us public," Reifsnyder conceded. "That would give them commissions on top of a fee, plus the chance to make a market in our stock. But the Street knows that in today's market, we'd be looking at two hundred seventy-five million, max, with a new issue. They also know a private placement could bring in close to double that. Trust me, we won't even have to tell whoever we choose which way to go."

"What about the due-diligence thing?" asked Chisholm, referring to the review the banking firm would perform to certify Caduceus 21's creditworthiness. Income and expenses would be examined, properties and inventories verified, contractual obligations and revenue projections analyzed. For a company like theirs, with assets across the breadth of America and many revenue streams, the process could take up to six months. "Any of 'em going to give us a rougher time than the others?"

"Century, everyone on this list is going to be damned thorough," Reifsnyder said. "That's the cost of doing this kind of deal. If we gave our business to some bucket shop, who's going to take us seriously?"

Chisholm turned over the first steak with a pair of tongs, then put on the last pair. Without looking up, he said, "You appreciate my concern."

"Sure. But there's a Chinese Wall between C-Twenty-One and you. The A.L.B. Foundation is a legitimate not-for-profit that did in fact provide us with generous seed money in the early days. So A.L.B. has every right to hold a sizable position in our company. If the IRS hasn't linked you to A.L.B. after what—thirty years?—a bunch of bankers with their eyes on the prize certainly won't."

"I suppose you're right." Chisholm checked the second steak and turned it over. Then he took out four plates and set them on the counter alongside the range. "Sounds like you all want Ms. Sepulveda doing our deal."

Reifsnyder tensed. In the decade that the people in the room had worked together, Chisholm had never overruled a unanimous recommendation made by the officers of Caduceus 21. Would this be a first? He, Wilkes, and Osteen exchanged charged glances, then nodded.

"The sale ain't rung up yet, friends," Chisholm said. "If I was a betting man, come next Election Day I'd put a little money on the Republicans. Which means throwing our business Merrill Lynch's way wouldn't hurt—especially if their guy gets Treasury. I also got to think about the fact Ms. Sepulveda's firm throws research dollars around like manhole covers. Not exactly a world-class rep, if I was the one being asked to buy something from 'em. So give me one good reason for going with her, and give it to me simple, in words an old man can understand."

"Hunger," Reifsnyder said. "Maggie Sepulveda is hungry. Her senior partners are hungrier. And this is not a deal they can afford to blow."

Chisholm again busied himself with the steaks. Finally he returned his attention to his guests and said, "Okay, so when we going to give Ms. Sepulveda the good news?"

"First thing next week," replied Reifsnyder, who could feel his muscles dissolving like a snowball in a furnace.

"Good," Chisholm said. "Now we can focus on enjoying ourselves."

Reifsnyder drained the last of his champagne but didn't set the flute down because he knew his hands were still unsteady.

"Almost done here," Chisholm announced, picking up the tongs. "Dr. Wilkes, would you kindly take the wine to the table? Reifsnyder, make yourself useful. Potatoes are done, you know where I keep the potholders and the spatulas. *Mmmmmm*, don't these look right tasty."

M O N D A Y
S E P T E M B E R   2 8

THE view through the rain-smeared window of the minibus was even more melancholy than Marguerite Kragen Sepulveda's mood. It might have been peak rush hour on the Long Island Expressway, but the vehicles in the adjoining Manhattan-bound lanes sat as motionless as her jitney.

Maggie looked decidedly out of place among her fellow commuters, having thrown on a ratty purple Washington Huskies sweatshirt, cutoff jeans, and a pair of steel-toed Doc Martens that would rate a thumbs-up from Tank Girl. Hair gathered into an unbankerly ponytail, she had the clear-skinned, firm-jawed good looks of a onetime cheerleader. Any notion of airheadedness, though, was instantly erased by her eyes; large and blue-gray in color, they bespoke a quicksilver intelligence easy to humor but hard to bullshit.

The jitney lurched forward several yards, then rocked to another stop. It had taken an hour and a half to speed from Sag Harbor, on the eastern end of the island, to within sight of the Manhattan skyline—and another forty minutes so far to crawl the last two miles to the Midtown Tunnel.

What a fitting end to a swell weekend, Maggie thought sardonically, one that was forcing her into a painful re-evaluation of the man she had been seeing since the summer of 1995. She and Paul Barry usually drove in from their country house late Sunday evening. But an incident at a party on Saturday had triggered in her an unnerving flashback to the life she thought she had put behind. Too stunned to confront Paul on it, Maggie had stayed on in Sag Harbor last night, citing her need to focus on a memo due that week. In truth, she didn't want to be around him until she could sort out her conflicted feelings.

Maggie unexpectedly found herself thin king back to her first beau, a high-school classmate, and how uncomplicated that relationship had been. Jerry, whose family owned a magisterial house in northeast Tacoma that overlooked Commencement Bay, was cute and a star jock, and he adored her. Like many teenaged couples separated by admission to different colleges, their tearful pledges of undying loyalty failed to survive the first year of campus life. She had last seen Jerry six years earlier, at their tenth Stadium High reunion. He was still cute and the tennis champ of his country club, and he adored his Jessica and their three towheads. Maggie couldn't have been happier for him; nor did she regret not becoming the wife of a vice-president of human resources for Boeing.

Simply put, her native Pacific Northwest could not contain Maggie's ambitions. Despite offers of a full academic scholarship from several of the nation's elite colleges, she had for the sake of her mother's finances become an "I-5 student" at the University of Washington, commuting to Seattle from Tacoma. But blowing off two hours a day in a junker deep into its second hundred thousand miles had not prevented Maggie from eventually getting to Harvard. She left Cambridge with an M.B.A. and a fiancé, a Harvard Law hotshot from Los Angeles so flamboyant that, early in their courtship, she had teasingly nicknamed him *el buscapleitos*, the Spanish equivalent of "ambulance-chaser."

Paul had known from Day One precisely why Maggie ended her marriage and moved to New York. So how could he commit an act straight out of her ex's playbook? A miserable day and a mostly sleepless night had left her no closer to an answer. To complicate matters, she was scheduled to take a vacation the following week. Sag Harbor in autumn was a bracing tourist-free paradise, but unless she could quickly resolve things, spending time there with Paul had all the allure of seven all-expenses-paid days in Chernobyl.

The jitney edged forward another dozen yards. A row of winking yellow lights drew Maggie's attention to a giant sign announcing that the two right-hand lanes were closed for repairs. She glanced at her watch and scowled; so much for that quick stop home. There was an onboard phone at the rear of the jitney. She voicemailed her secretary that she'd be late for her firm's top-of-the-week partners' meeting. Then, realizing how she was dressed, Maggie added a P.S.: please make sure the cleaners had returned her spare suit and blouse.

It was shortly after 9:30 A.M. by the time she darted out of the pelting rain and through the revolving doors of 638 Fifth Avenue. When the elevator stopped at the forty-third floor, Maggie dripped her way through the Marx Dillon & Neil reception area, past the conference room where the top-of-the-week was in progress, and down the hall toward her office.

"Morning, Boss." Dawn Mambelli, her secretary, had a Staten Island native's grating accent but a mind as agile as a currency trader's. Though only in her mid-twenties, she identified with the Hollywood heroines who had cracked wise through the screwball comedies of the Depression; hence, she always addressed Maggie as "Boss," and preferred to be called by her last name. "Bummer of a trip in, hunh?"

"For sure." Maggie continued into her office and dropped her knapsack and weekender. Bless Mambelli, she thought; a fresh bran muffin sat on the desk, the spare suit and blouse were hanging on the back of the door, and the blinds were drawn so she could change in a hurry.

Maggie was peeling off her purportedly waterproof windbreaker when her secretary came in carrying a gym bag.

Mambelli closed the door and pulled out a towel that she put to a quick sniff test. "Here," she said. "Only used once or twice."

"Thanks. You know, I can't believe the gridlock at the tunnel. You'd think they'd be bright enough not to start major road work during Monday-morning rush hour."

"Nah. It's their only way of getting even with guys like you, the big cheeses with the fancy weekend houses on the Island. Caffeine?"

"No time, but thanks." Maggie slipped off the band securing her ponytail and dolefully clutched a handful of rain-frizzied hair. "Look at this mess. Damn, I wish I had time to let Mr. Damian do something with it."

"As if. His shop isn't exactly the kind you drop in on."

"True," Maggie said. "Hey, how was dinner on Saturday?"

"Nasty. My folks think Howie's a cur," Mambelli said, referring to the new boyfriend she had taken home for the first time.

"Oh. I'm sorry."

Mambelli shrugged. "They're right. But hey, Howie's pretty buff. Plus which, he doesn't mind watching movies on AMC with me. Plus which, he's got season tickets to the Jets. Twenty-yard line, yet."

Maggie suppressed a smile and began to fumble with the sodden laces of her shoes.

"How'd your weekend go, Boss?"

"Fine."

Uh-oh, thought Mambelli, who after three years could read Maggie's every emotional nuance. It took more than a rotten commute to depress Boss like this; something pretty heavy must've gone down.

Maggie gave up on the laces and just stepped out of her Doc Martens, then began unbuttoning her jeans. "Any calls?"

"Four." Mambelli waved at the yellow slips on the desk. "Your mom and Paul left voicemail. Harriet, to confirm lunch today, and a Mr. Reifschneider from Knoxville."

Maggie froze. "Len Reifsnyder? Caduceus Twenty-One?"

"The very same."

"Oh, my God."

"What? What?" asked a startled Mambelli.

"When was my last trip to Knoxville? May? June?"

Mambelli started for the door.

"Use my computer," Maggie said, trying to fathom her first unsolicited call from Reifsnyder in the five years she had been paying visits to Caduceus 21.

The company was, in her opinion, the most admirable in the industry. Its ability to practice enlightened medicine while maintaining strict financial discipline had resulted in an extraordinary PEI rating. Though Reifsnyder and Osteen's Provider Efficiency Index still drew occasional fire from skeptics, rival health-care companies that had spent years trying to find fault with it were now busy trying to post numbers as high as Caduceus 21's.

Maggie always enjoyed her trips to Knoxville even though Reifsnyder had no foreseeable need of an investment banker. The situation must have changed, she reasoned; why else would he phone? And if several firms were being invited to make presentations, did that mean Marx Dillon & Neil was on the short list?

Mambelli popped a file up on-screen and said, "Last contact, July seventh, when he sent a note congratulating you on the partnership. Last visit to Knoxville, second week of May. Want me to read you your notes?"

"Unh-unh." Maggie didn't need jogging to remember

that she and Reifsnyder had for the first time been joined at lunch by Mary Osteen, the feisty CEO of Caduceus 21. She checked her watch. The top-of-the-week usually ran past 11:30. Should she wait until afterward to return the call or . . .

Maggie rebuttoned her jeans. "Better see what Reifsnyder wants."

"Isn't he the dude that always tells you, like, no way?"

"One of many."

"Yeah, Boss," Mambelli said as she stood, "but this one you care about. Want me to place it?"

"No need. One of the things I like about them is, they answer their own phones. Hold my calls. And Mambelli —wish me luck."

As her secretary left the room, Maggie opened her knapsack and retrieved a bright purple case, made of ABS plastic, that was slightly smaller but considerably fatter than a compact-disc jewel box. It held the removable 1.2-gig hard drive from her laptop. Like many who routinely worked at home on nights and weekends, she had become frustrated by the endless file-swapping required to synchronize the data on both office desktop and home laptop. Maggie's solution: install an adapter bay that enabled her office desktop to access the laptop's removable hard drive. This allowed her to keep in one place all her works-in-progress, plus all her software applications and some personal files she would just as soon not have on the Marx Dillon network.

Maggie slid into her chair and slotted the unit into her desktop's adapter bay. As she popped her address book up on-screen and spotted the cursor over Reifsnyder's name, a wave of anxiety swept over her. Damn, she thought, is this what guys feel like when they're about to phone a gal for a date? Be cool, she told herself, and clicked to launch the autodialer.

"Len Reifsnyder."

"Hi, Len. Maggie Sepulveda, returning your call."

"Maggie," he said warmly. "Nice to see that making

partner hasn't slowed your response time. Again, my congratulations."

"Thanks. It was nice of you to send a note."

"Now don't go spending your share of the profits all in one place."

She laughed. "Can't, Len. Even in New York, the stores close by nine. Anyway, you didn't call to hear me moan about my hours. What can I do for you?"

"Advice. For starters, let me say that C-Twenty-One's not auditioning investment bankers—you're the only call I'm making."

Maggie, suddenly giddy with anticipation, didn't trust herself to speak.

"Since your last visit," he continued, "we've developed a number of interesting options. We'd like to share them with you and hear your reactions. Which, I guess, is a fancy way of saying we want to pick your brain."

"What's left is at your command."

Reifsnyder chuckled. "You've already met Mary Osteen. This time, I'd also like you to meet our chief medical officer, Aurelia Wilkes."

"That'd be my pleasure, Len," she said, trying to contain her rising excitement. "I've read so much about her. When would you like me to come down?"

"Well, it turns out all three of us will be in K-town through the weekend. Then one or another of us is on the road until midmonth. If you're tied up this week, we could aim for the sixteenth or seventeenth—suit yourself."

"Give me a sec while I punch up my calendar." Though ready to hop the next plane to Knoxville, Maggie didn't want to appear that overeager. She popped her scheduler up on-screen. In anticipation of her vacation she had filled the coming days with appointments, but there was nothing that couldn't be moved. How quickly could she bring herself up to speed on Caduceus 21? Two days, Maggie calculated: "I could do it this Wednesday or Thursday."

"Thursday, the first, looks cleaner for Aurelia."

"Then let's say eleven A.M. Thursday, pending flight schedules. I'll have Ms. Mambelli, my assistant, confirm."

"Sold," Reifsnyder said. "Remember, casual dress. The only women who wear power suits in K-town are the trels."

"Trels?"

"Terrible real-estate ladies. Now, I've got a memo to send up, and it would probably be helpful for you to take a peek at our preliminary third-quarter earnings, too. They're not final—got a couple of days to go, so cut us some slack—but they should give you a reasonable snapshot. I can fax it to you in summary form, or I can shoot up my spreadsheet if you guys are glyph-capable."

Reifsnyder was referring to a technology introduced in the mid-1990s that ingeniously addressed a long-standing cyberproblem: how to safely transmit a binary file. The Net was speedy but now too thick with poachers and pranksters to entrust with sensitive material; a modem was highly secure but its send/receive software so offputting that many users would rather snail-mail floppies.

Yet research showed that almost everyone was comfortable with a fax machine, which was as secure as a modem. This finding had led Xerox to develop software that printed out a binary file as a series of glyphs, tiny slashes (/) and backslashes (\) that could later be reconstituted into a binary file. So foolproof was the technology that the sender could shrink the glyphs until they appeared as a background pattern and even write over them without garbling the underlying data. Better yet, it was simple to heighten security by encrypting the glyphs.

"We've got glyph software," Maggie replied. "But here at Marx Dillon we don't have private fax machines. Everything goes through our servers. It'd probably be more secure if you pipe the fax to my private Net account."

"Will do," Reifsnyder said. "Our half of the key will be, let me see, zero-four-four-eight-one. You know, I keep forgetting you used to analyze the computer industry. I can still remember the early PCs, and how only guys with pocket protectors and a personal-hygiene problem could debug the damn things. Now, when I've got a problem at home, I ask my nieces to play glitch-buster. Know what they love saying to me? 'User error, Uncle Len. Again. Really, why don't you try opening the manual?' "

"Probably the same reason guys won't stop at a gas station and ask directions," she quipped. "I'll have Ms. Mambelli forward you my e-mail address."

"Terrific. If you have any questions, Maggie, don't hesitate to call. If not, see you Thursday."

On ringing off, Maggie logged over to Marx Dillon's in-house database. The centralized servers to which her desktop was patched held the firm's proprietary research and CD-ROM libraries in addition to supporting voicemail, fax/modem traffic, Net access, online data services, and even cable-TV channels. The capabilities were awesome. For instance, Maggie could partition her screen so that as she wrote a report or reworked a spreadsheet, both the AP news-wire and market quotations scrolled by while an *L.A. Law* rerun played in its own separate window. And to think that her mother used to yell at her for doing homework with the radio on.

After a quick check of the in-house file on Caduceus 21, Maggie hit the Net and popped her private account up on-screen. She maintained it to keep private messages off the Marx Dillon system: billets-doux from Paul, gossipy e-mail from pals, and will-I-see-you-soon? notes from her mother, whom she had finally dragged into the computer age. Sometimes, though, the Net's growing hucksterism made her consider scrapping the service. Over the weekend, for instance, she had received thirteen unsolicited e-brochures for products ranging from Caribbean cruises to brokerage services to Saab leases. She deleted the junk mail, then reviewed what she had typed while talking with Reifsnyder.

Maggie usually took a minute to expand and prioritize

her notes before passing them on to Mambelli, but this morning she just hit the intercom: "Got a new laundry list for you. Ready? One, get my private Net address down to Reifsnyder. Two, book me to Knoxville Thursday morning, arriving around ten."

"You care which airport you fly from?"

"No. And if you can't get me down there by ten, then first available flight. Either way, confirm my arrival time with him. Three, ask Casselman to refresh the database on Caduceus Twenty-One. I'm showing the last update was early August. Four, cancel my lunch with Harriet and tell her I'll call her this afternoon. Five—you suppose I could talk Mr. Damian into a house call?"

"Sure, Boss. Just promise him a date with Richard Gere."

She laughed. "Last thing, Mambelli, I think I will have some coffee, in about ten minutes, thank you."

Maggie had changed into the industry's regulation tailored suit and pumps, and was trying to tame the last few strands of hair, when her terminal chimed to announce a letter hitting her private account.

She downloaded it, ran it through the glyph translator, and launched the software that enabled her to read the document.

The first few sheets were a projection of Caduceus 21's third-quarter earnings. She continued to click NEXT PAGE until she arrived at Reifsnyder's memo. Addressed to her, with cc's to M. Osteen and A. Wilkes, it summarized the company's proposed new alliances. These were concentrated in the Northeast, where Caduceus 21 was already a player, and Southern California, where its presence was minimal. At the core of the strategy: creating two more transplant centers that would act as regional magnets. The deeper she read, the more intrigued she became by this bold move: With sufficient new capital, Caduceus 21 could in five years expand into America's third biggest health-care provider.

A fresh mug of coffee was waiting when Maggie, now

formidably dressed and coiffed and carrying her clipboard like a shield, emerged from her office.

"Well, Boss?"

Maggie shrugged.

Mambelli's eyes narrowed. "Knoxville ain't Memphis, so I know you're not flying down to Tennessee to visit Graceland."

Maggie's poker face dissolved into the goofy grin that appeared only when she was truly elated.

"All right!" shrieked Mambelli, throwing up her right hand.

Maggie returned the high five, grabbed the mug of coffee, and strode down the hall. She paused at the conference-room door to try to put on her game face. Screw it, she finally decided, and turned the knob.

WEDNESDAY
SEPTEMBER 30

WAR had one benefit, Nguyen-Anh Dupree thought bleakly as he marched through the dark streets of the Mexican village; it left the night sky so clear that the stars glistened like signposts to infinity. The thirty-four-year-old physician had served in enough Third World communities to know that the air quality in them was usually foul. Each dawn villagers starting their rounds would kick up dust that thickened through the day, like the smog in Los Angeles, and linger until the unpaved streets were empty again. The pall settled early in besieged zones like Chiapas state for the simple reason that few ventured out after the sun went down and the *militares* began enforcing the curfew.

The temperature was rapidly dropping, for the highland village was situated a good seven thousand feet above sea level. Dupree pulled out a cigarette and his heirloom Zippo. He had not been this upset since the previous spring, when villagers led him to a clearing deep in the jungle. There in a makeshift grave lay five children, none older than eleven. The throat of each had been slashed open with a machete. Their crime? Having parents with Zapatista sympathies. Everyone knew who ordered it and who did it, but the men who owned the *fincas* and their goons had produced alibis the authorities chose to accept.

Tonight his anguish stemmed not from a fresh atrocity but from his fears for Guillermo Chacon. More than a month had passed since the teenager began his journey north, and three weeks since he was scheduled to cross the border, without any word from America. Yet not even Dupree had been alarmed, because the rebels and the *militares* were taking turns cutting the phone lines. The *patrones* didn't care, having paid for the construction of cell-phone relays, but the villagers were left mostly to the mercy of the infamous Mexican postal system.

Then, two days earlier, a rather peevish letter had arrived from Don Joaquin's cousin, twice-removed. The man worked on the grounds crew of a golf-and-ski resort outside Denver. When Guillermo failed to show up by September 15, as promised, the resort had given the busboy job to someone else.

Dupree heard the *militares* before he saw the silhouette of their Jeep parked several blocks ahead. The soldiers were playing gangsta rap from the mid-1990s on a boom box. The tightly rhymed, apocalyptic lyrics of the songs meant little to them; they just enjoyed the rumbling backbeat.

Suddenly the Jeep's spotlight flashed on. Its beam hovered around the tall *norteamericano* with the Asian face and the shock of dark brown hair, then pinned him in its glare.

Dupree shielded his eyes but did not break stride.

Target acquired and identified, the soldiers doused the spotlight.

Dupree had been asleep an hour ago when a boy came with the message that Don Joaquin wished a word with the doctor.

What the village elder had to report was not good. With telephone service momentarily restored, he had finally gotten through to the guide. According to this El Zopilote, the crossing had been a calamity; the green-shirts grabbed three of twelve runners, including Guillermo. Then where was the boy? According to El Zopilote, *la migra* had instituted a new centralized deportation policy, so possibly the teenager was now awaiting processing and return in one of five megacamps strung like gulags between Brownsville, Texas, and Portero, California. The guide had ended the conversation by promising that he and his associates in *el norte* would continue to seek news of Guillermo.

Don Joaquin believed the man.

Not Dupree, who for weeks had been nagged by a bothersome question: How would the elder of a remote village hear of someone like El Zopilote, much less know how to contact such a person?

Tonight, under gentle questioning, Don Joaquin told of traveling to the nearby city of San Cristóbal de las Casas in search of a frontier guide. He had been referred to an important gentleman named Barrera, who furnished him with a list of three and recommended El Zopilote as the best.

Was Señor Barrera a tall, clean-cut man of about forty? asked Dupree, desperately praying that he wasn't. With an office off Avenida 16 de Septiembre?

The very one, Don Joaquin had agreed.

Dupree was almost upon the Jeep.

"Dr. Kung-fu," the patrol leader called out with a mock salute.

"*Buenas noches,*" Dupree said.

"Doctors should not smoke," the patrol leader said, waving at Dupree's cigarette. "They say it is not good for the health."

His men snickered, but Dupree ignored the thinly veiled demand for the rest of his pack of Faros.

The patrol leader held up one arm and gestured to his wristwatch. "The curfew, Dr. Kung-fu," he said officiously. "You should not be out at this hour."

Dupree nodded in acknowledgment and continued on his way. In earlier days he would have visibly bridled at such petty arrogance. Experience had taught him to cork that urge, to save his ammunition for situations that mattered. Anyway, these soldiers were just kids, no different except for language from all the young toughs whose victims he had tried to stitch back together. Israelis vs. Palestinians on the West Bank; Serbs vs. Muslims in Bosnia; Hutus vs. Tutsis in Rwanda; Indonesians vs. Timorese in East Timor—he had been at the epicenter of each. The genocidal crusades of the 1990s might have been led by educated adults who gave vainglorious interviews to CNN, but Dupree knew firsthand that they were waged by illiterate children armed with awesome firepower and a bravado that could not disguise their fear.

He turned down a side street, interrupting several dogs snarling over a discarded bone, and came to the abandoned store that was now both his clinic and home. Don Joaquin had ordered a lock installed on the front door to protect the doctor's medicine and equipment. Dupree never bothered to use it; with its ungated windows, rotting back door, and tar-paper roof, the old building was easier to break into than his *grand-mère* Lulu May's cookie jar.

Unlike the telephone, the electricity was still out. The backup generator for the refrigerator in which he stored medicines and vaccines was humming away. He had a second unit to power the rest of the house, but his fuel supply was running low so he lit a hurricane lamp and carried it to the battered pine table at the back of the clinic. The bottle of Calvados that his supervisor had brought him in May was still in the cupboard, two-thirds full. If he started drinking tonight, he probably wouldn't stop.

Brooding about Guillermo was a no-win proposition, but he couldn't get the teenager out of his mind. Another of war's indirect casualties, he thought; for without the chaos that had taken his loved ones, Guillermo would not have been driven to head north.

It was at moments like this that Dupree was most aware of the central irony of his life: As much as he hated war, it had nevertheless given him his very existence and, later, a meaning to that existence. He lit another Faro, then studied the lighter. It, as well as the dog tags around his neck, had been his father's.

Major Lance J. Dupree left Mississippi in 1961 to serve as one of the first U.S. Special Forces advisers in South Vietnam. There he met and married Thieu Mei-lan, the daughter of a university professor. The couple had returned to his hometown of Yazoo City, where Nguyen-Anh was born, when President Lyndon Johnson decided that Ho Chi Minh could in fact be defeated if American troops not only advised but fought. Lance answered his country's call once more; in gratitude, his name was eventually chiseled, along with more than fifty thousand others, into the black granite wall in Washington, D.C.

Mississippi in the late 1960s and early 1970s was not an easy place for an Amerasian child. Nguyen-Anh finally gave up trying to fit in and concentrated on academics. He had been in his final year of residency at a hospital in Los Angeles when his mother died. With nothing left to keep him in America, he had spurned a number of job offers—talented minority doctors fluent in four languages were hard to find—to join Médecins Sans Frontières. That Brussels-based organization, known in English as Doctors Without Borders, sent its volunteers into regions riven by disasters. Some were natural, like earthquakes and droughts. Most were man-made; since 1990, Dupree had witnessed enough slaughter to make a combat vet shudder.

He had also witnessed the unseemly attraction that

such miseries held for one American organ-procurement company. In recent years, advances in transplant techniques and in suppressing host-body rejection had made the search for organs a global undertaking. Since the mid-1990s, Dupree and other veteran members of Doctors Without Borders had been trying without success to corroborate whispered stories of how the human vultures from MedEx preyed on the Third World.

The company's agents, it was said, bought organs from healthy peasants willing to live with just one kidney or one cornea in exchange for several hundred dollars U.S.—more than their families could otherwise earn in a decade. They ignored areas stricken by famine, where their blood money might do some good, because the body parts of those poor souls were too malnourished to recycle. They monitored weather reports to get a jump on the next killer hurricane in the Caribbean or the next big monsoon in the South Pacific. They cultivated both rebel and government leaders in war-torn countries to get advance notice of impending combat strikes. And as a hedge against times when the demand for organs grossly exceeded supply, they had even built a network of emergency suppliers comprising local law-enforcement officials; MedEx was thought to fund right-wing death squads from Brazil to Pakistan, from the Philippines to South Africa, from Czechoslovakia to, yes, Mexico.

It was MedEx's rumored alliance with Mexico's Federal Security Directorate, the shadowy intelligence arm of the Interior Ministry, that had set off the alarms back at Don Joaquin's house.

The village elder hadn't been surprised by Dupree's familiarity with one Señor Barrera of San Cristóbal; he assumed the *norteamericano* doctor would be acquainted with gentlemen of influence. In fact, Dupree knew Enrique Barrera de Barcellona, the regional head of the Federal Security Directorate, only because he had been personally interrogated by the thug. Mexico City viewed with deep suspicion any foreigner who took up residence in rebellious Chiapas state; hence, the DSF surveillance of him that continued to this day.

There was no longer anything to be done to help Guillermo, Dupree decided glumly. Besides, what actions could he initiate from this primitive village? He stubbed out the cigarette, picked up the hurricane lamp, and retired to his room at the back of the clinic.

Dupree looked at the room's Spartan furnishings: a bed, a swaybacked bookshelf crammed with CDs and well-thumbed paperbacks, and pegs for his clothes. He had busted his chops at a world-class medical school for this? The chance to run a clinic so poor that he was forced to boil used hypodermic needles and gauze pads for a second application, praying all the while that AIDS had not made its way to Chiapas state? So beyond the reach of normal supply lines that he had to hitch rides to Guatemala to buy black-market antibiotics with his own money? What the fuck was he trying to prove—that the world's downtrodden needed him more than he needed a Porsche or a projection TV or how about just a plain old bathroom with running water? Who did he think he was, the Albert Schweitzer of the 1990s? And then Dupree's rage subsided. Flush with self-pity and guilt—why hadn't he tried harder to persuade Guillermo to stay home?—he climbed into bed and snuffed out the lamp.

THE sky was still black, the streets still silent when Dupree's eyes opened. The luminous dial of his watch told him he had been asleep less than an hour, yet his despair was gone, replaced by a calm so absolute that his heart seemed to have stopped. He smiled thinly as a snatch of an old Doors song ran through his mind: *"The killer awoke before dawn / He put his boots on / He took a face from the ancient gallery / And he walked on down the hall . . ."* The last time he had felt this way was two months after his twelfth birthday: Yazoo City; early spring; the fight at dusk in Lintonia Park.

He lay in bed for several minutes, reviewing the game plan. It was so logical and so simple that he had needed his subconscious to assemble the elements.

Dupree got up, grabbed an old Mobil road atlas from his bookshelf, and padded out in bare feet to the clinic. After lighting the Bunsen burner to boil water, he went to the battered pine table and booted up his subnotebook computer. Only a half hour remained on the rechargeable battery, so he slapped in one of the dozen backups he had purchased, at considerable cost, because of the village's frequent power outages.

He made a pot of coffee and carried a mug back to the table.

Ever since that surrealistic day back in Lintonia Park, he had taken great care never to raise his hand against another living being. But the time had come for him to reclaim his roots. The father he never knew had been a warrior. Now, God help him, Nguyen-Anh Dupree was about to declare a war of his own.

He lit a Faro with his father's dented Zippo and popped his word-processing program up on-screen.

The pot of coffee was dry when Dupree finally reviewed what he had written:

Duchess & Data—
   Long time no chat. Hope you are both well.
   Consider this an S.O.S.
   A young man left my village for America in the third week of August. The last person to see him was the guide who was hired to sneak him into SW Texas.
   Tonight I learned that the guide now claims the U.S. Border Patrol picked the boy up about 20 miles south of Ruidoso on the night of 3/4 September. I've got my doubts. It turns out the guide was recommended by an officer of DSF (Mexican state

*security), which definitely fits the m.o. of a certain
company we've discussed in the past.*

*I'm asking you guys to hit the INS net to see
if there is a Guillermo Chacon, aka Guillermo
Echeverria, being held in one of the internment
camps along the border.*

*Assuming not, will you try to get into the
MedEx net? Because if what I most fear did occur,
each of his organs must be tagged with certain
medical data, including blood type, for it to be accepted for transplant. Guillermo's blood was
B-negative.*

*A second search parameter you might be able to
use is volume. We're told that two other young
Mexicans vanished on the same crossing. That
would mean three hearts, six kidneys, etc. entering
the system from the same point of origin. Harvested organs are highly perishable (transplantation must take place within 36 hours max) so I'm
guessing they would have been flown out from
some major airport near Ruidoso, perhaps El Paso.*

*Guys, I realize this is a real needle in the hay-
stack, but there's gotta be something out there.
You wouldn't think a chop shop could be that busy
and leave no traces.*

Thanks much and be well—N.A.D.

Satisfied that he had stated the problem correctly,
Dupree jacked in his cellular modem and then launched
an encryption program written by Duchess and Data, his
surrogate younger siblings. It was designed to query the
Net and generate a onetime, nine-digit key using an al-
gorithm that factored the previous day's closing indices
of five international stock exchanges. Which five markets
were chosen out of some fifty around the world was a
function of the day and hour (Greenwich Mean Time)
that the key was generated. Though not a true random
number, it was just as resistant to cracking.

He clicked ENCRYPT, typed his password, and clicked START.

Three minutes later a message popped up on-screen:

KEY READY. PROCEED WITH ENCRYPTION.

Dupree quickly disconnected from the Net; on his pinched budget, just sending and downloading e-mail was a luxury. He filtered his note through the encrypter, then scrolled through his electronic address book to Duchess and Data's joint mailbox and double-clicked it into the RECIPIENT field. The final option was routing. Should he pipe it to them direct or via a four-continent billiard shot that would make the message untraceable? He selected the four-continent billiard shot.

Last chance to cancel, he thought.

Dupree stared at the screen for a moment, then clicked SEND.

The windows of the clinic were still black with night. But it was almost 5 A.M. and too late to go back to bed; villagers would soon begin arriving at the clinic. Dupree felt good enough to indulge in a hot sponge bath, so he filled a kettle and turned the Bunsen burner back on. Hell, why not celebrate whole hog? He went to the cupboard and poured himself a shot of Calvados. The rest would keep until Guillermo had been avenged.

T H U R S D A Y
O C T O B E R   1

AS Leonard Reifsnyder dimmed the lights, Aurelia Wilkes pressed PLAY and grainy black-and-white images began to flicker onto the projection TV at the foot of the conference table. Maggie Sepulveda settled back in her chair; she hadn't expected that her visit to Knoxville would also include a trip back in time, to the very birth of Caduceus 21.

The videotape had been shot in a large room with a low ceiling and worn linoleum flooring. Some forty feet from the camera, a dozen folding metal chairs were drawn into a ragged circle. The men and women slumped in the chairs appeared to Maggie like mourners at a child's wake. The tape's soundtrack was fuzzy and echoic; though someone was talking, the words were impossible to make out. A time/date stamp in the lower right-hand corner of the screen read "21:56:08< ∙ >05/18/88."

Now a woman in the circle was pointing at the camera. The others in the group turned to look.

"Jacqueline Cox," Aurelia Wilkes said. She, Reifsnyder, and Mary Osteen were seated around the table with Maggie. "It was she who organized the Fairfax County Survivors Workshop. This was toward the end of our first session, and Jacqueline is asking if her son could tape us—she wanted something to show the foundation that gave her the seed money."

Soon, the woman was beckoning to the camera.

The picture grew shakier as her son started toward the group.

Maggie sensed the mood in the conference room changing. Since her arrival at Caduceus 21's headquarters in Knoxville a half hour earlier, her three hosts had been brimming with an easy hospitality. But now, as the tape continued to roll, they seemed to be retreating into themselves.

"Hi, I'm Jackie Cox," the group leader said, "and we're here in the basement of St. John's Episcopal Church on Fort Hunt Road in Alexandria, Virginia. Nick, is this enough light for you to shoot in?"

"Uhhh . . ."

"Then why don't you use the thingamajig, honey," she said.

A small spotlight sprang on, its pitiless illumination flattening Cox's features.

"That better?" She squinted into the glare, then refound her nervous smile. "Terrific. Now, I thought we'd go around the circle and have everybody give your name and the reason you've come here tonight. Okay? Terrific. Nick, why don't you start with Peter here on my left."

The camera began a clumsy traverse. Wilkes pressed the remote's MUTE button and said, "I realize Jacqueline comes across like the social director of a cruise ship. But you should know this was at the end of a very intense two hours, and this was a crucial night in her life."

"She was really out on a limb," Osteen interjected. "Spent six months trying to get funding for the workshop. She ended up dipping into an insurance company settlement to pay for the newspaper ads."

Maggie glanced questioningly at Osteen.

"Remember the Northwest flight that crashed taking off from Detroit, the one where only a baby girl survived? Her husband was on it. Jackie never made any bones about the fact that the workshop was as much for herself as for the rest of us." Osteen looked at the monitor. "Aurelia?"

Wilkes unmuted the sound.

On-screen, the camera was panning from the first workshop participant to Mary Osteen. The portrait was not flattering; her broad features were puffy with grief, her hair uncombed, her Wharton sweatshirt stained with food. Ten years earlier, Maggie knew from her research, Osteen had been an officer of a software firm that created inventory-control programs for small businesses.

Osteen might have looked frumpy, but the eyes she fixed on the camera glowed with rage: "My name is Mary Gossman, and I'm a widow with a young daughter and an infant son, and I'm here to try to understand just what the hell I did to deserve this. That's why I got a baby-sitter for my kids tonight, and that's why I'm here."

The camera hesitated, then started to swing to the next participant.

From across the table, Osteen cleared her throat softly; Wilkes again muted the sound.

Osteen turned to Maggie and said, ruefully, "Christ, wasn't I articulate that night. On top of looking like a bag lady. When was that tape made, May eighteenth? Norm's funeral was on the sixth. Thirty-five, never sick a day in the nine years I knew him. What a difference from Charlie, eh?"

Wilkes and Reifsnyder both smiled.

"The man I'm married to now's known around town as 'Mr. Second Opinion,' " Osteen explained. "If everyone in the country was as big a hypochondriac, C-Twenty-One would go belly-up in a month.

"Anyway, on the first of May, a Sunday, Norm and I go sailing on the Chesapeake with another couple. The next morning, he has a temperature of one-oh-five. Just a late-season flu, the doctor says, take aspirin and drink plenty of fluids. Shortly after midnight, Norm wakes up spitting blood. We drive straight to the hospital. One look, they put him in intensive care."

Osteen's eyes dropped to her coffee mug. "By dawn, he's dead. Turns out Norm contracted a bacterial pneumonia, we never found out exactly how. Easy to cure if you diagnose it fast, fatal if you don't. Same thing that killed that Muppet guy, Henson, several years later."

"I'm sorry," Maggie said, instantly regretting the inadequacy of the phrase.

The tape had continued to unspool in silence. Wilkes fast-forwarded past two other participants, then paused it on a man in his late thirties who possessed the chiseled features and self-assurance of a former college quarterback.

"Carl Haas," Wilkes said, "the other cofounder of C-Twenty-One. Our Fourth Musketeer."

Maggie's research packet had contained *New York Post* clips from 1993 that recounted Haas's fatal stabbing by a mugger as he was returning to his mid-Manhattan hotel. "Did they ever catch his killer?"

Osteen snorted. "Six-fifty in the evening, a violent struggle, a street full of witnesses, the cops can't even piece together a coherent description. The irony is, Carl wasn't fighting over his wallet, because he never carried more than fifty bucks in cash. But he had just bought a birthday present for his wife, a shoulder bag from Gucci. The killer dropped it making his getaway."

"Carl was still alive when the cops arrived," Reifsnyder said. "One of them found the bag and brought it to him. He clutched it and said, 'It was empty. I swear, it was empty.' Those were his last words."

Osteen slowly shook her head. "Giving that bag to Susan, his widow, was about as painful as burying Norm.

She was three months pregnant with their second kid, and then, boom. When your people get around to examining our books, Maggie, they're going to see the profit-sharing for the three of us is split four ways, with a share going to Susan."

"It's the least we can do," Reifsnyder said. "Carl's the one who convinced us to set up shop in K-town. He went to school here, the University of Tennessee. Office leases were dirt cheap and the labor pool educated. Sure, there were drawbacks, like trying to get airline connections to some of the places we had to go. But frankly, I don't think C-Twenty-One would've made it if we had started out in a high-rent town."

Maggie hesitated, then said, "I understand Mr. Haas used to be a Washington lobbyist."

"One of the best," Osteen said. "If he were still with us, he'd be our chief of government relations. Which, as you know, Maggie, may be the most critical headquarters job of all. We're up to our neck in bureaucrats, from the feds down to some local zoning board that wants to know why one of our hospitals needs a bigger parking lot."

"This may be impolitic, but . . ."

"This is business, Maggie," Wilkes said. "Nothing's impolitic. Speak your mind."

"Okay. I noticed that Mr. Haas mainly lobbied for conservative causes. Correct me if I'm wrong, but didn't he once work for Pat Robertson? And head one of Ollie North's defense funds? I guess my question is, wasn't he uncomfortable with some of Caduceus Twenty-One's policies?"

Wilkes regarded Maggie with fresh interest. "You're referring to the fact that where permitted by law, our facilities openly perform abortions on demand. And you want to know if we fought about that all the time. Or if Carl was the hypocrite of all time."

Maggie, surprised by Wilkes's bluntness, nodded.

"Medicine is about healing, not ideology," Wilkes said. "Yes, Carl hated that our facilities perform abortions. But Mary and Leonard and I, each of us has quarrels with our corporate policy.

"For instance, I as a doctor want each of our hospitals to own a magnetic resonance imaging unit. However, that's a diagnostic tool, not a vital piece of emergency equipment. Leonard has proven to me the wastefulness of duplicative resources, that lives don't often hang in the balance because the nearest MRI unit is an hour away. So I live with that, and dream of the day when those units will cost as much as a new Geo instead of a cruise missile.

"All three of us wish C-Twenty-One's transplant centers didn't have to rely so heavily on foreign organs. But we live with that even as we encourage our subscribers to consider becoming donors. As I believe you know, we automatically tissue-type them upon enrollment, and we remind them of the new law that grants a tax deduction for their organs—a law which, I might add, the medical community lobbied hard for.

"So Carl lived with our abortion policy while dreaming of the day his pro-life allies could craft legislation capable of surviving a Supreme Court challenge."

Wilkes stopped herself and blushed. "I'm sorry, Maggie. I didn't mean to slip into lecture mode on you."

"No, no," Maggie said, now fully appreciating why the doctor so often acted as Caduceus 21's spokesperson.

Wilkes unpaused the tape.

The man on-screen looked up at the camera and said, in a taciturn drawl, "Carl Haas, and I came here because of my poppa. He was a farmer. Till last fall, he worked a spread down in eastern Tennessee that's been in the family going back before the Civil War.

"Did okay, too. Never owed the bank a dime, 'cept short-term loans for spring planting. Sent me and my kid sister to college. Kept up on his life and medical premiums religiously so's if something went wrong, the farm'd be safe. Only hitch was, his broker sold him a medical policy from a company that went Chapter Ten. Bad real-estate loans or something."

Haas rolled his neck, as if to ease some invisible strain. "Poppa went straight to another company. That's when they found the cancer. Cancer of the prostate. Course, after that, no one wanted to insure him, preexisting condition and whatnot. So he looked into the odds of beating what he had, and the costs. And he figured . . . and he figured since it weren't early-stage cancer, it weren't worth betting the farm on. Nothing my momma nor my sister nor myself could say to make him change his mind, neither.

"Poppa died this spring. He would've turned fifty-nine come August, and I should've done more to see that he made it to the party."

As the camera began to pan to the next person, Wilkes fast-forwarded the tape again.

Maggie felt like a knee-jerk liberal—emphasis on "jerk"—for questioning Haas's convictions.

"We can stop anytime you like, Maggie," Reifsnyder said. "We thought this tape would be the quickest way to ground you in C-Twenty-One's origins. But then, we know it backward and forward. I think we failed to appreciate how unsettling it might be to an outsider."

Maggie shook her head. Articles about the company and its founders routinely referred to the chance encounter, at a therapy group, of a quartet of survivors nursing grievances against the health-care industry. The four had begun to meet in private to blue-sky a better system and, over the course of sixteen months, invented what became Caduceus 21. Reading about it had stirred Maggie; actually witnessing the genesis was profoundly moving. "I'd like very much to continue," she said softly. "Tell me, how often do you watch it?"

"Once a year," Reifsnyder replied. "Usually in mid-May. As kind of a refresher course, so we never forget exactly why we began this company."

"You don't show it to reporters, do you?"

"We did once," Wilkes replied. "Years ago. A *People* correspondent doing a profile on me—your typical minority-woman-makes-good kind of thing. The next day, the telephone rang, and Mary happened to pick up."

"One of Oprah's producers," Osteen said. "She's working on a segment about, so help me, the therapeutic value of weeping. 'Hey,' she says, 'a friend tells me you've got this fabulous tape of a bunch of people sitting around bawling their eyes out. We want to run some of that footage. And we want to fly a couple of you up to Chicago to tell our audience exactly how those tears changed your life.' Don't you ever wonder what the media would've done at the Crucifixion? Up-close-and-personal interviews with Judas and Pontius Pilate? Instant replays of the nails going in?"

Wilkes added, "The final irony was, the magazine didn't use any of my quotes on the tape. Their lawyers felt they were potentially defamatory."

"So now it pretty much stays in the vault," Reifsnyder said. "Doc?"

Wilkes pressed PLAY and the camera panned to the next participant. Maggie needed a moment to recognize the man in the grainy black-and-white picture. Len Reifsnyder's hair had been noticeably fuller then and his three-piece-suited frame a good twenty pounds heavier. At the time, Maggie knew, he was a senior analyst with the U.S. Department of Health and Human Services, a GS-17 specializing in health-care costs.

"I'm Len," he said, squinting up at the camera. "I'm here because I, uh, I saw the ad in the *Post* and I thought, uh, I thought talking about things might make me feel better."

Out of the corner of her eye, Maggie could see the present-day Reifsnyder gazing blankly at the pencil he was kneading between his palms.

"You see, my sister and her husband were in a car crash out in Colorado about three months ago," his earlier self continued. "Tom was killed instantly. Patty . . .

They got Patty to the hospital and put her on life-support, but she was brain-dead. It, uh, it took us almost three weeks to get them to . . . to stop their efforts." Reifsnyder's eyes welled. "I had to sign the papers authorizing them to pull the plug, and I don't feel very good about it."

Maggie swallowed hard as the words brought back searing memories of her own long vigils in an intensive-care unit. Petey, her half-brother, had spent his final weeks on life-support equipment as his worn-out heart collapsed and took down first one system, then another, after it. She could remember the frantic last-ditch search for a donor. She could remember the hopes raised by news of an available heart but dashed because it was deemed incompatible. Only when Petey slipped into a deep coma, and the doctors confirmed that his body had deteriorated beyond salvage, did she and her mother finally confront the unthinkable. Their talk had taken place in an all-night coffee shop a few blocks from the hospital. The plate-glass windows were turning gray with the false dawn when the two women finally bowed to logic.

Her mother could not bring herself to sign the consent form. So like Len Reifsnyder, it had fallen on Maggie to deal with the paperwork. A final private goodbye to Petey, so wasted and so unresponsive and yet so at peace, and then she was gently leading her mother from the ICU as the technicians slipped in to switch off the machines. Could that shared experience of having knowingly ended a loved one's life, Maggie wondered, explain some of the empathy that had developed between Reifsnyder and herself?

On-screen, the image shifted from Reifsnyder to a thin black woman.

Maggie leaned forward.

The Aurelia Wilkes in the video had been fully as striking as Iman or Naomi Campbell. Instead of modeling designer fashions in magazines and on runways, though, she had chosen the cotton scrubs of an orthopedic surgeon; in 1988, she was still on the staff of Walter Reed Army Hospital in Bethesda, Maryland.

"I am Dr. Aurelia Wilkes, Major, United States Army. I am present tonight because I failed my mother once, and I'm about to fail her again.

"When my folks retired, they moved back to Atlanta to be closer to their families. Six months later, Mom tripped and herniated a disc in her lower back. It became apparent she needed a lumbar laminectomy—a fancy term for removing a disc—so I located a specialist for her. Surgery was scheduled for twenty-four October, 1986.

"I had permission to fly down and be with her. But on twenty-three October, all leaves were canceled. Unbeknownst to us at the time, President Reagan was about to order troops into Grenada. That same day, the specialist we retained had a family crisis, a son who suffered a head injury at football practice. By this time Mom was already checked in. They persuaded her to let another doctor perform the surgery."

Until now, Wilkes had shown no emotion. Suddenly her face tightened: "Damn, we're talking here about an elective procedure! All those bastards cared about was losing one night's billing for a bed!"

She slumped back in the folding metal chair. "I'm sorry. It's just that I should've been there for her, I should've been down in Atlanta saying, No, we will wait, thank you. The doctor who, uh . . . The doctor who . . ."

Wilkes covered her face with her hand for several moments, then looked back at the camera. "The doctor who performed the procedure arrived at the hospital fifty minutes late. God, I wish he had never shown up at all because he botched it big-time—went in right past the disc and severed my mother's aorta. She died on the table.

"Know what the staff called that doctor? Jason, after the guy in the *Friday the 13th* movies. I also learned he'd lost another patient during routine surgery in the previous five years, and permanently maimed three others.

The insurance company sent a lawyer to the funeral home. Right there, in front of family and friends, he offered Dad fifty thousand dollars to sign a release absolving the hospital and the doctor of liability. I told the son of a bitch we'd sign it for free if they just fired that butcher and made sure he never practiced again, anywhere.''

Wilkes shook her head, a sad smile on her face. ''That didn't happen. Turns out the doctor's father was a prominent banker in Atlanta. And on the board of the hospital. And a big donor to the local Democratic Party, which might explain why our complaint to the state licensing board got nowhere.

''Now it looks like this war's over,'' Wilkes said bitterly. ''The doctor's father has a fishing buddy who's a U.S. senator. This senator happens to be a key player on the Armed Services Committee. Nine days ago, my CO called me in and ordered me to drop what he called my 'vendetta.' I asked him to put it in writing. He threw me out of his office. What's happening isn't right, but I am no longer confident I will ever win my mother justice.''

The camera started to pan to the next participant.

Wilkes punched STOP.

Reifsnyder got up and drew open the curtains. Sunlight cascaded into a room furnished out of a discount catalogue: a conference table that was veneered instead of hardwood, chairs upholstered in cloth instead of leather, a carafe that was plastic instead of silver. Maggie had visited direct-mail computer clone shops with more lavish facilities. Yet that was part of Caduceus 21's appeal; they didn't squander bucks on show.

Wilkes also stood and moved to the window.

''Did you nail that doctor, Aurelia?'' asked Maggie.

''After a fashion,'' Wilkes said, staring down at the street. ''His father's a member of Augusta National, and owns a house near the course. Just before the Ninety-one Masters, the police found the doctor there. Dead, of a cocaine overdose. The insurance company offered me one hundred thousand dollars to drop the lawsuit. My lawyer got them up to two-fifty and I signed. Dad had passed on by this time, and I'd resigned my commission to help launch C-Twenty-One, so I invested the money in our company.''

Wilkes suddenly checked her watch and turned back to the others. ''Goodness, we forgot all about lunch. It's such a nice day, I vote we skip Smoky Mountain in favor of one of the clubs. We could sit outside, plus it would give us more privacy.''

Reifsnyder said to Maggie, ''You in any danger of starving?''

''Not unless the club's in Memphis.''

''Okay, Doc, your club or mine?''

Wilkes smiled. ''You have the better golf course, Leonard. We have the better kitchen.''

THEIR table overlooked the ninth and eighteenth greens of Aurelia Wilkes's club. At this hour on a weekday afternoon, they had the terrace to themselves. The plentiful rains of summer and early fall had left the tree-lined fairways lush, and a slight breeze was sweet with the scent of fresh-mown grass.

Maggie was thankful for the decision to come here. The drive out, in separate cars, had given them all a chance to decompress from the morning session. She adjusted her sunglasses and tried to focus on the conversation at the table, but her mind kept drifting back to the videotape. Better than any interview or written report, it explained Caduceus 21's founders and their mission. Interestingly, Wilkes and Mary Osteen and Len Reifsnyder were now trading desultory industry gossip; it was as if, having allowed Maggie to glimpse their souls, they had become as skittish as a new lover on the morning after.

Maggie was finishing the last of her salad when she saw a Mutt-and-Jeff pair of girls in their mid-teens coming up the ninth hole. One, a rangy blonde, had a bag slung over each broad shoulder and the other, a rail-thin black a full head shorter than her pal, was hustling to keep pace.

"Sharri and Kelly, two of the best juniors in the region," Wilkes said. "Honorary members here until they become twenty-two. The clubs in K-town are very competitive. We stage clinics for preteens, then recruit the most promising ones the same way the high schools go after football and basketball players."

"Where's the phone?" said Reifsnyder with a mock scowl. "I'm calling the truant officer."

"Leonard's just jealous they didn't join his club," Wilkes said. "Actually, the girls schedule phys ed and study hall in the afternoon so they can get out here early."

"Why's the tall one carrying both bags?" asked Maggie.

"Kelly? She must have been the last to lose a hole. It's their way of betting without having to touch their baby-sitting money—whoever loses a hole caddies for the other until she wins again."

The girls stopped at the farthest ball, which lay some seventy yards from a severely contoured green guarded in front by a yawning bunker.

"A brutal hole," Wilkes said. "Only three of our women members can reach it in regulation. If either girl makes a four here, it'll be as good as a birdie."

Maggie watched as Sharri selected an iron, took two practice swings, and assumed her address. Her shot flew safely over the bunker and rolled to a stop nine feet left of the hole.

Wilkes beamed. "Sharri's probably the reason I'm a member of this club. They were already after her when I was asked to join."

"She's a relative?" asked Maggie.

"No, just black. I didn't integrate this place—two men joined in the late Eighties. But at the time, no club in K-town had a black single-woman member. They wanted

Sharri so badly they not only recruited me, but also waived my initiation fee. Part of the payback was taking her out on the course several times. Naturally, I never came within twelve strokes of her. And naturally, I never told the membership committee why Sharri ended up choosing us. We're the closest club to her home, just ten minutes by bike."

The girls had advanced to Kelly's ball, which sat thirty-five yards out. With her opponent already close to the pin, she tried to finesse in a delicate lob shot, but the ball barely carried the bunker and came to rest in the thick fringe, leaving her a difficult thirty-foot chip across a pronounced ridge. Kelly gave her wedge a long, sad stare, then disconsolately shouldered the two bags.

"Sharri's family doesn't have much, but Kelly has even less," Wilkes said. "A mom who works two jobs, a father who hasn't paid alimony or support in four years. Golf's the best ticket both these girls have to a college education—because of Title Nine, women must now get a fair share of a school's athletic scholarships."

As the girls neared the green, they spotted Wilkes on the terrace and waved.

"How's the match stand?" she called down.

"All even, Dr. Wilkes," Kelly said. "I put one in the lake on seven."

The waiter arrived and began to set out the main courses, but Maggie and her three hosts remained absorbed in the drama below.

Kelly studied her chip one last time, then lifted the club and forced it down into the heavy grass. The ball popped out, landed softly high up on the ridge, and began curling down toward the hole. Everyone watching realized the shot was going in a full two seconds before it actually found the bottom of the cup.

"Good four, Kell," Sharri said in a tight voice.

Kelly flashed a grin wide enough to accommodate an ear of corn sideways.

Sharri's confidence of a few moments earlier was visibly shaken; instead of putting for a win, she now had to sink it just to salvage a tie. She stepped up to the ball, then backed off to recheck the line and to wipe her palms on her shorts.

"Uh-oh," Wilkes murmured. "Grab those nerves, girl."

Sharri resettled herself over the putt, but her nerves remained ungathered. Her stroke was more of a stab; the putt was wide left all the way and ran a foot past the hole.

"Men insist the way to instill character is team sports," Wilkes said. "To which I say, bull. Watch."

Sharri, head low, hurried to her ball and tapped it in. When she retrieved it, Kelly replaced the flagstick. The girls waved to Wilkes, then walked off the green. Sharri stooped to heft both bags—having lost the hole, it was her turn to carry—before joining Kelly for the long walk to the tenth tee.

Wilkes took a sip of iced tea. "Sharri didn't miss that putt because Kelly was grabbing at her jersey or trash-talking her mama. She missed it because she lost her composure. Golf, unlike the team sports, is about individual responsibility. It's about coping with the mistakes you yourself make. Next summer, or the summer after, she'll face a putt that length to win a tournament. She may not sink it, but she'll put a better stroke on it. There's only one way to acquire grace under pressure, and that's to submit yourself to pressure."

"Tell Maggie where you learned," Mary Osteen prompted.

"Not on a golf course, I'm afraid," Wilkes replied. "Nineteen seventy-nine. Flint, Michigan, my first day of residency. I was working ER that night when they wheeled in a tall white female in her early thirties. What a mess. Her evening dress was soaked with blood and there was pulpy matter oozing out of a large perforation just above the left pelvic bone. It looked like she'd been gut-shot. As soon as I touched her skin I knew her temperature had dropped into the low nineties. I gave the standard instructions: get a line in, Solu-Medrol-and-morphine push, type and crossmatch, blood gas, check the BP, and for God's sake prep her for surgery like, right now!

"That's when the PA came on. There'd been a multi-vehicle pileup on I-Twenty-three, and all available medical personnel were to report to the ER entrance immediately.

"I was in and out of the scrub room in less than a minute. But when I got to the OR, the patient was still on the gurney and my entire team was gone except for one nurse. She finished taping down the IV tubes, then yelled that they'd be back as soon as they could and bolted out the door."

Maggie could feel her jaw sagging.

"I was just about hyperventilating," Wilkes said. "But then the training kicked in. The wound was in the patient's lower abdomen, so I grabbed a scalpel and started cutting away her dress from the hem.

"Partway up, though, I observed an anatomical anomaly.

"It was a penis. Which, as I watched, stiffened to reveal a word written in red Magic Marker: 'Gotcha!'

"Need I tell you the entire ER staff was watching on closed-circuit TV? The 'victim' turned out to be a fellow resident named Kirby Watt. He had gone so far as to shave his legs and spend twenty minutes in the cafeteria meat locker to lower his body temperature. It was their way of seeing if this new hotshot from the University of Michigan, not coincidentally a woman and black, was going to spaz out under pressure."

Maggie was surprised at Wilkes's lack of rancor; she herself would have been enraged beyond reason. "Aurelia," she said, "didn't you want to do something else with the scalpel?"

"Of course," Wilkes replied. "But do you think Lorena Bobbitt would've been allowed to walk if she'd been black? There are things you grow up attuned to—for instance, we women are far more cautious in a parking lot at night than, say, Leonard. Race is another. I am never unaware of the color of my skin."

The conversation drifted from Wilkes's cruel hazing back to the health-care industry, and to the explosive growth during the 1990s of the for-profit megachains. Most were bigger than Caduceus 21 but none had a higher Provider Efficiency Index rating. The result was an embarrassment of suitors calling Knoxville, asking to affiliate.

"You've analyzed the list I sent you, Maggie," Reifsnyder said. "I must tell you, we're frankly astonished by the interest we've gotten from California, considering how strong Kaiser is out there."

"The hospital in San Diego would be a real coup," Maggie agreed. "If you could turn around its transplant program, you'd suddenly have a really solid anchor in the Southern California market. But I see you're also proposing to develop a second transplant center in the Northeast, to supplement the program in Boston. The pressure's really going to be on to obtain sufficient organs."

"We've worked the numbers with our OPA," Wilkes replied. "The last three years, MedEx has been able to increase its supply to us by at least eight percent per year. There are several factors behind this. Transplants are now common enough that most hospital staffs are qualified to perform the harvest—you'll remember in the early days, Maggie, how we had to fly the transplant team to the donor to do the harvest, then fly it back?

"Also, Americans are finally starting to accept the notion of brain death, and of donating a loved one's organs. So are many Europeans, probably because of poor little Nicholas Greene," Wilkes said, referring to the nine-year-old American boy shot in the head by bandits while vacationing with his family in Sicily in 1994. His parents had donated his organs; seven Italians, ranging from youth to middle-aged, now owed their lives or their health or their vision to young Nicholas. "Virtually all cadaveric organs donated in Europe stay in Europe, but that still helps us. In the late Eighties and early Nineties, there were probably two, three hundred organs a year going from America across the Atlantic.

"Finally, Maggie, we've been following the field trials on swine-to-human xenotransplantation with great interest. Imagine the ramifications if the biotech companies succeed in breeding pigs with human-compatible solid organs—no more wait-listing of people in need of a new heart or liver or kidney."

Maggie, who had correctly anticipated this last line of reasoning, said, "You believe in the potential enough to start adding on transplant centers now?"

Wilkes nodded. "Five, ten years out, it won't be theory, it'll be reality. And we want C-Twenty-One ready and waiting."

Maggie nodded. Her crash review of the literature on xenotransplants suggested that what might appear to be an outrageous gamble was actually a fairly conservative bet. The transplant centers Caduceus 21 proposed to add in San Diego and Philadelphia were all but guaranteed to be revenue-neutral at worst just on the basis of the number of human organs currently furnished by MedEx. Add to that a limitless supply of swine organs, and the company would become a nationally dominant force in the transplant field—a strong selling point in attracting subscribers to its HMOs. "So all you need to make this grand design work," Maggie said, "is a little rainy-day money."

"Exactly," Mary Osteen said. "Question is, how're we going to raise it?"

Reifsnyder leaned forward and said, "I've filled in Mare and Doc on the mechanics of IPOs and private placements. Why don't you run down the pros and cons of each for us?"

"Fine." Maggie knew which option her senior partners preferred, but she also knew which was best for Caduceus 21. "Let's start with an initial public offering. An IPO's most obvious benefit is that it improves your cash flow immediately. Currently, in turnaround situations where a new affiliate hasn't begun to show a profit, you still hand out bonuses."

"In lieu of profit-sharing," Wilkes said. "It's the right thing to do. We're asking them to subscribe to a new management philosophy, and it's important to show we have confidence in our way of doing business. We think of it as an investment in the future."

"Understood," Maggie said. "But awarding shares of a publicly traded stock would accomplish the same thing without making you go out-of-pocket.

"A second benefit is higher visibility. Make no mistake, your IPO would be one of the Street's glamour issues, on a par with some of those Internet offerings a few years back. People seeing all the fuss might check out the services you offer and end up subscribing to one of your HMOs.

"Now, the cons. Caduceus Twenty-One is not for instant-gratification freaks. Your policies need time to phase in—I believe your quickest turnaround took a little over three years? That's not going to sit well with investors looking for a steady growth in quarterly earnings. You'll be under pressure to take shortcuts.

"You'll also be targeted by the full-moon crowd, the activists who buy a token share so they can attend your annual meetings. Pro-lifers throwing plastic bags of fake blood to get arrested in front of TV cameras. Antivivisectionists chaining themselves to the microphone to protest the immorality of xenotransplants. Maybe even trial lawyers ranting that your policy of settling malpractice cases is somehow unconstitutional—though I doubt they'd generate much sympathy. What I'm saying is, once you go public, you're fair game for weirdos.

"Most critically, I'm afraid an IPO would leave you short. I doubt you want to put more than fifteen percent of the company on the market. Even if we project an opening price in the low thirties, you won't realize enough to undertake the expansion outlined in Len's memo. How willing are you to perform a heavy triage on your wish list?"

Osteen scratched her brow. "I guess that depends on the downside of a private placement. For instance, would it kill our ability to secure future loans?"

"Actually, it'll help," Maggie replied. "Rob—Rob Dillon, the senior partner who would place the paper—will be going to large insurance companies and pension funds. Once the banks see that kind of conservative investor backing Caduceus Twenty-One, they'll be knocking down your door to see how much more money you might need.

"The downside of a private placement? You haven't created a public market, so you can't play balance-sheet games. I know Len doesn't believe in them, but trust me, nobody's immune to cash-flow problems. And, of course, the three of you don't become instant paper millionaires."

"Better cancel that Ferrari, Mare," Reifsnyder said.

"How much might a private placement bring?" asked Wilkes.

Maggie shrugged. "I'm reluctant to venture a number. But I'm confident that you'll be able to do most of the deals in Len's memo."

"Then that's what you're recommending? A private placement?"

"Yes. It lets you keep up with the big boys for now. Yet you retain full control of the company—you're taking on a loan, not selling off chunks of equity. Nor does it prevent you from going public at a later date." Maggie leaned forward. "Make no mistake, I truly believe in your company. You're here for the long haul. I hope to be, too, and I want nothing more than for you to prove that your policies work on a national scale. That way, when the time's finally right for an IPO, we can make it a once-in-a-decade event on Wall Street."

She sat back and reached for her San Pellegrino, suddenly worrying that she'd come on too strong.

Wilkes, Osteen, and Reifsnyder exchanged glances.

"As you can imagine, Maggie," Reifsnyder began gravely, "the three of us have spent a lot of late nights analyzing our options. Nothing we've heard here this afternoon has changed our conclusions."

Maggie set down her glass.

"First, a private placement is the way we should go." Reifsnyder could no longer contain his puckish smile. "And second, if Marx Dillon is willing, we'd like you guys to handle it."

"Thank you," Maggie said, flashing her goofy grin. "I believe we would be."

"It's a bit early in the day, but I think this calls for a toast," Aurelia Wilkes said. She signaled a waiter, who hurried out carrying a wine cooler packed with ice and a bottle of champagne.

"We've all gone to the bank to ask for a loan, but nothing like this," Osteen said. "How painful is this going to be?"

"Not very." Maggie started to reach for her knapsack. "Just six pages of triplicate forms, won't take you more than fifteen minutes to fill out."

The laughter at the table was punctuated by the pop of the cork.

"Actually," Maggie said, "I'll be preparing a report that documents the company's past and present and lays out projections for the future. A team from Marx Dillon will do the actual analysis of your books and contracts. They need to be down here in Knoxville, but they'll pretty much stay out of your way unless they need something clarified. I'll be down here too, as well as on the road visiting your various HMOs and hospitals. One of my key questions is something all the data in the world can't answer—how indispensable each of you three is to the company."

"What do you mean?" asked Wilkes.

"EDS survived Ross Perot's departure. Apple survived Steve Jobs's departure, at least for a good while. But any of you ever hear of Eagle Computer? I thought not. It was an early maker of PC clones with the potential to be bigger than Dell, bigger than Gateway. For all intents and purposes, though, the company died the day its founder skidded his Ferrari into a ditch."

"Each of us has been grooming a successor," Osteen said. "Sounds like you'll want to spend time with them."

"I do. As well as get feedback on them from your affiliates."

The waiter finished filling the last glass.

"Fair enough," Osteen said. "What's our next step, Maggie?"

"A preliminary letter of agreement spelling out the services Marx Dillon is to render and the fees we are to receive in connection with securing you a private placement."

"We do that with you?"

"No. Even if I liked doing it—and I don't—my firm has this quaintly chauvinistic belief that us gals are too shy to be effective negotiators. You'll be dealing with Rob Dillon."

"How long is that going to take?"

Maggie smiled. "You know that 'thrill-seeking gene' they found a couple of years ago? Well, who's got the bigger D-four receptor, Len or Rob?"

The three women turned to Reifsnyder.

"Gave up measuring mine when it stopped growing," he said dryly. "What about Mr. Dillon?"

A second round of loud laughter drowned out the clink of champagne glasses.

F R I D A Y

O C T O B E R   2

CENTURY Chisholm always took a work break at first light, a brisk thirty-minute walk around the grounds before sitting down to a hearty breakfast. It was the quietest time of day, he thought, God's gift to the weak. The nighttime predators had been chased back to their lairs by the sun breaking the eastern horizon, the daytime raptors were just starting to stir. He noted his condensed breath hanging in the crisp air like cigarette smoke, as well as the ghostly sheen of dew that drenched the piñons encircling the house. Autumn was descending and Chisholm longed to head for his beloved winter pasturage.

Come early November he would be in the tropics, where the mornings never left him all ashiver. Better yet, he would be watching Elspeth, the apple of his eye, prepare for her wedding. Too bad the month in between was nothing but busywork. A stream of executives from his various enterprises were coming down to Santa Fe to present third-quarter reports. Chisholm expected no surprises at these command performances—he monitored his empire closely—but experience had taught him the benefits of making 'em grovel every now and then.

He'd far rather spend the time on a personal project that sustained him in a way Lu would surely have appreciated. A smile stole across his weathered face. Before building this spread, he owned a small ranch not far from Oklahoma City on which he always kept a dog or two. Lu was a pick-of-the-litter border collie, an undersized bitch with more brains than a scientist, more heart than a gladiator. She also had one bad habit as a pup. True to her breeding, she would quiet the herd and sink to her belly in the watch posture. But no more than a half hour later she would spring up, bark her head off to scatter the herd, then go round 'em up again. Until he could mellow her out, his livestock had tongues that drooped to the ground. Small wonder the dog was his all-time favorite; she had instinctively understood that death was less an enemy than boredom.

Chisholm would've kept one of Lu's pups had he stayed on in Oklahoma. But the ranch had outlived its purpose, which was to let him sweat off the frustrations of building a business from scratch. Once the business took hold, he found himself too busy to do much ranching. Gallivanting here and there to stroke existing clients and drum up new ones wasn't all drudgery—prime seats at the Super Bowl and Wimbledon, Mardi Gras weekends, Pamplona for the running of the bulls, even a safari in Africa—but eventually it became about as exciting as brushing his teeth twice a day. More to the point, he had over the years assembled a portfolio of diversified enterprises best overseen in quiet.

Oh, sure, he sometimes missed the rough-and-tumble. Nothing stirred the blood like a fair fight, but those were now few and far between. The way he saw it, Americans had plumb run out of starch. It was a condition them politicians all blabbed about without doing much to solve. That's 'cause one thing you couldn't legislate was gumption. Back when he was growing up, didn't matter if you were a dirt-poor, eighth-grade dropout; a feller with a quick mind and no fear of close-quarters combat could make something of himself. Lots of quick minds these days, but not many of 'em had a stomach for blood. Let's be reasonable, they'd say, let's split the difference. That's when you measured 'em for the casket. Only it wasn't fun anymore; nothing that came too easy ever was. He could remember the last time he'd girded up for serious battle, to finagle that congressional waiver so's MedEx could set up shop. Needn't have even broken a sweat 'cause them do-gooding pantywaists on the other side had as much staying power as a trailer park in a tornado.

Chisholm, who never used to look back, could now understand the events that had shaped his life, could now put his past in some kind of perspective, because of the memoirs he was composing. With most of his enterprises running on autopilot, the project was the most interesting way he knew to pass the time. He started working on them in the early 1990s, inspired by the biographies he so enjoyed reading. Those books showed that the fellers who made history were as different from one another as night and day, yet similar in one important respect—each had demonstrated some trait in childhood that they rode to the top. Genghis Khan was ruthless early on, for instance, the same way Napoleon was grabby, Lincoln compassionate, Edison inventive, Hitler warped, Churchill tenacious, Nixon devious. His own success, he now saw, came from a willingness to answer opportunity's knocks.

Recollecting his achievements in detail wasn't always easy. First off, many were the kind of things you didn't exactly keep records of. And then there was the problem of connecting up all the things he'd done. The biographies made the great lives sound like a series of related challenges met and overcome. His own life was like one of those garden mazes in England. Felt like a hick at the time, laying out for a ticket to stroll through a bunch of hedges, but he surely got his money's worth; that maze had more twists and turns and dead ends and double-backs than a snake-oil peddler's spiel.

This past week, for instance, he had been setting down his thoughts on the Tashman project. It had been brought to him in the early 1980s by his Silicon Valley scout, who was on the lookout for high-tech start-ups to grubstake. Tashman, a retired doctor, had gotten together with his nephew, a computer programmer, and invented an electronic patient chart. Theory was, a doctor in Florida treating a tourist from Minnesota could dial up Minnesota and retrieve the patient's complete medical history, then update it with the services he performed. Fine idea but too far ahead of its time; it had needed the kind of universal twenty-four-hour online access the Internet now provided. Yet though the Tashman project ended up a dry hole, it had piqued his interest in the business of health care.

Which was why years later, when a young conservative lobbyist of his acquaintance mentioned a group trying to invent a better way of managing health care, Chisholm had been quick to provide seed money to Caduceus 21. The memory of that lobbyist, Carl Haas, still pained Chisholm. Sharper than most of his kind, more honest than most of his kind, willing to stand his ground. Signing Haas's death warrant was one of the hardest things he ever had to do, but if the boy hadn't stolen that MedEx staffing memo, who had?

Up ahead now Chisholm could glimpse his earth dish through the piñons. It was the latest model, installed this past spring, and linked him directly to his own breadbox-sized transponder on a geosynchronous communications satellite orbiting 22,300 miles overhead. Unlike most folks his age, he had no fear of new technology. Just like you didn't have to understand the innards of a carburetor to drive a car, you didn't have to understand how a computer worked to enjoy its fruits—as he had for more than four decades.

Somewhere in his files he still had the yellowing article about an antitrust settlement reached during the Eisenhower years. The deal was, International Business Machines could continue to manufacture and sell mainframe computers but not begin leasing hardware or offering computer services like data processing. He had come across the article while leafing through some old magazines in his dentist's waiting room, months after it ran in *Time*. The delay hadn't mattered; few folks in 1956 could grasp as readily as he the full implications of the IBM settlement.

At the time Chisholm wore several hats too many. During the week he was the business manager of a Bible college in northeast Oklahoma, a job depressingly beneath his talents. Yet he had sought it a decade earlier knowing that unlike some other places that were hiring right after World War II, the college wouldn't bother verifying his identity and past employment record. They may have been trusting fools, but they also paid something awful; as the flood of Korean War vets taking advantage of the GI Bill shrank to a trickle, so did salary increases. Things got so bad, the college encouraged the staff to moonlight. Most weekends, Chisholm motored around the Southwest hunting for secondhand construction equipment to buy and ship south of the border, and one day a week, he consulted for other nonprofits in the region.

One of these was a charitable foundation run by a large petroleum company. He could still remember the day the foundation head proudly took him to see the petroleum company's latest investment. There, in an immense air-conditioned room, sat an IBM mainframe surrounded by lab-coated technicians fussing with the tubes and coding the punch cards. By the end of the month, Chisholm had the foundation's data digitized. Three months later, after a judicious bribe to a technician, the data for his other clients and his machinery deals were on punch cards as well. The ability to carry around so much information in a large briefcase astonished him. So did the fact that the petroleum company turned off its mainframe from 5:30 P.M. to 8:30 A.M. every weekday, and all weekend long.

The *Time* article got Chisholm to thinking. If IBM was limited to making hardware, someone else ought to start up a business storing and retrieving data. By early 1958 he had built a list of potential clients within a day's hard drive and, just as important, technicians looking to make a few extra bucks. At that point Chisholm offered to lease the petroleum company's mainframe every Saturday for a thousand dollars per month plus, of course, the cost of extra electricity. They thought he had been munching too much locoweed, but sent over a one-year contract before the week was out.

All but one of Chisholm's initial data-processing clients were small manufacturers and retailers. The exception was two boys from Wichita whose Ivy League schooling had given 'em smarts but not too much common sense. In the days before junk mail began spreading like kudzu, they anticipated the wealth of subtle detail you could plumb from public sources, like census data and vehicle registrations, and private sources, like credit agencies and magazine subscription lists. Crunch all that data on the mainframe the right way, you had yourself a list of prime mail-order candidates. Only trouble was, them boys set their sights on a bum target: fellow evangelical Christians to peddle religious literature to. They soon went belly-up and stuck him for nine thousand dollars, a dark cloud whose silver lining was not yet apparent.

Chisholm left the Bible college the next year, shortly before its doors shut forever. By then he was leasing the petroleum company's mainframe from 6 P.M. Friday until 6 A.M. Monday, plus two nights during the week. He had incorporated five different companies in three states to shelter a workforce grown to eighty and to diddle various tax agencies.

At about that time the Wichita deadbeats ran into one of their college classmates and happened to mention

Chisholm's operation. The classmate flew out to Oklahoma to share a singular vision: In a TV jungle increasingly ruled by merchants of sacrilege and smut, he would buy a station and establish an electronic pulpit from which to preach the Lord's word. That part of the feller's business plan was about as exciting as watching metal rust. The part that woke Chisholm up had to do with soliciting tax-deductible donations on-air and selling merchandise no good Christian home ought be without, like aprons with various Proverbs printed on 'em. Experience had taught Chisholm that where cash flowed, there were sure to be leaks. That afternoon he wrote the feller a check for thirty-five thousand dollars in return for a contract to process all the station's pledges and sales. Tearful homilies and on-air faith healing proved irresistible; the teleministry raked in so much money that if anybody noticed the one percent Chisholm was skimming on top of his rightful fees, they weren't saying.

Getting in bed with the minister soon paid more dividends. In the early 1960s, some in his circle saw that a whole lot of Americans were fed up with Big Government. For a generation Washington had been tilting the playing field away from God-fearing white folks and toward work-dodging minorities. To seek out the faithful, these conservatives needed mailing lists—and who better to handle the job than a man with fundamentalist credentials, a staff versed in fulfillment services, and his very own mainframe? Chisholm's new clients lost big their first time out, backing Barry Goldwater, but they went on to construct the Silent Majority that five times in the next six general elections put a Republican in the White House.

Chisholm's direct-mail business had exploded in the 1970s, the angriest decade in his long memory. Just about everybody wanted to raise money to finance their version of the right thing. The gun nuts, long solid clients, were joined by pro-lifers hopping mad about *Roe v. Wade* and by PACs, or political action committees, spawned by post-Watergate campaign-financing reforms. And then there were the semi-American hotheads: Jewish-Americans who wanted all of the West Bank settled, Palestinian-Americans who wanted all of Israel back, Cuban-Americans who wanted Castro dead, Irish-Americans who wanted the British out. . . . The list was endless and, like the dear, departed *contras* of Nicaragua, these true believers were the easiest folks of all to gouge. The only folks he wouldn't touch were survivalists, the crazies who kept scanning the skies for them black helicopters carrying UN attack teams. First, not many of 'em had mailboxes. Second, not many of 'em had much cash laying around after buying their lifetime supply of freeze-dried meals.

The skim from his direct-mail empire grew so vast he needed a front to wash it. Having seen firsthand that few folks paid much mind to the activities of nonprofit organizations, he had set up the A.L.B. Foundation. A.L.B. channeled most of the money offshore while keeping up appearances by investing a smidge in legitimate American start-ups. The Tashman project had been one such enterprise, as had Caduceus 21 and then MedEx, a Chisholm brainstorm he entrusted to a feller he met while scaring up money for the *contras*. These days A.L.B. even had a piece of a couple of them biotech companies trying to breed pigs with organs that humans could use. The notion of a swine's liver inside his own body gave him the willies but hey, a buck was a buck.

Chisholm found himself at the front of the house again, his constitutional complete. Turning up the stone path flanked by beds of cacti, he paused by the door to slip from his dew-soaked boots into dry moccasins, then went inside.

A mixture of savory aromas greeted him. There was strong coffee, freshly brewed; bread just out of the oven; and best of all, a kettle of *feijoada* that Placida was simmering for tomorrow's lunch.

Chisholm hung his down-filled vest and broad-brimmed Stetson on pegs by the door and headed for the kitchen.

"*Bom dia*, Placida," he said.

"*Bom dia, Tío.*" The cook, a handsome woman in her late thirties, was stirring a pot of oatmeal. Did *Tío* want eggs and bacon as well this morning?

"*Dois ovos, por favor.*"

As Chisholm and Placida chatted in Portuguese, he dipped a spoon into the *feijoada*, a hearty stew of black beans, pork, sausage, bacon, and beef, and *mmmmmm*'d his approval. Over the next few minutes, the rest of the staff wandered in from their quarters to the kitchen: Natalie, the housekeeper; Lino, the pilot; Pedro, the chauffeur; and Nestor, the gardener.

Placida rinsed two soft-boiled eggs in cold water and put them on a plate. Chisholm carried it, along with his bowl of oatmeal, to the table and took a seat between Natalie and Lino. As he reached for the silver salver that held his daily regimen of pills and vitamins, Lino poured him a mug of coffee.

Meals were now the social highlights of Chisholm's day. That was by design; hell, he couldn't even go to opening night at the local opera house without being pestered about willing his artwork to the new O'Keeffe museum in town. The staff gathered around the table knew little about his holdings and his business affairs and cared less; they wanted nothing from him except his satisfaction and approval. The conversation this morning centered on their impending departure from Santa Fe. Chisholm patiently elicited from them the type of gifts they wanted to take home to family and friends, then announced that on the next two weekends Lino would fly everyone to Dallas and Los Angeles in the Gulfstream for some proper shopping.

Shortly after 8 A.M., his breakfast finished, Chisholm excused himself from the table. He walked past his bonsai collection to the single door on the long wall hung with O'Keeffes and pushed through it to his private quarters. Damn, it was chilly this morning, he thought, swinging by his bedroom to slip a woolen vest over his chambray shirt before continuing to his office.

The furniture in it—a large, rough-hewn table he used as a desk, several hutches that served as bookcases—was painted in the gaudy azures and yellows favored by the seventeenth-century artisans of colonial Spain. There was only one chair, his, because he held no meetings here. Executives of the companies he controlled came to the ranch periodically, but none had so much as glimpsed this room.

Only one had ever asked to. "Century," Duane Strand, the chairman of MedEx, once joked, "I'd love to check out the rumor about the hot Vermeer hanging over your desk." To which Chisholm had replied, "No need, Strand. First off, it's a Rembrandt. Second, it ain't hot. Third, if it was over my desk, I'd have to crick my neck to admire it, now wouldn't I?"

Not long ago, the room had been dense with office machinery: computer, printer, stock-quote terminal, database retrieval terminal, telephone answerer, fax, copier. Today most of these services were accessible through the single monitor on his desk.

He fingered the touchpad and called his electronic in-box up on-screen.

There was a note confirming that his personal physician would be coming to Santa Fe in midmonth to give Chisholm his semiannual checkup.

There was also a report from Leonard Reifsnyder summarizing Maggie Sepulveda's visit to Knoxville. As predicted, she was recommending a private placement. Negotiations with her firm, Marx Dillon & Neil, would take a week, mainly because Reifsnyder planned on playing hardball on the expenses he would allow the investment bankers to bill to Caduceus 21. After that, Sepulveda and several associates would arrive in Knoxville to begin their analysis of the company. She planned to finish her creditworthiness report by mid-January, in which case the placement should be concluded by March 1.

Chisholm stared at the screen for several seconds, then eased himself into his chair and began plucking his upper lip. Like a grizzled coyote whose hackles rise at a faint scent from a far valley, he felt the icy touch of an unnameable anxiety. He had always been reluctant to expose Caduceus 21 and, of course, MedEx to close scrutiny. Reifsnyder's assurances at their recent dinner rang true; yes, all ledgers and contracts were in order. But Chisholm had been a party to too many deals undone by complexity. He knew from experience that the best lie was always the simplest, that loose threads invited yanking.

Forewarned is forearmed, he thought, finally deciding on his course of action. Chisholm made an electronic copy of Reifsnyder's report, then appended to it a cover note:

D.S.—
FYI, SOME STRANGERS ARE GOING TO BE PUSSYFOOTING AROUND KNOXVILLE. YOU MIGHT WANT TO CHECK OUT THE MDⓔN PLAYERS AND MONITOR THEIR ACTIVITIES.
—CENTURY

He addressed the document to the personal electronic inbox of Duane Strand, chairman of MedEx, and clicked SEND.

Time's a-wasting, thought Chisholm, eager to get back to his memoirs.

He stood and crossed to a seven-foot-by-five-foot oaken panel set in the west wall. At chest height to the right glowed a square of luminescent plastic, a scanner programmed to authenticate his palm print and that of his housekeeper, Natalie. When he palmed the square, the oaken panel parted in the middle.

• • •

JEFFERSON Y. T. Leong splashed water on his boyish face, then checked the men's-room mirror to make sure he had rinsed off the last of the shaving cream. Never in his four-plus years as director of MedEx's worldwide computer networks had New York called a videoconference on twenty minutes' notice; such sessions were normally scheduled days if not weeks in advance. Some tectonic shift was under way, but what?

At thirty-one, Leong rarely paid attention to dress codes. His job was to tweak systems, not social-engineer humans. Yet even he knew it would be rude to greet the corporate suits wearing a four-day stubble and a Speed Racer T-shirt. Good thing he had a spare shirt and jacket in the office. The borrowed tie didn't go with the jacket, but it would have to do.

Leong left the men's room and went to the elevator bank. As he waited for a car he looked down on his domain, a half-acre expanse of workstations buried fifty feet underground. The basement was the most secure part of the building, and its lower ambient temperature noticeably reduced the air-conditioning bills. Manning the Unixes were serfs who called their bunker "Mushroom Farm" and their boss "Cap'n Fungi." That derisive tag carried a nasty racist overtone; coined years earlier during the O. J. Simpson trial, it alluded to the hapless LAPD criminalist who had wrecked the perception of Asian-American superiority almost beyond repair. The wise-asses on his staff would be toast if only Leong could find the time to recruit replacements. Serfs were expendable because they patrolled the ninety-eight percent of the MedEx systems dedicated to legitimate data. They had no inkling of sites like SEECUBED and the Caduceus 21 trap-door; access to this dark core, as Leong thought of it, had been given only to him and his deputy, Rusty.

A soft *bing*, and the elevator doors slid open. He stepped in and pressed the top button. The car ascended past SB1, which housed the building's core utilities, and two parking levels before stopping at the ground floor.

The view out the lobby's glass doors depressed Leong almost as much as his staff did. The executive offices of MedEx were in Manhattan but the bulk of its operations rested in a sunbaked industrial park on the outskirts of Dallas/Fort Worth International Airport. The company had copied the efficient hub-and-spoke concept perfected by Federal Express: the organs it collected worldwide were all funneled through DFW on their way to the various Caduceus 21 transplant centers. Of the major airports in the midcontinental United States, DFW experienced the fewest weather delays—a crucial consideration when dealing with commodities that were highly perishable.

Leong made his way to the videocon room, a windowless cubicle in the center of the building. A sign by the door reminded visitors that recording devices were not permitted; transcripts of MedEx's videocons were preserved only in digital form, on one of the dark-core sites even Leong couldn't access. Palm-print check, cleared. Metal-detector check, cleared. He entered the room. It contained a glass table flanked on one side by three chairs and on the other by a camera and a thirty-five-inch monitor that at the moment displayed the MedEx logo. Leong settled himself into a chair, then absentmindedly took off his glasses and polished them with his tie.

Promptly at 3 P.M. the logo on the monitor dissolved to reveal the caller.

Leong reflexively straightened his posture, surprised to find himself face-to-face with the chairman of MedEx.

Duane Strand, who was in his late fifties, had a square face, deep-set eyes seemingly devoid of lashes, and a haircut that virtually demanded a salute. He reminded Leong of that brusque Air Force general from the Iran-*contra* hearings of a decade ago.

"Good afternoon, Mr. Leong," Strand said. "I received your communiqué on the attempted hack the other day. Any damage?"

"No, sir," Leong replied. "He hits our gateway with a password-cracking app. Way uncool—like, you'd have better luck getting inside Fort Knox with a slim-jim? He's bright enough to mask his calling number, but no phreak can resist my Trojan Horse. So while the little pinhead's downloading my virus, we trace him to Minneapolis? Just some kid at a boarding school autodialing around, some dweeb who's now got himself a seriously wrecked C drive."

"You stand by that analysis?" asked Strand.

Leong nodded. "Our gateway gets misdialed every day. My firewall only targets hackers who try to log on—maybe one per month, average? They're rarely such buttwipes, though. Eighties shareware right off a BBS? A ninety-six-hundred-baud modem? My God, talk about . . ."

"You'll keep me apprised, Mr. Leong?" Strand often interrupted when Leong started to veer into jargon. "Thank you. Now, what's the status of our Caduceus Twenty-One penetration?"

Leong tensed—he preferred to think of his patch-ins as "visits" rather than "penetrations"—but quickly recovered: "Our trapdoor remains transparent."

"Meaning they don't have a clue we're inside their net?"

"Yes, sir."

"I'm also interested in their offices," Strand said.

"Knoxville? Full surveillance on selected users. That means clickstreams on their boxes, seines on the PBX. Everything they type or say, we know."

"What about new employees coming aboard—you have to go back inside the building with screwdrivers and pliers?"

"No, sir. Since we're inside their hubs and routers, I can acquire and lock on new users from here."

"Outstanding." Strand's tight smile was like a benediction. "Your handiwork will be important in the days ahead. Now, Mr. Leong, another little matter's come up that requires your prompt attention. Stay right where you are, and M.T. will call back and brief you in five minutes."

"Of course, sir." But mention of an urgent new task caught Leong off-guard; he blurted, "Er, am I permitted a question, Mr. Strand?"

Strand looked as if he'd just spotted a cockroach waltzing across his T-bone.

"Prompt attention? Does that mean, like, this weekend? You see, I . . ."

"M.T. will brief you in five minutes," Strand repeated evenly. He swept his arm from left to right, MedEx etiquette for terminating a videocon, and his image dissolved back into the corporate logo.

Leong knotted his fists in despair. He had embarrassed himself to Strand for no good reason. So what if the new assignment interfered with his plans for a long weekend in New York City? Leong loathed Texas, which he considered a wasteland of gun-crazed hotheads, fat-tired pickup trucks, and unspeakably foul Chinese food. He fled it at every chance, be it by chat-rooming with Net pals most nights after work or the occasional trip home. But life was a trade-off, and he had opted for professional gratification over personal happiness.

Leong lived to write code. His serfs swore he could actually think in machine language; certainly his programs were more concise and articulate than his staff memos. Fluency in cybertongues was common among a tribe of lost boys from America's middle class, nerds who found it easier to bond with their PCs than with their peers. Leong's first computer, a primitive TRS-80 received for Christmas, had booted him into a meritocratic realm where intelligence and logic ruled over brute force. It was like *Star Trek* in real life. So what if the neighborhood Klingons shook him down for his lunch money; Leong could mess with their grades or scramble their parents' bank accounts from the safety of his bedroom.

His obsession with computer security dated to his senior year of high school. By then, Leong was diligently scanning the software he poached for viruses. But someone sneaked a Trojan Horse past all the safeguards; once loose on his hard drive, it began deleting data—including two years' worth of notes on the project he was preparing for the nationwide Westinghouse Science Talent Search. Leong graduated from Stuyvesant High at age sixteen and studied programming at Carnegie Mellon and MIT. His master's thesis, not surprisingly on network firewalls, had won him wide notice in the computer community as well as a brace of job opportunities.

Back in 1989, accepting the National Security Agency's offer had seemed a no-brainer. NSA, charged with procuring SIGINT, or signals intelligence, was equipped with the latest and the best of everything.

As Leong quickly learned, though, his new employer's vaunted wizardry sometimes had Oz-like consequences. For instance, the agency had covertly jacked into every telecommunications system in the world. That meant it captured enough raw product each minute to occupy its analysts for weeks. To cope with this overflow, NSA developed powerful software to scan files for key words. But that in turn required converting audiotapes into digital files, and a digitized ten-minute conversation took up more disk space than the full text of *War and Peace*. Without analysis, it was impossible to tell whether a file contained Saddam Hussein discussing troop deployment around Basra or merely Prince Charles raunching it up with his fair Camilla. Meanwhile, the file had to be parked somewhere; small wonder the agency was a prime supporter of data-compression research.

Leong's arrival at NSA's Fort Meade, Maryland, stronghold also coincided with events that soon rocked the agency: the leveling of the Berlin Wall and the fissuring of the Soviet Union into an enormity of warring ethnicities. With no more Iron Curtain to penetrate, NSA lost not only its limitless funding but also its sense of mission. Compared to, say, decoding Moscow–Tehran intercepts, eavesdropping on Colombian drug lords or

Airbus salesmen or Matsushita executives was stoop labor.

Four years later Leong was stuck in a particularly unworthy job, helping engineer NSA's misconceived "clipper chip." He started thinking seriously about going freelance. The agency from time to time hired outside security consultants, and they weren't always top-shelf. One, a self-important geek from San Diego, actually managed to lose the goodies stored on his supposedly impregnable home workstation to an Israeli hacker, but saved face—and landed a seven-figure book-and-movie deal—by helping jail a harmless fugitive American cyberprankster. Definitely not a cool moment in NSA history.

Before Leong could leave the agency, Duane Strand had come calling. Strand offered an extraordinary salary-and-bonus package plus full authority, backed by an open checkbook, to keep MedEx's hardware state-of-the-art. What clinched the deal, what made Dallas worth the hassle, was the freedom Leong won to develop the killer firewall described in his master's thesis.

A flicker now on the monitor. Leong looked up as the MedEx logo dissolved to reveal Morris Tomczack, the company's director of operations. M.T., a man in his late forties so unprepossessing that he could disappear in a crowd of three, was the most informal of the New York suits. When Strand made a rare tour of the Dallas facilities, he treated Leong like a pencil-neck. Tomczack, whose duties brought him down at least once a month, took a genuine interest in the rigors of maintaining a global net.

"How goes it, Jefferson?"

"Same old same old. Listen, M.T., did I say anything just now that, like, tripped Mr. Strand's circuits?"

"Not that I could tell."

"Great." Leong blew out his breath in relief. "What's up?"

"Something you can do in your sleep," Tomczack said. "Ready?"

"Go."

"We're setting up a new listening node."

Leong blanched. Covert electronic surveillance was strictly dark-core, which ruled out using any of his uninitiated serfs. "I don't have the resources," he protested. "It's in writing. The memo I wrote right after Knoxville? It's . . ."

"Strand and I reread the memo this morning," Tomczack interrupted. "What you wrote is true. But Jefferson, shit happens. And when the going gets tough . . . Well, you know the rest, right?"

Leong nodded glumly.

"The target's a small investment-banking firm," Tomczack continued. "I'm guessing there won't be more than a half-dozen candidates for twenty-four-by-seven coverage. Total staff of about a hundred, but it's a replay of Knoxville. We only track the whole office until we're sure of who's who."

"Oy." Leong had a hellish vision of the datastream generated by one hundred people: clickstreams and audio totaling several gig per day. Trying to suppress the whine in his voice, he said, "Only me and Rusty are cleared to sift the output from a listening node. Jeez, M.T., we're logging four, five hours a day between us just keeping current on Caduceus data. Plus, like, we got a net to run?"

"Understood," Tomczack replied. "After you set up the new node, all data from it will be processed by freelancers."

Let rent-a-dweebs loose inside the dark core? Talk about compromising the system he had built—why not just post the MedEx access codes on CompuServe? Leong's thoughts immediately turned to self-protection and to the recording of this video con that was being written onto a disk deep in the basement: "I can't be held responsible for anything the freelancers do."

Tomczack's eyes seemed to detonate in anger, but it could have been a trick of the lighting because a millisecond later the security chief winked reassuringly. "Of course not," he said. "Listen, Jefferson, I anticipated your concerns and expressed them to Strand. Got him to agree to a stand-alone node that's not patched into our net."

Leong grunted, partially mollified.

"It's my job to find the freelancers, vet them, supervise their work," Tomczack said. "FYI, some of the new targets will be working out of Caduceus for several months. If you can set up a pipeline, I'll have my men monitor their Knoxville datastreams too."

"No problemo," Leong replied.

"Outstanding. So your job now is to tell me how many freelancers we need. Be advised that budget is not a consideration. Same goes for hardware—whatever you say it takes, I get."

Leong scratched his head. "How much time do I have?"

"We want in by this time next week, so I need your shopping lists ASAP. Gives me the weekend to start lining up personnel and matériel. Meanwhile, you can be scoping their software and writing the patches. I assume you want me to take their system down and get you a seat on the resusc team?"

Leong nodded. "Like, why not kill two birds with one stone? We take the time to hardwire the PBX, they can't spot the tap without unscrewing everything. A cold boot's also the best time to plant the clickstream wad. I can do it by remote from Dallas but somebody notices the file spec changes, they suspect a hack. I show up on-site, I got a reason to tweak the OS files. Anybody asks about the reconfigs and like, hey, I'm only debugging the glitches that crashed your system."

"Outstanding," Tomczack said. "I understand you had plans for this weekend, which is why I saved the good news for last. The target's in midtown Manhattan, so Mrs. Leong's favorite son gets to eat some home cooking after all, courtesy of MedEx."

"Cool!"

"I think that about covers everything, except for the target's dial-up number. Got a pencil?"

Leong jotted it down, then said, "How about I e-mail you the shopping list overnight? And unless this company has some outrageous configs, I shoot for coming up to New York, say, Wednesday night?"

"Sounds perfect, Jefferson. Let's talk in the morning." Tomczack swept his arm from side to side and his image dissolved back into the MedEx logo.

It was a little after 3:15, which meant 4:15 P.M. in Manhattan. Leong wouldn't be dialing up the Marx Dillon & Neil system for another ten hours, so he remained seated, trying to make sense of his back-to-back videocons. Strand hadn't been as complimentary since his recruiting dinners with Leong. Tomczack had worked overtime stroking him. The two men wanted to pass off the new listening node as some casual afterthought, not a project requiring a budget that might easily run into seven figures.

Leong realized why MedEx needed to be patched into Caduceus 21; the first duty of a parasite was to do its host no harm. But an investment-banking firm? Last time Leong looked, his employer wasn't exactly in the financial-services racket. Finally he sighed and stood. New York wanted the node up and running within seven days. So little time, so much to do.

WEDNESDAY

O C T O B E R   7

WHENEVER Maggie Sepulveda entered Central Park after midnight, she imagined herself transported back to a Manhattan long since vanished. The fragrance of leaves and grass, so rare on this concrete-clad island, and the soft light from the cast-iron streetlamps lining the footpaths combined to suggest the city that existed before skyscrapers started sprouting like stalagmites. It was a pastoral illusion dangerous to joggers and pedestrians but not to someone safely cocooned inside a dial-a-cab cruising up Park Drive East.

The ride home usually allowed Maggie to decompress from the tumult at Marx Dillon & Neil. Not tonight, though. Days like this made her wonder why she continued to work in investment banking. In America, she thought darkly, high-testosterone males who dropped out of high school often wound up behind bars, but those who made it through business school often wound up in Hollywood or on Wall Street. Case in point: Rob Dillon, the senior partner assigned to placing the Caduceus 21 paper.

Though he was the logical choice, Maggie had decidedly mixed feelings about working closely with him for the next several months. Of the many concepts alien to Dillon was that of compromise. For instance, he was still bickering with Len Reifsnyder over the terms of the Caduceus 21 letter of agreement by way of ever more bellicose faxes. Dillon would storm into her office, the latest salvo in hand, to rant about "that fucking lunatic down in Knoxville." Maggie knew it was really about ego—at issue were nickel-and-dime expenses—but that didn't make the interruptions any less distracting. She was supposed to be organizing and briefing the in-house team that would verify the health-care company's creditworthiness, not listening to her boss vent.

At least the firm had acknowledged the importance of the Caduceus 21 account by granting her pick of the staff. Maggie was opting for intellectual nimbleness and perseverance over seniority and rank. Her key aides were both in their late twenties. The team of number crunchers going down to Knoxville would be headed by Teddy Quereshi, with whom she had worked on previous health-care projects, while Jill Unger, a former college volleyball star turned financial analyst, would be performing almost half the on-site visits to Caduceus 21's far-flung facilities.

Despite Dillon, Maggie's preparations were more or less on schedule; she even had a shot at salvaging one day of her vacation. The thought did not thrill her. Though not by nature a procrastinator, she had yet to come to terms with Paul's behavior at that party the other weekend. How could a man with whom she'd shared so much for so long end up as much of a stranger as a blind date?

Paul, who managed classical musicians, had been the first to not make an issue of Maggie's seventy-hour workweeks and extensive travel. Perhaps he was such a low-maintenance guy because, with clients performing on three continents, his schedule was even crazier than hers.

For that reason they still maintained separate apartments; since the start, finding time for each other had been as taxing as it was romantically reaffirming. Maggie could remember the joy of bailing out of her office at 2 A.M., eyes numb from spreadsheets, and heading down to SoHo, where one of Paul's postrecital bashes would still be in full swing. Of him flying out to Minneapolis or Denver or Atlanta to assuage, if only for a night, the loneliness of her research treks. And of cashing in her frequent-flyer miles to jet off to Europe for intense weekends divided between the backstages of concert halls and the beds of five-star hotels.

In the beginning they had also shared the pressures of undertaking significant career gambles. She was entering negotiations to switch from Goldman Sachs to Marx Dillon & Neil. He, meanwhile, was building a stable of young, conservatory-trained soloists who were also highly photogenic, and redesigning their acts to play to the mosh-pit crowd.

The industry had smirked at this bizarre fusion of classical and grunge until one of his studmuffins recorded a catchy synthesizer version of Bach's *Goldberg Variations*. Paul talked the label into releasing the first three variations as a single and commissioning a video that segued its bare-chested star through a variety of settings—mountain meadow, deep desert, raging surf—as he pummeled the Kurzweil and rippled his pecs. The single, titled "GV 1-2-3," crossed over onto the Top 10 charts, the video went into heavy rotation on MTV, and the CD earned a Grammy nomination. A *New York Times* critic had spoken for many when he fulminated against "a new breed of organ-grinder influenced less by Albinoni and Mozart than by *American Gladiators* and *Melrose Place*."

Among those undeterred by the bad notices: Linzy Kirsch, a young opera superstar in the market for her third manager in five years. Kirsch knew of Paul by reputation. Wanting a firsthand look, she arranged to have him invited to a party being given for her in the Hamptons. Maggie wouldn't have made a special trip out to attend it, but since she was already at the Sag Harbor house, she had agreed to tag along. Big mistake.

The driver of the dial-a-cab slid into the left lane to follow the 72nd Street transverse as it curved toward the Upper West Side. To Maggie's left loomed the bandshell and to her right, down twin flights of majestic steps, lay Bethesda Fountain and the rowboat lake. When she first moved to the city, into a 350-square-foot studio apartment whose main window faced an airshaft, she had used this area to read the Sunday *Times* and to rendezvous with friends. Today she had a real backyard out in Sag Harbor but, ironically, zero urge to use it.

All because of that damned party. It was such a snore —she hadn't seen so many business cards exchanged since the last medical-equipment convention in Las Vegas—that Maggie spent the first two hours watching a video with the host's kids.

Then, shortly after 10 P.M., she happened to spot Paul and Kirsch across the crowded living room. Maggie knew from his body language that he felt on top of his game and from Kirsch's face that Paul's soft-sell was working. Just at that instant, the diva drew him close. A quick exchange of whispers and then he was nodding and turning away with that eager-to-please smile Maggie detested.

She had looked on with foreboding as Paul moved through the crowd to the side of a TV talk-show host. The man was notorious for his philandering; not as well known was the habit that had cost him his job as a network news reporter. He and Paul traded backslaps and a few words, then left the room together.

Maggie refocused on Kirsch. Two admirers had replaced Paul but the diva, who looked suddenly drawn, listened halfheartedly to their praises as she darted edgy glances toward the front door.

Less than five minutes later, Paul came back into the house and headed straight upstairs. Kirsch excused herself from her fans and followed.

Maggie's suspicions were confirmed when the diva soon rejoined the party, her eyes bright, her color high, her mood recharged. Paul sauntered downstairs a few minutes after, equally ebullient. And why not? Cocaine was popular precisely because it worked.

The driver of the dial-a-cab exited the park and continued west on 72nd Street, then turned north up Amsterdam Avenue. Once past the cluster of singles bars in the seventies and eighties, he made good time. Maggie thought of asking to be dropped at the pizza parlor at the corner of 96th Street, the only takeout place in her neighborhood still open at this hour, but she had been in there the previous night; microwave potluck it would be.

The doorman emerged to help her out of the cab. It had taken her months to find the right co-op; in the end, a fashionable address had mattered less than a front desk manned around the clock and an apartment with the high ceilings, thick plaster walls, and parquet floors common to Manhattan's pre–World War II buildings.

Maggie collected her mail and took the elevator up to her apartment on the sixteenth floor.

Greeting her was the soft chirp of her answering machine. She hung up her coat, went into the bedroom, and pressed NEW MSGS.

"Congratulations!" boomed an unctuous male voice. "Marguerite K. Sepulveda, you've won a sun-splashed vacation for two to the fabulous Bahamas! To claim your valuable prize, just call . . ."

Maggie punched STOP. She should have guessed it would be a boiler-room solicitation; sadly, everyone in her life—her mom, Paul, her pals—knew that their best chance of reaching her, no matter what the hour, was at the office. It was ironic that her chosen field of investment banking was thought to be on the crest of a postindustrial wave that would enable professionals to lead more efficient and benign lives. Just the opposite was true. Databases never called it a day, so why should those who made their living trolling them for information?

Her eyes fell on the two framed photographs next to the answering machine. One snapshot showed her and Petey, both wearing Seattle Pilots T-shirts, sharing a playground swing back in Tacoma. The squirt must have been about three and she about six because she still looked like Tweety Bird. In the facing picture, also of the two of them, her kid brother had matured into a gauntly handsome young man of twenty-four. It had been taken in the same playground, at Petey's request, three weeks before his death in 1991.

The photographs summed up why Maggie put up with the stress, the succession of post-midnight dial-a-cabs home.

Had she continued to specialize in the computer industry, she would be out of investment banking by now. Talk about knee-deep in the hoopla: Would John Q. Hacker fork over an extra five hundred dollars for a new lithium-laminate battery capable of powering an active-matrix laptop for eight hours between recharges? Would the latest release of Microsoft's operating system finally iron out all the glitches in the ho-hum Windows 95?

The noble dream of making the PC as affordable and as ubiquitous as the television had been sidetracked by the Barnumesque philosophy of planned obsolescence. Maggie was no Luddite; she rather enjoyed her state-of-the-art setup at Marx Dillon. Yet so much of what passed for progress was merely product enhancement. For instance, the most minimal word-processing programs now imported graphics and could set type in columns in case users wanted to publish a newsletter; even low-end personal-finance programs now generated pie charts in 256 colors. Trouble was, how many users published newsletters or needed pie charts? And such bells and whistles, by hogging ever more memory and disk space, rendered older machines obsolete.

Nothing epitomized the frivolity of the industry more than screensavers. These were programs that, on detecting user inactivity, generated animated images of flying toasters or wacky aquariums; touching a key or the mouse restored whatever had been on-screen. Screensavers dated to the dawn of the home-computer era. They were created to prevent "burn-in," a phenomenon whereby an unchanging image eventually etched itself into the monitor. The problem still plagued the low-resolution monitors found in ATMs; often, the words of the bank's welcome screen remained in ghostly view throughout the transaction. The monitors now sold for office and home use were no longer susceptible to burn-in. Yet screensavers—ranging in theme from *Star Trek* to Sonic the Hedgehog to Calvin and Hobbes—had become the equivalent of the rock-star posters with which teenagers plastered their bedroom walls: useful only for proclaiming attitude. And the companies that produced them, once an amusing little niche industry, now demanded the attention of analysts. All of which grabbed Maggie as much as an announcement by Ferrari that this year's Testarossa featured titanium commuter-mug holders.

Health care was different. The industry's first wave of consolidation had shown that cost containment often came at the expense of compassion. Someday, somewhere, someone with a fresh philosophy was going to build a system better able to save the Peteys yet to come. And if it turned out to be Caduceus 21, she would have helped.

After a while, Maggie got up and headed into the kitchen. The pair of *Sesame Street* refrigerator magnets on the freezer door, a birthday gift from her college roommate's daughter, usually cheered her. Tonight, they were a baleful reminder of how little time she spent at home. She used Oscar the Grouch to post notes and money for the apartment's only regular visitor, Mrs. Allen, who came every other Monday to clean. And Grover held a sheaf of notes to herself—*Buy orange juice. Pick up dry cleaning. Zabar's: coffee & filters. Low on toilet paper!*—

grown so thick that the magnet's grip had become tenuous.

As she opened the freezer, the slips of paper cascaded to the floor.

Maggie cursed softly, took out a container of clam chowder and placed it into the microwave, then knelt to gather the notes. It would have been easier to transcribe them onto a single sheet than to coax the magnet into holding, but she was not in the mood.

When the microwave buzzed she carried the soup out to the living room. Letterman was over so she began to channel-surf. On one of the cable networks, a psychotherapist was promoting her new best-seller, *Women Who Always Win (Except in Love)*. Maggie put down the remote.

Damn, that's a book I could have written, she told herself, or at least provided some firsthand research. Men tended to bond through competition; when they got together socially, conversation always seemed to revolve around the next poker game or tennis match or business coup. Women tended to bond through empathy; when they got together, conversation unerringly focused on the fault lines in their romantic lives.

Maggie's girlfriends had been there for her when she was agonizing over leaving *el buscapleitos*. In return, she had served as their sounding board and counsel. Yet after a decade and a half of gals-only lunches and late-night telethons and running-with-the-wolves weekends, the riddle of the inappropriate mate remained no closer to solution. BMOC, rebel without a pause, starving artist, adoring doormat, Master of the Universe: all cute in their own way at some point in life, but someone to spend forever with?

She had not begun her relationship with Paul casually. He was bright, ambitious, and impulsive—as was Sebastian Sepulveda. For that reason Maggie had consciously judged him against *el buscapleitos* before following her heart. Making Paul's actions even more inexcusable was the fact that he knew she had nursed her ex through a successful rehab out in Palm Springs before filing for divorce. How could Paul then try to win a potential client by scoring cocaine? And worse, snorting a few lines to be sociable—the same way her ex had become addicted? Linzy Kirsch's favor was worth winning, but the man with whom Maggie had originally fallen in love would have politely declined and walked away. Or did she not truly know the man with whom she had fallen in love?

Tired of beating herself up, and mindful that she had to be back at Marx Dillon in less than eight hours, Maggie powered down and called it a night.

T H U R S D A Y
O C T O B E R   8

NINE months earlier it was the storeroom of a public library in the South-Central district of Los Angeles. Now the dusty shelves and musty cabinets were gone, replaced by a dozen plywood carrels that each housed a PC or Mac. Every computer was in use by a member of Boot Up the 'Hood, a nonprofit workshop that taught hardware basics and the ABCs of popular applications.

The students, earphones jacked in, were busy inputting commands, then checking the screen to see exactly what they had wrought. All were in their teens and three were girls. Yet the scene would not have interested the agencies that produced commercials for IBM and Microsoft and Apple. For one, not a face in the room was white; the group consisted of five blacks, five Chicanos, and two Asians. Worse, there wasn't a shopping-mall ensemble in sight; indeed, a majority of the participants sported the colors of various neighborhood gangs.

But Boot Up the 'Hood's sole rule—check your hostilities and your mouth at the door—was rigorously enforced by its two founders. Over the course of their inaugural ten-week session, cofounders Ignacio Tejada and Phillipa Walker had expelled half the class of eight, and three of nine during the second session. Word got out. This session there had been a record twenty-six applicants; the twelve they accepted had all made it into Week Eight.

The slender Tejada, wearing his usual rude T-shirt and baggy jeans, could have passed for one of the students. He was in fact a twenty-one-year-old senior at the University of Southern California, majoring in computer science. As he steered a Korean girl through the idiosyncrasies of a leading desktop-publishing app, his weight rested on a hand-carved ebony cane sent him from the city of Malacca, in Malaysia, by Nguyen-Anh Dupree. At age eleven, while playing in front of his home, Tejada had taken several rounds from a street-sweeper meant for his brother Javier, then second-in-command of a gang called Tres Equis. The ER doctor, Dupree, had saved Nacio's life that night on the operating table and then again in later years by acting as a surrogate big brother who walked on the right side of the law.

Tejada's partner, a watchful black woman of twenty-five in a silk blouse and linen slacks, was slouched in a folding chair by the door. Phillipa Walker, who answered to "Leepi," munched on an apple as she stared at the open PowerBook on her lap. Walker was the chief programmer for MorpHaus, a small firm that created computerized special effects for movies, television commercials, CD-ROMs, video games, and amusement parks. Her title and her talent made her one of the handful of young blacks achieving behind-the-camera prominence in the new Hollywood.

Logical analysis was Walker's strong suit, intuitive insight Tejada's. When the pair jointly tackled a project, they had few peers on the electronic frontier known as cyberspace. Yet never in their five-year collaboration had they encountered a problem as vexing as that posed by Doc Dupree.

His request seemed simple enough: Hack two networks, neither a part of the ultrasecure U.S. defense system—though Walker and Tejada had roamed around inside there too.

The Immigration and Naturalization Service network proved easier to enter than a bank's ATM; its access codes were posted on a dozen Net sites. As Dupree had feared, there was no trace of a young Mexican surnamed Chacon or Echeverria being nabbed by the Border Patrol in southwestern Texas or languishing in one of the INS gulags.

Hacking their next target, MedEx, proved a different story.

Walker and Tejada were well versed in the ways companies guarded their gateways. When someone dialed up, the host would identify itself and prompt for a password. A valid response led deeper into the network and a second level of authentication. It was customary to permit two attempts at the password before disconnecting, since even careful typists sometimes hit a wrong key.

Nor were they strangers to extremely stringent security protocols. Access to their own outlaw board, named NUROMNCR after William Gibson's seminal cyberpunk novel, was limited to other *otakus* with whom they'd collaborated in the past. If the feds had one-tenth the intelligence, gleaned from elegant hacks of major American corporations, that was freely exchanged on NUROMNCR, white-collar crime would plummet by half. No chance of that, though; their board automatically beamed a new password, valid only for the next twelve hours, to all users in good standing twice a day, at 0300 and 1500 hours GMT.

In all their many sorties, Walker and Tejada had never encountered a firewall as user-unfriendly as MedEx's. The Code Boy who wrote it was too twisted for even such hotbeds of paranoia as the National Security Agency and the weapons lab at Livermore.

It had taken them several hours of browsing medical Websites to find the company's (800) dial-up number.

When they first hit the gateway a week earlier, the call was answered by the familiar susurrant hiss that hackers called "modem breath." Then came . . . absolute nothingness. Had they input the correct telephone number? Yes. The screen remained blank, but then why did both of them experience the same unnerving sensation of being watched?

Nacio had reflexively punched ESC and said, "Like, welcome to *The Twilight Zone.* This has got a real nasty feel to it, Leepi. I say we wait an hour, then go in with Baby Huey." That was a program they had written to simulate the primitive password-cracking apps commonly available in the 1980s on outlaw bulletin boards, or BBSes. In fact, Baby Huey used the preliminary dialogue between machines to probe the host system. To further the deception, Walker and Tejada had retarded their modem to 9600 baud, which was like ramping onto the information superhighway on a tricycle, and routed their second call through the switchboard of some prep school in Minneapolis.

The precautions paid off.

Dial-up; modem breath; blank screen.

After a few moments Tejada, not knowing what else to do, hit ENTER.

A message appeared on-screen:

MEDICAL EXPEDITING SYSTEMS INC.
PLEASE ENTER YOUR PASSWORD:

Tejada launched Baby Huey. As soon as their app generated its first random password, a new message popped up on-screen:

PER OUR BULLETIN OF 05 OCT, RELEASE 7.31 OF THE MEDEX NAVIGATOR IS NOW AVAILABLE. DO YOU WISH TO DOWNLOAD AT THIS TIME?

Walker and Tejada exchanged nervous glances. It was almost inconceivable that Baby Huey had spit out a valid password on its first try; something was wrong. But this was a reconnaissance mission so they clicked YES.

Eight minutes later, the file transfer finally complete, a fresh message popped up on-screen. Under an ominous skull-and-crossbones was the telephone number of the Minneapolis prep school—MedEx must have used the download time to trace the call—plus these words:

THE PENALTY FOR HACKING IS A *SERIOUSLY*
FATAL DISK ERROR. WISE UP AND LIVE LONG.

At which point MedEx disconnected.

Walker and Tejada were almost certain that "MedEx Navigator 7.31" harbored a virus. They also knew that a virus could not begin its nasty mission spontaneously; it needed a trigger. Leaving their machine on, they scanned the drive and spotted not one but two new files. They copied both to a floppy, then ran a diagnostic utility.

The main file was gibberish; a staggering seventy thousand lines' worth, apparently to keep a hacker online until MedEx could trace the call. The second file held a boot-sector virus that, if Walker and Tejada read the code correctly, commanded the hard drive's head-arm to access a cylinder that did not exist.

Would the virus work?

Reboot, followed by a lengthy hang during which the keyboard and mouse were inoperative, and then a sickening grinding sound. Opening up the box, Walker and Tejada found the hard drive beyond repair.

Their study of the vicious virus, which they named Pit Bull, had yet to yield clues. The MedEx net was ultimately hackable—everything was—but they needed more time and, perhaps, outside help.

"Yo, Leepi."

Walker saw that Nacio was still helping the Korean

girl, so she folded down her laptop screen and went to field the call.

"Wassup, bro?" Walker was fluent in the dialects of four distinct subcultures: the streets, whose syntax she used with childhood friends and here in the workshop; white suburbia; high-tech; and Hollywood. The pop therapists who wrote self-help books would consider her ability to effortlessly move from one world to another a sign of a dangerously compartmentalized life. She thought of it as a survival skill.

The young Chicano asking for help slipped off his earphones and waved at the screen: "This motherf . . . Sorry, Leepi. This sucker keeps malfing on me."

Rafael was a sixteen-year-old who had not been inside a school in two years. Tattooed on his right forearm were four small teardrops, one for each rival gang member he had capped. Walker and Tejada had been surprised when Rafael signed up for the workshop. It turned out the teenager saw computers as his ticket from drive-by marksman to a more substantial—and less risky—role in his gang. Perhaps even at his young age Rafael was starting to feel mortal or perhaps, as word on the street had it, his Connie was pregnant; whichever, he had proven himself an unexpectedly adept, if terribly undisciplined, student.

Walker tried mousing his system back to life. "Yup, you crashed it again. What we been saying about watching system resources? About shutting down apps you don't be using?"

"Yo," Rafael said, "I didn't do no overload on this sucker. You telling me sixteen meg of RAM can't be handling a spreadsheet and a word processor and do a download at the same time?"

"And what else?"

"And nothing else." He scratched his scraggly goatee. "Well, maybe Doom Four."

Rafael was lying, but did she want to call him on it? Walker said, "Why don't you just reboot?"

" 'Cause, like, I got stuff on my spreadsheet, y'know?"

"Stuff you forgot to save."

Rafael nodded morosely.

Walker didn't mind that the stuff was probably his gang's financial records. Just as she and Tejada were careful not to share hacking tricks, Boot Up the 'Hood was not in the business of teaching society's dos and don'ts. In any event, she failed to see any moral difference between Rafael's use of a PC to log drug revenues and Ford's use of a mainframe to calculate that it would be more cost-effective to pay off burn victims than to redesign the Pinto's crash-vulnerable gas tank. Like any technology, a computer was neither good nor bad, just a tool. Same as dynamite, she thought, which Alfred Nobel invented to help farmers clear their fields of tree stumps, not blow up fellow human beings.

Rafael's dilemma, though, gave her an opportunity to drive home an important lesson about knowing a box's limits. She glanced around to make sure the users in the adjoining carrels had their earphones on, then squatted down beside the youth: "I can save your stuff. But I got to run a batch file that shows me every app you be running. And you know that I know you ain't just got up a spreadsheet and a word processor and a downloader and maybe Doom Four. You don't want me to see what you been up to, reboot. Your call."

"Aw, Leepi, I got an hour's work in there! C'mon, girl, don't be doing this to me."

"I'm doing nothing to you, Rafael. You don't like the way it is, give it the three-finger salute," she said, referring to the PC warm-boot procedure of simultaneously depressing the CONTROL, ALTERNATE, and DELETE keys.

He squirmed for several moments, then nodded.

Walker reached into her pocket for her "911" disk and slotted it into the floppy drive. Then, depressing four keys simultaneously, she launched a homemade utility that overrode the stalled operating system. A list of Rafael's active apps popped up on-screen, along with a time stamp that told her the machine had been hanging for almost ten minutes. She also spotted the reason for the crash: on top of everything else, Rafael had been connected to a Website that posted nude photos of celebrities. Hiding a grin, she said, "Who you be downloading, bro?"

He blushed.

Walker knew the answer, for the download file carried the singer's name. "So what happens is, you start the download and because it's such a big file with a mega transfer time you go over to Doom and then after a couple games you go back to your spreadsheet. And everything be cool until you go do a three-year projection. Wham—no mouse, no keyboard. That about what happened?"

Rafael was dumbfounded.

"Shut your teeth before a fly wanders in," Walker said. She typed in a few commands and hit ENTER. "All yours. The game's what took you down. The box don't know you wasn't playing Doom Four so it's still grinding away to process the graphics, which are bitchin'. Like me and Nacio keep saying, close down apps that ain't in use. By the way, that download of yours be in gorgeous living color?"

"Sure is."

"Might as well trash it, Rafael. Looking at the byte count, you only sucked in her face and neck before you crashed the system."

The boy hesitated, as if to screw up his courage, then said, "Her face and neck, nowhere near as butter as yours."

Walker now understood why Rafael hadn't immediately reported the malf; he wanted Nacio fully occupied so she would have to answer the call. She was not unaware that some men found her attractive, but what was the kindest way to cancel this child's wet dreams? "Thanks," she said, ejecting her 911 disk. "But I look like a nurse to you?"

"Hunh?"

"They say patients think no one's foxier than their nurse. Situational gratitude or something."

"Whatever. I just thought maybe we could go do something after class."

"I think not, Rafael."

"Aw, c'mon, Leepi," he persisted. "I want to show you how much I 'preciate what you and Nacio be doing."

Walker flashed him a world-weary smile and said, "Then make sure you go to every last Lamaze class with Connie."

She strolled back to her chair by the door. Boot Up the 'Hood never ceased to amaze; no nerd had ever hit on her before, but then Rafael was hardly your average nerd. As much as Walker looked forward to the workshop and its surprises, her continued participation was being threatened by career pressures. For instance, after tonight's class she had to squeeze in a meeting with her agent before pulling an all-nighter on a project that was loathsome to her but profitable to MorpHaus. Yet phasing herself out during the next six months would put her partner at risk.

Nacio's USC education was being financed by Javier, now undisputed *jefe* of Tres Equis. Though Javier had deliberately insulated his kid brother from gang affairs, Nacio was tempted to repay the debt by using his smarts to steer Tres Equis into legitimate enterprises. It was like a Hispanic *Godfather*, Walker thought, only she didn't want to see her friend wind up like Al Pacino. Nacio would make his decision the following spring, after graduation. Until then, she and Doc Dupree—and the computer workshop—were stabilizing influences in his complex life.

Walker could still remember the afternoon she first met Nacio. The math tutorial program of their high school had matched her, an honor-roll senior, with him, a brainiac freshman with a bullet-crippled body. Their intellectual rapport was immediate, their interests similar; for instance, both had joined the school's computer club even though the only machines then available were antique Apple IIe's. Despite the racial barriers dividing not only the student body but all of South-Central, their friendship blossomed. Their lives had become so entwined that they stayed in daily touch even after she enrolled in UCLA as a psychology major. Along the way Walker met the other key outsider in Nacio's life, Nguyen-Anh Dupree. She had long since worked through her unrequited crush on him, but Doc was the only adult besides her aunt around whom she could sometimes still behave like a flustered teenager.

Walker's hacking collaboration with Nacio began in the spring of 1993, on the morning after the first Rodney King verdict. Nacio had phoned her dorm and asked her to brave the ongoing riots to come to the Tejada compound. When she got there he explained that the previous night, on seeing neighborhood crazies start to terrorize white motorists and loot stores that sold appliances and liquor and clothing, he had given Javier a wish list. Shortly after 3 A.M., four Tres Equis members pulled up a van and began unloading cartons.

Nacio then took her to his study, at that time in the basement. There sat two brand-new, fully loaded, top-of-the-line 486 DX66 computers and three shelves packed with apps, some retailing for $899 a copy.

Walker was livid. Screaming that she would not risk her hard-earned scholarship for a possible bust on an accessory-to-felony, she had stormed out of the house. Yet on returning several days later, whom should she find in the basement, checking out an online medical database, but Nguyen-Anh Dupree? For some reason Doc didn't seem the least bit disturbed by Nacio's loot. That was good enough for Walker, who within a month was so hooked that she switched her major to computer science.

Boot Up the 'Hood had been conceived by Nacio as an antidote to the teen workshops so commonplace in Los Angeles. He considered these little better than the bogus trade schools that advertised on late-night TV. Hewing to a narrow and patronizing definition of computer literacy, they only drilled students in the specific software applications needed to gain such low-level jobs as data-entry operator or graphic-arts apprentice.

Nacio understood that despite its obvious utility as a workplace tool, a box was not just a souped-up typewriter or a no-error calculator or a paint-free artist's palette. Far more significant and subversive was its potential to teach skills that truly empowered. One of computing's earliest axioms was GIGO—garbage in, garbage out. Want a correct result? Enter correct data. That in turn demanded that the user employ organization, reason, and discipline, traits that did not come easily to many inner-city teens. But those who acquired a problem-solving mind-set would forever view the world through more confident and self-reliant eyes.

Walker had instantly bought into the concept. First she and Nacio persuaded the community leaders of South-Central to make a library storeroom available. Then she used her contacts in the motion-picture and advertising communities to secure donations of discarded machines. The boxes were virtually cherry high-end screamers, but those industries upgraded hardware as routinely as Hollywood stars their limos.

Walker noticed that across the room, Nacio was checking his watch. He said something to the girl he had been helping, then made his slow way to his partner's side. "Yo, you wireheads," he announced, "it's cleanup time."

The workshop participants reluctantly began closing apps.

It was a Boot Up the 'Hood tradition to end each session with one of Tejada's trick questions: "Okay, listen up, listen up. Bet's the same—you get the answer right, me and Leepi buy pizza next week. Blow it, you owe us apples." He turned to Walker. "Was tonight's apple good, girl?"

"Yummy," she said.

"Everyone in? Okay, the question is, Does Earth weigh more now than it did two thousand years ago?"

Nacio was full of such stumpers, which was why Doc Dupree had once called him "Data," the tag he proudly used on the Net. Her cyberhandle had come from the relative for whom she was named. Uncle Phillip, a devotee of doo-wop music, owned more than six hundred singles from the 1950s that she had been allowed to play as soon as she was old enough to operate a turntable. One song in particular had captivated her with its totally silly lyrics. On hearing his young niece spin "Duke of Earl" for about the tenth time in a row, Uncle Phillip had harmonized with Gene Chandler to sing, ". . . *You are my Duchess / Duchess of Earl* . . ." He had called her "Duchess" from that afternoon until the day he died.

After consulting the other students, the cocky young man who usually acted as their spokesperson said, "Earth weighs more now."

"Why's that, Kadeem?"

"Like, buildings. There wasn't no big buildings around two thousand years ago. Well, okay, maybe the pyramids, but nothing like what we got downtown, or in New York."

"That's cool," Tejada said. "But think about the pyramids. Where did the Egyptians get the stones?"

"Someplace else—I don't know."

"Right. They got them from someplace else. Where does wood come from? A tree that grows someplace else. What about concrete? Right, cement and sand and gravel and water, all from someplace else. If everything's from someplace else, how can Earth be heavier?"

Kadeem scratched his head, then consulted the others again. "Okay, we say Earth be heavier now 'cause of all the people. What we up to, five billion?"

"Almost six," Tejada said.

"And how many people was around in the old days?"

"Under two hundred million."

"Nothin' but net," Kadeem said triumphantly. "Even

with midgets and babies and all them sisters on diets, got to be a whole lot more pounds now."

"How much you weigh, Kadeem?" asked Tejada.

"One seventy, one seventy-five."

"Where that come from?"

"Like, food, man. You know, Mickey D's and a bucket o' fries. And pizzas, like you and Leepi got to buy us next week. By the way, no anchovies."

The other workshop participants chortled and cheered. Tejada quickly sobered them: "How much a cow weigh after Mickey D be through with him? Or all them tomatoes Pizza Hut cuts up? You eat that junk, their weight goes into you. And when you be dead from that junk, Kadeem, you don't be weighing no one seventy, one seventy-five. You be dissolving back into elements—and those elements be making some plant grow tasty enough that some other cow's going to eat it so it can get fat enough for Mickey D. Think about it, man. Planet Earth be a closed system. What goes around comes around."

"That the answer?" said Kadeem. "That Earth weighs the same?"

"Basically. Whatever we gain when meteorites fall down on us, we lose whenever NASA and the Russians and them other dudes shoot rockets into space. Don't believe me? Check it out with Ms. Ferrer," Tejada said, invoking the name of a science teacher at the high school. "Okay, same time next week. And don't be forgetting them apples for me and Leepi."

On that note, the teenagers collected their belongings and started to file from the room. When the last had departed, Walker said, "Great question, Nacio. You know, you ought to think about teaching."

"Nah. I don't work for no chump change."

"We'll talk career plans some other time. Let's huddle up—got to go meet Treasure for a fast drink before I head back to the sweatshop."

"What you working on?"

She grimaced. "Cigarettes that do an Astaire-and-

Rogers kind of shtick while they sing in Chinese. Way sick, but the client thinks the commercials'll triple sales on the Mainland."

Tejada broke into a singsong chant: " 'Oh, good-ee, tobacc-ee! But know what-ee? No puff-ee, no kill-ee!' Damn, girl, this the company you always be bragging on?"

"Shut your face, Nacio."

He shrugged. "So what you want to talk about, MedEx?"

"Unh-hunh." Walker hesitated, then said, "Nothing personal, okay? That account happens to be a real sore spot."

"No sweat, Leepi. Your conscience, not mine."

She shot him a mock glare, then raised the screen of her PowerBook to consult her notes. "I think your hunch about the MedEx gateway's right on—anyone authorized to dial in has a handshake built into his hardware. So we can try to grab a box and eyeball the code. More realistically, we post a line-by-line of Pit Bull on NUROMNCR and maybe a couple of other *otaku* boards. Code Boy didn't just wake up one morning and say, 'Yes!' He learned from writing earlier versions. Some friendly's going to flash on his style and point us to him."

Tejada scowled. "No way, girl. Duchess and Data don't beg for help."

"Listen, we going to worry about how much your *cojones* weigh or we going to help Doc Dupree?"

He ran his fingers through his hair. "Okay. But we got to get his permission about posting the problem. You going to e-mail him, or me?"

Walker smiled and punched Tejada affectionately on the shoulder. "You mind? I've got to go make some cancer sticks dance."

S U N D A Y
O C T O B E R   1 1

THE valet-parking station was unmanned when the Mitsubishi Spyder, its retractable hardtop open to the sky, pulled up at the foot of the driveway. Paul Barry surveyed the solid rows of cars lining both shoulders of the leafy two-lane road, then turned to Maggie Sepulveda and said, "Why don't I drop you off here."

"I don't mind the walk."

Paul shifted back into gear. He passed several BMWs, Saabs, and Mercedes station wagons that looked right at home in Bernardsville, New Jersey, a community that allowed Manhattan executives the illusion of horse-country squiredom in return for a brutish commute. Most of the cars, though, suggested an invasion of the hoi polloi: Celicas and Geos and even a few jalopies whose ability to pass an emissions test seemed dubious.

They finally saw a valet but Paul signaled that he would park it himself.

A quarter of a mile beyond the driveway he tucked the Spyder behind the pair of yellow school buses Marx Dillon & Neil had chartered to transport its lowest-salaried employees out to Bernardsville. "Guess we know what the poor folk are doing this afternoon," he said, nodding to the buses. "Do they really have to help clean up to get a ride back?"

Maggie wasn't rankled by Paul's sarcasm; she shared his sentiments on the party they were about to attend.

In much the same way some suburbanites tried to cloak the newness of a custom-built house by staining the siding a weathered gray and filling the rooms with reproduction antiques, so Maggie's firm had sought to disguise its youth by manufacturing instant corporate traditions. Exhibit A: the annual Columbus Day outing at the estate of Rob Dillon.

Dillon was known as the firm's "go-to guy," the senior partner who "stepped up big" when "the chips were down." Of the women on staff, Maggie was the least perturbed by his rainmaker personality, having observed such traits from inside a marriage. At a recent office pour to mark Dillon's thirty-seventh birthday, the most apt gift had been a bumper sticker that read, I *NEVER* BRAKE FOR ANIMALS. And then there was the framed needlepoint above his desk:

> WE EXPECT TO WIN
> WE PREFER TO DOMINATE

Nor was Dillon above intimidating his own staff. Attending his party wasn't mandatory, but no employee to date had mustered the nerve to skip it.

Maggie had almost become the first, having given up all but a day of her vacation to prepare for Knoxville. She had even begged off going out to Sag Harbor for the weekend, though in truth that was primarily because she still hadn't confronted Paul about the Linzy Kirsch incident.

But he had pressured her to attend the party because of the touch football game that was its centerpiece. Paul played for the team captained by senior partner Larry

Marx, whose Monsters had lost last year's game on a late touchdown by Dillon's Dirtbags. It was time, he figured, for a little payback.

They got out of the car and stretched. Both wore the T-shirts that doubled as party invitations: The fronts were emblazoned with the date, time, and driving directions and the backs with the firm's logo. Each year the shirts came in a different color. This year they were olive drab with a camouflage pattern, Rob Dillon's subtle way of saying that the U.S. Marines weren't the only outfit that was *Semper fi.*

Paul reached into the tiny backseat of the Spyder for his gym bag, which held their swimsuits and his game jersey, then joined Maggie for the hike back to the house.

"So listen," he said, "let's say I have a clean shot at Dillon. You know, make him a candidate for a hip replacement, something that'll keep him out of commission until this Caduceus deal goes down."

"Let's say you do."

"What's it worth to you?"

He still doesn't sense my estrangement from him, Maggie thought, not sure whether to be mad or relieved. "That Burberry you've been eyeing?"

"Sold."

The seven-foot-high phalanx of hedges that shielded the Dillon estate from passing traffic was eventually interrupted by the driveway. Waved through by the valets, Maggie and Paul turned up it and beheld a sprawling stone mansion that, with its ten-plus acres of land, was probably worth three or four million dollars. Not bad for a man not yet forty, but Dillon had married into it; his wife, Deirdre, was the only child of a shopping-mall developer. Deirdre taught autistic children and was active on the state's Special Olympics committee, impeccable résumé entries to support her goal of following role model and neighbor Christine Todd Whitman into high elected office.

"Son of a bitch," Paul said at the top of the driveway,

detouring to the vehicle on which Dillon had plastered the gag bumper sticker. A pearl-gray Hummer—the civilian version of the military's wide-track, all-terrain HumVee—sat there like a mechanized carnivore with an eye peeled for supper. "How much you suppose one of these costs?"

"A half-dozen Hyundais," Maggie guessed. "Worth every penny, too, for those family outings to Safari World. Oh look, isn't this cute?"

Paul saw the small RLD monogram painted on the driver's door and snorted.

They followed a flagstone path around to the back of the estate, where some 250 people in camouflage shirts were milling about.

"Jesus," Paul quipped, "did we make a left turn and end up at Camp Lejeune?"

Immediately before them was one of the umbrellaed pushcarts scattered across the property to dispense wine, beer, sodas, and iced tea. The Olympic-sized pool teemed with youngsters being tutored by the instructors Dillon had hired for the afternoon. Beyond the pool, the lush lawn was chalked into an eighty-yard-long gridiron. And off to their left stood the large food tent.

From parties past, Maggie knew the menu. First would come a dazzling array of antipasti and a raw bar, catered by Trattoria dell'Arte in Manhattan. Then, lobster; Two-Alarm chili that Deirdre insisted be made with chunks of filet mignon instead of ground chuck; grilled free-range chicken; and burgers and hot dogs for the tots. Finally, fresh-baked apple and pumpkin pies, plus visits by two trucks: one a Good Humor, the other a Mr. Softee. Maggie had never been comfortable with the grandiosity of Dillon's bash, even if the leftovers were donated to a soup kitchen in a nearby community. Now, having been exposed to the admirable low-rent philosophy that guided Caduceus 21, she felt embarrassed by the let-'em-eat-shellfish opulence set out before her.

Maggie and Paul armed themselves with drinks before she started to scan the crowd for their host.

He and his fellow senior partners were by the tent.

Rob Dillon had already donned his navy blue Dirtbag jersey, rugby shorts, and rubber-cleated shoes.

Larry Marx, forty-three, was the nonplaying captain of the Monsters and the firm's strategic director. Though furtive in demeanor and stumbling of speech, he could absorb a CD-ROM's worth of data on select companies and then mentally recrunch the value of each after a glance at its latest earnings report. But in this Lotus 1-2-3 age those skills no longer guaranteed a partnership at Goldman Sachs. When it became clear that Marx's social clumsiness was no asset either, he and Dillon, at the time a hot young Goldman trader, had gone off on their own. Marx alone of the guests was in shirt and tie, worsted trousers, and dress shoes, though his dignity was somewhat compromised by the garish scarlet jersey he wore like a sweater.

Completing the troika was Nigel Neil, forty-two, a large, moon-faced Australian recruited by Marx from Sydney to provide the new firm with expertise in the burgeoning Pacific Rim markets. Neil, who was fond of posing as a boorish colonial boy, had an endless larder of anecdotes that he usually dispensed with one meaty hand wrapped around a can of Foster's ale. His tales of outhaggling the native wallahs while sitting around the bar of Raffles in Singapore or the lounge of the Peninsula in Hong Kong were mostly true; in all of New York, no investment banker was more solidly networked into the financial tigers of Asia. By default, Neil was the most approachable and tactful of the senior partners and handled all personnel matters save for firings. Those were, of course, Dillon's pleasure.

Maggie pasted on a smile and led Paul toward her bosses.

"The Healthmeister!" boomed Dillon, who had taped

every *Saturday Night Live* since its 1975 premiere and regularly recycled the show's moldy routines.

"Hi, Rob . . . Nigel, Larry. You all know Paul?"

"Hell, yes," Dillon said, punching Paul on the biceps. "Good to see you, guy. Ready to get your butt kicked again?"

"Hell, yes," Paul shot back. "Worth it for the chow alone. I keep telling Maggie you guys serve the best damned cheeburger-cheeburger-Pepsi-Pepsi in New Jersey."

Dillon laughed immoderately. "Funny stuff, guy. I'll have to remember to tell it to Deirdre."

Larry Marx made a strange little grunting noise, his way of signaling that he had something to say. "Er, Maggie, I think you weren't in on Friday? Just as well, considering the power failure. Thank God that capable young Chinese technician got us back up without any loss of data. Anyway, I think you'll be pleased to know our lawyers and the lawyers down in Knoxville have finally reached an agreement in principle."

"Pardon my French," Dillon interjected, "but that Reifsnyder's a fucking lunatic. World-class. Just what is his problem?"

Marx blushed, then continued: "The important thing is, we're all on the same page now. Which is not to say that we won't feel better when the paperwork is signed— but, er, I think it safe to say that Caduceus Twenty-One is now a client. Our congratulations."

"I smell . . . bonus!" proclaimed Dillon.

It was a tired gag, but Maggie played along: "Really?"

"No! Not really!"

"Er, Maggie," Marx said, "you should expect calls from several reporters. The good folks in Knoxville are allowing us to announce that we've been retained as their advisers."

"Isn't that a bit premature, Larry?"

Marx shook his head. "It serves two purposes. It announces to the industry that Caduceus Twenty-One is ours. And it saves Rob not a few phone calls—I suspect he'll be hearing shortly from a number of interested portfolio managers." He paused to bestow a smile on her. "Three purposes, actually. It gives you a chance to get a little press."

"Gee, thanks," Maggie said, trying to keep a straight face.

"You the man!" Dillon said to her, pumping an exhortative fist. "Think Schwarzkopf, Maggie, think Iran. That's how I want you and your guys to hit Knoxville. Fast. Decisive. No prisoners."

Maggie felt Paul's eyes on her; was she going to set Dillon straight on the country Desert Storm had been waged against? Tempting, but instead she said, "Fast. Decisive. No prisoners. Can do, Rob, if you'll sign my requisition for a couple of Tomahawk missiles."

Even Larry Marx smiled.

Maggie and Paul engaged in small talk with the troika for a few more minutes, then excused themselves.

"Paul," she said as they began to circulate, "that rah-rah speech back there about being fast and decisive. I'm not?"

"Dillon's just being Dillon."

"Yes and no. His little digs never come out of nowhere. Maybe this goes back a couple of years, to a project that . . ."

"Look," Paul said, "you're one of the quickest studies around, so that part's bullshit. But the other stuff may not be, in his mind. It's not that you're indecisive, Maggie, but you can be awfully deliberate. The more data you have, the happier you are."

"Isn't that true about everybody?" she said, hating her defensiveness.

"Yeah, and the Supreme Court's still trying to figure out what the guys who wrote the Constitution really meant. You've read some of those business-management books. 'Paralysis by analysis.' "

"Right," Maggie retorted. "Why take a day when really good managers can make decisions in one minute."

"Are we having an argument?"

She sighed. "No. I'm sorry. I'm asking you to decode something, and getting huffy about what I'm hearing."

"There's things about guys that you understand but don't fully appreciate. Never underestimate ego. If Dillon ropes in the firm's biggest deal in two years, you're his cute little Nancy Drew, off to ferret out secrets. You rope in Caduceus, what's he got to brag about except how fast he can place the paper?" Paul paused by the edge of the swimming pool. "Here's what I think it was really all about. Remember when he said, 'no prisoners'? Dillon's not sure you have it in you to go for the jugular, to finish something off."

"But this isn't some *mano-a-mano*," Maggie protested. "It's a business deal between two consenting companies."

"Like the book said, men are from Mars and women from Venus."

A T the time of the firm's start-up its oldest founder, Larry Marx, had been in his late thirties, so most of the staff was Maggie's age or younger. That probably made for higher morale, since Marx Dillon was not burdened with the aging burnouts that collected like driftwood on Wall Street. Yet peer bonding only went so far. As was the norm at office parties, the guests had subconsciously segregated themselves by rank: managerial, support staff, and clerks and messengers. And then there was Reggie Jamaal. Ostensibly hired to deliver packages, in truth the former junior-college wide receiver was on the payroll for this one day each year, when he was expected to run down Rob Dillon's passes.

Maggie and Paul eventually settled into a circle that included Dawn Mambelli, accompanied by her beau Howie, he of the Jets season tickets, and the firm's brightest junior analyst and best athlete, the tall and rangy Jill Unger.

Mambelli had significant news: by hook and crook, she had managed to get her boss an emergency hairstyling appointment. "Mr. Damian consents to squeeze you in at ten-fifteen Wednesday morning," she reported. "He will be most cross if you're even one minute late. Want I should pick up a box of Teuschers for you to take him?"

"That's not a bad idea, Mambelli."

Paul studied Maggie's hair, which fell over her shoulders, and said, "Didn't you just have it trimmed?"

"Yes, but hello? I'm going down to Knoxville, remember?"

"They must have haircutters down there."

"Would you trust yours to one?"

Jill Unger felt her own hair and said, "Any chance Mr. Damian would make two exceptions?"

Mambelli's eyes narrowed: "Don't even think about it, Unger."

After a while they were joined by Marx Dillon's odd couple: six-foot-three-inch Teddy Quereshi of Karachi, Pakistan, and five-foot-five-inch Sterling Nussbaum of St. Louis. Lovers since their days at Princeton, Nussbaum did freelance proofreading at the firm to supplement his meager income as an Off-Broadway actor while Quereshi was the peerless number cruncher who was heading the team that would vet Caduceus 21's books.

During a lull in the conversation, Quereshi said to Maggie, "I am sorry to have not finished my memo on time."

"No sweat, Teddy." Because Caduceus 21 was privately held, and had therefore never disclosed much about itself, Quereshi needed to assimilate considerable research to make sense of the company's myriad units.

"When are you leaving town, Maggie?"

"I was hoping Tuesday night or Wednesday morning. I'd like to visit my mom before going to Knoxville. Why, something the matter?"

"Well," he said, his soft eyes uncharacteristically grave, "I am reading all of the reports and the flow charts that Mr. Reifsnyder is so kind to send up, but there are a few matters that still remain a bafflement."

"Listen, Teddy, you're not playing this afternoon, right?"

He smiled and shook his head.

"I'm not big on watching blood flow, either. Why don't we use that time to talk things through?"

"That would be most appreciated, Maggie. Thank you."

Shortly before 3 P.M., Rob Dillon trotted up to the group with Nigel Neil in tow. "Okay, guys, game time," he said to Paul and Sterling Nussbaum. "And Dawn, maybe you ought to check out the cam."

Mambelli nodded and started for a minivan parked alongside the football field. On its roof stood a tripod-mounted, network-quality camcorder. Years back, when Dillon learned that Mambelli's brother was a cameraman for a local television station, he had permanently assigned her to tape the game she privately referred to as "the Toilet Bowl."

Dillon said to Unger, "Jill? How about pulling on a shirt this year?"

"Shucks, Rob, no can do."

"Why not?"

The junior analyst, who stood a good three inches taller than Dillon, slid down her sunglasses and looked him square in the eye. Then she smiled sweetly and said, "Wouldn't want to hurt you."

Dillon gamely joined in the laughter before turning to Quereshi: "Hey, big fella, you going to let your buddy Sterling have all the fun?"

"I am sorry, Rob, but this is not the football that I know," Quereshi replied. "Now, if you say that you will play World Cup–style football, well, then, perhaps Nigel and I could be enticed to stand everyone else by ourselves. Right, Nigel?"

"Spot on, mate," replied Neil.

Dillon made a rude noise, then cast an appraising eye at Mambelli's date, Howie; the extra-large T-shirt she had ordered for him stretched tautly over his chiseled torso. "What about you, guy? You must've played ball in college."

"All four years, sir."

"Well, all right! We could use some fresh blood."

"But sir?" said Howie. "I'm afraid my sport's also soccer."

"Nigel and Teddy I can understand, they're foreigners," Dillon said, shaking his head in disgust. "You, I don't. Any game you can't touch the ball with your hands is . . . why, it's goddamned un-American!"

Just then the zebra—an assistant football coach at the local high school glad to pick up a quick seventy-five dollars for an afternoon of refereeing—shrilled his whistle and signaled the two captains out for the coin-toss. Most of the guests began gathering along the sidelines, where Deirdre Dillon had thoughtfully restationed the beverage carts.

Maggie and Teddy Quereshi headed the other way, for the shelter of a shade tree, and began to discuss his questions about Knoxville.

She had resolved most of them when he glanced at his watch and then the field. "My gosh, Maggie, I believe the game is nearly over."

"Sure hope it was as good for them as it was for me," she said, accepting a hand up.

They made their way to the minivan atop which Dawn Mambelli was taping. Maggie said, "What's the score, Mambelli?"

"Bummer, Boss. Eighteen–thirteen, Dirtbags, their ball with under two minutes to go."

Maggie winced; Paul would be insufferable on the ride home.

Out on the field, the players on both teams definitely looked the worse for wear; several, including Paul, wore patches of dried blood on their limbs like campaign badges.

The Dirtbags broke their huddle and lined up.

The zebra called out, "One minute left, guys. One minute."

"The fat lady's sung," Maggie said to Quereshi. "They'll just run out the clock."

Indeed, Rob Dillon took the snap and started to kneel while most of his teammates turned to congratulate each other.

Maggie caught a sudden blur of motion.

Dirtbag wide receiver Reggie Jamaal was running directly at defender Sterling Nussbaum, freezing him with a head-fake, then sprinting past with more hustle than he ever showed making pickups and deliveries.

Now Maggie saw Dillon straighten up and dash quickly to his right.

Paul was the first Monster to realize that Dillon was going for a gratuitous, in-your-face touchdown. He bolted after the retreating quarterback and flung out a desperate hand that grazed Dillon's jersey—but there was no whistle. Paul spun around to glare at the zebra, who looked away.

Capitalizing on the home-field advantage, Dillon drifted to his right a few more steps, reared back, and launched a pass far downfield.

Reggie Jamaal was in full stride near the goal line, his neck arched back to track the incoming ball. Sensing not only a touchdown but also a generous bonus close at hand, he stretched for the perfectly thrown spiral.

It never reached him.

Sterling Nussbaum, as if climbing an invisible ladder, rose to tip the pass away and then while falling somehow managed to gather in the loose ball. Players and spectators alike stood rooted for several heartbeats, trying to digest the human highlight film they had just seen. Only it wasn't over: Nussbaum picked himself up off the turf and set off for the goal line seventy-five yards away. He deftly eluded one tag after another until there was but a single player left to beat—the quarterback who had coughed up the interception.

Maggie glanced at Rob Dillon and knew by his expression that he wasn't planning to just gently tag Nussbaum. She wanted to look away, but couldn't.

Nussbaum was clearly running out of steam and seemed to have pulled a muscle to boot because he was limping noticeably as he cut toward the near sideline.

Dillon adjusted his closing angle until he was certain of range and distance. Then he surged forward with enough force to gouge a divot out of the lawn and dove for his diminutive prey's gimpy knee.

That's when Nussbaum not only miraculously lost the limp but also, like a sprinter sighting the tape, summoned up a final burst of speed. As Dillon thudded to earth empty-handed, Nussbaum sped past the minivan and a line of cheering spectators to the goal line: Monsters 19, Dirtbags 18.

Maggie yelled up to Mambelli, "Sure as hell hope you didn't run out of tape."

"No way," came the jubilant reply. Then Mambelli saw who was approaching and quickly busied herself with the camera.

Rob Dillon looked like a character out of a Kabuki play. His grimacing face was caked with sideline chalk and he walked listing to port as he protectively clutched his left shoulder.

"Good game, Rob," Maggie said.

Dillon ungritted his teeth and said, "Not as good as last year's."

MAGGIE took the wheel of the Spyder for the trip home, Paul having overcelebrated the victory. Not that she minded; driving was something she enjoyed so much that several years back, she had spent a three-day weekend at a racing school in the Poconos. And driving at night with the top down was to her one of life's simplest but truest pleasures: seamless black sky overhead, dark wind ruffling her hair, radio tuned to an oldies station and cranked up a notch, the sounds and smells of the passing environment unfiltered and sharp. Maggie had come of age in the early 1980s, when few automakers were producing ragtops. In college, though, her first date had been with a senior who owned a fully restored aquamarine '57 Chevy Bel-Air convertible. Alas, there had been no paradise by the dashboard lights with him, she recalled, only a feeling of ineffable regret that such a fine car should be owned by such a jerk.

The Manhattan skyline was piercing the horizon when Paul awoke.

"You okay?" she said.

"Yeah, but I won't be in the morning. Damn, that champagne was fine. Tasted even better seeing the look on Rob's face."

Maggie grinned. "He's probably going to be up all night reviewing the tapes and drawing up new plays for next year."

"What's the word on his shoulder?"

"A slight separation. He'll be in the office Tuesday."

Paul groaned. "Does that mean no Burberry?"

"Yup."

"Darn."

Traffic thickened as they neared the tollbooths guarding the Holland Tunnel.

Maggie felt Paul's eyes on her. He reached over to turn down the radio, hesitated, then said, "You're pissed at me, aren't you?"

She was too surprised to respond.

"I'm pretty sure I know why," he continued. "That party for Linzy Kirsch a couple of weeks back—you saw something."

In thinking he had been oblivious of her recent moods, Maggie had underestimated how well he knew her. Was this a battle she was prepared to fight right now? Why not? "What did I see, Paul?"

He looked away.

"I wasn't spying on you," Maggie said defensively. "What you do is your business."

"That's what it was, Maggie. Business. Client management. You know what signing her would mean to the agency."

She downshifted, shunted the Spyder into a shorter line, and angrily fumbled a bill from her wallet.

"Wrong choice of words," he murmured. "I know that's what the ambulance-chaser used to say, too. I'm sorry."

"About what? About the fact that I saw you do it? Or about what you actually did? What if this Kirsch signs with you—you going to become her dealer?"

"What's your next question—do I still beat my wife?"

Maggie jammed her change into a pocket, pulled away from the booth, and dipped into the tunnel.

The air was suddenly fetid, the fluorescent glare depressing as it bounced off white tiles that decades of exhaust fumes had stained as yellow as an old dog's teeth. The tunnel throbbed with the captured vibrations of a hundred vehicles. As Maggie gained speed the lights began to flash by in a stroboscopic rhythm that reminded her of the claustrophobic opening scene of $8^{1}/_2$. She suddenly wished she had stopped to raise the top.

Paul didn't speak again until they had climbed the incline at tunnel's end and emerged in Manhattan. "Listen," he said, "head up the West Side. I'll drop you at your place."

"You're in no shape to drive home."

"Aw Christ, now you're going to bust my chops for drinking, too?"

"Get a life," Maggie retorted. "This isn't about what you've done, it's about what you're willing to do."

"Might be willing to do," Paul corrected. "I told you I haven't figured things out yet."

"Oh? And when might you?" She braked abruptly enough for a red light to draw glares from pedestrians entering the crosswalk.

"Midmonth. I'm meeting her and her lawyer as soon as she gets back from Milan."

"Linzy, dah-ling," Maggie said with steely scorn. "Forget La Scala, forget Verdi. Two words: classic rock. A cover of 'Girls Just Want to Have Fun' with your sweet pipes? Can't miss. Or 'Chain of Fools,' or maybe 'Bohemian Rhapsody' to grab the head-bangers? And oh, and if you've got a mirror handy, I've got some marching powder."

"Stop shouting," Paul said. "Please. You're making a scene."

Maggie wheeled around. The driver and passengers in the cab alongside them were gawking, as were several passersby on the sidewalk. Damn, why hadn't she put up the top? "What's the matter?" she shrieked at the onlookers. "You never saw an argument before?"

"Yo, guy," shouted a bottle-picker standing next to a Dumpster. "Yeah, you in the fancy car. Can't you shut the bitch up?"

Despite the red light Maggie, seeing no traffic approaching on the cross street, banged the Spyder into first and gunned it through the intersection. They rode in silence across town and up Third Avenue. On 31st Street she took a left and slammed to a stop in front of Paul's building.

"It'll be in the garage on Ninety-Fifth and Broadway," she said.

Paul hoisted his bruised body from the passenger seat and retrieved his gym bag without a word.

As she pulled away he called out something, but it was lost in the *blat* of the muffler.

She took the 86th Street transverse through Central Park to the Upper West Side and pulled into the garage. The bored attendant watched while she transferred the keys to Paul's apartment from her own ring to the Mitsubishi's. Not until fifteen minutes later, after she had walked the two blocks to her apartment, did the tears begin to flow.

Maggie went to the kitchen for a glass of juice. Turning on the light, she recoiled: The floor was littered with the scribbled reminders she kept magneted to the freezer door. Had someone broken in? No, Grover was still in place and, more important, the hundred dollars for the housekeeper, Mrs. Allen, was still pinned under Oscar the Grouch. But what had jarred her notes loose? Then she noticed the window was open several inches, just as she had left it. That's what happened, she thought; must've been the wind.

WEDNESDAY

OCTOBER 14

SHORTLY after 10:45 A.M., a 1952 Ford pickup eased past the bustling outdoor market of a village in Chiapas state and sighed to a halt in front of the clinic run by the *norteamericano*. Nguyen-Anh Dupree, sitting in the passenger seat, felt light-headed from an all-night obstetrics vigil that had come on top of a full day of treating patients. But anyone who had survived a medical residency, as well as several tours of duty in war zones, was no stranger to fatigue.

He thanked the proud new father for the ride, grabbed his medical bag, and hopped down from the truck.

A girl squatting in the shade of the building rose. Only fifteen herself, she carried a one-year-old under one arm and, under the other, an infant Dupree had brought into the world two months earlier. He shook off his weariness and greeted Fabiana warmly even as his heart went out to her. The girl lived five miles away but she had trekked in, probably setting out before dawn, to have him examine her children and inoculate the older. The previous evening he had posted a sign that said the clinic would be closed until noon. Even if Fabiana could read, what was she to do—walk all the way home and come back another day?

"Dr. Kung-fu?"

Dupree turned back to the truck.

The farmworker was holding up a string bag that held a squash, two tomatoes, and several onions, the payment he had insisted the doctor take for delivering his child. Dupree hadn't left it in the truck by accident. Though humble, the offering was still more than the family could afford. But now was the time to be gracious so he accepted the bag, then asked a favor: Would the man be so good as to wait fifteen minutes and give Fabiana a ride home?

Dupree took down the sign, ushered the girl and her babies inside, then went to the refrigerator for a Coke that he handed Fabiana. As he began examining the children, he couldn't help but think of the American politicians who regularly voted against granting aid to international health organizations that promoted birth control. How many of those legislators' daughters were on the pill? Or had obtained an abortion in a state-of-the-art Beltway clinic? Yet by shamelessly pandering to the right-to-lifers, they were dooming the world's Fabianas, as well as their families, to an inescapable poverty.

He returned to the refrigerator for a vial of smallpox vaccine. The one-year-old wailed like a banshee when the needle pricked his arm but fell silent when he saw the small banana in the doctor's hand.

Dupree told Fabiana her children were in excellent health. Bring the infant back in February for a routine checkup, he added, picking up a fluorescent-yellow three-by-five card printed with the numbers 1 through 180. Having learned early in his travels that the biggest barrier between his patients and him was neither language nor culture but illiteracy, he had devised an ingenious appointment reminder. Dupree circled the "120" in red and gave Fabiana the card; she would simply cross off a number each day until it was time for the next visit.

He walked the girl and her children out to the truck.

No other patients had gathered, for which he was grateful. Dupree checked his watch and saw he had an hour to himself. A short nap would be welcome but food was more important. He was about to head around the corner when he remembered that the farmworker's string bag held the makings of a meal a damned sight fresher and healthier than anything the cantina served. Plus, the mere act of cooking would help him relax from his most grueling day in months.

Yesterday had started with a predawn emergency appendectomy. Then after closing the clinic in late afternoon he had taken the bus into San Cristóbal, as he did every Tuesday, to consult on cases at the local hospital. Dupree welcomed the arrangement, because in return the hospital sent out a physician to cover the clinic when he needed to travel. Plus it meant dinner with a group of the more cosmopolitan doctors and nurses on staff. Dupree was passably fluent in Spanish, as well as the major local Mayan tongues, and never lacked for conversation here in the village. But discussing events and ideas beyond Chiapas state was another matter. Tuesday dinner was thus the social high point of his week, an intellectual counterpoint to his every-other-day workouts. The previous evening he had just returned to the village from San Cristóbal when a worker at a nearby *ejido*, braving the curfew, had driven in with word that his wife had gone into labor.

Dupree measured a half cup of rice into a pot, covered it with water, and began to knead the grains. Unlike most boys raised in America, he had been taught to cook at an early age. He grew up thinking the ability a curse; when news of it leaked out to his grade-schoolmates, the bullies quickly added a new pejorative, "apron-head," to their taunts. Only after leaving Yazoo City did Dupree come to appreciate the skills acquired in *Grand-mère* Lulu May's kitchen. One night during his junior year of college, well before Cajun cuisine became the rage, he had prepared for a date blackened catfish, sautéed okra, and corn bread. Her way of complimenting the chef had been to declare herself the dessert. Since then, he had grown adept at using whatever was at hand to whip up something tasty in even the most alien of environments. And because few Third World kitchens boasted multiburner stoves, he now treasured his wok and bamboo steamer almost as much as his medical instruments.

He finished rinsing the rice and dumped it and a half cup of water into the wok, which he covered with the lid of his steamer. The Bunsen burner lit with a soft pop. Next he sliced up the squash and an onion. Placing the vegetables into the steamer, he drizzled on soy sauce and sesame oil, then set them aside.

As he fished out a cigarette, Dupree realized it had been two days since he'd checked for e-mail. He booted up the subnotebook, used his scheduler to set a pair of alarms, and uplinked through his cell phone onto the Net.

There were three messages waiting. He usually downloaded files and read them offline to save money. The return address on one, though, suggested it was probably from either Duchess or Data. If so, it would require a decryption key. He opened the file:

Sender: visitor@forum22.uscla.edu
Received: from stovell.ozrelay.intercon.com by
mexico.centamer.medsans.com (8.6.10/5.950515)
     id ‼‼‼‼‼‼; Tue, 13 Oct 22:27:21 −0400
Received: from tsutomu.nara.nippon.com by
stovell.ozrelay.intercon.com
     id ‼‼‼‼‼‼ Thu, 15 Oct 06:08:18 −2000
Received: from denebrink.berlin.deutschl.com by
tsutomu.nara.nippon.com

> id ‽‽‽‽‽‽‽; Thu, 15 Oct 04:44:24 +1900
> *Received: from visitor@forum22.uscla.edu by*
> *denebrink.berlin.deutschl.com*
>   id ‽‽‽‽‽‽‽‽; Wed, 14 Oct 08:17:18 –0100
> *To: nad@mexico.centamer.medsans.com*
> *From: visitor@forum22.uscla.edu*
> *Date: Tue, 13 Oct 23:16:37 PDT*
> *Message-Id: <**!%)%(%‽‽‽‽‽@case.uscla.edu>*
> *Mime-Version: 1.0*
> *Content-Type: text/encrypted; charset="us-ascii"*

The rest of the file was gibberish, a dense string of characters such as Φ, $<\delta\upsilon$, $<\Xi\upsilon$, and $<\chi\tau\cdot<\sigma\tau\ni<\nu\tau\Theta<\pi\tau$ $\overline{<}E\tau\cdot<\Gamma\tau$ generated by Duchess and Data's encryption program.

Scanning the circuitous header, Dupree realized his friends were spooked, encryption or no. Their message would have ordinarily been piped from a terminal on the University of Southern California campus in Los Angeles straight to the Médecins Sans Frontières BBS in Brussels. It had instead been routed through remailer boards—services that stripped incoming traffic of all IDs—in Germany, Japan, and Australia. That three-hour odyssey rendered the message untraceable even if it were to be intercepted and its code broken.

Dupree downloaded all his e-mail, then remained on-line while he popped his encryption software up on-screen and selected DECRYPT. He typed in his password and the original time of transmission—19:16.37 P.M. Greenwich Mean Time on 13 October—and clicked START.

As the program began to scan the requisite stock-market indices to generate the key, he occupied himself updating his medical log on Fabiana's kids.

Finally a message popped up on-screen:

KEY READY. PROCEED WITH DECRYPTION.

Dupree quickly logged off the Net and ran the letter through the decrypter. The salutation told him it was from Duchess:

Hi Doc,
Remember the haystack you asked me and my friend to search? Damn if we didn't find a needle. Don't go dialing 911 just yet though because the bad news is, MedEx's name isn't on it anywhere. But we think the evidence shows that organs that were planted inside 15 patients on 09/04 and 09/05 all came from Presidio, a 1 zipcode town in West Texas.

We started with what you said about how organs have got to be hand-delivered and transplanted ASAP. My friend processes this and goes into his Spock mode. Like, you don't just walk into ER and ask for a new heart. Those organs got to go to hospitals that do transplants, right? Most likely by plane? The way my friend figures it, even if some body-snatchers can firewall off their own data, no way they can triple-wipe their tracks off everybody else's systems.

So we pull threads on a couple of medical sites. They clue us to the Organ Procurement and Transplantation Network, a national online registry which tracks who needs what organ and how bad. So we dial up OPTN and query for all hearts, livers, kidneys, and pancreases transplanted on 09/04 and 09/05. Total of 81, in 26 U.S. cities. The list also tells stuff like blood type but not where the organs come from.

Here's where my friend's thinking gets truly fine. The map says the biggest airports near where your Guillermo disappeared are in Texas and across the border in Chihuahua. So we dial up the FAA and query for all flights on 09/04 *from* Texas or Chihuahua *to* our 26 cities. The count is in the

100s, which is a lot of noise. But when we filter out scheduled airlines like American and Delta it's like, film at 11.

The airports at Boston, Indianapolis, Birmingham (AL), and Portland (OR) all log in Learjets taking off from Dallas/Fort Worth Airport. We scan DFW and see 4 Learjets taking off between 0312 and 0326. Dallas is maybe 500 miles from where Guillermo disappeared so we scan what flew *into* DFW shortly before the 4 Learjets leave. Mostly courier services like Emery and DHL plus, at 0249, a turboprop which took off from Presidio.

So we run the registrations of the 1 incoming and 4 outgoing DFW planes through the CAB. Damn if it ain't a small world after all—same company leasing all 4 Learjets also chartered the turboprop. Only it's not MedEx, like you thought. It's an outfit called Wings of Mercy Ltd. of Georgetown, Grand Cayman. (Isn't that where that Tom Cruise movie says white collar crooks set up bogus companies?)

Anyway, then we sort the OPTN data from only the 4 cities the Learjets flew into by type of organ. 3 hearts (2 type A, 1 type B-negative like Guillermo). 3 livers (2 A's, 1 B-negative). 3 pancreases (2 A's, 1 B-negative). 7 kidneys (4 A's, 2 B-negatives, 1 O). Not counting the extra type O kidney, the organs sure look like they came from the same 3 people in West Texas, no?

Maybe this doesn't connect the dots for Judge Wapner, but me and my friend are buying.

Not to worry, Doc, we haven't quit on the MedEx hack. Even if they're not involved, we want to carbonize the ankle-biting asshole who coded their security. Soon as we're in, you'll be the third to know. Meanwhile, yell if there's other things for us to do. But remember, you already owe me and

my friend, big. So come up to L.A. and give us that
dinner and some face time?
:-)

Dupree was rereading the letter for the third time
when his computer's speakers suddenly blasted out the
guitar licks that launch Midnight Oil's "Beds Are Burning."

He blinked. Then, remembering why he had set the
alarm, he got up and placed the steamer with the vegetables atop the wok.

By the time the computer sounded its second alarm, to
signal that lunch was ready, Dupree had a screenful of
notes and questions. He brought the food to the battered
pine table and began to write.

D&D—
I am awed and humbled by your artful work-
around. Next time I'm up, dinner for sure wherever
you say. Two dinners, in fact, if you'll consider an-
other question—namely, how can we get enough
evidence to call 911?

Seems to me we must start by making sure the
Presidio connection isn't just an innocent coinci-
dence. Most hearts, livers, and so forth come from
people in excellent health who are in an accident
that leaves them brain-dead. For obvious reasons
the victims can't have sustained massive internal
injuries. Could some accident in the Presidio area,
say a capsized boat, have produced three such un-
traumatized victims at the same time? If so, the
local papers should have run stories.

Meanwhile, can you pipe me the complete typo-
logical data you downloaded from OPTN? Maybe I
can sift it and link those 16 organs to three specific
donors.

I'm also curious about the hospitals in Boston,
Indianapolis, Birmingham, and Portland. What

might they have in common? Ownership, affiliations, board members?

I'm afraid we read the same thrillers. The Caymans bring to mind Somerset Maugham's description of Monaco: A sunny place for shady people. My image of the islands is also that of a haven for dummy corporations run by local fronts. Any ideas on how to pierce the veil? If you were to ask me to triage priorities, at this moment I'd rank getting inside Wings of Mercy Ltd. higher than hacking MedEx.

But like you, I'm not giving up on MedEx either. Can you tell me some databases to scan? I want to know everything about these bastards—their principals, when they started, where they're based, the scope of their operations, and so forth.

Thanks much and be well—N.A.D.

Dupree cell-phoned back onto the Net, waited for a fresh key to be generated, then encrypted his reply and sent it on its way.

There was a soft tap at the front of the clinic.

Through the open door he could see perhaps a half-dozen villagers lined up outside. Time to go back to healing, he thought, closing the lid of his computer and taking away his plate of barely touched food.

THURSDAY

OCTOBER 15

FIFTEEN hours after she had originally planned to arrive, Maggie Sepulveda made her way through the familiar terrain of Orlando International Airport. She was ticketed to fly down the previous evening, but enough brush fires had cropped up at the office to turn a dial-a-cab to JFK into her usual 1 A.M. ride through Central Park.

A large freestanding display case in the main terminal caught her attention. She stopped to study its array of high-end golf and tennis gear and designer swimwear. The sign read, "Here for grown-up fun? We sell grown-up toys." Pretty punchy, she thought, though in truth anything was better than the old slogan: "For all your sporting needs, visit the Rec Room—Orlando's finest selection of equipment and apparel." She made a mental note to compliment her mother, who managed the store, and continued past the baggage-claim area. A jumbo-jetload of Scandinavians were milling around, winter parkas in hand, dazed from their flight across six time zones and almost two seasons.

Maggie had been coming to Orlando since her mother moved here six years earlier. Time had not erased her unfavorable first impression of a place that, like Venice and Bali, owed its prosperity to humoring a transient flow of tourists. Venice at least boasted fifteen hundred years of history and a half millennium of art, Bali tropical beauty and an exotic culture. Orlando was little but a parade of theme parks rising up out of the charmless central Florida scrubland. She had to admit, though, that this city of grimly smiling vacationers with travel-weary children in tow had afforded her mother a second life.

Edging through the crowd, Maggie slipped on her sunglasses and stepped out into the bright haze of late morning.

The curb directly out front was hogged by three tour buses that sat idling with their luggage-compartment doors open.

She scanned the pickup zone and finally spotted a woman in her mid-fifties standing alongside a dark blue Saturn. Maggie smiled, heartened to see how fit Helen Wagner looked, shouldered her knapsack and weekender, and started toward her mother.

Helen had moved to Florida shattered in both spirit and health. The immediate cause was Petey's slow and sad death, of course, but there had been earlier tragedies and heartbreaks as well.

The girl born Helen Culver came of age in the time and place so lovingly recalled by the movie *American Graffiti:* the early 1960s in Modesto, California. In her second and final year at a community college, she had defied her family and married Jeff Kragen, a local legend on whom director George Lucas was said to have modeled Milner, the laid-back hot-rodder portrayed by Paul LeMat. Jeff soon enlisted in the Army to learn a trade. After basic training he was posted to Fort Lewis, Washington, where he was joined by his bride. Two months before Maggie was born in nearby Tacoma, Jeff died in an on-base helicopter accident. The daughter he never saw inherited her mother's eyes but her father's firm jaw, goofy grin, and, perhaps not so oddly, his love of high-performance vehicles.

Rather than return home to Modesto, Helen had taken a sales job at the Tacoma Mall, one of the earliest built in the Pacific Northwest. It was one year before she accepted a date, and another year before Maggie found herself playing flower girl at her mother's marriage to a man a decade her senior.

Barney Wagner sold passenger jets. His employer, Boeing, manufactured the hottest commercial plane in the world—after Pan Am broke the ice, orders for the brand-new 747 virtually wrote themselves—so he could well afford the big house with the nice lawn, the annual Hawaiian vacation, the new Bonneville convertible every September.

None of that could compensate for the fact that behind Wagner's hail-fellow-well-met facade lurked a control freak intent on wiping away all traces of Helen's first husband. For instance, he allowed no photographs of Jeff to be displayed in the house. Nor would he add Maggie to his health insurance until he was permitted to adopt the little girl and legally change her surname to his. Wagner was at his worst on Friday and Saturday nights, when there was no compelling reason to meet the morning sober. One night in 1973, when Maggie was nine and her half-brother, Petey, six, Wagner went beyond emotional abuse. He awoke the next afternoon to find Helen and the kids gone.

Neither Maggie nor Helen ever again set foot in that big house with the nice lawn. Petey did for a time, under the visitation provisions of the divorce decree. But Wagner soon lost interest in his ex-family. He was facing court action for falling more than a year behind in alimony and child support when he left Tacoma to take a job with McDonnell-Douglas. Rather than pursue the son of a bitch all the way to St. Louis, Helen let go of the past and went back to work. Fifteen years later, Petey had specifically requested that his father not be told of his failing health. After the funeral, though, Helen felt obliged to write Barney at his last known address. Her letter was neither returned nor acknowledged.

"Hi, Mom," Maggie called out.

As Helen turned, her smile of anticipation froze. "What have you done to your hair?"

Maggie self-consciously fingered Mr. Damian's handiwork. "You don't like it this short?"

"It's a bit severe, isn't it? And those circles under your eyes don't help." Helen frowned. "You're not getting enough sleep. Or exercise, either."

"This is true, so why not add vegetables to the list?" Lighten up and back off, Maggie told herself; you're in her world now, not New York. She set down her bags and stretched out her arms. Maggie had surpassed her mother in height almost two decades earlier, but it still felt clumsy and disorienting, even vaguely inappropriate, to be taller than the woman in her embrace. "Hi, Mom. Good to see you."

"Hi, sweetie," Helen murmured. "I'm so sorry I didn't recognize you. The hair threw me. And I was looking for someone carrying a computer."

Maggie laughed. "I'm on vacation, remember? But know why I had to play Mule Girl all these years? Because you were the last on the block to chip up."

"I still say you wasted all that money buying me a laptop. Why not just pick up the phone more? This e-mail business, it's unnatural."

"Like licking an envelope and shoving it in a big blue metal box on the corner isn't?" said Maggie. "Anyway, remember when that techie I retained came to the store and added something to your desktop?"

Helen nodded. "What is that doo-hickey?"

"An adapter bay. Now your daughter doesn't have to schlep her laptop down here, just a removable hard drive that works on both your machines."

"Oh."

Maggie lifted her weekender into the trunk of the Saturn. "Listen, sorry I didn't make the flight yesterday."

"So am I," Helen said. "You missed the Dahls."

"Really." Maggie cocked her head; her mother's friends from Tacoma usually vacationed in Florida in January. "What brings them down this time of year?"

"Visiting Christina over in Sarasota," Helen said. "Remember how you used to baby-sit Christina? Well, she just had her second son—hint, hint. Anyway, Eric and Trudie stopped by for dinner, and they were disappointed not to see you."

"Probably wanted to check the battery on my biological clock," Maggie joked. "Why don't I drive?"

Helen pulled the keys out of reach. "My car, I drive. And I don't want to hear a word about how I've become a menace on the road. If you really think I'm such a Thelma . . ."

"It was Louise who drove off the cliff, Mom."

"Well, if I'm such a Louise, the taxi stand's right over there."

Maggie shook her head ruefully and climbed into the passenger seat. Had there been the remotest chance that her mother might enjoy living in New York City, where cars were optional, Maggie would have tried to entice her north. Here in Florida, though, automobiles were as essential as oxygen, and harping about her mother's growing lack of concentration behind the wheel was as useless as urging her to ask for the raise she deserved.

"Did you eat on the plane, sweetie?"

Maggie shook her head.

"Good. After I check in at the shop, we'll go out for a nice lunch," Helen said as she pulled away from the curb. "How's Paul?"

"Fine."

Helen glanced sharply at her daughter. "You two have a fight?"

"Yes." Maggie felt herself tensing. Her mother was always cordial to Paul, but never showed him half the warmth she had to *el buscapleitos*.

"You know I don't like to pry . . ."

"Well, you're prying." Maggie softened and added, "Sorry, I just don't want to discuss it right now."

"Well, there's something I've been meaning to get off my chest for some time now. I promise I won't bring it up again this weekend—unless you start nagging me about my driving or my paycheck. Deal?"

Steeling herself, Maggie said, "We haven't had this kind of talk since I was in college, but okay, deal."

They were almost out of the airport. Helen ignored the turnoff to the Beeline and continued north on local streets to save time and a toll. After a few moments, she said, "Don't you find Paul a bit too . . . too accommodating?"

Maggie frowned. "What's that supposed to mean?"

"How many times have I met him? Several dozen?"

"Between our trips down here and your visits to New York, that sounds about right."

"Well," Helen said, "I've never once heard him express an opinion."

Maggie groaned. "I assure you Paul has lots of opinions. On lots of topics."

"Did I say he sits there like a clam? Sorry, shoptalk doesn't count. How good is this musician? How bad is that concert hall's lighting crew? How crooked is this record company's royalty department? Imagine how you'd feel if I only carried on about the sales of Big Berthas or whether hiring more security guards reduces inventory shrinkage. What I mean is, I've never heard Paul say anything about his past except the battles he's won or lost. Same goes for his future—nothing except the deals he wants to pull off."

"Well, excuse us! Next time I'll make sure we discuss the progress of the Serbian war trials and America's trade deficit!"

"Why bother?" snapped Helen. "After all, who wants

the opinion of some old lady who never got a college degree? Somebody living so far out in the boondocks she turns on Peter Jennings to find out what's happening? Because that's how Paul makes me feel. And so do you when you're with him."

Maggie, stunned by this uncharacteristically resentful and sarcastic outburst, could only stare at her mother.

Helen blinked, and then her shoulders sagged. "You must be wondering what set me off. Well, one thing you have a lot of in Florida is time. I've been using mine to do some thinking. About me, about you. Sweetie, there's no easy way to say this, so I'll just come right out with it. There's things about Paul that remind me of Barney."

"What!"

"I don't mean that he's an abusive bully," Helen said. "Actually, Paul's quite charming. But what will he fight for besides a bigger contract? Does he really give a damn about anyone or anything? Or is he just a silver-tongued opportunist like Barney Wagner?"

Maggie heard her mother's words but they registered dimly, like sentences in a foreign language. Her mind was suddenly vacant, her face numb, her palms moist. Finally she broke the lengthening silence: "Wow. This is pretty heavy. I've got to take it under advisement, okay?"

"If you want to talk about it, I'm here. If you don't, a deal is a deal."

Maggie leaned back into the headrest and said, in a soft voice, "Maybe my buddies are right. They've all been seeing shrinks for years, and think I'm nuts because I don't. Paul and Barney. Funny, until now I assumed I've been so edgy because of this deal I'm doing."

Helen decided it was time to change the topic: "Is the deal as hard as that Silicone Valley merger you worked on a few years back?"

"Silicon Valley, Mom. Probably harder, because I was just an analyst then. Now I know how a seabird feels during hurricane season—you sense something out there but you don't know how big it is, how fast it's coming, how hard it's going to hit. I've got all these people to keep track of, as well as a zillion facts. Why didn't you tell me the downside of being a manager?"

"You never asked."

Maggie smiled. "You said something about time hanging heavy. I hope you're not trying to lay a guilt trip on me for not coming to Orlando more. I know for a fact that you've got friends here, that you're always going out to dinners and parties. Plus, you get lebenty-leben channels on your dish . . ."

"Haven't you clicked your way through them all and found not one single show that interested you? You know, I think there's a lot of truth to that old saying about ignorance being bliss."

"What do you mean, Mom?"

Helen paused to gather her thoughts, then said, "Remember that time several years ago when you were complaining about 'data overload'? I think many people suffer that these days, and it's making them crazy. Did you know that when I was a girl we only had two TV networks? There was an ABC but nobody watched it except me. Half an hour each Tuesday night, so I could gaze like an adoring puppy at the first boy I ever had a crush on."

Maggie regarded her mother with interest; she had never heard this juicy confession before.

"The show was called *The Adventures of Ozzie and Harriet.*"

"You had a crush on Ricky Nelson? Get out of here."

Helen blushed. "He wasn't like that back then. Or if he was, we didn't know it. Stars didn't go on Barbara Walters or Jay Leno and reveal how shallow they were. Neither did politicians. We only saw them in newsreels, dedicating highways or making speeches. I'm sure if there had been a Larry King back then, or C-SPAN, they would've sounded just as silly as Newt or the vice-president or that dreadful little toad from New York, what's his name, D'Agostino?"

"D'Amato, Mom."

"Here's an example of how times have changed, sweetie. My parents told me that after Franklin Delano Roosevelt died, everyone was shocked to find out he needed a wheelchair and crutches—they simply hid his polio from the public. For four terms. Can you imagine?

"Anyway, the point I started to make is, in the early days of TV they could've put on pig races, we were so happy just to have something to watch. But with all these channels nowadays, if you can't find a show that entertains you, you don't blame the people who make them. You ask yourself, 'What's wrong with me?'" Helen shook her head. "Listen to me prattle on about data overload. You're more swamped than me. How do you deal with it?"

"By vegging out in Orlando. Oh, I meant to tell you, nice slogan in that lobby display."

"Why, thank you." Helen was clearly pleased her daughter had noticed. "But is it too . . . too New Yorky?"

"Nothing wrong with a little attitude, Mom. Especially since so many of your customers are from New York—believe me, we city slickers know from aggressive. Since you ask, though, I think the slogan should be even blunter."

"Oh?"

"Yup. How about, 'Not enough balls? We've got plenty'?"

"Marguerite Rose Kragen!" said Helen, trying to keep a straight face. "You never had a mouth like that when you were growing up."

"In Tacoma?" replied Maggie. "Who did?"

THE store Helen managed was on the brief stretch of International Drive where the dreary march of motels, fast-food outlets, and discount liquidators gave temporary way to high-rise hotels, white-linen restaurants, and upscale shops. As her mother pulled into her reserved parking space in front, Maggie remembered the abject dismay she had felt on first entering the place.

Right after Petey's death, Helen had taken a two-month leave from her job in Tacoma and gone to Florida with her friend, Trudie Dahl. She was leafing through the local paper when she noticed an interesting employment ad. Two interviews later, she called Maggie—who flew down that same night.

Back then, the Rec Room was a cavernous bare-bones warehouse outlet, its merchandise inelegantly sandwiched between high banks of fluorescent lights and a concrete floor painted battleship gray. "This is the pits, Mom," Maggie had whispered. Helen agreed, but a quarter-century in retail had trained her to see the store's potential. She accepted the position of manager only after the owner agreed to a budget that would permit her to do a complete makeover. Judging by the size of the lunchtime crowd, Helen had spent the money wisely.

"What happened to the tennis stuff?" asked Maggie, slipping off her sunglasses. "Didn't it used to take up this whole area?"

By way of a reply, Helen asked, "Do you still play?"

"Nope."

"Neither do a lot of other people. There's no excitement anymore. Look at the pros. Even that mushy singer I don't much care for, what's his name . . ."

"Julio Iglesias?"

"No, the bozo from Las Vegas."

"Wayne Newton?"

"Exactly. Even Wayne Newton has more charisma than most of the pros. Tennis sales are down so much, we halved the stock and moved it to the back."

One of the clerks approached.

Helen listened for a few moments, then said to Maggie, "Something's come up. Want to look around or wait in my office?"

"Might as well check my e-mail."

"I thought you were on vacation."

"It's just mail, Mom." Maggie made her way to her mother's office, a modest cubicle back near the dressing rooms. One wall had a window that looked out into the store. Another was covered with photographs of Helen's children.

All were familiar, but Maggie hadn't looked closely at them in years. It gradually dawned on her that every shot of Petey showed him in his physical prime, before the *Baywatch* body fell victim to its faulty heart. She went back and scanned the photographs of herself. The most recent was a snap of her with *el buscapleitos* at the Palio in Siena, sent from their honeymoon in Tuscany. Maggie could understand why her mother hadn't posted later pictures of Petey. But why were there no shots of her from the past decade? Was some part of her mother retreating to a time when her kids had been healthy and happy? Or, thought Maggie with a guilty start, was it perhaps that a lonely woman's only daughter had been too self-absorbed to mail home fresh photographs? And too smug to consider availing herself of her mother's wisdom and perceptions?

The door opened behind her.

"I thought you were going to check your e-mail," Helen said, noticing the darkened computer.

"I'm on vacation, remember? Ready to go?"

"I'm sorry, sweetie, this thing I have to straighten out is knottier than I thought. But then I can take the rest of the day off. How about we order in some sandwiches, then go do something nice?"

"Sure."

"There's a deli menu on my desk," Helen said. "What do you want to do this afternoon?"

"When's the last time you spread a blanket on Cocoa Beach?"

"The last time you were down, I'm sure. It's so . . . so tacky there."

"Like, Orlando isn't?"

Helen laughed.

"Sunny day, Mom, and my bikini's in the car. I vote for baking the old brain cells a few hours, then repairing the damage with a few margaritas and some fresh seafood."

Helen sighed. "My swimsuit's at home, which is clear in the other direction."

"You got three aisles of suits out there."

"Those are for toughbodies."

"Hardbodies, Mom. Okay, isn't there a Salvation Army shop between here and the coast? Or a Senior Depot?"

Helen giggled. "Okay, you win. Cocoa Beach it is."

Maggie phoned in their lunch order, then opened her knapsack, took out her removable hard drive, and slotted it into the adapter bay on Helen's desktop. Booting up, she logged over to her own drive, dialed up her Net provider, and popped her private account up on-screen.

Only one solicitation today, from the driving school in the Poconos that she had attended several years earlier.

She left it there unread, then dialed up Marx Dillon. There were two messages that could wait, and a note from Rob Dillon she didn't have the stomach to read, plus a message from Dawn Mambelli she promptly opened.

Evidently the public-relations firm that represented Marx Dillon & Neil had started its spin-doctoring, because three business journalists had called that morning to request brief interviews with Maggie on the Caduceus 21 placement. Mambelli had included phone numbers for *The Wall Street Journal*'s "Heard on the Street" columnist, a *USA Today* reporter, and a producer from CNN's *Moneyline.* Next to the cable-TV financial show she had added a note: *"Larry and Rob *really* want you to do this one."*

Might as well get it over with, Maggie thought, reaching for the phone.

Twenty-five minutes later, Helen returned with a paper bag. "Problem solved. And here's lunch."

"Mom, mind stopping at a TV station on our way to the beach?"

"Of course not. Why?"

"CNN wants to tape a short segment on this deal I'm doing."

"You're going to be on TV?"

Maggie nodded.

Helen's eyes narrowed as she studied her daughter's attire. "Did you pack a suit or a nice dress, sweetie?"

"Of course not. I'm on vacation, remember?"

"But . . ."

"But what am I going to wear? They're only shooting me from the waist up so I thought I'd borrow a Rec Room T-shirt, maybe one of those tasteful fuchsia numbers. You know, give the shop some free advertising."

Helen's eyes widened in horror.

"Joke, Mom. There's a clean blouse in my bag. All I need's an iron."

"Nonsense. I know an outlet store nearby that carries Donna Karan and Anne Klein."

"Do they also have bathing suits for, ahem, women of a certain age?"

"Come to think of it, I believe they do."

Maggie grinned. "Why don't we eat in the car, then?"

F R I D A Y
O C T O B E R   1 6

AT 3:00 A.M. sharp the timer clicked and the reading light atop the night table sprang on. Century Chisholm's eyes fluttered open. As had been his habit for some years now, he remained in bed staring at the ceiling while he worked out today's date. The exercise, more difficult than it might seem, served two purposes: It oriented his mind and it reassured him that senility had been kept at bay for another day. He settled on the sixteenth of October—thirteen days before he and his staff left Santa Fe to head south for the winter—and then glanced at the clock/calendar on the night table. Bingo.

Next drill: Summon up the coming day's agenda. Sometime this morning he would learn the results of his semiannual physical. Duane Strand of MedEx owed him a memo on the Sepulveda woman, whose team would be arriving at Caduceus 21 headquarters shortly; so far the phone taps and clickstreams of Marx Dillon & Neil in New York had raised no alarms. And he had to begin briefing himself for his meetings next week with the managers of two more of his direct-mail companies.

Chisholm threw off the comforter. Though the thermostat in his bedroom was set to a toasty seventy-eight degrees, he found himself shivering. As a young man he had slept buck naked even in winter; this past summer, he had taken to wearing flannel pajamas. He had discussed the symptom with his doctor the day before. Was his metabolism slowing as a normal by-product of aging —or did it hint at something more serious? No use fretting about news until it was delivered, he thought.

He pulled on a pair of heavy socks, stepped into his slippers, and drew tight a silk dressing gown. The chill that seemed to pervade his marrow was worse in the morning, especially the hours before dawn. This, though, was when the rest of the Americas slept, leaving him free to work uninterrupted on his memoirs.

Chisholm left his large but austere bedroom and padded down the hall to his office.

The lights, keyed to a motion sensor, came on as he entered.

He stopped at his monitor to check the overnight messages. Nothing that couldn't wait, so he continued to the seven-foot-by-five-foot oaken panel set in the west wall of the room and palmed the luminescent plastic scanner.

When the panel parted, he boarded the elevator and pressed DOWN.

Before the start of construction on the house, Chisholm had taken the contractor aside and presented himself as a right-wing zealot who wanted protection against the inevitable World War III. Hell, Los Alamos is almost within spittin' distance, he had said, and you just know them Russki bastards got a couple of nukes aimed right at us. Such reasoning, plus an under-the-table fifty thousand dollars, had persuaded the contractor to excavate a fifteen-hundred-square-foot basement that did not appear on the building plans filed with the county.

As Chisholm stepped from the elevator, the overhead lights sprang on.

In a sense, his claim about wanting a survival bunker was true. Behind the door to his right, in a room commanding two thirds of the subterranean complex, sat state-of-the-art diagnostic, surgical, and intensive-care equipment that the most modern hospital would covet. It was here that he had undergone his physical the previous day.

The space directly before him used to contain not much beyond a kitchenette built into the far right-hand corner. They had stored odds and ends down here until Chisholm began his memoirs, which he meant to keep as private as Genghis Khan's tomb. Earlier in the decade a Japanese syndicate had sunk several million dollars into scouring the Central Asian steppes with high-tech equipment for the final resting place of his favorite historical figure. It tickled Chisholm no end that the Mongol chieftain had managed one final posthumous victory; after 750 years, his battle gear still lay untouched.

Not wanting to leave his recollections lying around upstairs, Chisholm had cleaned out this room and brought in an old pine table and straight-backed chair. Atop the table sat his work tools, a computer with a twenty-one-inch monitor, a microphone, and a halogen lamp. And to inspire himself, he had filled two walls of the windowless den with the type of personal memorabilia so noticeably absent from the rest of the house.

The wall opposite the elevator bore a large weathered wooden sign:

WELCOME TO
BENJAMIN
OKLAHOMA TERRITORY
POP: 266

Flanking the sign were photographs arranged as formally as a museum exhibit. To its right was a poster-sized print, in black-and-white, of an abandoned farm-house standing on a bleak prairie. Grainy from enlargement, it possessed the pointillistic elegance of a Seurat painting. On the other side was a group of sepia portraits whose subjects were posed against impossibly hokey backdrops, as was the custom in the early days of studio photography.

Photographs also adorned the long wall to his left, but they were more a festive collage-in-progress.

In the center was a cluster of framed black-and-white photographs, a few of them dating back at least five decades. One showed the young Chisholm, dapper in morning coat and spats, alongside an exotic-looking woman with café au lait skin wearing a wedding dress. Fanning out from this core were several hundred color snapshots pushpinned to the wall. Some had begun to fade but most seemed as fresh as yesterday's pickup from Fotomat. Chisholm appeared in about a third of them, posing with people of various genders, ages, and ethnicities, including his Santa Fe staff. He appeared happiest in the company of a gal whose growth was photographically traced from button-cute tyke to a willowy young woman of exceptional beauty. Seemed like just yesterday he was dandling Elspeth on his knee, and now she was a popular television reporter set to marry, in less than three weeks' time, the heir to a major telecommunications fortune.

Finally, a bookcase set against the right-hand wall held his work to date. This consisted of a row of composition tablets, the kind with the stiff, black-and-white marble-ized covers, and an acrylic diskette case filled with some three dozen backup floppies. Chisholm had begun his memoirs in longhand even though writing had never come natural to him; fact was, the sentences filling the composition tablets made him wince, they were that clumsy. Then one of his people sent him some new voice-recognition software that actually worked. He had set up a computer down here, taking care to pull the network card and modem so's to keep out hackers. Now he just talked into the microphone. The software transcribed his words right up on-screen while storing them in a file he could touch up later. Since the switch he'd made much faster progress. Better yet, the memoirs were sounding more like him.

Chisholm stopped to boot up the computer, then continued to the kitchenette and took from the mini-refrigerator the fresh-squeezed orange juice Natalie had brought down the night before. He poured some into a tumbler and carried it back to the table.

The transcription software's password prompt had popped up on-screen.

Chisholm spotted the cursor in the PASSWORD field, picked up the microphone, and said, "Marpessa."

The characters ******** appeared on-screen but the software recognized the password and presented its opening menu.

He called up the file named UNOS. Chisholm had previously described how the notion for MedEx had come to him and how he'd recruited Duane Strand to turn that idea into reality. The current file dealt with removing the one stumbling block to MedEx's start-up, a damnfool law that said before you could go shipping organs around the country, you had to get permission from them do-gooders at United Network for Organ Sharing.

Strand believed Chisholm had obtained the waiver by bribing a couple of subcommittee chairmen to tack it on as a rider to some minor pork-barrel bill, then ram the bill through during one of those end-of-session all-nighters when nobody much cared what they were voting on. Well of course that's what he'd done; it was the American way of turning special favors into law. Hadn't cost all that much, either. If your average citizen knew how cheap you could buy a congressman, his opinion of politicians would be even lower.

Funny thing was, Strand had phoned him a half-dozen times while the bill was being voted on, nervous as a turkey the day before Thanksgiving. Couldn't understand how Chisholm was able to remain so calm. Simple; Chisholm had mastered tricks that not even a shrewd feller like Strand suspected.

Scrolling down the file until he reached the point where he'd left off the previous day, Chisholm picked up the microphone.

"You reach for your checkbook in front of a politician," he said, watching his words form on-screen, "only thing he's going to ask is 'How high you want me to jump?' Bribing a do-gooder ain't as easy. I'm not talking money here—no one's ever cost me more than seventy-five thou—I'm talking the guilt they lay on you. I don't know how them priests can hear confessions day after day, year after year. 'Cause that's what you feel like, a priest, doing business with a do-gooder. Before they say yes, you got to put up with their sniveling. They think they're committing a sin against the cause, every last one of 'em. Once, just for the hell of it, I offer this feller an extra five grand if he'd just quit his blubbering. Might as well've tried stopping the Mississippi with a pitchfork.

"Anyway, what Strand didn't know, and still doesn't, is I bought myself a do-gooder long before I bought myself the subcommittee chairmen.

"You say the word 'lobbyist,' and everyone thinks of one of them fancy Dans running around Washington trying to get their big-business clients another tax break. That's only half the picture. Do-gooders try and influence legislation too. Maybe they call themselves 'pro bono lobbyists,' maybe they order alfalfa sprouts instead of red meat and Perrier instead of martinis, but the job's the same. One thing any lobbyist's supposed to do is keep your ox from getting gored, and one way to do that is study upcoming bills for end runs like the MedEx waiver.

"I had my people nose out the lobbyists working for the various organ-transplant interest groups. They find one way over his head financially. Idealistic as all get-out, quit a decent job to become a lobbyist after one of his kids' life was saved by a transplant, only now he can't make ends meet on a do-gooder's wages. Well, once we know we have him, it's a simple matter to find out which subcommittees he monitors. Those were the chairmen I bought, one feller from New York and the other from Texas. Two days before they tack on the rider, the lobbyist takes his family on vacation. By the time he gets back, the waiver's a done deal."

Chisholm stopped to review what he had just dictated. Then he checked his watch and saw he had another three hours before his constitutional. Good, because he was recalling fresh details that would flesh out the story. It always happened this way, one memory unlocking another. That's why this project never bored him.

THE bungalows on Chisholm's estate were situated west of the main house. As he started his constitutional he heard the thin strains of music coming from the partially opened window of one of the guest rooms. Chisholm knew damn little about rock and roll—next to his beloved sambas, it was just unholy caterwauling—but he recognized the song from those old TV commercials with the animated raisins. How did it go: *I heard it from the grapevine*? He glanced over and spotted a lanky, balding man in his mid-fifties hunched over a laptop.

The doctor was a flawed man, he mused, but who amongst us isn't? In the early 1970s, Chisholm's longtime personal physician in Oklahoma had found a partially obstructed bile duct and sent him on a precautionary visit to a gifted young thoracic surgeon in Pittsburgh. Naturally he had the new man, Lester Haidak, checked out beforehand. Such caution was not uncommon among the rich. During Ross Perot's first run for the presidency, it became known that he had vetted the beau of one of his daughters. Chisholm likened the resulting outcry to the baying of chihuahuas; anyone with a net worth in the billions would be a damn fool not to make sure such a suitor wasn't a gold digger or worse.

The snoops learned that Haidak lived his personal life on the edge. So did many successful folks who had money to burn and a thirst for adrenaline rushes. Others tested their invincibility with damnfool hobbies like car racing and sky diving and whitewater kayaking; Haidak gambled. Chisholm did too, but only on events whose outcomes he could control. The daily sports bets Haidak placed with his bookie were harmless enough, as were the day trips to Atlantic City. Not so the four-day weekends in Las Vegas or the Bahamas and the annual trip to the private clubs in London. It was these binges, when he'd remain at the tables twenty hours at a stretch, that seriously fucked his finances. The snoops also learned that Haidak was covering his markers by falsifying Medicare bills.

All this was known to Chisholm before his first appointment, during which the surgeon impressed him by correctly predicting that the obstruction would clear itself up. When he moved to Santa Fe and needed a new personal physician, he offered Haidak the job. Things got a little dicey when the feds found out about the bogus Medicare bills. Haidak pleaded no contest, agreed to make full restitution, and lost his medical license for six months.

Chisholm tried to help the surgeon stay on the straight and narrow—after all, he had entrusted his well-being to the man—but it was not to be. Eight years later, when government investigators finally unraveled the bewildering maze of dummy corporations Haidak had created to render phantom services, prosecutors were in no mood to plea-bargain. This time he was tried, convicted, sentenced to three-to-six, and barred for life from the practice of medicine.

Two weeks after Haidak's release from Lewisburg Federal Penitentiary, the Gulfstream brought him west to Santa Fe to hear a proposition that was short and sweet. No law kept Haidak from marketing his unquestioned medical expertise to others, so Chisholm would create him a consulting firm. He would throw in a baboon lab so Haidak could legally keep up his surgical skills. And he would bring the consulting firm a legitimate contract with the only client it would ever need.

The client, a start-up company called MedEx, wanted someone independent to watch over its organ-expediting protocols and procedures. The fees for that service would be reported to the IRS, just to keep things aboveboard. The bonuses MedEx was offering, on the other hand, would be paid to a numbered account in Geneva. To earn 'em, all Haidak had to do was travel the world harvesting involuntary donations, plus occasionally perform transplants on patients able to afford total discretion.

Finally, Chisholm himself was willing to pay a right handsome annual sum into the Geneva account if Haidak would again serve as his personal physician.

Today MedEx was happy; the global harvesting operation set up by Haidak ran like a Swiss watch. Haidak was happy; the MedEx bonuses were so generous that he no longer put up with the punishing trans-Pacific flights, having subcontracted a Thai surgeon to handle all harvests on the continent of Asia. Happiest of all was Chisholm; he was again under the care of the physician he trusted most.

Chisholm had finished his constitutional and was lingering at the breakfast table, chatting with Natalie and Placida, when Haidak made his entrance.

"Morning, Doc," he said. "Breakfast?"

"No thanks, Century. Coffee's fine." Haidak set down his clipboard to pour himself a mug and fuss with the cream and sugar.

Chisholm, who could read others the way a shark could detect a drop of blood a mile away, noted the tension in the doctor's jaw, the guarded look in his eyes. He shot quick glances at Natalie and Placida, who promptly left the table.

Haidak finally carried his mug and clipboard to the table and took a seat opposite Chisholm. Then, adjusting his horn-rimmed glasses, he began running down the standard tests.

Chisholm's hemoglobin was fine, as were PSA, overall cholesterol, and HDL counts. LDL, the so-called bad cholesterol, was, at 147, a bit elevated.

Usually at this point the two of them engaged in a little dialogue as familiar and comforting as an Abbott-and-Costello routine. Haidak would say, "You still wolfing down three or four steaks a week?"

Chisholm would nod sourly.

Haidak would say, "You might think about halving that, Century."

Chisholm would grouse, "I know, I know, and cut down on the eggs and the butter and the cream. Hell, why don't I just curl up in a corner and die? Them things's most of what's worth living for."

This morning, though, Haidak briskly flipped to the next sheet on his clipboard. "Your static EKG looks fine, Century, but when we put you on the treadmill . . ." He unfolded a graph and passed it across the table.

Chisholm glanced at the sinuous wave that rolled across the paper and said, "What'm I looking at?"

"Why you're feeling so cold lately. There've been significant ischemic changes since your last stress test six months ago."

"What the hell's that mean?"

"It suggests cardiomyopathy . . ."

"In English, Haidak, in English."

"You're suffering a viral inflammation of the heart muscles. Technically, the condition is known as endocarditis."

Chisholm set down his coffee. "You damn sure about this?"

"Yes. We've been discussing this possibility for what, a year and a half?"

"But why now? After all these years? I've been taking my medication."

Haidak shrugged. "A new strain of virus, perhaps. To

be absolutely sure, I faxed your EKGs to cardiologists in Boston, Pittsburgh, and Cape Town. The second opinions came back this morning. They all concur."

"The look on your puss tells me it's nothing you just go in and fix."

Haidak shook his head. "A hardening artery, definitely. Valves, maybe. But muscles, no. I'm sorry, Century, the consensus is, transplant."

"Shit." At Chisholm's age few things came as a complete surprise, but this was definitely an unforeseen complication. He thought about Elspeth's pending wedding, about his annual New Year's fete—and about all the affairs he needed to put in order should the surgery fail. "You up to the job? Putting 'em back in ain't exactly the same as ripping 'em out."

"Understood," Haidak replied. "Check with Strand if you want, but since June I've replaced one heart in Cali and another heart and a kidney in the Middle East. That's on top of the three or four baboons I do every month. So I'm up to the job, Century. And I've lined up someone to assist me."

"Who?"

"Same guy I used in Tripoli, a South African."

Chisholm nodded, then said, "Okay, how much leeway I got?"

Haidak knew MedEx had him scheduled for a harvesting trip to Eastern Europe in late November, but Duane Strand would understand that nothing could interfere with the well-being of the firm's most important client. He replied, "I'd like to do it within the next six, seven weeks."

"What's the risk of putting it off until mid-January?"

"How close do you want to cut it?"

"Not close enough to risk dying, you fool," Chisholm said, instantly regretting his loss of composure and the signal that might send Haidak.

"Then I wouldn't advise waiting that long."

"I can travel three weeks after the operation?"

"Assuming no complications, yes."

Chisholm absently plucked at his upper lip, then said, "Okay, order me up a heart for the end of November."

"Fine. I'll post the specs on the MedEx net the week before Thanksgiving. I believe you'll be out of town? How much notice do you need to get back to Santa Fe?"

"Twenty-four hours," Chisholm replied. "Anything I got to do to protect myself until the new one's in?"

Haidak smiled weakly. "Have a well-marbled steak every day, wash it down with heavy cream if you want. It won't matter once we do the procedure."

"Make sure you get a good one, Haidak," Chisholm said. "I don't want to be doing this again."

"Of course, Century."

"We done here? Good. Let Lino know when you want to fly out." Chisholm abruptly rose from the table and headed back toward his private quarters.

T U E S D A Y
O C T O B E R   2 0

IGNACIO Tejada had better places to be than some *gabacho*'s estate in the Hollywood Hills, more important things to do than listen to a pair of mooks run their mouths. Yet his big brother asked so few favors that he couldn't refuse Javier's request: Please accompany me to hear a business proposition. He hadn't grasped the importance of the meeting to Javier until the two of them had rendezvoused here. Nacio was wearing a Butthole Surfers T-shirt over baggy jeans, but his brother was in his Sunday best, a bronze-colored Armani suit that nicely complemented the green Tres Equis bandanna covering his razored-slick skull.

The Tejadas sat across from their hosts on a redwood deck that soared out over a rim of Topanga Canyon. Tres Equis protocol called for Javier to be flanked by at least three bodyguards whenever he ventured off the gang's turf. His human shields remained out in the driveway of the two-million-dollar aerie, though, watching *Oprah* in the back of the limo, because muscle and firepower were of no use to their boss this afternoon. And if mere brains and cunning had been enough, Javier would have brought Esai Ayala, the Tres Equis consigliere. Instead, he required someone not only smart but also wise to the ways of a certain class of Anglos; he needed his kid brother.

Sunlight bathed the deck, which seemed to Nacio as vast as the flight deck of an aircraft carrier. A gentle breeze was redolent with the fragrance of the jacarandas blooming on the steep hillsides below. The table before him bore platters of hors d'oeuvres, and a nearby cooler held an assortment of Mexican beers and two bottles of Chardonnay. Nacio was less than thirty miles from the flats of South-Central but everything was different here: the light, the landscape, the air, the lifestyle. Most surreal of all was the monologue being delivered by the younger of the two Anglos, a screenwriter in his early thirties.

"So it's the dead of night," Erik said. "Miguel, our hero, is on the lam with his little nephew, who's got a big old bullet hole in him. Like, what's top speed on one of your low-riders? Hundred? Hundred-twenty? Then we're talking primo white-knuckle shit, *amigo*, stuff any director'd cream his jeans to do.

"Anyway, Miguel sees the flashing turret lights gaining on him—no way he can outrun the rogue cop forever. But suddenly, up ahead, he spots a big store, maybe Robinson's over on Broadway. It's his only chance so *pow*, he rams his car right through the display window."

Erik shook his head sorrowfully. "Some fix he's in, hunh? Cornered by a rogue cop. Black-and-whites rushing up to seal off all the exits. A SWAT team on the way. Worst of all, his little nephew's going to bleed to death unless he gets him to a hospital.

"Remember, though, Miguel's still got that videotape his nephew shot. And remember what's on the tape—the rogue cop raping a young Chicana prostitute, then offing her. Think that's enough to ignite East L.A. and South-Central? Damn right it is. We're talking riots that'd make

Rodney King look like a marshmallow roast. But what can our hero do from inside the deserted store?"

Melodramatically raising his mirrorshades, Erik leaned toward Javier: "Like it so far?"

"Is not bad," Javier allowed.

Nacio bit his lip to keep from smirking. He had sat through old *Cisco Kid* episodes on late-night cable with better plots.

"Fuckin' A, it's not bad," declared the fourth man on the deck. Dean, their host, was a producer in his late forties who wore painfully thick glasses and had some kind of scaly rash on his balding forehead. "*Jefe*, sure I can't have the maid run some beers out to your boys?"

"They no drink on duty," Javier said.

Dean shrugged and poured himself some more wine. "Erik's a genius at dreaming up story lines that grab you by the nuts and never let go. But who was it that said there's only seven basic plots in the world?"

"Shakespeare?" volunteered Erik. "Or maybe Dickens."

"Exactly," Dean said. "And know what? This town's done 'em all. So how do we convince the masses to open their wallets? With texture, with authenticity, *Jefe*, which is why it was so important that I have Erik meet you."

Nacio masked his disgust by toying with the handle of his ebony cane. Not only was he sweating a killer term paper for Greek Mythology 306, but he should be spending this time working on Nguyen-Anh Dupree's posting of the previous week.

The search for background information on MedEx, and on the hospitals that had transplanted the suspect organs, would be performed at that night's Boot Up the 'Hood session, where he and Leepi Walker would unleash the kids on a host of specialized databases. The exercise would spare the two of them that time-consuming task while giving the new class, now in its third week, some firsthand online experience.

Digging up data on Wings of Mercy Ltd. was another matter. He and Leepi had attacked various sites on the Cayman Islands with Baby Huey and run into firewalls as staunch, though not as ferocious, as MedEx's Pit Bull. By pulling threads on several *otaku* boards, they learned why. In the early 1990s, those who ran the shell corporations and private banks saw their Caribbean sanctuary becoming ever more dependent on electronic transfers. That is, drug-money launderers and embezzlers and income-tax cheats no longer arrived at Georgetown International Airport lugging suitcases bulging with newly minted dead presidents; they just wired in the money. With the various American intelligence agencies and the IRS hiring hackers to sniff out cybertrails, the white-collar buccaneers of the Caymans had banded together to fortify online security.

Serious hours of hacking would be needed to gain access. But here he was, stuck in Topanga Canyon, all because several weeks earlier his brother had been in the wrong after-hours club at the wrong time.

That was the night an actress named Lourdes dropped by the club. Lourdes, a minor South-Central celebrity for playing a Latina temptress on one of those raunchy Fox sitcoms, had just come from a screening. Javier had invited her and her date to his table. The date turned out to be Dean, who professed an interest in casting Lourdes in a movie but probably just wanted to screw her brains out —which, Nacio reflected sourly, shouldn't take more than a couple of seconds.

When Dean learned that Javier headed a gang, he mentioned that one of his writers was developing a script on "the Zorro of East L.A.," an honorable badman who fought for Chicano justice. Might Javier be interested in helping on the project? Evidently so, because here they all were.

". . . so what we've got at the moment is a bankable story that lacks one crucial thing," Erik was saying. "Sure the hero's named 'Miguel,' but let me be straight up with you, we could change it to 'Mike' and make it a Brad Pitt vehicle. That's not what Dean and I want to do. We think this story's more important than that. We think it's a way to make the whole world realize the hardships that you and your people endure."

Uh-oh, thought Nacio, cue the violins.

"When's the last time you saw a mainstream picture portray the barrios as they really are?" continued Erik. "Where decent, hardworking immigrants are raising their kids as best they can? But where the community is being bled dry by *gringo* shylocks who live in Nine-oh-two-one-oh? Where honorable men such as yourself have to go outside a system that is corrupt to do the right thing?

"That's why this project needs you, *amigo*. If the story's about Wall Street or NASA, no problem, I just hop a jet to Cape Canaveral or New York. But you know better than me, no way this white boy can do research in South-Central unless someone of your stature vouches for me."

"Is no problem," Javier said magnanimously. "I put the word out you ain't no narc, okay? I tell my people Erik, he just want to hang in the 'hood. You be safe, my friend."

Erik hesitated, then said, "There's more, Javier. I want face time with you so I can get inside your skin. What are your dreams? Your fears? What's the most bodacious thing Tres Equis ever did? My story line, your anecdotes —we're talking a script here that's going to green-light itself. Right, Dean?"

"Fuckin' A," Dean agreed. "Just between us girls, guess who I'm thinking of taking it to first? Antonio Banderas."

"No way, man," said Javier, clearly flattered.

"Absolutely. Now I happen to know Tony's up to here in projects, so I have in mind a couple of designated hitters who ain't exactly chopped liver either. Andy Garcia and Jimmy Smits."

Javier said to Nacio, "What you think, bro?"

Dean and Erik turned with curiosity to the rudely dressed, gimpy-legged young man who had remained mute since arriving.

Nacio said, "I think you should be played by Chong's buddy, Cheech."

When Javier laughed, so did Dean and Erik, though a bit nervously.

Nacio glanced over the railing of the redwood deck and saw that purple shadows were beginning to shroud the ramshackle cabins on the floor of the canyon far below. Damn, time to stop getting dissed by these Anglos, time to dust these mooks. "Yo, Erik," he said. "How's your picture going to end?"

Erik gave him a patronizing smile. "That's got to grow organically out of life in the barrios, *amigo*, which is why your brother's participation is so important. But I got a couple aces up my sleeve."

"Good to hear, man," Nacio said. "For a while I'm worrying, maybe you just take the easy way out."

"Oh? What might that be?" Erik leaned forward to smear a five-grain cracker with pâté.

"Well, I say to myself, so *pow*, hero rams his low-rider through this big window. Store like that's got lots of big windows. Maybe one of them's got a dozen big-screen TVs all playing *Monday Night Football* or something, you know?

"So after a while hero says to himself, how come these big-screen TVs all be playing the same shit? So he checks it out and damn if they don't all have cables sticking out the back. So he follows the cables down to the basement and damn if they don't all go into the same junction box. So hero goes up to the electronics department, snatches a VCR, and jacks it into the junction box.

"*Ker-chunk*—that be the sound of him slotting in his nephew's tape.

"And *whoa!*—that be the sound of the pigs outside getting a load of what's going down and turning their thirty-eights on the rogue cop."

Erik looked as if his pâté had turned into a turd.

"Hey, not bad, bro," Javier said. "Maybe you could do a screenwriting class or something over at USC."

"Nah," Nacio said. "I kind of ripped that off from a picture that was on TV the other night, *Three Days of the Condor*. I bet Erik can make up something fresher. Yo, Javier, gotta make tracks."

Javier nodded and started to stand.

"Hold up, *Jefe*," Dean said, reaching for his briefcase. "We haven't discussed our deal."

Javier gestured to Nacio: "Bro here be my main man on details. You make him happy, you make me happy."

"That one of them whatchamacallits?" said Nacio, looking at the papers in Dean's hand. "A deal memo? Why don't you messenger it over to my agent."

"You got an agent?" said Dean with open amusement. "Sure, what the hell. Who is he?"

"He's a her," Nacio replied. "Treasure."

Dean's eyes widened: "Treasure Geltman? Over at CAA?"

Nacio nodded. Just the mention of Leepi Walker's high-powered agent should be enough to back down this creep, he thought; if not, Treasure would gladly tell Dean where to stick his deal memo.

The four men left the deck and made their way to the front door. As they carried out the obligatory round of effusive goodbyes, one of the Tres Equis bodyguards hustled to get the door of the limo.

Javier waved him off and fell in step with Nacio as his brother started hobbling toward his own car.

"So," Javier said. "What do you think?"

"Puro pedo," Nacio muttered.

Javier frowned. "You will explain tonight?"

"Mañana. I got a workshop I'm late for, then there's something I got to do for Doc Dupree."

"Mañana, then. Hey, bro—thanks for coming."

"Por nada." Nacio slid his cane across the front seat and then climbed into the car he thought of as a

geezermobile. Javier had wanted to give him the keys to a Ferrari or a Jaguar. Thanks but no thanks, Nacio had said; his leg made those low-slung roadsters difficult to get in and out of, unlike this geriatrically oriented Buick Park Avenue fitted with hand controls.

Slotting in a Selena CD, he sped up the driveway and through the security gate. But when he reached Topanga Canyon Boulevard, the northbound lanes that led to the Ventura Freeway were bumper-to-bumper and stalled. Nacio sighed and reached for the car phone.

SAM Cooke crooned sweetly through Phillipa Walker's earphones as she sat in the Boot Up the 'Hood workshop editing a file on her PowerBook. The document on-screen was a list of databases the class would hit first that evening. The file itself actually resided on one of the machines in her Santa Monica office. But since experiencing an epiphany in late 1995, Walker had put up with the minor hassles of remote networking because it allowed her to harness the MorpHaus servers to majorly simplify her life.

One day, rushing to leave her apartment to meet a prospective client, she had reflexively slipped on her beloved khaki photographer's vest. Though grungy, the vest had manifold pockets that readily absorbed all the necessities of the typical Angeleno's car-centric life: sunglasses, keys, cell phone, and pager. Normally she would have continued out the door without a second thought. On that morning, however, Walker couldn't help but notice how ludicrous the vest looked over a Norma Kamali suit.

Shortly thereafter she had cobbled together an app so useful that more than one associate had urged her to market it. Once, friends and colleagues had to maintain six separate numbers for her: voice both home and office; fax both home and office; cell phone; and pager. Now they just had to remember her direct-dial at MorpHaus. The company's servers could differentiate voice and fax calls.

Faxes were routed straight to her queue. On a voice call, the servers simultaneously rang her office, home, and cell phones, as well as messaged her telephone-capable computers. If Walker didn't pick up by the third ring, the caller could choose between leaving voicemail or messaging her pager.

Suddenly Sam Cooke was interrupted by the soft tinkle of wind chimes as a thumbnail-sized photograph of a young Don Ameche popped up in the upper-left-hand corner of the screen. Walker double-clicked on the Ameche icon to toggle her earphones from the laptop's CD-ROM drive to the incoming call, then said into the built-in microphone, "Yo. So how'd the meeting go?"

"You don't want to know," Ignacio Tejada replied. "All our little wireheads show?"

"Every last one's already whaling on a box. Fact is, half of 'em were hanging at the door when I got here, and I got here twenty minutes early."

"Don't be making me feel bad, Leepi."

"Me? I wouldn't do that to someone who had to take a meeting with Dean. Ain't he some piece of work?"

"Javier ought to whup Lourdes upside the head," Tejada muttered. "Any woman who'd give that creep so much as the time of day, she be a disgrace to the sisterhood. By the way, Dean wanted to lay a deal memo on Javier. Told him to send it to Treasure."

Walker laughed. "Hope he does. It'll make her day."

"Listen, girl, KFWB says they took down the Ventura. It be another hour before I show."

"Thanks much."

"Don't mention it. See you when I see you."

Walker closed the Ameche icon and copied her on-screen document from the MorpHaus servers to the Boot Up the 'Hood LAN, or local area network. Now each workshop participant could access and annotate it, even at the same time. Then she messaged all twelve screens simultaneously:

Yo—Showtime. Leepi

A dozen heads turned her way.

Walker waited for the kids to take off their earphones, then said, "Tonight, we surf the Net. Which be a step up from last week, when you logged onto the white-boy services. Pretty lame, hunh?"

"Truth, sister, truth," a boy called out from the back.

"Totally sad," one of the girls agreed. "Why people be paying good money to use them? I'm going into this wave-file library on AOL? To see if there be some bad sounds to use as an alarm? Like, ain't we all sick of this?" She clicked her mouse and the speakers on her box spat out the opening bars of Beethoven's Fifth. "But know what's in there mostly, what those Caspers be so busy devising and posting? Big belches and monster farts, that's what."

"White boys," the class murmured, shaking their heads.

"Okay, listen up," Walker said. "Tonight we be exploring some databases so's you can find some stuff for me and Nacio. There's a new queue on the network called 'DOC.' The file in there called 'LIST' tells you the topics we're after and what sites we want searched.

"Go into LIST and sign up for a topic by putting your initials next to it, then go do your search. Dump your downloads into DOC. Depending on the stuff you dig up, I'm going to be thinking up new queries, so check the LIST file from time to time for fresh topics and fresh sites."

Walker paused. "These be grown-up sites which charge grown-up prices. Some bill you by how much time you spend online, some by how much you retrieve. Do the workshop a favor—use your time wisely."

"Can't you and Nacio get us inside them free?" asked one of the boys.

"Course. But we going to teach you those tricks? Nope."

"Why not, Leepi?"

"It be illegal, Akim."

"Then why you and Nacio do it?"

"We don't. Much."

"Word is," said a girl named Inez, "Nacio ain't paid for a long-distance call since he was twelve."

"You're confusing two things, Inez," Walker said. "There be phreaking and there be hacking.

"Not that I'm saying Nacio does it, but phreaking the phone company's like, no harm, no foul. They be pissing and moaning about us stealing a billion here and a billion there. Bull. Say you see a bitchin' jacket or some choice CD or a phat new app. You boost it, now that be theft 'cause the store's out the money it paid for the merchandise. If the phone lines always be full, and phreaks be keeping off paying customers, then AT and T got a point. But every second their lines ain't one hundred percent full—which is always—that's an unbillable second that never comes around again. It's like an empty seat at a Lakers game or on a flight to New York. Any way to recycle those? Nope. So what phreaks do is, we see that some of those AT and T moments don't go to waste.

"Hacking's a whole 'nother matter," Walker continued. "That's busting into somebody's system. Me and Nacio only do it if we think a particular somebody be messing with the 'hood or with a tight friend. Then we might go in and see what's what. Remember that stink a year or two ago, when they caught those banks saying no to brothers and sisters wanting a loan so they could buy a house? Didn't matter if they had good jobs, answer was still no. Well, white folks call that 'redlining,' and you can't do it."

"You and Nacio put the collar on 'em?"

"No way," Walker said. "We look like the Man to you? But me and Nacio, we familiarized ourselves with their electronic archives so we could tell the lawyers what documents to subpoena."

She hesitated. It was time for the kids to get cracking on the searches. Yet Week Three of the workshop was when she or Nacio usually gave a cautionary talk about digital security, a topic to which the discussions so far this evening were a perfect lead-in. Go with the flow, she thought.

"There's an important lesson here," Walker continued. "Used to be, the way to keep your goodies safe was put a real thick wall around them—which is what they still do with stuff like gold and jewelry and great artworks. Before anyone can grab them, they got to use a lot of force and time just breaking in.

"Today, some of the most valuable stuff in the world is electronic data. Funny thing about electronic data is, you can't touch it, can't weigh it, can't smell it. So how do you protect it?"

"Yo, Leepi, that be easy," said a boy named Ramon. "Put it on a box that ain't got no network card and no modem. Wanna button it even tighter? Pull the floppy drive and the printer cable. Now someone wants your stuff, he gotta come boot up your box and read it on your screen."

"That'll work, Ramon," agreed Walker. "But let's say you have some data that can help a bunch of your pals. You gonna make 'em come to your room and copy it down? And what if one of 'em lives in the Valley?

"But the moment you slot in a communications device, it's like, kiss security goodbye. For the first time in history, other people don't be needing to blast down walls to get at your goodies. They just need a cheap box and enough brains to outsmart your firewall.

"What I'm telling you is important. All of us keep secrets on our box. Some just be embarrassing if they get out, like the names of our old love-toys. Others be enough to get you five-to-ten courtesy of the Man. So remember, you got incriminating data, you also got a security problem."

Ramon raised his hand. "Let's say I copy all my secret stuff onto a floppy."

"Then delete the file from your hard drive?"

The boy nodded.

"Deleting a file ain't the same as physically erasing the data, Ramon. Deleting just tells the operating system certain tracks are now available for overwriting with fresh data. Nothing actually gets deleted except the OS address of the old file. Old data stays right there."

"But Leepi," Ramon persisted, "ain't there a workaround? Like, write directly onto the floppy so there be no data touching the hard drive?"

"Now you got a security problem with the floppy, don't you?" said Walker. "You going to build some walls around it? Hide it under the mattress? Carry it in your shorts? And another thing—say the data on it can land you some hard time? Well, floppies don't flush down the toilet like paper. You can't chew 'em up and swallow 'em, neither.

"Okay, I'm all lectured out. Time to hit LIST and go to work."

THE workshop was in its last hour when Ignacio Tejada finally arrived. He reviewed the query Walker had written asking their fellow NUROMNCR users for help in penetrating the electronic security of the Cayman Islands. After posting it, they turned their attention to the mountain of data the class had already pulled in that evening.

The daily news indices of a number of papers in West Texas, plus transcripts of local news programs, revealed that during the first week of September none reported an accident or cluster of accidents claiming at least three victims.

Credit reports and newspaper articles on the hospitals in Boston, Indianapolis, Birmingham, and Portland laid out each's ownership, affiliations, and board of directors. Walker had asked for a full biographical search on every member of the four boards. On noticing that all four hospitals were affiliated with the same Knoxville,

Tennessee–based health-care corporation, she had also requested credit reports and articles on that company, which was named Caduceus 21.

But the pickings were slim on MedEx—a few scattered articles, mostly from medical trade papers—and slimmer still on Wings of Mercy Ltd.: no data online anywhere.

"How much stuff we pulling in, girl?" asked Tejada.

Walker launched a utility, tagged the files, and read off the byte count: "Two hundred meg already. How many hours that going to take Doc to download on his old fourteen-four modem? Damn, Nacio, we're talking almost three and a half days. And I don't even want to think about the cell-phone fees."

Tejada nodded glumly, then broke into a grin. "Wait," he said. "There's a better way."

WEDNESDAY

OCTOBER 21

THE rasp of the Zippo broke the stillness of the room. Nguyen-Anh Dupree, lying in bed with a paperback novel propped on his bare chest, eyed the lighter's guttering orange flame and made a mental note to pick up a can of fluid on his next run into San Cristóbal. Maybe he should just quit smoking. Why bother, he thought, as long as he continued to expose his lungs to the equally noxious kerosene fumes of the hurricane lamp by his bed? Dupree took a drag on the Faro and returned his attention to *The Magus*, which he was reading for perhaps the tenth time.

Before joining Médecins Sans Frontières, Dupree considered fiction something to put up with for the sake of various required lit courses. Long years abroad, though, had taught him that the library of tattered paperbacks he now dragged from one country to the next was his principal reality check. The news was never far from hand: his radio had a shortwave band, Don Joaquin's dish picked up CNN, and American newspapers and magazines were available online if he wanted to pay the exorbitant cell-phone fees.

But events that the Western media considered newsworthy impinged little if at all on his daily life here in Chiapas state; Dupree regarded the stories as dispatches from an alternate universe. On the other hand, the novelists he had grown to treasure—be it Conrad or Tolstoy or Malamud or Fowles—magically transported him back into his once and future culture. Their tales resonated with characters and values and motives and dilemmas as reassuringly familiar as the face he shaved every morning. Dupree could ask for no better companions than his novels at day's end, as the lights began to wink out and the streets quieted in his remote little village.

That calm was suddenly shattered by a loud burst of vintage rock and roll. Dupree blinked in astonishment. Who around here could possibly own a recording by Sly and the Family Stone, he wondered, even as "Hot Fun in the Summertime" was abruptly muted in midsong.

Then a young boy called out, *"Esa es la clínica del Dr. Kung-fu,"* followed by the solid *thunks* of car doors slamming shut.

He set down his book, slipped on his sarong and a T-shirt, and was padding out of the bedroom when he heard three firm raps on the front door.

Dupree opened it and found himself staring at his past. Two homeboys with green bandannas around their necks —one wiry, the other as big as an NFL tackle—were standing nonchalantly in front of a dusty white Thunderbird convertible. He had not laid eyes on them since his last visit to South-Central in what, the mid-1990s?

"Qué cura, Esai?" said Dupree, extending a clenched fist. "And wassup, Large?"

"Yo, Doc." First Esai Ayala and then the hulking Anthony Quintanilla returned the ritualistic four-step pound that was the Tres Equis greeting. Ayala turned to Quintanilla: "What I say to you, Large? You see surprise on this man's face? No way—Doc Dupree, he one chill hombre."

"To what do I owe this pleasure?" asked Dupree.

"Well, we just passing through the 'hood and Large, he have to pee," Ayala said gravely, before breaking into laughter. "Actually, Nacio sent us. FedEx says they don't do no deliveries to this part of the planet."

A few of the locals had followed the Thunderbird to the clinic. It was a toss-up as to which mesmerized them more: the car or Quintanilla, who towered over the tallest villager by a foot and outweighed the beefiest by eighty pounds.

Dupree glanced at the tired faces of the two young men, then at the Avis sticker and Guatemalan plates on the car. "Long day, hunh? You guys catch the dawn flight out of L.A.?"

Ayala nodded. "Nacio say we can go to a closer city, but they only got night flights, so we save like almost a day. I don't know about that."

"True, Esai. There's airports in Villahermosa and Tuxtla, but the roads from there are worse than what you took up from Guatemala City."

"No way," Quintanilla objected. "Esai, he look at the map and say, 'Two hundred ten miles, Large, we make it in three hours easy.' They call it a highway, I call it one damn long pothole. How many hours we in that car, man? Maybe like nine? Sheesh."

"Every time we start to go good," Ayala said, "boom, another roadblock and there be a soldier with a gun, like, 'Open the trunk, *por favor*.' What gives, Doc?"

"Didn't Nacio tell you this province is still under martial law?"

Ayala shook his head. "All he say is, don't be packing down there."

"Smart advice," Dupree said. "Listen, you guys must be thirsty and hungry."

"Both," Quintanilla said mournfully. "Nacio say don't be eating nothing you don't know, don't be drinking nothing that don't come in a bottle. So we ain't had but a couple of Cokes since those itty-bitty bags of peanuts on the plane. Doc, you know that there ain't one Mickey D or Pizza Hut between here and the airport?"

"Lot of food on the highway," Ayala said, "but it all be roadkill or inside a wagon and still alive. Yo, Large, how long we behind that chicken truck? A half hour? Damn, those suckers give off a nasty smell."

"Welcome to Central America," Dupree said. Realizing that he had little by way of food and drink in the clinic, he scanned the crowd, which seemed to be growing by the second. Curfew was still some twenty minutes off, so he motioned over a twelve-year-old boy named Paco and asked him to run two errands: check the village's lone guesthouse to see if it had vacancies for the night, then go to the cantina around the corner and bring back six cold *cervezas* and a half-dozen burritos. Wait, he said, eyeing Quintanilla, make that nine burritos.

Dupree was ushering the two men inside when he saw headlights rake the side of the clinic and heard the whine of fast-approaching vehicles. Uh-oh, he thought. *Militares.*

Two Jeeps slewed to a halt behind the Thunderbird and a half-dozen soldiers piled out clutching their rifles. Several shooed back the villagers encircling the Thunderbird so that they themselves could get a better look.

The patrol leader swaggered up to Dupree: "*Buenas noches,* Dr. Kung-fu. We have alarming reports of desperadoes asking directions to your house."

"The men who ask directions to my house are not desperadoes," Dupree replied. "They are my friends."

A murmur swept through the crowd; it was good to see Dr. Kung-fu stand up to this officious *pedazo de mierda.*

The patrol leader frowned. "You are expecting them?"

Dupree nodded.

"Why was I not informed?"

"I know of no regulation that says I must report the comings and goings of friends," Dupree said. Then, seeing the impact of his words—the villagers were greatly pleased by the patrol leader's sudden anger—he tried to defuse the tension with a more conciliatory tack. He took out his pack of Faros, offered one to the patrol leader, and lit both. "My friends tell me they pass through many checkpoints on their way here," Dupree said. "If one of your fellow officers thinks they are dangerous, they would be behind bars by now, no?"

The patrol leader mulled it over. He could not fault the *gringo's* logic but needed to save face. "I will see their documents. And that of the car, also."

Dupree turned and said, "Esai, Large? The captain here needs your passports, driver's licenses, and the rental agreement on the T-bird."

Quintanilla's emergence from the clinic stunned those who had not yet glimpsed him. Among them: the patrol leader, who rocked back and reflexively dropped his hand to his holster, a reaction that drew not a few snickers.

Dupree quickly gathered the papers. The patrol leader carried them back to the Jeep and picked up the radio.

Ayala looked over the *militares* and said, scornfully, "These *putas* . . ."

"Speak English," Dupree hissed.

"These assholes the local heat? Hell, up in South-Central, they couldn't hack it as meter maids."

"No," Dupree agreed, "but they carry M-sixteens and they don't always remember to engage the safety. Be cool, Esai."

"I hear you, Doc."

The patrol leader was still on the radio when young Paco, wobbling under his burden, emerged from the crowd. Dupree relieved him of the tray of food and the plastic bucket containing the bottles of beer, handing them to Quintanilla. Paco whispered something in Dupree's ear, then ran back to his parents.

A murmur swept the crowd. Dupree looked up in time to see Quintanilla shove a burrito in his mouth and consume half of it in one bite.

"Ain't these villagers got something swifter to do?" asked Ayala.

"Nope. You guys are the best show to hit town since Don Joaquin brought in a band last Carnaval."

The patrol leader strode back to Dupree and reluctantly returned the papers of Ayala and Quintanilla. "You must go inside instantly, Dr. Kung-fu. It is the curfew." He turned to the crowd and yelled, "Do you hear that? The curfew has started! Go home!"

Dupree led his guests inside.

Ayala and Quintanilla went immediately to the battered pine table and dug into the food. Dupree was reaching for his Swiss Army knife, which had a bottle-opener, when Quintanilla uncapped a beer with an easy flick of his thumb.

"We're at seven thousand feet, guys," Dupree warned. "Those beers are twice as potent."

Quintanilla nodded, then slaked his thirst by chugging the bottle.

"Yo, Doc," Ayala said, "me and Large, we didn't see no Motel Sixes coming into town."

"*Mi casa es su casa*," Dupree replied. "I'm afraid the guesthouse in town's showing 'No Vacancy.' Probably wants to save its furniture from Large. You guys'll stay with me tonight."

Ayala dubiously surveyed the Spartan clinic.

"There's a bedroom with a single bunk through that door," Dupree said, "plus sleeping bags. How long you planning to stick around?"

"Don't know," Ayala said. "Me and Large, we got open tickets back to L.A. What's to see and do round here, anyway?"

"Not much that's glitzy," Dupree admitted. "There's shopping in San Cristóbal, stuff like embroidery and weavings and *huipiles*, which are really nice cotton smocks. There's some Mayan ruins up near Palenque, about four hours away. And there's the Lacandon rain forest, one of the best in Central America."

Quintanilla said, "Mayan ruins sounds cool, Esai. Disneyland and Busch Gardens, they get boring after a while, you know?"

Ayala made a face. "Maybe we go shopping in San Cristóbal. Get the women something. Speaking of women, Doc, any, like, whorehouses around?"

"As a matter of fact . . ."

"The girls be clean? I want to take home something to Rita, but nothing like that, you know what I mean?"

"I give them checkups once a week. Who's Rita?"

"My old lady," Ayala said. "You know her, Doc. Rita Lopez?"

Dupree scratched his head. "Didn't you used to go with a Rosa Lopez?"

"Same girl," Ayala said. "After the O.J. trial, people give her so much shit, she change her name."

It turned out Ayala and Rita were the proud parents of two young children. Esai had worked his way up through the Tres Equis ranks from gofer to Javier Tejada's consigliere, a position that effectively removed him from the mean streets of South-Central.

Large Quintanilla's story was not as happy. Despite earning all-state defensive tackle honors in high school, his abysmal classroom record had scared off every university except one major West Coast football factory, which packed him off to a junior college in hopes that tutors could raise his grades and ACT score. For the first time in his life, Quintanilla hit the books. By his second season he had squeezed his ACTs into the low twenties and made himself academically eligible to transfer to the university the following year. Then he blew out a knee during a game. On learning that the damage to Quintanilla's anterior cruciate ligament was so severe he could never play again, the university withdrew its scholarship offer. To the rescue had come Ayala, Large's best friend from sandbox days. Tres Equis sponsored a gamut of after-school sports teams ranging from soccer to basketball to track; Quintanilla now helped run them.

Dupree drank in their stories like a dry sponge. And in listening to his guests, he realized what he missed most about Los Angeles, indeed about the United States. Life as an expatriate doctor had allowed him to have a greater impact, and experience more vivid highs and keener lows, than any practice in America. Yet downtime in the Third World was like running out of gas on a dirt road ten miles from town. This village, like most of the others in which he had served, seemed governed by the same internal clock. Everybody arose, ate, and went to sleep at the same time. Daily life held no surprises.

Back home, he remembered having to constantly check his watch, always under pressure to make the next decision, see the next patient. The sheer velocity of American life was draining, but those able to handle it could also change their destinies. It was not nostalgia that Dupree felt, but appreciation. Esai Ayala could have remained a Tres Equis foot soldier and risked being capped. Large Quintanilla could have worn out the rest of his body muscling crates for a living. Instead, both had bettered themselves.

What choices did the people of his village face: little Paco? Fabiana and her babies? Don Joaquin? Even the best doctors at the hospital in San Cristóbal were doomed to remain in Chiapas state for the rest of their careers, Mexico being as class-conscious as England. And then he thought of young Guillermo, whose quest for a new life had cost him the one he had.

Quintanilla was polishing off the last burrito when Ayala yawned, stood, and went out to the Thunderbird. He returned a minute later with a pair of nylon gym bags, which looked like they had been scavenged from a Dumpster, and a gaily gift-wrapped package.

"What's with those?" asked Dupree, nodding at the gym bags. "Javier tightening the Tres Equis travel budget or what?"

"Yo, Doc, me and Large dig seeing you and everything," Ayala replied, "but it's not like we volunteered to come down here. Tres Equis ain't exactly the outfit you join if you want to see the world, know what I mean? Like, when we go back, think we ain't going to make some Customs sucker's day? One look at our passports, Guatemala and back real quick, and he be saying to himself, 'Hot damn, bonus time—caught me some *cholos* running some coke.' So while me and Large're in the back room letting some faggot get off doing a cavity search, they be cutting our luggage looking for hidden compartments. So the Louis Vuitton stays in the closet, know what I mean?"

Ayala handed the gift-wrapped package to Dupree.

Dupree hefted it, a look of bemusement on his face. "Too heavy to be a sweater or a fruitcake," he said. He gently shook it and heard a rattle. "Doesn't sound like a book."

"Go ahead, Doc, open it," Quintanilla urged.

Dupree undid the wrapping paper carefully, so he could give it to the local school, and beheld three cartons of his favorite cigarettes—available in San Cristóbal, but at almost ten times the price of Faros—and a shoebox.

Inside the shoebox was a high-tech CARE package as thrilling as any Christmas present from his youth. There were a half-dozen spare batteries for his laptop. And a cell-phone-capable PCMCIA card that could transfer data at 28800 bits per second, or twice the speed of his current modem. Lastly, there was a plastic box stamped IOMEGA that came with a power cord and a centronics cable.

"That be what Nacio call a 'jazz' drive," Ayala said. "Him and Leepi say it so full of goodies, it take you more than a day to downpull everything they put on there. Whatever that means."

"It means you and Large saved me a zillion-dollar phone bill. Thank you."

Ayala yawned again. Quintanilla, refueled by seven burritos and four beers, looked as contented as a baby in search of a burp and a nap.

Dupree broke open a carton of the cigarettes. Lighting

up a Benson & Hedges Light, he savored the moment, then stood and fired up the Bunsen burner to heat water for coffee. "I think it's time to get you guys tucked in," he said. "Come on, I'll show you where you're sleeping."

"How 'bout you, Doc?"

"I think I'll stay up awhile and scope out what's on this Jaz drive."

F R I D A Y
O C T O B E R   2 3

F ROM Maggie Sepulveda's Manhattan bedroom she could glimpse slivers of the Hudson River between the high-rises that lined the avenues to the west, Broadway and West End and Riverside Drive. From her bedroom here in Knoxville she had an unobstructed view of the Tennessee River flowing past under the shadow of the Great Smokies. There were less felicitous differences as well. Back home at 7:30 A.M., she would be skimming the *Times* and *The Wall Street Journal*, coffee in hand and one of the network news shows droning in the background. There was no such easing into the day in Knoxville.

Few experiences cranked the stressometer more than an extended on-site assignment in a distant city. She and her fellow analyst, Jill Unger, were at least accustomed to life away from home and to the awkwardness of spending long days inside a targeted company, searching through old ledgers and memos for the kind of ghastly corporate skeleton that could doom a half-billion-dollar deal. Teddy

Quereshi and his squad of number crunchers weren't. With her office hours taken up by part-time den-mothering, meetings, and phone calls—including at least three a day from an anxious Rob Dillon—Maggie had come to reserve early mornings for paperwork and for what was left of her personal life.

For instance, one e-note in her private account this morning was from Paul Barry. They had spoken but twice in the past ten days. He was six time zones away, in Italy, because Linzy Kirsch had decided to treat herself to an extended vacation; more likely, thought Maggie uncharitably, the diva was in some fancy clinic, recuperating from a septum transplant on her cocaine-ravaged schnozz. In any event, Paul expected to briefly swing through New York at the end of the month before hitting the road again. Might she be in town then?

Maggie had yet to reply, being too preoccupied with a pair of memos aimed at smoothing her staff's transition to Knoxville.

The first dealt with the so-called conjugals. To entice New York staffers onto the Caduceus 21 project, Marx Dillon had promised to pay the airfare to reunite each volunteer with spouse or lover for one long weekend per month, plus all major holidays, in New York or in Tennessee. Yesterday her team had submitted their wish list of dates for conjugals.

It came as no great surprise that everyone signed up to take them in New York. Only Teddy Quereshi had enjoyed his first week in Knoxville, having discovered the city's sizable Pakistani community. In fact, there were enough students from his homeland enrolled in the University of Tennessee's engineering, computer-science, and medical programs to support a grocery store that carried staples like basmati rice, red lentils, and goat meat. Plus, he had met someone at the student union with a complete collection of CDs by Nusrat Fateh Ali Khan, his country's foremost *qawalli* singer. Teddy was eager to show Sterling Nussbaum around Knoxville, but not until he had a better read on how their sexual orientation would be received down here.

Maggie's task was to devise a schedule that honored as many first choices as possible without leaving herself shorthanded.

Her second memo dealt with some mundane aspects of the relocation. The letter of agreement over which Rob Dillon and Len Reifsnyder had sparred so heatedly called for Caduceus 21 to foot the bill for living quarters, office space, and a warm body to answer phones. The New Yorkers had lucked out on accommodations, having been installed in a quartet of corporate apartments some fifteen minutes by car west of downtown. The two-bedroom units were impersonal but as comfortable as a Marriott or a Wyndham—and far less depressing than a Motel 6 off I-40. That still left the visitors clueless as to the best supermarkets, the most dependable dry cleaners, the hippest video stores. At Maggie's request Reifsnyder had queried the Caduceus 21 staff for recommendations, which she was collating into a home-brewed Baedeker.

Damn, she thought, but playing boss involved a lot of scut work. Funny how they never dwelled on that in biz school or at the "breaking-the-glass-ceiling" seminars the women's networking groups were always sponsoring.

At 8:15 A.M. she heard a tap on her door.

"Come on in, Jill." Maggie hadn't bunked with a woman since grad school a decade ago, but the junior analyst seemed less a roommate than a kid sister. Both of them liked to unwind by cooking; both had the same taste in takeout food, music, and sitcoms; and neither was a cosmetics slut, which made bathroom-sharing tolerable.

The rangy Unger was wearing a bright orange University of Tennessee football jersey, white compression shorts over black tights, and knee guards. She carried a pair of Rollerblades and a helmet in her hands and her day's wardrobe in a trim little Fendi backpack slung over one shoulder.

"I'm off," said Unger, who was taking advantage of the mild weather by blading the aerobically strenuous five miles to and from work in lieu of daily workouts. "See you at the factory."

"Cute outfit. Might land you on Page One."

Unger blushed. Two days earlier the Knoxville *News Sentinel* had rescued a dull news day with a large photograph of her captioned, "These Boots Are Made for Gawking." Unger, who stood six-five in blades, had been captured waiting for a downtown light to change, oblivious of the driver of the convertible alongside. That gentleman, mouth agape, was gazing up in awe at her industrial-strength butt.

"By the way, there's still some coffee in the pot," Unger said.

"Thanks. See you in a while." Maggie checked her watch, stored her memos-in-progress, and started an e-note projecting her itinerary through the end of November. Dawn Mambelli needed the information to start booking flights, cars, and hotels.

Late the following week it was Birmingham, Alabama, to visit a Caduceus 21 affiliate. From there she would fly to New York to meet the head of MedEx, the outfit that supplied the majority of organs for the health-care company's ambitious nationwide transplant program. Next stop, back to Knoxville, where the New Yorkers would be treated to a U.T. football game, complete with tailgate party, by Reifsnyder, Osteen, and Wilkes, along with their respective Number Twos. Then, after a three-day call on another affiliate, in Indianapolis, Maggie planned to head down to Orlando for Thanksgiving. Assuming, of course, she wasn't strapped in a straitjacket and bouncing off padded walls.

Maggie finished the note and beamed it to New York. Then, because she was being such a good girl this morning, she batted out a reply to Paul: How about they meet on Wednesday, November 4, in Central Park?

• • • •

TRAFFIC on Cumberland Pike was moderate as Maggie drove down the hill past the University of Tennessee campus and, slightly farther east, a sorry edifice left over from the Knoxville World's Fair of 1984. The Sunsphere, as it was called, consisted of a skinny tower topped by a large ball made of multifaceted panes of gilt-tinted glass. From a distance it looked like Joan Collins's idea of a classy dildo. She continued to Gay Street, made a left, then turned onto a side street to a garage halfway down the block. Unlike in Manhattan, parking was a cinch. In the 1970s the downtown stores had fallen victim to the malls sprouting to the west and south, throwing Knoxville's old business district into a desuetude from which it had yet to recover.

Maggie shouldered her knapsack and started for 420 South Gay. Caduceus 21 occupied the top two floors of that nondescript building, a onetime department store that dated to the 1920s. Because of the health-care company's rapid success, space was tight, so Len Reifsnyder had leased part of another floor for the Marx Dillon team.

On Monday the eight New Yorkers had unfolded like circus clowns from their fleet of two compact-sized rental cars and trooped up to view their temporary offices for the first time. The large room, measuring fifty feet by thirty-five feet, was freshly painted but contained only seven chairs and five desks. Further, the three PCs on hand were hand-me-down 486s whose bare bones lacked telecommunications devices like network cards and modems. Not that a modem would have helped; the room also had only two telephone lines, one of which was hooked to a fax machine so antiquated it regurgitated curly thermal paper.

Maggie had resisted her first urge, which was to scream, and her second, which was to parachute in Dawn Mambelli on the first available flight. Instead, she had waited for her blood pressure to drop back into the

double-digit range, then gone upstairs for a chat with Len
Reifsnyder.

The inadequacies of their workspace turned out to result from clashing corporate cultures. Caduceus 21 depended on cash flow and believed all invoices should be
either collected or paid within thirty days. Marx Dillon &
Neil followed the fiscal policies of Larry Marx, who believed in easy come but not easy go; the firm's bean
counters routinely delayed disbursements so the funds
could be put to profitable use by way of short-term CDs
and T-bills. Bottom line: Marx Dillon had refused to advance the money to properly set up the office and to lease
enough cars for its people, and Reifsnyder was refusing to
make an interest-free loan.

Maggie's first call, to Rob Dillon, had been a formality.
At one point Dillon may have been willing to mud-wrestle
Reifsnyder over the protocols, but the negotiations had
been a sport. So much profit was in the offing that he
didn't "give a rat's ass" if Maggie leased everyone their
own town house with butler and limo. "Just on general
principle, tell Reifsnyder to eat shit and die," Dillon had
said. "Then go beat some money out of Larry. Let's not
get hung up on nickels and dimes, kiddo."

Unfortunately, the firm's managing director had once
been aptly described as a man who threw nickels around
as if they were manhole covers. Larry Marx told Maggie
to lease her own car and top-of-the-line equipment, but
insisted the junior staff should fend for itself. She thought
this nonegalitarian mind-set typical of his generation: I
made mine, you go make your own. After an intermina-
ble argument, she finally managed to wangle a fifteen-
thousand-dollar allocation for properly equipping the
office.

Marx tried to salvage his bruised ego by digging in his
heels on the issue of transportation. "Eight people, two
cars," he had whined. "The government's optimum ratio
for carpooling. What the hell more do you need? If you

think this firm is going to subsidize your weekend joy-riding, let me disabuse you of that notion right now."

"Cars aren't a perk outside of Manhattan, Larry," she had replied. "But fine. You're the managing partner, so you get to choose from the following menu of options.

"Press 'one' if you want us to move into a hotel within walking distance of work. Room rates start at sixty bucks per head per night.

"Press 'two' if you want us to come in and leave exactly on time.

"Press 'three' if you want anyone who comes in early or works late to expense-account a cab. You should know that a one-way ride to our free apartments runs ten bucks. Before tip."

On Wednesday, when Maggie took her team to lunch, they traveled to the restaurant in a fleet of cars newly grown to five. Each person now had an individual cubicle defined by chest-high sound-dampening partitions and fitted with a desk, proper desk lamp, lumbar-supportive chair, and two-line telephone. Their computers were current and networked not only to Caduceus 21 but also, via a remote server, Marx Dillon so they could exchange e-mail and research files with New York. Best of all, they had done something about what Jill Unger had dubbed "the Screensavers from Hell."

Maggie smiled as she recalled her staff's outrage when their computers were patched to the Caduceus 21 servers. The health-care company had installed a system-wide screensaver with a "medical" motif that was impossible to disable and automatically kicked in after just one minute of user inactivity. Worse, there were but three choices of scenes: patients in wheelchairs drag-racing down hospital corridors; orderlies pushing gurneys through wacky obstacle courses; or amorous doctors and nurses chasing each other across the monitor. It had taken a memo from Reifsnyder to make the techies reconfigure the system so the Marx Dillon team could individually disable the obnoxious cartoons.

The struggles to get her people operational had given Maggie a fresh perspective on the 1991 Gulf War. Despite what Rob Dillon might think, the miracle of Operation Desert Storm wasn't the Norman Schwarzkopf–directed hundred-hour rout of Saddam Hussein. Rather, it was the skills of the anonymous Allied logisticians who had managed to assemble a four-hundred-thousand-strong expeditionary force—with requisite gear, fighting vehicles, ammo, and fuel—and deliver it to Ground Zero in less than four months.

She got off the elevator, pushed through the door into the Marx Dillon suite, and greeted Chloe, the temp who tended the phones and coffeepots.

Maggie's first order of business was the daily "green sheet." She had participated in enough full-scale background checks to realize that although Marx Dillon and Caduceus 21 had a common goal—producing a report that would induce investors to ante up vast amounts of money—friction was inevitable if the two staffs kept getting in each other's hair. So each day before noon she sent Reifsnyder a memo, on green paper, summarizing her team's latest queries. He would obtain written responses from the appropriate department or, if the subject was especially complex, bring his specialists to a meeting at day's end.

As soon as Maggie logged in she saw a message from Teddy Quereshi.

She filled her mug with coffee and went to his cubicle. "What's up, Teddy?"

"I wish to discuss C-Twenty-One's bookkeeping and reporting system," he replied. "Is this a good time?"

It really wasn't, but Maggie nodded and dragged over a chair. She knew from past projects that Teddy needed to talk through a problem to set it firmly in his own mind.

"One of C-Twenty-One's secret weapons is their high degree of computerization," Quereshi said. "The system is remarkably efficient. Mary Osteen should be quite proud. If I might give you an overview?"

"Please."

"Maggie, I have never encountered a company of this size so fully networked." He picked up a personal digital assistant, a stylus-operated computer the size of a paperback book. "Every employee at every facility, from the custodians to the top administrators, is issued a PDA like this. No matter if they routinely work on a desktop computer, they still get one. These PDAs communicate with the central servers via infrared beams. Every room has at least one infrared port—even the public lavatories, so custodians can report the amount of paper towels and toilet tissues that they replenish.

"The reasons for such an elaborate system are threefold.

"Most immediately, it saves time and labor," Quereshi continued. "Each C-Twenty-One client is assigned a unique electronic file accessible throughout the system. Say John Doe is enrolled in a health-care plan in Philadelphia. While on vacation in California, he experiences chest pains and visits an affiliated hospital. The ER doctor can use his PDA to instantly call up Mr. Doe's complete medical history and check preexisting conditions, contraindicated pharmaceuticals, et cetera. The serology and X-ray technicians can enter results into that same file. Say Mr. Doe requires a brief hospitalization. The nurse who dispenses medication, the therapist who helps with the rehabilitation, both can append data on the spot, via their PDAs, rather than take notes back to their desktop machines.

"Second, the PDAs afford everyone instant access to his or her daily calendar. An administrator can see appointments and calls. Doctors and nurses can see which patients are coming in when for what, scheduled surgeries, et cetera. The kitchen can see exactly how many trays to prepare for a given meal, which patients are on special diets, et cetera.

"Finally, the PDAs upload data continuously. That permits the facility to maintain a precise inventory of all supplies used, as well as create an accurate time sheet for every staff member. Why do you frown, Maggie?"

"It sounds kind of Orwellian to me, Teddy. You know those places that clickstream their employees, like insurance companies and mail-order houses? To catch workers taking a seven-minute bathroom break when they're only allowed five? This sounds even more Big Brotherish. Why aren't affiliates across the country rebelling?"

Quereshi smiled. "Orwell's Big Brother was oppressive. C-Twenty-One is not. I do not know who is responsible—Leonard, or perhaps Mary Osteen or Dr. Wilkes—but the system is programmed to recognize that nobody works for eight hours straight. When staffers are not in performance of their duties, they need not specify their activities. They just log what is called 'X-time.' A personal telephone call? A slightly longer lunch? A cigarette break? No matter. Only those staffers whose X-time gets out of hand are spoken to."

"Nice concept," Maggie said wistfully. "I could probably sell Rob Dillon and Nigel Neil on X-time. But that leaves Larry Marx . . ."

"Who would rather sip his own urine than acknowledge human frailties," Quereshi said, noting that she had grasped his reference to a perfectly horrid custom practiced by devout Hindus. "The C-Twenty-One system has one other great benefit. Every affiliate uses identical software. This means, Maggie, the data transmitted to K-town every eight hours need not be translated, a step that of course can only induce errors. Mary Osteen's computers are thus able to crunch the numbers straightaway, and produce accurate reports thrice daily.

"Which brings me to my problem." Quereshi paused to sip his tea. "The one thing I am having great difficulty comprehending is how they determine local coefficients. For example, C-Twenty-One purchases bedpans by the truckload for one set fee. Yet they bill an affiliate in Florida, a high-cost state, more for a bedpan than they do one in Kansas. As you will remember, Maggie, there was much skepticism in the early years of C-Twenty-One about its Provider Efficiency Index. About how they must be fudging the numbers to make their own PEIs look better."

Maggie nodded. "They stopped those whispers by releasing an independent audit affirming that the books weren't cooked. But you're right, Teddy. Some people might have long memories, so we should address the issue in our report. Mary Osteen's the logical person to walk you through it. I think she's out of town until next week, so why don't I put it at the top of today's green sheet? Maybe Len will have time to meet with us."

"That would be greatly appreciated, Maggie. Finally, I want to ask your permission to randomly select perhaps four C-Twenty-One affiliates and analyze their expenses against those of local competitors."

"How much time is that going to take?"

"Not much," he replied. "I propose to pick sites where the competition is allied with a publicly traded company. If I start the research immediately, the actual cross-checks should add no more than a few days to the process."

Maggie thought about the request for a few moments, then said, "Why not. Rob's going for a half-billion-dollar placement. It can't hurt to have a report that dots all the *i*'s, crosses all the *t*'s, and also anticipates questions that very few people will even think of asking. By the way, Teddy, you still planning to spend Thanksgiving in St. Louis?"

"The Nussbaums are quite insistent. Sterling does not look forward to the trip because he says his mother's turkey is virtually inedible. I told him the only time turkey is ever edible is in a good curry."

"Touché," she said with a laugh. "Listen, if you want to take a few extra days, feel free."

"Thank you, Maggie, but I think three days in the company of Mr. and Mrs. Nussbaum will more than do."

. . .

THE sun was setting earlier each day. Though it was not yet 6:30 P.M., the windows of Caduceus 21's sixth-floor conference room were already black with the coming night. Gathered at one end of the long table were Maggie Sepulveda, Teddy Quereshi, Len Reifsnyder, and Stephanie Bock, who was Mary Osteen's deputy and one of the health-care company's PEI specialists.

For the past five minutes, Bock had been patiently describing the company's formula for billing centrally purchased supplies to affiliates in different parts of the country. "We factor in localized cost-of-living figures from Commerce plus reimbursement indices from several of the biggest insurers," she said. "Didn't Mary give you a copy of PEI Appendix D?"

Quereshi flipped through the thick bundle of manuals he had brought to the meeting and shook his head.

Maggie looked at her watch. Caduceus 21 was very much a nine-to-five company and Knoxville very much an early-dinner town; Reifsnyder and Bock were the last people here. She was just about to suggest they push the matter until Monday when the phone rang.

Reifsnyder picked it up and said, "Caduceus Twenty-One. Oh, hi, honey. Hold on a minute, okay?" He cupped the mouthpiece and turned to the others. "My wife. I'll just be a second."

"Why don't we call it a night," Maggie suggested. "This'll hold."

He shook his head. "We're almost there. Stephanie, Mary's office is locked but mine isn't. Why don't you get my copy of Appendix D? It's on my desk."

Maggie said, "I'll go. I want to hit the ladies' room anyway."

Reifsnyder nodded. As Maggie left the conference room, she could hear him telling his wife that he'd be another half hour and suggesting that the two of them meet at the restaurant.

After a quick visit to the john, Maggie continued through the deserted corridors to Reifsnyder's office, which was even more Spartan than Osteen's and Wilkes's. The only personal touches in it were family photographs and numerous pieces of grade-school artwork courtesy of his twin nieces.

High stacks of paper flanked his monitor, which was displaying the cavorting-doctors-and-nurses screensaver. Maggie felt a fresh twinge of guilt. Reifsnyder liked to end the day with a clean desk but this mess would take at least fifteen minutes to straighten, further delaying his dinner. Not wanting to rummage through the papers, she dialed the conference room.

"Should be midway down the stack to the right of the terminal," Reifsnyder said. "Bluish-green binder."

"I see it. Be right back." Maggie punched off the speakerphone, started to slide out the document—and was startled by a sudden movement at the edge of her vision.

Gone from Reifsnyder's screen were the cartoon figures that had obscured the file he was working on. She spied the mouse cord disappearing under the stack; in extricating the document, she must have jostled the papers enough to activate the mouse and override the screensaver.

Maggie started to turn away but something on-screen caught her eye:

TO: Century Chisholm / 23 October
      cc: Mary Osteen, Aurelia Wilkes
FM: Len Reifsnyder
RE: Marx Dillon & Neil Queries
Attached are copies of the last two "green sheets" containing MD&N questions. You'll see that many of them are pretty incisive. As we expected, Sepulveda's people are being thorough. But it doesn't look as though

Maggie had met more than fifty Caduceus 21 employees since arriving in Knoxville earlier in the week. None that she could remember had the unusual nickname of "Century." Whatever misgivings she might harbor about reading someone else's mail were outweighed by her concern over Reifsnyder's apparent breach of trust. The green sheets, taken together, revealed much about how Marx Dillon & Neil planned to position the placement. In her view they constituted privileged information. To whom was Reifsnyder releasing it? An outside adviser she didn't know about?

Heading back to the conference room with Appendix D in hand, Maggie made a mental note to search the Caduceus 21 phone list for anyone, either in Knoxville or at an affiliate, surnamed "Chisholm."

S A T U R D A Y
O C T O B E R 2 4

THREE computer monitors graced Phillipa Walker's office, but she chose to view the rough cut of a major MorpHaus commercial-in-progress on the twenty-seven-inch Mitsubishi TV against one wall; might as well see it the way America would in three months. She patched the feed from the server over to the Mitsubishi, spotted her cursor on PLAY, and clicked.

On-screen, a computer-generated ape drew back his arm like a bowler, then flung a huge thighbone high into the air. As the bone spun upward it morphed into a rocket. The rocket continued to climb into the velvety blackness of near space, whereupon its nose gracefully swung open to disgorge a satellite. Cut back to Earth, to a cave outside which a satellite dish had been installed. Tracking shot following the dish's cable snaking into the cave and ending up jacked into the back of a large-screen television. Around the television sat the ape and his family, mesmerized by the scene from *2001: A Space Odyssey* in which Keir Dullea yanks HAL's memory boards.

Walker thought it pretty lame to tout a new movie-on-demand satellite service by visually quoting a generation-old motion picture. But the ad agency's checks were generous and the project did present intriguing technical problems.

There were alternative ways to film the commercial—miniatures for the space stuff and monkey-suited actors for the apes—yet computer-generated images were cheaper and just fine for special effects, as shown by recent hits like *Twister*, *Independence Day*, and *Titanic*. Indeed, from the frame in which the bone left the ape's hand until the ape reappeared with family, the MorpHaus footage was almost flawless. The shadows that were off a tad and the reflections that seemed a bit hot were easily tweaked.

Unfortunately, the apes themselves looked like specimens in a taxidermy shop, even on a low-res TV monitor. Walker was in the office on a Saturday because for the past six months she had been trying to enhance realism with advanced data-compression techniques. Although not formally assigned to the *2001* ad, she had been asked by the head of MorpHaus, Glen Piscatelli, to test her experimental work on the twelve-second reel. Unless the apes could be salvaged by midmonth, the client was going to rent some monkey suits.

Out her window, the lights of the Santa Monica Pier floated above the darkening Pacific. In several hours the concessionaires would begin shutting down and the homeless would begin foraging in the Dumpsters laden with half-consumed hot dogs and french fries and popcorn. The street people here had a different skin color than those in her 'hood, but they were just as hungry.

On that cheery thought, Walker swung around to one of her desk monitors and isolated the most difficult sequence to make look natural—the ape heaving the bone—and started to work.

An hour later she had to admit that though her mind was in it, her heart wasn't. Maybe a few hands of Hearts would help. She shrank the app to an icon and started to punch up the card game. That's when she remembered she hadn't checked her NUROMNCR mailbox since the previous evening.

Was it a case of approach-avoidance? Usually queries posted on that board drew answers in days if not hours. It had been a full two weeks, though, since she and Nacio sent up flares on Pit Bull, MedEx's killer feedback virus. They had received tips on some two dozen pizza-faces capable of such rude work, but were as yet unable to associate any of the suspects with MedEx.

Under most circumstances the next step would be to go onto other boards. Unfortunately, there was zero degree of separation in their cyberspatial peer group. *Otakus* who didn't regularly exchange e-mail were sure to cross paths in private chat rooms or on various outlaw boards. As sure as night follows day, the author of Pit Bull whiled away his downtime online. She and Nacio were thus unwilling to seek help outside their trusted circle of NUROMNCR users; why alert Code Boy that someone was out to fry him?

Equally frustrating, the Fortress Cayman problem had been posted for more than three days without eliciting any useful feedback. Most probably, Walker thought, cracking a commercial firewall was low on the *otaku* priority list.

She logged onto NUROMNCR and saw a fresh message in the DUCHESS+DATA queue, which they used when posting jointly. No doubt there were nerds out there who imagined her and Nacio to be Siamese twins, joined at the cortex.

The message was from Slingshot, a Singaporean who routinely circumvented his government's wholesale electronic eavesdropping by satcomming onto the Net. Talk about a hacker with a righteously bent sense of humor; six months earlier, Slingshot had the audacity to hack the servers in the new gazillion-dollar mansion built by Bill Gates outside Seattle. These controlled, among other things, the giant high-res flat-panel displays on which Mr. Microsoft threw up art masterpieces to which he had purchased all digital rights. Slingshot seized the servers in the middle of a cocktail party Gates was hosting for Wall Street honchos. After wiping the Michelangelos and Rembrandts and Picassos off-screen, he had thrown up in their stead a portrait of a grinning Steve Jobs.

Now Slingshot was passing along a tidbit gleaned during a routine hack of a Singapore brokerage firm. It seemed a certain bank in Georgetown, the Caymans, had not yet upgraded a firewall in which a trapdoor had been identified the previous week. A trapdoor was something an app's developer secreted amid the millions of lines of code to allow himself or herself emergency access in case of a crash. Slingshot had thoughtfully provided the high-speed ISDN, or integrated services digital network, gateway for the bank and the magic string—24RTC6BA5N—that not only unlocked the trapdoor but also gave its user root access, or total control of the system.

Even a password-cracker more powerful than Baby Huey would have taken forever to arrive at that one, Walker thought. 24RTC6BA5N admirably followed the recommended guidelines for passwords by randomly mixing letters and numbers. It wasn't a word that could be found in the dictionary. Nor did it appear to be the name/birthday/phone number of a parent, spouse, lover, friend, or child, a cardinal mistake made by novices unaware of how susceptible such data was to social engineering.

In fact, the password seemed too perfect. How could anyone remember it for years on end without writing it down, another cardinal mistake?

The more Walker studied it, the more it resembled a half-finished *Wheel of Fortune* board. Then she happened to glance down. Could the solution be that simple? Her office box had a standard 101-key keyboard, the right-hand side of which contained an eleven-key cursor control/numeric pad. In default mode, the following grid was operative:

HOME	⇑	PG UP
⇐	[disabled]	⇒
END	⇓	PG DN
INS		DEL

Number crunchers wanting to quickly enter data into a spreadsheet hit the NUM LOCK key, located above HOME, to toggle the grid into its numeric mode:

7	8	9
4	5	6
1	2	3
0		[.]

The configuration was different on laptops, which were limited to eighty-five keys. On those machines NUM LOCK toggled seven alpha keys to numeric. Thus M=0, J=1, K=2, L=3, U=4, I=5, and O=6, with the numeric keys 7, 8, and 9 remaining themselves.

Feeling as self-conscious as Vanna White, Walker visualized the laptop NUM LOCK pairings and re-typed 24RTC6BA5N, substituting letters for numbers: KURTCOBAIN. Whoever installed this trapdoor had obviously been a fan of the grunge band Nirvana and its late leader.

Her curiosity satisfied, Walker dialed the number in the Caymans and at the prompt entered the password. Five seconds later she was in the system. Activity was nil, as she would have expected on a weekend. She scanned the root directory, snagged a few files, then logged off.

It was hacker custom to e-mail each other or, if the message was seriously urgent, to effect a modem link and type directly onto the other person's screen. Walker was too old for such nonsense. Humans talked a lot faster than they could bat out words, so she punched up her electronic address book and speed-dialed Ignacio Tejada's number.

"Yo, Nacio. Watcha doing?"

"Greek Mythology Three-oh-six. Wassup, Leepi?"

"NUROMNCR just paid off big-time. Slingshot posted the key to a bank in the Caymans. I just tested it. Sucker works, so I pulled some sysop files. Know what? We got about thirty-six hours before the bank opens Monday."

"You at home or the office?" asked Tejada.

"Office."

"See you in thirty minutes," he said. "Might as well make use of your ISDN line."

"Make it forty-five," she replied. "Sounds like a high-sugar night, so save us a trip later and pick up some doughnuts or Li'l Debbies on your way over."

"Done."

Walker stood and headed for the MorpHaus kitchenette. Nacio would also bring several two-liter bottles of Jolt! but she couldn't stomach that extra-caffeine cola. Time to brew herself some fresh coffee; it was going to be a night of little or no sleep.

WEDNESDAY
NOVEMBER 4

MAGGIE Sepulveda's home leave would amount to less than a day, but she was grateful for small favors at a time when her road-warrioring was gathering velocity. Few Americans would complain about staying in an expense-account hotel where the maid put a Godiva chocolate on the pillow every night, or in a nicely appointed corporate suite in Knoxville. Accommodations notwithstanding, living out of a suitcase for weeks on end inevitably took a toll that was both physical and psychic. The best balm: waking up in her own bed for the first time in three weeks.

She reached over and dialed her clock radio from its wake-up setting to an all-news station. Temperature, fifty-two; forecast, sunny with increasing afternoon breezes. Nets and Devils win, Rangers tie, Knicks lose. Topping the headlines: incumbents returned to office in the statewide races for governor and U.S. senator. She shook her head in chagrin. Why had she bothered to rush for a flight out of Birmingham, Alabama, that had gotten her back to town in time to vote? The majority of her fellow citizens were perfectly happy to reelect the Beavis and Butt-Head of New York politics.

Maggie slipped on a robe and headed for the kitchen, lugging a large shopping bag into which she had chucked several pounds of accumulated junk mail. She fetched the single-serving orange juice purchased at McDonald's the previous evening—any larger container would spoil before her next return to New York—and reviewed the coming day as the kettle heated.

At 10 A.M. she would call on MedEx, the privately held firm under exclusive contract to obtain and deliver organs to Caduceus 21's seven transplant centers.

The Marx Dillon & Neil research department had turned up little on MedEx: a Dun & Bradstreet credit rating and a report from Technicmetrics, Inc., that contained a plain-vanilla rundown of the company's activities and a few stale clips from trade publications. The paucity of information didn't surprise Maggie. MedEx probably did not actively court attention. No matter how many heartwarming press accounts of yet another plucky child saved by an anonymous stranger's final kindness, many people still perceived transplants as a macabre act against nature.

In fact, she thought, if OPAs, or organ-procurement agents, were included in the surveys measuring public approval of various occupations, they would probably rank lower than even telemarketers and politicians and lawyers. Was that because the transplant deck seemed stacked in favor of the rich and the famous? Or because the notion of prolonging life with another's heart or liver conjured up unnerving images of certain black-and-white movies from the 1930s in which spectral figures skulked through fogbound graveyards, shovels in hand? Maggie only knew that if a replacement heart had been available for Petey, neither her kid brother nor their mom nor she would have hesitated.

After MedEx, she would swing by the office to reassure

Rob Dillon that the Caduceus 21 project was on track. Dillon had two major pension funds panting to participate in the placement, and would pressure her to crank out the report faster. Maybe she could spike his coffee with a couple of Ritalins, that drug for hyperactive kids? Then she would collect Dawn Mambelli for their lunch date at Café des Artistes; there was much office gossip to catch up on.

The kettle began to whistle. Maggie scooped fresh grounds into the plunger, added boiling water, and waited for the coffee to steep.

Her 3 P.M. meeting was one she did not relish. That's when she would see Paul for the first time since the Toilet Bowl. Their recent long-distance communications had been tellingly impersonal, with neither extending an olive branch. Though it was tempting to leave matters as they stood, it hadn't seemed right to seal the coffin over the phone or, tackier still, via e-mail.

Finally, Maggie was booked on a 5:30 P.M. flight back to Knoxville, there to join Jill Unger, Teddy Quereshi, and the rest of her team for a working dinner. Life in the fast lane, she thought, ain't it grand?

MEDEX's headquarters were in a high-rise on Sixth Avenue across from Radio City Music Hall. Maggie obtained a pass from the visitors' desk in the lobby and continued to the elevators. Though most of the building was occupied by large corporate tenants, the forty-third floor housed small companies. She ventured down a long corridor past a number of two-partner law offices, export-import firms, and commercial realtors before coming to a rosewood door bearing the MedEx logo.

Maggie pushed through the door into a cramped reception area. The company's operations might have been global, but it occupied a suite no larger than many of Manhattan's three-bedroom apartments.

"Hi, I'm Marguerite Sepulveda," she said. "Mr. Strand's expecting me at ten o'clock. I'm a bit early."

The young receptionist informed her that Strand wasn't in yet.

Maggie hung up her coat, took a seat, and reached for a travel magazine; maybe she could find a sunny destination to chill out in after the Caduceus 21 placement went through.

Fifteen minutes later a bland-looking man in his late forties emerged from one of the offices and approached her: "Ms. Sepulveda? Morris Tomczack, director of operations."

Maggie stood and shook his hand.

"Duane just called from Grand Central," Tomczack said. "His train got in late. Asked me to entertain you until he got here—unless you prefer the charms of our luxurious waiting room."

She smiled.

"Care for some coffee? Tea? Juice?"

"Coffee'd be great, Mr. Tomczack, if you've got some brewed."

"Call me M.T. Everyone else does."

"And call me Maggie."

"Our pot never runs dry," he said. "How do you take yours?"

"Why don't I do my own?"

Maggie followed Tomczack to the coffeemaker, which was in a room mostly given to videoconferencing equipment.

"Duane says you're interviewing him."

She nodded.

"Who do you write for?"

"I'm an investment banker."

Tomczack's eyebrows shot up. "That mean my stock options might be worth something after all?"

Maggie laughed.

"Duane suggested we go into his office. Not much to look at, but it's the biggest. Rank has its privileges."

Tomczack led her to a large corner office perfunctorily decorated in standard executive male. Outside of several framed photographs showing groups of men posed in front of airplanes, the only personalized touch was a bookcase that held an interesting array of books and videotapes. She gestured to them and said, "Do you mind?"

"Help yourself," Tomczack said. "Duane collects novels and movies that deal with transplants. Go figure, but hey, it's his money."

The most prominently displayed item was a magazine, the Christmas 1884 issue of the *Pall Mall Gazette*, preserved in a Lucite case; the cover trumpeted a new Robert Louis Stevenson story titled *The Body Snatcher*. The books, all first editions in mint condition, appeared to be arranged in chronological order. The oldest was *Frankenstein*, published by Mary Wollstonecraft Shelley in 1818. The rest were of more recent vintage. Maggie was familiar with *Coma*, by Robin Cook, having devoured it in one sitting as a teenager, but not such novels as *A Change of Heart, Corazon, The Magic Bullet, The Fourth Procedure*, and *Harvest*.

"Any of these worth reading, M.T.?" she asked.

"You'll have to ask Duane. I'm more up on the videos. Easier to sit through a dumb movie than a dumb book."

Maggie turned her attention to the videos, which were divided into two groups. Those with illustrated slipcovers were commercial releases; those with neatly typed labels were made-for-television movies taped off the air. Topping the collection: more than a dozen reworkings of the Frankenstein myth. Among them were the mainstream Hollywood versions starring Boris Karloff and Robert DeNiro as the monster and Elsa Lanchester and Jennifer Beals as its mate. Strand had also acquired the idiosyncratic Andy Warhol and Mel Brooks adaptations, as well as outright trash like *Blackenstein* and *Frankenhooker*.

She spied *The Body Snatcher*, also with Karloff; *Coma*; and *Body Parts*, which she had noticed in video stores but never bothered to rent. "I've seen *Donovan's Brain*. It's not really about transplants."

"Duane couldn't resist," Tomczack said. "The mousy little ingenue in it grew up to be a much-feared First Lady."

"I didn't know Hillary used to be an actress."

Tomczack chuckled. "Mrs. Reagan, née Nancy Davis."

Maggie held up the garish slipcover of something called *Blood Salvage*. "And what about *B.O.R.N.*? And *Night of the Bloody Apes*?"

"Grade-Z, like most of the ones you never heard of. *Blood Salvage* is about a white-trash family that chops up tourists so they can sell off the parts. Second one, the title stands for 'Body Organ Replacement Network.' Last one's a Mexican flick about xenography."

"You mean transplanting organs from another species?" she asked.

"Yes, ma'am. Doctor tries to save his dying son with a gorilla's heart. Idea's better than the execution. Matter of fact, sixteen years after the movie came out, they gave that baby girl out in California a baboon's heart."

She picked up a two-cassette movie whose slipcover read *The Kingdom*.

"*Twin Peaks* goes to Denmark," Tomczack said with a wince. "It's set in a hospital and you have to read subtitles for about five hours. One of the subplots is about a terminal patient with a very rare liver cancer. His family won't let the doctors run tests on it. There's some loophole in the law, though, that says the patient can't refuse a transplant, so an ambitious researcher swaps his perfectly healthy liver for the diseased one. Figures it's a small price to pay for a Nobel. Very weird, but then the Danes are the folks who gave us Hamlet."

Of the made-for-TV movies, Maggie knew only of the network docudrama based on the bittersweet case of Nicholas Greene, the boy shot to death while vacationing with his family in Sicily.

"I guess *Astro-Zombies* needs no explanation," she said. "What's *Beyond Forgiveness* about?"

"Cop's kid brother gets whacked," Tomczack said. "Cop tracks the perp to Warsaw and discovers a black-market-organ ring. Know how they're sending hearts and livers into the U.S.? Disguised as cans of Polish ham."

Maggie laughed. "No wonder the last can I bought at Zabar's tasted a little strange. *Donor Unknown*?"

Tomczack shrugged.

"*The Harvest*?"

"Did see that one," he said. "Unrelated to the novel of the same name. Hack screenwriter goes to Mexico to research a murder plot. Screenwriter gets bonked on the head, wakes up in a derelict warehouse minus one kidney. Bad guy's the producer who sent him down there. Seems the producer has a kidney problem and is bored with dialysis."

"An amusing little B-movie," said a voice that was not Tomczack's.

Maggie turned to see a stocky man in his late fifties enter the office.

"Duane Strand," he said, extending his hand. "Sorry I'm late, Ms. Sepulveda. Metro North was its usual efficient self this morning. I trust M.T.'s been a good host?"

"A terrific host. We were discussing your video collection. I probably owe it to myself to rent some of them."

"May be hard to find," Strand said in the flat, right-stuff cadence of an airline pilot. "Most are not major-studio productions. You run into problems, let me know. I'll dub you a copy."

Tomczack started for the door.

"Feel free to stay, M.T.," Strand said.

"Love to, but I got an eleven-o'clock teleconference with Jefferson so I'd best go over my notes. Oh, by the way, Maggie was asking about some movie I never saw—what was its name, *Donor Unknown*?"

Strand thought for a moment, then said, "Insurance executive suffers a severe coronary. His wife calls in a celebrity heart surgeon with a knack for obtaining new organs in a hurry. Turns out he has a silent partner, a racist ex-cop who murders illegal immigrants on demand."

"Now how the heck did I miss that one?" Tomczack turned to Maggie and broke into a grin. "Doesn't Mark Fuhrman, OPA, sound more plausible than counterfeit Polish hams? My pleasure meeting you, ma'am."

After Tomczack left, Strand gave Maggie an overview of MedEx. The firm's operations were primarily in the United States, where its sole client, Caduceus 21, was based. But MedEx also procured organs on every continent except Australia and Antarctica for delivery to the seven Caduceus 21 transplant centers.

A key to his firm's success, he observed, was a fleet of fourteen corporate jets leased on advantageous terms in the early 1990s, when the market for such aircraft had been soft. Seven were based domestically, with two each in South America, Africa, and Europe, and one in Southeast Asia.

"Are those planes capable of crossing oceans?" asked Maggie.

"Absolutely. But commercial long-hauls are faster. We usually go to one of the scheduled carriers. They're happy to help—the flight gets 'lifeguard' designation, which means priority routing and landing. Anyway, soon as the coolers land Stateside, we transfer them to our own craft for final delivery." Added Strand, "We're damned good, ma'am. In better than four years, we've only had two organs time-expire on us, and one was marginal from the get-go. Using our own fleet, commercial long-hauls, and local charters as needed, we can move a shipment from anywhere in the world to any of C-Twenty-One's centers in under twenty-two hours."

"Very impressive," she said. "How did you get into this business?"

"That's a long and roundabout story. Sure you have the time?"

Maggie nodded.

"Ever hear of Air America?"

Her brows furrowed, and then she had it: "The air-charter company the CIA ran in Southeast Asia during the Vietnam War? To supply the hill people, what were they called, the Montagnards?"

"The Hmong and the Meo tribes. Very good. I didn't think people your age cared much about that part of this country's history."

"They made a lame-o Mel Gibson comedy about it a while ago," she said. "I happened to come across it on cable."

Strand nodded. "Hollywood blew a great opportunity. A lot of what we did was much funnier than that movie. Anyway, Air America's the outfit that got me into the aviation industry. Stayed with them into the early Eighties. But at some point in a man's life, he needn't be flying night missions in and out of Peshawar and Quetta, if you know what I mean."

"Peshawar. Isn't that in Pakistan?"

"So's Quetta," Strand said. "After Ivan invaded Afghanistan, the Company set up shop there to support the *mujahedeen*, the resistance movement next door. There were two objectives. One, get under Ivan's skin. Two, score brownie points with militant Muslims—this was at a point in time, you might recall, when Khomeini's Shi'ites were booting the Shah out of Iran."

He sighed. "Big mistake in retrospect, cozying up to the ragheads. I dealt with them on a daily basis. Sure they hated communism, but think that meant they loved democracy and capitalism? That blind sheik, the rabid little Egyptian we nailed for the World Trade Center bombing? Made his acquaintance in Eighty-one or Eighty-two in Peshawar. Guess who was giving him the grand tour. CIA chief of station, Karachi, a guy who hated to travel upcountry.

"As I said, ma'am, I was getting too old to play Sky King so I came home. A lot of us vets hung it up right

about then, which is why the Company got caught with
its pants down in Nicaragua."

"How so?" asked Maggie, fascinated by this unexpected detour into a murky world she had glimpsed only
in paperback thrillers.

"Langley's air force went slack," Strand said. "Fly
against the North Vietnamese or Ivan, you're locking up
with the A-Team. Sandinistas? Strictly JV—hell, the only
SAMs they had was outmoded stuff Moscow couldn't
dump elsewhere. Ms. Sepulveda, the aircraft CIA used to
supply the *contras* were a disgrace. The Southern Air
flight that went down in the jungle, the one where they
captured that poor son-of-a-bitch Hassenfus? Held together with duct tape and Juicy Fruit. Pilot ought to have
scrubbed the mission. He paid for his carelessness with
his life."

"It's a long way from covert operations to mercy missions," she observed.

"Told you it was a roundabout story," Strand said with
a smile. "Reason there's a MedEx today is that in Eighty-
three, which is when I returned to the States, the commercial airlines were full up on pilots. All the left-hand
seats were taken by guys my age, fighter jocks from Nam
smart enough to get out at the right time.

"Best I could do was drive corporate jets. As it happened, though, the company I hired on with was real
civic-minded. Used to lend their Gulfstreams to transport
donated organs. I did a lot of those runs. Some made
sense. As you know, the clock's running soon as the organ's harvested. You have one coming available in some
place hours from a major airport, like Potsdam, New
York, or Weyers Cave, Virginia, a mercy flight's the only
way. But Boston–Pittsburgh? L.A.–Indianapolis? Why not
just pack the cooler on a commercial flight?"

"I thought they did," Maggie said.

"Once upon a time, maybe, before airline dereg.
You've heard the old joke—don't matter if you're going to
Heaven or Hell, gotta change planes in Atlanta."

She smiled; it was a chestnut among road warriors but funny nonetheless.

"These days it's all short-haul or long-haul," Strand said. "Anything in between, you change planes. Hub-and-spoke's good for revenues but bad for passengers and worse for organs. So I started looking into putting together an outfit like MedEx. Same time, some other folks were putting together C-Twenty-One. We kind of found each other."

"A good fit," Maggie said. "Aurelia Wilkes told me because of MedEx, the number of transplants they perform has grown an average of nine percent per year. One of my questions, though, is what happens to their program if something were to happen to MedEx?"

"You mean like us going Tap City?"

She nodded.

"It'd slow them down nine months to a year, until they got another service up and running. That's not false modesty, ma'am. Doctors are the ones who have to be able to do brain surgery. We're just couriers."

Maggie thought a moment, then said, "Are you concerned that MedEx might be made redundant in five or ten years by xenotransplants?"

"Swine organs? Not at all."

"Oh?"

Strand leaned back in his chair. "Ms. Sepulveda, let me explain something about this business. The rewards are considerable, and I don't mean just money. The pressure's also something else. I know it's a cliché to talk about life-or-death situations, but you simply do not have a margin—one snafu and two people are dead instead of just the donor. Know the worst thing about flying out of North Dakota on a snowy night in February with a liver that's borderline? It's recognizing that you might be investing a lot of energy and emotion and maybe your life in something that's not going to work.

"Swine organs are going to help an awful lot of real sick folks get better. The way I read the research literature, though, some patients will always need a human organ. There's also going to be patients not yet on the crit list who'd prefer to take a pass on a pig's kidney. Xeno-transplants are not going to end our service. If our volume goes down a third, I cancel the leases on five Gulfstreams. And in a way, scaling back MedEx wouldn't be such a bad thing."

"How's that?" asked Maggie.

"One, we only make flights where the chances of success are good," he said.

"Two, we don't have to go into ICUs and twist arms. Despite all the success stories, most Americans still think giving organs is something the other guy should do. One thing that's helped is Caduceus Twenty-One's policy of tissue-typing everyone they cover. It makes their subscribers think about the issue. We're experiencing three, four extra donations per facility, per year—may not sound like much, but you factor in the multiplier effect, and that's progress.

"Still, ma'am, there are about fifteen thousand cases a year where a brain-dead accident victim possesses organs suitable for donation. Know how many families agree to harvesting?"

"Fewer than six thousand," Maggie replied, all too aware that those stingy numbers had been as fatal to Petey as his damaged heart. "I've always thought OPAs had a terrible task—persuading a family that's just lost someone to donate the organs. Is that the toughest part of your job?"

"Toss-up between that and the fact we have such a bad rep," Strand said. "You think the tobacco industry gets rotten press? M.T. walked you through my collection, right? According to the novelists and screenwriters, if we can't find the right organ, we go out and make a fresh corpse."

"It may be unfair but I can understand why," she said. "Those writers hear the same rumors I do, and spin them into melodramas."

"Those rumors reach a lot of people, ma'am. Let me fetch something that might interest you." Strand turned to his computer, keyed in a file name, then swiveled the monitor around.

Maggie saw that in the first ten months of the year, MedEx had fielded calls from every network news department, every major newspaper, and every weekly newsmagazine.

"So many reporters call us to check out rumors, we decided to keep a log," Strand explained. "Nowadays, if you're famous, the only way to die in peace is in a hurry. Linger awhile in intensive care, someone's bound to start whispering about last-ditch transplants. In a way, I can appreciate that. If well-connected people like that Pennsylvania governor and Larry Hagman can get a new body part so easily, think what they must've done to try to save the Pope and Yeltsin and Deng Xiaoping. But far as I can ascertain, ma'am, in the last five years only one minor Saudi royal bought his way atop the wait-list. That any more outrageous than that Dominican drug king?"

"Not really," Maggie agreed. In 1993, a man charged with murder, kidnapping, and running a cocaine ring was diagnosed with terminal heart disease. Charges were dropped. The man somehow convinced a Philadelphia hospital to give him a new heart—the four-hundred-thousand-dollar transplant was paid for by Medicaid—and then fled the country.

"Sorry I'm so wound up about this," Strand said, "but remember the wild stories about Beijing? The ones that came out of Jesse Helms's Senate hearings? Testimony was, China systematically executes political prisoners to obtain a compatible liver or kidney for its senior leaders, and just throws away the other organs. Doesn't make sense. Those folks are world-class when it comes to frugality. Hell, they invented recycling—Chinese have been eating things like pig ears in aspic and braised duck feet for thousands of years. I'll be frank with you, ma'am, if there were in fact leftover organs, I'd be in Beijing trying to negotiate for us to acquire them."

"What about the black-market trade?" Maggie asked.

"Well, that nonsense out of Guatemala finally quieted down."

"You mean how Americans are adopting babies for their organs?"

Strand nodded. "Absurd on the face of it. A baby's organs are too small and immature to transplant into an adult. What's a *gringo* to do—fatten up the baby like veal for ten, twelve years? By then you're dead of whatever's ailing you."

"How did such a farfetched story get started?" said Maggie.

"KGB disinformation."

"You're joking."

"Negative. Ivan floated it all across Central America in the early Seventies, just about when American adoption services began bringing up babies from those countries." Strand's eyes brightened. "Talk about opening Pandora's box. You've heard the rumors coming out of Russia."

"I have," she said. "Government-sanctioned mortuaries are cutting up cadavers and exporting the organs for hard currency. It doesn't make sense. An organ from a dead person's useless."

"Exactly, and you'd think the press would wise up to that simple medical fact," Strand said. He looked at his computer screen. "Spelled it out for some top gun from *Time* in February. He came back around Labor Day with a fresh twist. Now it was Russian Mafia death squads working out of Budapest, targeting migrant Turkish workers and refugees fleeing Bosnia."

Maggie shook her head. "And there's supposed to be a gang that roams the Southwest killing undocumented Mexicans. They remind me of the stories we used to tell by the campfire. Like the one about the couple parked on a lover's lane near a prison? They hear a radio bulletin about a jailbreak, some serial killer who's got a claw for one hand, so the boy drives the girl home. When he goes to open her door, there's a bloody claw dangling from the handle."

"Same story made the rounds when I was a pup," Strand said with a chuckle. "Some writer labeled them 'urban myths,' even published four or five books of ones he'd collected. Fascinating stuff. Seems every age needs a new tale to scare the kiddies. Yes, OPAs like us profit from death. But we don't take lives, we save them. So don't you find it ironic, ma'am, that we've become society's latest bogeymen?"

AUTUMN had stripped away Central Park's green canopy and carpeted its lawns with a crazy quilt of yellow and red and orange leaves. As Maggie hiked east across the Sheep Meadow, trying to work off her decadent lunch with Dawn Mambelli, she noticed a cold front had moved in, clearing the azure skies of clouds but also dropping the temperature a good ten degrees since morning. The crisp tang in the air, the low sun that provided little warmth, the long shadows, reminded her of late-season college football games at Huskies Stadium.

She reached the 72nd Street transverse and paused at the balustrade overlooking Bethesda Fountain and the rowboat lake beyond.

A pair of nannies were wheeling carriages across the brick-paved plaza. Paul Barry was perched on the rim of the drained fountain, reading the new *Variety*.

Two wide sets of stone steps led down to the plaza. Were these elegant staircases in London, thought Maggie as she skipped down them, they would have rivaled the balcony at Buckingham Palace as a backdrop for royal photo ops.

Paul heard her approaching and lowered the newspaper: "Hi."

"Hi yourself. Congratulations on the Linzy Kirsch deal."

"Thanks. Signing her was the easy part. Now we've got to think up some songs for her to record." He smiled ruefully. "Remember what you suggested in the car the night of the Toilet Bowl?"

Maggie shook her head.

"Covering old rock hits sung by women and girl groups? I know you meant it sarcastically, but I happened to mention it to Linzy. Next thing I know, she's back from the Virgin superstore with six feet of new CDs. Every time I see her now she's trying out something by Cher or Tina or Carly or Carole King."

The conversation was not going as Maggie had expected. Was Paul always this absorbed in his clients? Probably. Then why hadn't she noticed it before? Or had she noticed, and just never cared?

"Remember this?" he said. *The wayward wind / Is a restless wind . . .*"

"Vaguely."

"By someone named Gogi Grant, a big hit back in the Fifties. Our parents probably dated to it."

"Gee."

When Maggie showed a similar lack of interest in several more titles Paul mentioned, they turned to the only unresolved issues between them. Each had things like clothing, books, and CDs at the other's apartment; they decided to swap cartons through Maggie's doorman. That left the country house, the lease on which ran until May 15. Given their workloads, neither anticipated using it much over the winter; in the event either wished to, he or she would check with the other before heading out. Finally, they agreed to put off divvying up the joint purchases out in Sag Harbor until it came time to surrender the keys.

Maggie was struck by the cut-and-dried tone of it all, as if the two of them were wrapping up a business deal rather than dropping the curtain on a three-year relationship. She felt none of the surging indecision and roller-coaster emotions that had attended her breakup with *el buscapleitos*. What had she expected of herself? Or, for that matter, of Paul? Would she be happier if he were angry, spewing put-downs? Or on his knees, contritely begging for another chance? Perhaps her mom was right. Perhaps Paul was only a convenient low-maintenance harbor in which she had moored a shade too long. Then again, perhaps he felt the same way about her.

And then they were out of things to discuss.

Paul hesitated, not sure of whether to shake Maggie's hand, pat her shoulder, or kiss her cheek. He did none of the above and just said, "Well, take care."

"Yeah. You too."

Because he was headed back to his office on Madison Avenue and she to her apartment, they parted company at the fountain, Paul taking the eastern staircase back up to the transverse and Maggie the western.

M O N D A Y
N O V E M B E R   9

TWO Whoppers, hold the pickle," Ignacio Tejada said into the pole-mounted speaker unit, raising his voice as the night air suddenly filled with the grumble of a jumbo jet on its final approach to Los Angeles International Airport. "Small fries, two large chocolate shakes."

"Missed the last part," replied the static-streaked voice of the Burger King attendant. "Say again?"

Tejada sighed—if working eight hours a day directly under a flight path didn't mess with your hearing, nothing would—and repeated the order.

"Anything else?"

Nguyen-Anh Dupree and Phillipa Walker both shook their heads.

"That be all, bro," he said, and began inching his geezermobile ahead in the drive-through line. "Damn, Doc. Don't seem right, you eating this crap your first night home in almost a year."

"Sorry?" Dupree was distracted by the thunder of the passing jet, the song on the car stereo, the hums and honks of passing traffic; since landing twenty minutes ago, he had been exposed to more ambient noise than his remote little village produced in a month. God, he missed America.

"I said, least me and Leepi can do is buy you a nice steak."

"Steaks aren't hard to find down my way, Data," Dupree replied. "And they're not bad, either—ask Esai and Large."

"Some seal of approval," Walker snorted. "Pavlov spent years learning what we all know. Wave food in front of Large, he starts drooling."

"Leepi's kind of gent," Tejada said slyly. "Yo, Doc, ever sample this girl's cooking?"

"Shut your face, Nacio," Walker snapped. Sitting beside Dupree just reinforced the humiliating memories of the dinner she had tried to fix him long ago, when she was still in the throes of her crush.

Dupree suppressed a grin. So Data was still jerking Duchess's chain over that meal; or, more correctly, she was still allowing her chain to be jerked. He said, "We can do steak or whatever tomorrow night, on me. Right now, this is exactly what the doctor ordered. Soon as you asked me to fly up, I started dreaming about things like junk food. And spending a couple of hours in some big drugstore like Rexall or People's."

Walker and Tejada exchanged puzzled frowns.

"Benson and Hedges Lights," Dupree explained. "Edge shaving gel. Blades for my Sensor. Dental floss. Lighter fluid and flints. Birthday cards with rude messages. You have no idea of the little things that cost a fortune in the rest of the world, if you can find them at all. I even brought an empty knapsack to fill with stuff like that."

There was a soft honk from behind them. Tejada crept the geezermobile up a car length.

"Enough about my guilty pleasures," Dupree said, his mind switching back to the urgent flare that had brought him north. He had wanted to fly to Los Angeles sooner, but it took almost two days to arrange for proper coverage of his clinic. "Duchess, you were filling me in on all the things that are going down."

"Me and Nacio finally got a good sort on those bank records we pulled on Wings of Mercy," she said. "You'll see it at the compound."

"They be a dead end, girl," Tejada muttered. "We can track routine disbursements, but not the ones with big numbers that go into a numbered account in Geneva. Plus, the deposits are always wired from a Miami bank that's known as 'Maytag,' they wash so much money."

"Don't mind bro, it's that time of month for him," Walker said. "Anyway, the real reason we asked you to come up is, me and Nacio got a toe inside MedEx. But the next move's dicey. We blow it, all the alarms get tripped and they go directly to Defcon Four."

"Rewind time," Tejada said, inching the car forward again. "Doc, you remember how last month we posted the code for the Pit Bull virus? Asking if anyone recognized a signature? Lots of leads but no positive makes. So last week we chain all the replies and post them as a thread."

"Which brings rain," Walker said. "Someone remembered a nasty thesis on 'proactive system safeguards'—a euphemism for trashing an unauthorized caller's box— submitted in the late Eighties at either MIT or Rice. We went online both places. Bingo. There's a paper at MIT that postulates a defense system like the one the Army's using on its tanks."

"What do you mean?" asked Dupree.

"Ceramic armor," she said. "You can't build conventional armor thick enough to stop modern tank-killing sabots. So they developed ceramic shields laced with explosives that go over the armor. When an incoming round hits the shield, both detonate, saving the tank. Code Boy suggested a similar concept, a line of defense before an intruder can get to the firewall. He even suggested how to do it—by using customized baud rates in the handshake protocol."

Tejada snuck a glance at Walker: interesting how she was unconsciously drifting out of homegirl mode now that Doc was in the car.

"Clever," Dupree said. Though not nearly as computer-literate as his young friends, he used the modem enough to know about the handshake protocol, a preliminary string of commands that allowed two machines to check their compatibility and to synchronize. One essential part of the handshake was the baud rate, the exact speed at which the two computers would transmit data during the ensuing session. Baud rates were usually set at one of the conventional speeds: 300, 1200, 2400, 9600, 14400, 19200, 28800, and 33600 bits per second. It wouldn't be hard, though, to program a computer to accept calls only from modems transmitting data at an unconventional speed, say 13100 baud.

Walker said, "Suddenly everything made sense. Most firewalls start when you enter a password. Two wrong passwords, session terminated. At first we thought perhaps MedEx was just on the far side of harsh—one wrong password and Pit Bull cons you into downloading a fatal virus? But then me and Nacio realized if that's how a company set up its firewall, who'd risk calling? I mean, the penalty for a typo is a wrecked drive?"

"Only one other possibility," Tejada chimed in. "Pit Bull ain't there to punish bad typists, it be in place to fry hackers. But how can the system know someone's a hacker before they even hit the first screen? Code Boy's paper spells out a way: by messing with the handshake. Get it right, you're in the log-in loop. Get it wrong, you're toast."

"The thesis allowed us to go from two dozen suspects to one," Walker said. "So we launched a full-scale press on Code Boy."

"Whose name be Jefferson Leong," Tejada added.

"Wait till you see the dope we got on him. An extreme dickhead."

The geezermobile finally reached the head of the line. Tejada passed over a bill and the Burger King attendant slid back the food and his change.

Dupree promptly pulled one of the shakes out of the bag, uncapped it, and virtually poured the drink down his throat.

"Don't tell me," Walker said in awe. "You and Large—separated at birth?"

An impatient honk from the car behind brought a gape-jawed Tejada out of his trance: "Gee, Doc, didn't they feed you on the plane?"

As they made their way south to Imperial Highway, Dupree listened to Walker and Tejada replay their stalk of Jefferson Y. T. Leong. To be able to post knowing queries, they had first scoured online databases like those maintained by motor-vehicle bureaus, telephone companies, and credit-reporting agencies.

Leong had grown up in the New York City borough of Queens, where his family still lived. One month after earning his master's at MIT, he had registered his first car, listing an address in the town of Silver Hills, Maryland.

"Same zip code as Fort Meade," Tejada said, "home of the National Security Agency. We know Code Boy didn't go down there to become a sysop for the local utility company. Nope, the dude done signed on as a cyberspook, a fact we later confirmed."

In mid-1993 Leong moved from Maryland to Dallas.

"His first apartment was maybe twelve minutes from DFW," Walker said. "The credit agencies confirmed he went to work for MedEx, whose system is based near the airport. They must pay pretty good. Code Boy's gone from renting a studio to owning a condo, he's traded up from a Hyundai to a high-end Beemer, he's bumped his unsecured credit line from under ten thou to almost two hundred thou."

"Doc, I keep telling this girl, be on the next flight to Dallas," Tejada teased. "If this homey ain't her kind of hardworking, Chee·tos-scarfing, money-grubbing brainiac, I don't know who is."

Walker grabbed one of the remaining fries from Dupree's container and caromed it off Tejada's face before continuing with the story. She and Nacio had then posted their dossier on Leong on NUROMNCR, along with a request for relevant personal tidbits from anyone who knew him.

"We got back stories all the way to his high-school days," she said. "Seems even then, he was short a couple of chips on his reality interface. His world revolved around computers and science fiction. First on his block to tape all the *Star Trek* episodes, sat through *Star Wars* fifteen times the week it came out, that kind of thing. Same pattern at college. Someone who lived in Code Boy's dorm said he was a one-man Trekkie convention— even tried to arrange his room so it looked like the bridge of the starship *Enterprise*.

"Anyway, Leong's thesis proved to be a rough blueprint for the MedEx firewall. He knew his plan was clever, but also that you can't secure a gateway with a single customized baud rate. Someday, some user's going to slip by because his modem was inadvertently set to the magic speed. It's like if you put typewriters in the monkey house, one of them's eventually going to bang out *The Bridges of Madison County*.

"That's why he proposed using a prearranged sequence of baud rates. Here's where we caught a break. A classmate from Carnegie Mellon remembered that Code Boy rigged his answering machine so the beep was actually something from his most favorite movie ever."

She whistled five notes: D, up to E, down to C, down an octave to another C, and up to G.

Dupree cocked his head. "*Close Encounters*? The handshake with the aliens?"

"Told you Doc would know it," Walker said to Tejada.

"Anyway, me and Nacio translated the notes into five baud rates having the same proportions and tried it on the MedEx gateway. Took us right to the log-in prompt."

"Terrific!"

"Yes and no," Tejada said. "We disconnect pronto. Any creep willing to sic Pit Bull on a stranger's got worse things in mind for a hacker making it past his firewall. Way me and Leepi see it, there's only two ways to get what we need, which be a valid password. One, run a sortie on MedEx's top sysop."

"You mean go after Leong's password?" said Dupree.

Tejada nodded. "Get it and we get root access—the whole net be ours."

"And if that doesn't work?"

"Me and Leepi go to Dallas for some social engineering. Girl here just loves to cruise Taco Bells, looking for a MedEx nerd to shake her booty at."

HEADING east on Imperial, Tejada crossed Avalon Boulevard and made a right. Several blocks farther on, deep in the heart of Hispanic South-Central, he turned again and slowed before the driveway of a two-story building that had been remodeled into a gatehouse.

At the approach of the geezermobile, the gate swung open.

When Dupree made his initial house call on Data, six months after the near-fatal shooting, the boy had lived with his parents and brother on the same street, in a modest house two doors down. Today four generations of the family were gathered in a compound Walker jokingly called "Hyannisport *Oeste*."

As head of Tres Equis, Javier Tejada could easily afford a four-acre mansion in an upscale zip code, but he had seen the fate of rivals adopting the Twinkie lifestyle of a *pocho*: resentment among the troops that inevitably soured into jealousy and then anarchy. That was why he had chosen to purchase over time five adjoining houses, fronting on two streets, and reconfigure them to his needs. Mindful of all those who wished him dead, Javier had considered building a high wall around the compound. Trying to re-create a traditional *finca*, though, would have isolated him as surely as moving to Beverly Hills.

In the end, an award-winning Los Angeles architect had designed a brilliant if iconoclastic compromise.

She began by reversing the orientation of each house from the street to the backyard and merging the six small backyards into a central courtyard landscaped with shade trees, beds of bright flowers, and a small playground. This enabled her to clad all the street-side walls in thick stucco and bulletproof glass brick. She also ripped out the driveways of five of the houses. This enabled her to create a single gated entrance to the compound and frame the entire property with one continuous lawn. And she bridged the spaces between houses with chest-high rows of *Berberis thunbergii erecta*, or upright barberry, a beautiful but dense and thorny hedge used on corporate campuses to keep out trespassers.

When the compound was finished, Javier was heard to boast that the enemies of Tres Equis now needed their own air force to attack him.

Enemy ganglords, of course, were not the only outsiders interested in taking down Javier Tejada. It had fallen to Nacio to shield the compound against electronic surveillance by the feds and the local cops. Every room was swept for bugs twice weekly. White-noise generators were installed to nullify the Drug Enforcement Agency's prized laser eavesdropper, a gizmo that measured the vibrations made by voices on a windowpane, then converted them back into voices. Business calls were placed only on scrambler units modeled after the government's STU III sets. Digital communications were funneled through an off-site remailer board; in the unlikely event the authorities stumbled into the basement storeroom of a housing project a half-mile to the northeast, there was no way to connect the computer in it with the Tejadas.

Javier had given one house to the two surviving Tejada grandparents, another to his and Nacio's parents, a third to his in-laws. He, his wife, and their kids lived in the fourth house, the focal point of the compound by dint of its enormous kitchen and communal dining room. The fifth contained the Tres Equis offices and an upstairs suite that Nacio had moved into on starting college. The sixth house served as a gatehouse, lounge for Tres Equis bodyguards, and parking lot.

Tejada pulled the geezermobile into its slot, waited for Dupree to get his under-the-seater and laptop from the trunk, then led his friends to his house in the compound.

The offices on the ground floor resembled those of a small insurance company; however arresting the architecture of the compound, Javier had resisted the temptation to furnish it like a *Miami Vice* don.

The second floor had three rooms. Dupree dropped his bags in the guest bedroom, then joined the others in Data's study.

On the floor by the couch was a stack of books. Dupree knelt to examine them. The paperbacks were tragedies by Aeschylus, Sophocles, and Euripides, and the hardcovers were scholarly commentaries on the Athenian writers. "It's nice to see someone's still teaching the works of dead white Euromales," he said. "I took pretty much the same course at North Carolina. 'Greek for Geeks.' "

Tejada grinned. "At USC it's called 'Trojans Without Lubrication.' "

"Figures," sniffed Walker, an alumna of UCLA.

"Yo, Doc," Tejada said, "any of your old term papers be handy? I got one due before Thanksgiving and I ain't even got a topic."

"As a matter of fact, I received an A-minus for comparing and contrasting Euripides' two versions of the Iphigenia legend. It's back in Yazoo City. I could have my lawyer find it and mail it out, but know what, Data? As one of America's great presidents said, 'That would be wrong.' "

"Aw, come on, Doc . . ."

"Stop your whining, Nacio," Walker said. "Doc won't give you his paper, but he gave you a topic. Quit while you're ahead."

Tejada made a face at her, then went to his desk to fetch two reports.

Dupree started with the one on Jefferson Y. T. Leong. The level of personal information Duchess and Data had compiled on the programmer was a disquieting reminder of how tenuous the notion of privacy had become. For instance, credit-card records revealed Leong as an un-imaginative gift-giver, sending to a small circle of rela-tives and colleagues the same mail-order smoked hams and fruit baskets at Christmastime and FTD arrange-ments on birthdays.

He traveled in a pattern almost as predictable as a mi-gratory bird's. On his annual calendar were Las Vegas on the same dates as COMDEX, the computer-industry con-vention, and Pittsburgh coincidental to a computer-security seminar sponsored by a not-for-profit foundation that was in truth a front for his alma mater, the National Security Agency. He flew to San Jose, California, five or six times a year, undoubtedly to keep abreast of new de-velopments in Silicon Valley. And he returned to New York for long weekends every six or eight weeks; the lack of hotel bills except from his most recent visit, in mid-October, suggested that he stayed with his family.

Leong was not one to spend his free time cruising Dal-las's freeways, though, purchasing on average only about twelve gallons of gas per week.

He habitually grocery shopped on Saturday nights at a Tom Thumb in Las Colinas. A check of the customer-preference database the supermarket had built by scan-ning bar codes showed he tended to fill up his cart with microwaveable meals-for-one and the ingredients for Fluffernutters, the breakfast of dweebs. The recipe:

Skippy peanut butter and Fluff marshmallow topping, sandwiched together on untoasted Wonder bread. In addition, on the first of each month Ah Ling's Food Emporium, a store in Flushing, Queens, FedExed him a large cooler that Duchess and Data guessed contained Chinese delicacies not commonly available around Dallas.

Leong bought most of his wardrobe over the phone: size-M shirts and coats, according to the files of several clothing companies; pants with a thirty-inch waist and twenty-eight-inch inseam, uncuffed; size-8 shoes.

He patronized several major mail-order videocassette retailers and had over the years built an astonishing tape collection of sci-fi movies. He also maintained accounts at three local video stores whose databases spelled out his preferences: the occasional Jim Carrey comedy and XXX-rated fare like *Poke-a-Hantas* and *Rosie Fingered Dawn*, which turned out to be a girl/girl title.

Leong had not borrowed a book from the public library since 1995. He did, however, subscribe to the *Dallas Morning News*; six computer magazines; three sci-fi/fantasy publications; a periodical put out by Mensa, an organization for those with IQs certified above 150; and a sci-fi book club through which he had ordered every volume of William Shatner's *Tekwar* series in hardcover.

He paid for a range of premium cable-TV services but his set was generally in use only between midnight and 3 A.M., Dallas time, usually tuned to the Sci Fi Channel.

And Leong had two telephone lines in his condo. His voice-call records were those of a man who diligently called his parents twice a week, but otherwise reached out to few friends either locally or via long-distance. The second line was an ISDN link for accessing the Net and, most probably, the MedEx servers on a twenty-four-by-seven basis.

"This boy clearly needs to get a life," Dupree said. "How do you plan to get his password?"

"Thought about breaking into the condo and scoping the box that's patched to MedEx," Tejada confessed.

"Some Dallas-area *amigos* Javier does business with took a ride out to Las Colinas. But Code Boy bought into a gated complex that's buttoned real tight. Armed rent-a-cops, those claws that pop out of the pavement and shred tires—get this, they even palmprint the maids and delivery boys. Pulling off a B-and-E without tipping him looks dubious."

"And if he's tipped, the first thing he does is change his password," Dupree said glumly.

"Smile, Doc," Walker said. "There's more than one way to carbonize Code Boy's motherboard. Nacio's working with a NUROMNCR pen pal in Dallas to tap Leong's ISDN line. If we can take down the line, he'll have to relog onto MedEx. That's when we can capture his password."

"Your pen pal's going to disguise himself as a lineman?" asked Dupree. "And go up in a cherry picker?"

"This ain't Hollywood," Tejada said. "The way it's done in real life be so ordinary, no one would pay to see it. You think an FBI agent with a warrant be climbing a pole? No way. He just goes to the phone company, hands over the paper, and they patch in right at the switching station. Our pen pal does freelance troubleshooting for the phone company in Texas, which gives him physical access to the boards that handle Las Colinas. He thinks they'll call him in sometime this week."

Dupree nodded and turned his attention to the second report, which was on Wings of Mercy Ltd.

The first Georgetown bank that Duchess and Data had hacked, the one with the vulnerable trapdoor, contained no trace of the company. But it provided them a platform from which to easily attack other Cayman institutions. The third bank they hit held the jackpot: ten months' worth of Wings of Mercy transactions.

The account was controlled by the company's chief operating officer, a Georgetown lawyer. A check of the commonwealth's public records revealed the lawyer to be the sole registered representative of not only Wings of Mercy, but also half a dozen other shell companies.

Deposits into the account, as Data had said, invariably came by electronic transfer from a Miami savings-and-loan with a dubious lineage. According to the financial press, the institution was a BCCI-like front for Middle-Eastern petrodollars. The allegations remained unproved because several federal probes of the bank had been derailed by a State Department fearful of offending America's anti-Saddam allies.

The debits from the Wings of Mercy account fell into two categories: those going to recipients that were easy to trace, and those that did not.

Most disbursements in the first category involved transportation. Each month, funds were drawn to cover the leasing, hangar, and landing fees for fourteen corporate jets, half based in the U.S. and half overseas. There were also scheduled payments to truck-storage depots in the American Southwest, Europe, South America, and Southeast Asia. And from time to time, checks were cut to air-charter services around the world.

The second category consisted of sporadic wire transfers into fourteen accounts, all in overseas banks. Two numbered accounts at Leclerc & Cie, a private bank in Geneva, received payments that always totaled either $90,000, $135,000, or $180,000. Duchess and Data were set to follow the trail inside Leclerc & Cie until a couple of NUROMNCR buddies convinced them it would be a waste of time. Though in this electronic age the private Swiss banks accepted wire transfers, they assiduously guarded against online mischief by keeping the names of their clients in handwritten ledgers. The other dozen accounts, scattered across four continents, received payments that always totaled either $8,000, $12,000, or $16,000. Those banks were not as immune to hacking. Duchess and Data managed to unearth the identities of all twelve account-holders but a search of their names on the major news databases had turned up zip.

Although the fourteen payees remained a mystery, Wings of Mercy always paid them two at a time: a big transfer to Geneva and a small transfer to one of the other banks. What's more, the coefficient was always identical; that is, if Leclerc & Cie received $90,000 (two times $45,000), one of the other banks would receive $8,000 (two times $4,000).

Duchess and Data had spotted a more subtle pattern when they looked at the Wings of Mercy disbursements by date. The most recent paired payment had been made a week ago, on November 2, precisely sixty days after Guillermo was to have crossed the border. The amount wired to a bank in Geneva was $135,000 and to Mexico City $12,000—and Guillermo had been one of three young men who disappeared.

Coincidence? They picked another paired payment, in which the smaller sum had been wired to a bank in Prague. Sixty days earlier, one of the two corporate jets maintained by Wings of Mercy on the Continent had flown from its base in Berlin to Prague, touched down briefly, then continued on to London's Heathrow, which offered the most frequent transatlantic flights out of Europe. Duchess and Data went further back and located a paired payment in which the smaller sum had been wired to a bank in Manila. Sixty days earlier, the corporate jet maintained by Wings of Mercy in Singapore had flown to Baguio on the Philippine island of Luzon, touched down briefly, then continued on to Hong Kong, which offered the most transpacific flights out of Southeast Asia.

"So it looks like the smaller payments are bounties collected by the locals lining up the victims," Dupree said. "And the big ones?"

"The way me and Leepi see it," Tejada said, "they got to be for whoever takes out the organs."

"Agreed. Trouble is, will anybody besides us buy this story? And nothing you've dug up to date ties Wings of Mercy to MedEx, does it?"

Walker and Tejada shook their heads.

"Only way to make that link," Walker said, "is get inside MedEx."

"Or inside Caduceus Twenty-One."

"How's that, Doc?" asked Tejada.

"You know how they cracked the Watergate cover-up? By following the money. Which is what you guys are doing. But the Wings of Mercy account is near the end of the trail, and when you try to backtrack into MedEx, you get stonewalled by that bank in Miami. Why not jump to the head of the trail and work forward? The Caduceus Twenty-One hospitals that performed the transplants must've sent checks to someone to pay for the organ deliveries."

Walker looked over at Tejada and said, "Nacio, shut your teeth before a fly wanders in."

"Still, you've done great work," Dupree said. "I . . . Hold on, I just remembered that there was something I wanted to show you."

He hurried from the room but quickly returned carrying his computer case. As he unzipped it he saw a Polaroid lying atop his subnotebook: "My friend Guillermo. It was taken at his farewell party, the night before he headed north."

In the photograph Dupree stood next to a skinny teenager who barely came up to his chest. Guillermo was displaying his going-away presents—a watch, clothing, new shoes—and the dark eyes above broad Mayan cheekbones were wide with pride and anticipation.

Walker reached for the tissues on Tejada's desk. She pulled out a sheet, blew her nose, then said in a thick voice, "Shit, he was just a child."

"Young and trusting," Dupree agreed, booting up. "And very healthy, just the way MedEx likes them. Here it is, something buried in the files you sent down with Esai and Large.

"The four hospitals receiving the organs the day after Guillermo disappeared are all affiliated with this Caduceus Twenty-One, right? Well, a couple of newspaper stories from mid-October report that Caduceus Twenty-One is trying to raise money to finance an expansion. They've hired a New York investment banking firm called Marx Dillon and Neil. I think a partner named Marguerite K. Sepulveda's handling the deal, because she's who *The Wall Street Journal* interviewed. Let's see what we can find out about these people."

"No problem," Tejada said, jotting down the names.

WEDNESDAY
NOVEMBER 11

THE view through the large plate-glass windows of the Admiral's Club at O'Hare International Airport in Chicago reminded Maggie Sepulveda of one of those paperweights that create a short-lived blizzard when tipped upside down. Problem was, the snow that had closed the runways shortly after dawn had swirled not from a giant paperweight but out of the Plains States, and it showed few signs of abating.

Maggie kept up memberships in a batch of frequent-flyer clubs for just such occasions. The rest of O'Hare was a bedlam; every chair, every baggage carousel, every other square yard of floor space was staked out by a grounded and grumpy passenger. The American Airlines lounge was also uncomfortably crowded, but as one of the earliest to arrive, she had managed to snag one of the carrels set up for laptop users.

Up on the large TV in the corner of the room, CNN had on a bow-tied environmentalist to talk about the unusual weather gripping the nation's Heartland a full two weeks before Thanksgiving. The man, a public-television fixture who addressed the anchorwoman as if she were science-challenged, had a ready culprit: global warming. While conceding that it might seem counterintuitive to blame harsh winters on Earth's rising temperatures, he insisted the two were in fact linked for the simple reason that warm air held more moisture. Thus the record snow-falls of '96, as well as today's storm, resulted from the greenhouse effect. He was gloomily describing a future not unlike that of Kevin Costner's *Waterworld*, in which melting polar caps imperil humankind, when it was mercifully time for a commercial break.

Maggie went back to reviewing her research on the Caduceus 21 affiliate she was en route to visit, a hospital in Indianapolis. This delay would actually have been a heaven-sent opportunity to catch up on some routine paperwork, away from all interruptions, were it not for the rare opportunity she was about to miss.

Originally, she was to arrive at the hospital in midafternoon. Then late yesterday Maggie learned of an interesting surgery that had just been scheduled for 8 A.M. today; in all her years of observing operations, she had never witnessed a transplant. But though Indianapolis was only three hundred air miles from Knoxville, there were no direct flights between the two cities—an example of the hub-and-spoke nightmare that had propelled Duane Strand to start up MedEx. The only way Maggie could catch most of the operation was to drive deep into the night or lay over in Chicago and take the first flight out of O'Hare. She had chosen the wrong option.

A murmur swept the lounge.

Maggie looked up. Someone had switched the TV to the Weather Channel in time to catch the latest update. The storm had not continued east over central Pennsylvania, as originally forecast, but was instead looping south toward the mid-Atlantic states.

Great, she thought, now I won't even be able to fly back to Knoxville. Yet she had to concede that things could be worse. After almost a month on-site, her team was not only up to speed but making great progress. Teddy Quereshi's number crunchers were ahead of schedule, and the quality of Jill Unger's reports on the affiliates she had visited exceeded Maggie's expectations. The only fly in the ointment: Rob Dillon. The pressure of being courted by institutions wanting in on the placement seemed to make Dillon even more hyper than usual; he had taken to barraging her with e-mail and phone calls that all conveyed the same impatient query: Couldn't her team work still faster?

"Howdy, stranger."

She glanced up and saw a fellow health-care analyst approaching. Tom Joslyn, a tweedy man in his early fifties, was a highly respected and highly outspoken senior partner of Everett-Joslyn.

"Care for some company?"

"Absolutely." Maggie looked out at the falling snow and said, in puzzlement, "Did you just fly in?"

"Nope. Been over in the United lounge all morning, but some yuppies grabbed control of the zapper. I'm not a big *Gilligan's Island* fan."

Maggie smiled as she cleared some space so Joslyn could perch on the table. "Where you headed?"

"Home," he said. "If the storm takes the new track, though, Gwen's going to spend another night alone. You?"

"Indianapolis."

"Not White River General Hospital, by chance?"

She nodded.

"Congratulations on the Caduceus account," he said. "I'm real happy for you. Not for the creeps you work with but for you, personally."

"Thanks, Tom—I think."

Joslyn hesitated, then added, "Keep your eyes open in Knoxville, okay? And trust your intuition."

Working hard to keep her face neutral, Maggie said, "What do you mean?"

"You hear a lot of sour grapes in this industry," he said. "Most of the time it's in one ear and out the other. But I got to tell you, kiddo, too many other health-care companies—and I'm talking the good ones, not the fast-buck consolidators—too many of them still have a bone to pick with that index Reifsnyder and Osteen dreamed up. I know of several truth squads digging away, and the players on them are all A-Team."

She felt her concerns evaporate. If there was anything fishy about the Provider Efficiency Index, Teddy Quereshi would ferret it out. Yet was Joslyn's thinly veiled warning just smoke, or did he know something? She decided to probe: "What's your take? Is C-Twenty-One cooking its books?"

"If I knew that for a fact, you'd get the first call and *The Wall Street Journal* would get the second."

Maggie thought through his non-answer, then said, "Let me put it another way. Say Reifsnyder had asked you to do the deal. You would've passed?"

"Damn, you have a knack for asking uncomfortable questions. Truth is, I'm not sure we would have. But I'd make sure I kept my all-weather radar on, which is all I'm asking you to do."

"Fair enough, Tom. Thanks much for the heads-up."

"I'm still sorry we couldn't lure you down to Baltimore," Joslyn said. "We do have the Orioles and a new ballpark, you know, plus one slightly tarnished pro football franchise."

"And you know what a crabcake slut I am," Maggie responded quickly, grateful for the change of topic.

"I rest my case."

"At the time, New York just felt like the right place for me to be," she said, wondering if that was still true now that Paul was no longer a part of her life.

"Well, when you get sick of life in the passing lane or working for the Three Stooges, whichever comes first, I hope you'll keep us in mind."

"Why, Tom Joslyn, are you propositioning me?"

"Guess I am, kiddo," he said. "Am I out of line?"

She shook her head.

"So what do you want to do now, gossip about enemies and friends?"

She grinned and nodded.

Shooting each other conspiratorial looks, they began dishing industry dirt.

Shortly after 10 A.M., Maggie was surprised to hear her flight paged. She turned to the plate-glass windows. Not only had the snow stopped, but a few planes had even pushed back from the gate and were now taxiing toward the runway. The fresh Weather Channel map showed the storm moving east of both Chicago and her destination, Indianapolis.

"Hey," she said, gathering her things, "if I'm getting out of here, you probably will too."

"No such luck," he replied, glancing at the TV. "That mess is tracking straight for Baltimore. Do I try to fly into La Guardia and rent a car, or do I just book a room here?"

Maggie stood and bussed Joslyn on the cheek. "Gwen's more fun than a Sheraton. Brave the blizzard, and say hi for me when you get home."

O NE sure gauge of a hospital's stress level: the number of employees finding time to squeeze in a meal. The blizzard that had brought Indianapolis to a standstill had also packed the cafeteria of White River General Hospital with staffers savoring a rare leisurely lunch. These included most of the ER personnel; with few traffic accidents or street crimes expected in the next few hours, their main concern was snow-shovelers suffering heart attacks. But there was bad news mixed with the good. The liver transplant Maggie thought she had missed had been put on hold; at last word, the plane delivering the replacement organ was still over southern Illinois en route from Dallas.

Maggie was sharing soup-and-salads with Elizabeth

O'Leary, a senior White River administrator in her late forties with an appreciation of medicine far beyond that of most hospital bureaucrats.

"In a sense," O'Leary was saying, "you could view surgery as the failure of medicine."

"How's that?"

"It's saying that if we can't cure it, we cut it out."

At that moment one of her assistants approached the table and said, "Betsy? Sorry to interrupt, but we just got word from Weir-Cook. The MedEx flight's landed."

"Thank God," O'Leary said. "The transplant team's been notified?"

"Yes, ma'am. They've already started pre-op."

O'Leary turned to Maggie. "If I remember correctly, the organ was harvested about twenty-seven hours ago, so we're really sweating its viability. Anybody else but MedEx, we would have given up hope."

"I met the founder of the company the other week," Maggie said.

"He's in New York, isn't he?" O'Leary stood and picked up her tray. "I should make it a point to go there to thank him. Without them, our transplant program is about as efficient and predictable as the bus service in this town."

The two women hurried up to the scrub room, where they donned gowns and masks.

There were already a half-dozen other observers in the OR.

The boom box was playing Elton John. Maggie had observed enough operations to have picked up geographical and demographic patterns in the musical tastes of surgeons. Once, in Minnesota of all places, she had sat in on a hip replacement performed to gospel. It was usually rock, though, with pockets of classical and jazz on the coasts and C&W in the Sunbelt. The exact type of rock was a tip-off to the age of the chief surgeon, who chose the music. Those at the forefront of the Boomer generation tended toward golden oldies. Those in their late thirties and early forties preferred middle-of-the-road artists from the 1970s and 1980s. Maggie had never heard grunge, because that generation had not yet begun graduating to First Scalpel. Nor, for that matter, heavy metal or rap, which was just as well; it was unnerving to contemplate some surgeon cutting away to the doom-laden beat of Megadeth or Snoop Doggy Dogg.

Maggie and O'Leary took their places behind the head of the table, alongside the anesthesiologist.

The surgical team had already incised the patient's abdomen and was beginning to peel back the layers of muscle.

The woman on the table, the wife of a construction worker and the mother of four, was about Maggie's age. O'Leary explained that she had developed primary hepatoma, or liver cancer. An exhaustive metastatic workup—CT scans of the lungs and bones, sophisticated blood tests—suggested the tumor was probably confined. But one area had given an ambiguous reading; the surgeons would thoroughly check her peritoneal wall before performing the transplant.

"What if they find that the cancer's spread?" asked Maggie.

"We have another candidate waiting in his doctor's office."

Maggie regarded the upside-down face of the unconscious patient. What a harsh world, she thought. Not because of cancer—diseases happened—but because the availability of a healthy liver had raised more hopes than it could fulfill. If the cancer had spread in the woman on the table, she would be sewn back up and sent home to die. If it hadn't, the candidate waiting in a doctor's office upstairs would be given some encouraging words, then told to go home and wait some more. But at least the standby was now at the top of the wait-list; her brother Petey never even made standby.

Thirty minutes later, O'Leary nudged Maggie forward to the chest-high partition at the head of the table. The team had finished excavating; the patient's skin and abdominal muscles were neatly clamped to the rim of the wound, her viscera and blood vessels cleared aside. As always, Maggie was astonished by the lack of blood. It was a point made by good medical documentaries but not Hollywood: a skilled surgical team prided itself on stanching hemorrhages before they arose. From her new vantage point, she had a clear view of the woman's liver, which was medium red in color, pulsing gently, and surrealistically large.

The chief surgeon strapped on a device that provided him with 3x magnification. The carcinoma was on the left side of the liver, so he gently manipulated the organ to expose the tumor, then bent over and began to examine closely the adjoining peritoneum, the membrane lining the abdominal cavity.

The tension in the room was thick enough to curdle.

At last the chief surgeon raised his head and said, "She's clean."

Maggie could feel relief flood the OR in a palpable wave. As the team regrouped to begin the next phase, she noticed another observer, one of the older men in the room, quietly head for the door. She said to O'Leary, "Is that the other candidate's physician?"

O'Leary nodded.

One prayer was about to be answered, another had already been dashed; Maggie's heart went out to the standby and his family.

A short while later, the team finished clamping the portal and inferior vena cava as well as the biliary ducts. Now, using lengths of plastic tubes, the surgeons started on the veno-venous bypasses that would reroute the patient's blood past her shut-down liver.

One of the nurses left the OR, returning a few minutes later pushing a small wheeled cart. Atop the cart sat a large stainless-steel bowl containing the replacement liver, grayish-brown in its chilled saline bath.

As soon as the bypasses were completed, the chief surgeon said, "How's she doing?"

"All signs stable," the anesthesiologist replied.

The team began to cut the native liver free. They took great care in severing the blood vessels and bile ducts, for these same vessels and ducts had to be sutured to the replacement organ.

The chief surgeon glanced up at the wall clock—during this phase, the greatest enemy was time—then reached in with both hands and began to manhandle the liver, much like a baker kneading a large lump of dough. Maggie quickly understood why; extricating an organ the size of a five-pound rib roast was probably as difficult as delivering a baby. Finally the surgeon gained the clearance he needed. He lifted out the liver and placed it in a plastic tub, which a nurse rushed from the room.

"Pathology?" asked Maggie.

O'Leary shook her head. "No need to biopsy—we know it's cancerous. More likely it'll end up in the forensic lab, a sample specimen for our residents."

The chief surgeon had stepped away from the operating table to examine the replacement organ with his team.

O'Leary listened in on the discussion, then said, "One of the veins on the new liver looks questionable. They don't want to take any chances, so they're going to perform a venous bypass."

The chief surgeon lifted the replacement liver and maneuvered it into the abdominal cavity.

At the same time, one of the assisting surgeons swabbed the patient's left inner thigh and made an incision.

The chief surgeon stitched the organ in place, then pulled his magnifier back on and joined his assistant in attaching one end of a freshly removed length of the patient's femoral vein to her inferior vena cava and the other end to a valve in the new liver. After the venous bypass came the painstaking job of vascular reconstruction, or anastomosis. This procedure consisted of sewing together the narrow, circular vein endings with Prolene, a plastic-coated synthetic thread.

Maggie moved forward again to the chest-high partition.

A task that couldn't have been easy under the best of circumstances was complicated by the fact that the surgeons had to work deep inside the abdominal cavity. With insufficient room for their hands, they had to use long, scissorlike clamps to grasp a curved needle that was a junior version of the kind used to sew leather. Watching them patiently push and pull the needle through the slippery, easily ripped tissue, she was struck anew by the skills, the discipline, the stamina, the self-confidence all good surgeons possessed. No wonder some developed a godlike sense of infallibility. No wonder many developed a unique occupational disability, a creeping numbness to their hands and arms; the physical stress of standing hunched over the operating table for hours on end led to herniated disks that themselves required surgery. And no wonder most developed an ability to work the room like a stand-up comic, using wisecracks to fight fatigue and tension.

Coming up on the four-hour mark, Maggie suddenly sensed all around her another sudden spike of adrenaline.

Anastomosis complete, the surgeons stepped back.

"Time for a test-drive," the chief surgeon said lightly.

The clamps were released and the patient's blood began coursing through her rebuilt circulatory system, and then there were murmurs of satisfaction from around the room as the grayish-brown replacement liver began to pulse and pinken.

"Well, it's just another goddamn miracle," the chief surgeon said.

His team laughed appreciatively, knowing that the ritual incantation was a direct lift from Keith Reemtsma, the transplant pioneer under whom their leader had trained.

One of the nurses slapped a small bottle of chilled Evian into the chief surgeon's hand.

"Halftime," O'Leary explained. "They need a break to grab some coffee, go to the bathroom, whatever."

Several members of the team maintained a vigil over the patient but others began ducking out of the room. Not the chief surgeon, though. Maggie noticed that even as he and a few others began to discuss the exact combination of immunosuppressants that would go into the antirejection cocktail, his eyes never wandered for long from the transplanted liver.

Ten minutes later, the team reassembled to begin the least dramatic phase of the operation. Hemostasis involved tying off all the little leaks that inevitably sprang from the sutured veins. Before the team started reconstructing the biliary ducts through which the liver's excretions flowed, the abdominal cavity had to be bone dry —a condition that might take six more hours to achieve. The tools required for this tedious procedure: Bovies, which were handheld battery-powered cauterization probes; sutures; cotton and gauze packing; and an immense reservoir of patience.

A half hour into the hemostasis, an attendant hurried into the operating room and sought out Maggie.

"Ms. Sepulveda? You have a telephone call. They say it's urgent."

Damn it, Maggie thought, if that was Rob Dillon again, she would fly directly back to New York and personally shove thirty tabs of Ritalin down his gullet. She followed the attendant out to the nearest station, where the nurse handed her the phone.

"Maggie Sepulveda here."

"Maggie?" It was Jill Unger, who sounded as if she'd been crying.

"Jill. What's wrong?"

There was a brief silence, then a wet sniffle, and then Unger took a deep breath and said, "It's Teddy. He's dead."

T H U R S D A Y
N O V E M B E R   1 2

AS the rising sun pushed the temperature into the upper seventies, the pool began filling with young 'uns. Century Chisholm longed to be down there listening to their yip-yaps, getting himself splashed every now and then; hell, that was half the fun of coming south every winter. On this gorgeous morning, though, he watched from behind the French doors of his second-story study, which were tightly shut to seal in the warmth of the fire blazing in the hearth. Until Lester Haidak slapped a healthy ticker in him, he was only comfortable in heat that could wilt an orchid.

Chisholm didn't know what bothered him more, his condition or the fact folks were noticing it. Here at the house everybody was too polite to say anything about how he wore a down vest whenever he left this room, even to the dinner table. Elspeth's wedding had been something else. Wonderful ceremony, held outdoors at the groom's estate on the kind of hot afternoon they invented linen for. The other guests hadn't remarked about his woolen suit and vest, but did wonder aloud about why his hands were a tad puffy and cold to the touch. What could he tell 'em 'cept he was battling some kind of bug?

He moved away from the French doors, depressed at how poorly this visit was going, at how he was having to huddle in this study like some sodbuster waiting out a blizzard. Reading helped some. What he really needed to make time pass was his memoirs. Couldn't chance bringing 'em along, though; this house wasn't like Santa Fe, with a private sanctum. Spending hour after hour dictating, then locking the door to the study at night, would both be totally out of character and set a lot of tongues to wagging.

Chisholm started for his Eames wingchair—he was halfway through a new biography of Alexander the Great —then decided to first make his daily check for e-mail. That was the only way his people could communicate with him when he was down here; no reason for any of 'em to know his exact whereabouts. He opened the door of an antique hutch, took out a laptop, and booted up.

Among the messages in his electronic inbox was one Duane Strand had sent the previous afternoon:

Century,
This is to advise you that an incident did occur on the MD&N watch. It was ascertained that one of their accountants posted to Knoxville went beyond the parameters of his assignment and acquired data of a potentially damaging nature. Early this morning the accountant did undergo interrogation. A review of his clickstreams and telephone calls supported his statement that no one else has seen the data. At that point in time the accountant was terminated and the data was erased. I am therefore pleased to report that our rapid response to the situation did result in successful damage control.
—D.S.

Chisholm felt anger course through his veins like lava. Damn that bunch of fools. All they had to do was keep to the tall grass for another two months. But no, Strand went and bungled a routine surveillance mission, then made things worse by unleashing his fucking attack dog. Oh, he knew which one did the dirty work, all right. All them ex-cowboys were alike. Government trains 'em to kill, they think it's their God-given right. Didn't give a damn about the consequences, neither. Just wiped off the blade and left the mess for somebody else.

He was also livid about how much the note left unsaid. Anytime a feller like Strand started using that mealymouthed briefing lingo, he was covering someone's ass, probably his own.

Chisholm checked his watch. It wasn't 8 A.M. yet on the East Coast; Strand should still be home. Whose turn was it to house-sit in Santa Fe? He remembered Placida had gone back up after the wedding. Good, that gal knew how to relay a call through the uplink dish so's it couldn't be traced.

Six minutes later, he heard Duane Strand's secure phone begin to ring.

As soon as Strand picked up, Chisholm said, without preamble, "Just what kind of stuff was this accountant feller acquiring?"

"Hello, Century. He was analyzing that index C-Twenty-One uses. Played a couple of long shots and came up with some data the folks in Knoxville might not've liked."

"How long he been on that trail?"

"Less than two weeks," Strand replied.

"Two weeks and not a one of you noticed? Strand, according to your memo of twenty-two October, and I quote, 'They can't fart without us knowing about it.' So explain it to me simple, in words an old man can understand."

"Begging your pardon, sir, the accountant and his team are pulling in a tremendous volume of outside material. I believe that's par for the course during a due diligence? It took a while to spot the extraneous data and understand what he was up to."

"What you mean to say is, your folks were too busy jacking off to notice. Who's in charge of the monitoring operation, that Chinaman?"

"Negative. He set up the node but his plate was full, so a team of freelancers was hired to do the day-to-day."

"For Christ's sake," Chisholm exploded. "Freelancers? That's like buying the Mona Lisa and giving it to Helen Keller. What the hell was going through your thick skull?"

"We didn't just yank guys off the street," Strand replied defensively. "It's easy to find techies who can process the clickstreams and voice taps, but people who can make sense of sophisticated financial data? And are willing to do a job like this? M.T. did the best he could."

"It wasn't near good enough, was it?"

"Century, like I said in my note, the damage has been contained."

"Until somebody notices this accountant feller's missing."

There was a long pause. Finally Strand said, "We didn't disappear him. But the cops think it was a random attack, same's with Carl Haas."

Chisholm absently plucked at his upper lip. "You sure he didn't let on what he was doing to the other accountants? Or to Ms. Sepulveda?"

"Negative. No e-mail, no calls. Even kept his workfiles encrypted so nobody could read them."

"Still, he found the trail. Someone else can too."

"Unlikely, sir. He was the best they had, and like I said, it was a one-in-a-million shot. Rest assured we're now on full alert. Any of the other accountants requests the same data, we'll know it in a hurry."

"Then what?" said Chisholm. "Send in a commando team? Some of your men would like that, wouldn't they?

Listen, Strand, between now and when the C-Twenty-One deal goes down, no more fuckups. And you don't 'terminate' anybody without clearing it with me first. Hear?"

"Loud and clear, sir."

F R I D A Y
N O V E M B E R 1 3

BENEATH the civilized veneer of ancient Hellas, reckoned Ignacio Tejada, there had lurked a love of conspiracy that would put Oliver Stone to shame and an untempered blood lust that would give a junkyard dog pause. The epic poems he was reading for Greek Mythology 306 were up to here in intrigue and vengeance, the gorier the better. So how come the *gabacho* elite was so full of praise for the classics but so down on rap and on homeboy action movies?

Tejada yawned and pushed back from his desk. Was it Euripides glazing his eyes or sleep dep? The night was young—barely after 1 A.M.—yet he found himself envying Leepi Walker, sacked out on the couch across the room, and Nguyen-Anh Dupree, slumbering in the guest bedroom. It was the first time since Doc's arrival in Los Angeles that any two of them had managed to grab zzz's at the same time. They had been too busy hacking through the early-morning hours, when their target systems were tended by sysops too junior or too inept to escape the lobster shift.

The good news was, they had penetrated the four Caduceus 21 hospitals and discovered the payments made to MedEx in late September and early October, a month after the disappearance of Guillermo and his two fellow border-crossers. The sums involved totaled more than eight hundred thousand dollars; evidently killing people for their organs paid even better than trafficking dope.

The bad news was, MedEx had deposited the money with the same Maytag bank in Miami used by Wings of Mercy Ltd.

The ugly news was, he and Leepi had encountered something sinister while probing the New York City investment bankers retained to raise money for Caduceus 21. The Marx Dillon & Neil network's firewall was so flimsy, the opening screen might as well say HACK ME. Someone had, big-time: in snooping around, they came across a hidden program that was recording the clickstreams from select terminals, compressing the data, and piping it out through an ostensibly unused com port. Among the Marx Dillon users being monitored: Marguerite K. Sepulveda.

Tejada took another swig of Jolt! and forced his attention back to his box. On-screen were his preliminary notes for the Greek lit paper due all too soon. In truth, though, it was not Euripides keeping him up at this late hour, but rather his decision to volunteer for the night's first Jefferson Leong watch.

Fourteen hours earlier, he had been attending a sociology lecture when his pager vibrated. The call came from area code (214)—the NUROMNCR pen pal who freelanced for Southwestern Bell. The hack of Code Boy was good to go.

In early afternoon the pen pal reported that he had successfully run a tap from Leong's ISDN line to an unused number. He also provided Tejada with the password of a phone-company sysop who was on vacation until next Monday.

Shortly before 2:30 P.M. from this very chair, with Doc and Leepi looking over his shoulders, Tejada patched together a relay that ran from the compound in South-Central to the remote server a half-mile away to Raleigh, North Carolina, to the city of Terrell, Texas, some twenty-five miles east of Dallas. Then he used this untraceable connection to dial up Southwestern Bell and log onto its network with the borrowed password.

Tejada had spent enough time inside phone companies to know exactly where to go and what to do. First, pull up the schematic of Leong's neighborhood in Las Colinas. Second, identify the junction box into which Leong's two lines ran. Third, identify the workstation that supported the junction box. Fourth, log over to the workstation and locate the file that controlled the junction box. Fifteen seconds later the junction box was offline and Tejada was disconnecting. Total time of operation: less than six minutes.

"This surgical bombing be time-consuming," he had casually remarked to Dupree. "In half that time, I could've taken down all of two-one-four."

The wait for feedback, though, was nowhere as quick. Last word from the Tres Equis *amigos* in Dallas keeping an eye on the MedEx parking lot was that Code Boy's car was still in it.

JEFFERSON Leong finished archiving the previous day's dark-core files, launched a housekeeping utility, and wiped his bleary eyes. Good thing Morris Tomczack's rent-a-dweebs were processing the clickstreams and voice seines on those bankers temporarily working in Knoxville; he and his deputy, Rusty, had their hands full with the data from the health-care company's permanent staff.

As the utility program triple-wiped incriminating material from SEECUBED and the Caduceus 21 trapdoor, Leong glanced out over the skeletal crew manning the MedEx workstations on the midnight-to-eight shift. Damn, he loathed his office. Only an architect with a couple of circuit boards loose would have installed a plate-glass wall in a windowless underground complex. In theory, it allowed him to watch over his serfs. In practice, it also allowed them to stare back.

For instance, Leong needed five monitors to keep tabs on his intricately linked nets. If he arrayed them along the back wall, people down on the floor might be able to make out what was on his screens; yet if he arranged them against the side walls or turned their backs to the glass wall, all those unworthy technopeons were in his field of vision.

And then there was the problem of all-nighters. Like most hackers who went on marathon work burns, Leong had trained himself to take ten-minute catnaps. No way he could just close his eyes in this office, though; any such public sign of weakness and he'd be an even bigger target of derision.

The mindless task keeping him past 2 A.M. tonight could have been done more comfortably from his home, with an *Outer Limits* rerun on in the background. But it would take him three times longer, because the box in his condo communicated with the MedEx servers by way of an ISDN line. Perhaps he should ask New York for the money to install himself a way-fast T1 line. If they sprang for it, he could cut his time in this hellhole by half.

As was his preshutdown routine, Leong tagged a batch of files he wanted piped to his home box and pressed a hot key.

The message that popped up on-screen woke him up, fast:

REMOTE TERMINAL DISCONNECTED AT 16:34:22

Leong punched up his autodialer and double-clicked APT.

After four rings, he heard his own voice on the answering machine.

If not a fire, a burglary? He moved his cursor down to LONE STAR SECURITY and double-clicked. The operator who answered put him on hold while she checked the computer, then returned to say everything was fine.

Why then was his remote terminal not responding? He dialed Southwestern Bell repair and finally breathed easier; according to the customer service rep, some type of disruption in midafternoon—probably a power surge—had interrupted service to parts of Las Colinas for twenty minutes. There had been a similar disconnect two Julys ago, after a major thunderstorm.

He powered down and gathered his things. The wall clock read 2:17. Damn, at this hour the only fast-food joints open were in the wrong direction.

As Leong turned his BMW 750iL east out of the MedEx lot, he paid no attention to the darkened car parked across the street, a low-rider in which the driver was picking up a cell phone.

Fifteen minutes later Leong wheeled into the gated complex in Las Colinas and pulled into the reserved slot in front of his condo. He hurried up the walkway, unlocked the door by palming the glowing plastic square under the bell, then stepped inside and quickly disarmed the multiple security systems.

If the apartment resembled a combination showroom for Pier 1 and Circuit City, that was because those were precisely the stores where he had spent one long day shopping until dropping. The home-entertainment rig was top-of-the-line. The furniture clearly wasn't, but since his social life sucked, why blow money to impress himself?

Leong went directly to the bedroom that had been converted into an office. The message on the monitor read:

16:34:22

SESSION TIMED OUT

ERROR 002484: 60 SECONDS NO RESPONSE
16:34:22

The line wouldn't have gone down if it was a T1, he thought as he reached for the keyboard. Leong relaunched his app, typed his password, and logged back onto the MedEx net.

ALL fatigue, not to mention all thoughts of Euripides, had vanished with the heads-up from the Tres Equis *amigo* tagging Jefferson Leong. Now, twenty minutes later, Ignacio Tejada was staring at the intercepted string of numbers and letters that had just popped up on-screen: -4E00AEB. Truly random. Good thing he and Leepi hadn't tried logging in; they would have ended up another snack for Pit Bull.

Tejada considered waking his friends, then decided to let them sleep. Code Boy might be online with MedEx for a while, checking the interface for glitches, and it definitely would not do to have two -4E00AEBs running around inside the system at the same time. He'd give it until 3 A.M. his time, or five in the morning in Dallas.

He set an alarm to remind himself to go downstairs in an hour to brew a pot of fresh coffee for Doc and Leepi. He was about to minimize the window containing the password, and return to poor unsuspecting Iphigenia, sailing from Mycenae to Aulis and her destiny, when he remembered the NUM LOCK trick Leepi had flashed onto during her initial Cayman hack. He retyped the odd string, came up with PUEMMAEB, and grinned.

All the manuals urged changing passwords every couple of days. Easier said than done, for it didn't take more than a couple of weeks to run out of easily remembered combinations. Yes, humans could write programs capable of generating random strings, but because humans didn't have brains that were etched like a RAM chip, retrieving the umpteenth random string became a problem. Tejada was comforted by the thought that everybody—even an *otaku* like Jefferson Leong—fell back on easy mnemonics when it came to passwords.

Even non-Trekkies would recognize PUEMMAEB backward: BEAM/ME/UP.

S A T U R D A Y
N O V E M B E R 1 4

THE tragedy brigade was still besieging the funeral home on Manhattan's Upper West Side when Teddy Quereshi's mourners began emerging from the private memorial service. The streetscape was white with the eight inches of snow dumped by the late-week storm, a powdery fall that would linger for days. The police had sawhorsed off a path across the sidewalk to a line of waiting dial-a-cabs. The cameramen and reporters behind the blue barricades hadn't shrunk in ranks over the past hour, just gotten colder and meaner, thought Maggie Sepulveda as she stepped through the door, supporting Jill Unger on her arm.

All it took to send the journalists into a feeding frenzy was one glimpse of the statuesque Unger's tear-flooded cheeks.

"Keep walking, Boss," muttered Dawn Mambelli. Anticipating just this kind of media circus, she had asked her TV cameraman brother, Frankie, for a couple of tips. Frankie was always filming perp walks, those photo ops where cops led shackled suspects to the paddy wagon. Mambelli took a deep breath, released Unger's other arm, and hurried over to the nearest camera. She ignored the shouted questions until the other reporters nearby had shoved their microphones in her face. Then she said, in a loud voice, "Listen up, I got two statements to make on behalf of the family and friends."

Mambelli stepped back and snapped open her overcoat to reveal a hand-lettered T-shirt:

WE'RE GOING TO
DISNEY WORLD!

The whispered curses, the sour air of sudden consternation, validated Frankie's advice. Want to stay off TV? Don't bother making like Pretzel Boy, trying to twist a coat or sweatshirt over your head. Just mock a major advertiser; no station was going to air footage that might cost it a sponsor.

"Also, power down, guys," Mambelli said. "We are not public figures and we definitely do not agree to be photographed."

"Suck my dick, lady," the nearest videocam operator snarled without taking his eye from the viewfinder.

"Sorry, I forgot my magnifying glass," she retorted, moving to block his view.

The cameraman barked another obscenity at her but continued to pan in search of Jill Unger.

Mambelli reached into her pocket, pulled out a small can, and sprayed the jerk's lens with black model-airplane paint.

The enraged cameraman shoved his now-useless instrument onto a colleague and was halfway over the barricade when he felt an iron tug on his collar. He wheeled and launched a roundhouse punch that he managed to pull just before it connected with the police sergeant in charge of the scene.

Mambelli took advantage of the diversion by turning

and brandishing her can of Testor's at the journalists behind the opposite barricade. In their haste to back away, two collided and went sprawling into a two-foot drift.

"Arrest that cunt!" the cameraman screamed, wildly waving his arm at Mambelli.

"What's the charge, pal?" The sergeant, who had yet to release his grip, was working manfully to keep a straight face. "You a building or a monument? Then it can't be graffiti."

"I got your shield number, you prick."

The merriment faded from the sergeant's eyes. "Did I just hear the p-word? Out of the same mouth that just used the c-word? Want to go back to the Two-Zero, pal, so we can look up 'public nuisance,' or you going to calm down?"

By this time Maggie had bundled Jill Unger into a dial-a-cab and given the driver Unger's address and a voucher. As the dark sedan pulled from the curb Maggie turned and flashed Mambelli a big thumbs-up. Because Teddy would be buried in his native Pakistan and no wake had been planned, she had the rest of the day to herself. Her apartment lay fifteen blocks north up Amsterdam Avenue. Deciding her need for fresh air outweighed the biting cold and the hassles of partly shoveled sidewalks, Maggie hiked up her collar and set off on foot.

Everyone feared Teddy's service would be a tabloid circus once details of his death began to come out. The *Post*'s front page was quick to oblige:

GAY NY BANKER
BOBBITTED
& SKEWERED

It was the most gratuitous of the headlines, but not by much; even *The New York Times* had deigned to assign coverage. As Mambelli's brother had pointed out, the story was every editor's dream. Snow dumped by a blizzard soon melted. A gruesome crime, though, might play for a week, even for months if the victim was from the privileged classes: the model with a hideously slashed face, the preppy strangled during kinky sex, the Central Park jogger gang-raped and left for dead—and now sweet, gentle Teddy Quereshi.

Shortly after dawn on Wednesday, even as Maggie sat snowbound at O'Hare, Knoxville police had been summoned to an alley near the Greyhound station to the north of Caduceus 21 headquarters. At night the area around Central and Magnolia was frequented by homosexuals seeking trade rougher than that normally found in such Old City bars as Antoine's. It was evidently not unusual for the police to come upon johns who had been robbed and battered unconscious. But none had ever been left in a condition that caused one responding officer, an eleven-year veteran of the force, to instantly vomit.

The coroner determined the victim had been methodically beaten over the course of several hours. Half the bones in his face, as well as half his teeth, were shattered, along with both knees. Several of his ribs were broken and his spleen ruptured. His penis had been severed and crammed into his mouth. Only then did Teddy Quereshi's killer or killers deliver him from his agony with one clean plunge of a double-edged knife through the heart.

By the time Maggie fought the bad weather and the frustrating hub-and-spoke airline routings back to Knoxville, Jill Unger was under sedation. As the senior member of the Marx Dillon team on hand, she had been responsible for identifying the corpse before its release to the coroner.

The detectives who interviewed Maggie were classifying the case as gay-bashing. She disagreed. Maggie acknowledged Teddy's homosexuality but insisted the circumstances surrounding his murder didn't add up. First, Teddy was in a long-run monogamous relationship. Second, she knew from Quereshi's condo mate, a fellow Marx Dillon accountant, that Teddy's idea of a night on the town was hanging out with Pakistani students on the UT campus, not cruising the Old City. Third, Caduceus 21 computer records, as well as the sign-out sheet at 420 South Gay, confirmed that Teddy had worked until well past 2 A.M. Wednesday, by which time the pickup bars were emptying. Fourth, Teddy's leased car was still in a lot near Caduceus 21, almost a mile from the Old City; why would he have walked that distance on a bitterly cold night? The police had dutifully taken down Maggie's statement, but she knew it was destined for the back of the file cabinet.

Had they been able to return Teddy's body to New York on Thursday or early Friday, perhaps some dignity could have been preserved. But the storm delaying Maggie in Chicago had looped south as projected, then unexpectedly veered up the Eastern Seaboard, snarling all travel. Her team had been trapped in Knoxville and Teddy's benumbed parents in London, en route from Karachi. By Friday afternoon, Caduceus 21 headquarters, as well as the Marx Dillon offices in New York, were encircled by reporters.

But the hysteria had not diminished the turnout of mourners. In addition to family, friends, and the Marx Dillon staff, Len Reifsnyder, Aurelia Wilkes, and Mary Osteen were in attendance, along with several Caduceus 21 financial staffers with whom Teddy had worked in Knoxville.

In Maggie's eyes, Rob Dillon had gone far to redeem himself by so ably taking charge of the crisis. He had organized the service, booked a larger chapel as the number of respondents continued to climb, and even made sure the ushers double-checked each arriving mourner against the guest list. This last safeguard, which prevented two reporters from sneaking in, proved farsighted. Five minutes into the first tribute Sterling Nussbaum, Teddy's companion of a decade, had risen from his seat in the audience, taken two steps toward the closed casket, then collapsed onto the carpeted floor.

• • •

A short nap and a long shower failed to revive Maggie's spirits. The wasteland of sports and infomercials on TV held no appeal. Neither did the prospect of phoning up a friend for a chat, or the stack of unread magazines next to the couch, or even food. By 4 P.M. she was tired of aimlessly wandering the rooms, of wallowing in the disorientation, the emptiness.

While making herself tea, Maggie remembered that she hadn't checked her e-mail and messages since the night she spent in Chicago, before flying to Indianapolis. Going back to work in Knoxville on Monday—another unbearable thought—would be easier if at least her electronic inboxes were weeded.

She carried the mug into the bedroom and without much enthusiasm booted up her laptop.

Nothing urgent awaited her on either the Caduceus 21 or Marx Dillon net. She punched her private account up on-screen—and felt sudden tears begin to well. Leaping out from the usual clutter of solicitations was a message Teddy Quereshi had sent her at 2:18 A.M. Wednesday, just minutes before he walked out of the Caduceus 21 offices for the last time.

Maggie dried her eyes, then opened the file and frowned. It was not e-mail, but rather a fax of a note typed on speckled gray stationery:

TO: M. Sepulveda   11 November
FM: T. Quereshi
RE: "Conjugals"
Per your Policy Directive #36642, requiring written applications for conjugal visits: I ask you to reverse your decision of 8 Nov. I demand the whole of Thanksgiving week off so that I may spend it in New York with Sterling. The time is more than owed me. You see, Maggie, I have reluctantly come to agree with your rather tart observation that I

*seem to be going "dotty" backgrounding myself on
C-21's operational patterns; if only the target were
stationery. A fast answer is therefore appreciated.*

Maggie was stunned by both Teddy's uncharacteristic
belligerence and by the many misrepresentations he had
made in such a brief note.

She had never issued "policy directives," much less
ones with numbers.

She had never asked for "written applications for conjugal visits."

She had never denied him a conjugal at Thanksgiving;
in fact, he had declined her offer of extra days off because
he would be spending the holiday in St. Louis with Sterling Nussbaum's family, a trip he didn't relish.

She had never criticized his ability to master complex
details; quite the contrary, she could remember her positive reaction when he recently mentioned that he was
almost done with his analysis of Caduceus 21's vaunted
PEI.

Equally baffling was the fact that Teddy had communicated by way of a fax to her private account. Why not
simply e-mail her on either the Caduceus 21 or Marx Dillon system? And if he was going to the trouble of laser-
printing it on fancy stationery, why not just leave it on
her desk in Knoxville?

As Maggie reread the note, one sentence caught her
eye: *You see, Maggie, I have reluctantly come to agree
with your rather tart observation that I seem to be going
"dotty" backgrounding myself on C-21's operational patterns; if only the target were stationery.*

Some of Teddy's word choices, like "dotty," "backgrounding," and "operational patterns," were downright
weird. Nor did he often perpetrate a misspelling; "stationery" didn't mean "unmoving," it meant—writing paper.

Maggie blinked, then sat back and stared not at
Teddy's words but the speckled gray paper they were
printed on.

dotty. backgrounding. patterns. stationery.

On a hunch, she moved the cursor up to the menu bar, clicked VIEW, spotted the cursor on two hundred percent, and clicked again.

Suddenly Maggie's nape hairs bristled.

Magnified on-screen, the stationery's grayish background was actually a series of /'s and \'s—Teddy had printed his note on a sheet of glyphs, the coding system based on slashes and backslashes.

She punched up her glyph software, entered 36642 in the key field, and started the decryption process.

Maggie,

My prayers are answered, for you have seen through the persiflage of my silly note. I was hoping to speak with you before you left for Indianapolis, but Chloe said you took an earlier flight. All this cloak-and-dagger with the glyphs, Maggie, is occasioned by two sinister findings.

Firstly, C-21's stellar financial performance appears to be predicated on what we accountants might deem "infracompany misappropriation allocation irregularities"—that is, the deliberate over- or understatement of departmental performances.

Laymen call it cooking the books.

The fraud really is quite subtle, but I shall try to summarize my findings. You'll remember I requested permission to compare C-21's fees and expenses in select cities against those of similarly sized competitors. On doing so, I found the fees charged by our client for a wide array of standard services to be slightly below average and expenses significantly below average. On the face of it, then, C-21's PEIs seem on the up-and-up.

But one thing bothered me, Maggie. None of the competing medical facilities against which I compared the C-21 affiliates operates a transplant center. There is nothing sinister in this per se; rare is the community capable of supporting more than one transplant center. Still, I felt it would be derelict to not attempt an extrapolation. It took some time to identify centers that can truly be considered commensurate, for few perform the sheer volume of transplants as does our client.

C-21's transplant fees turn out to be spot on norm—but its expenses are without fail dramatically higher. I can place only one interpretation on this disturbing fact: C-21 is using its transplant centers to absorb a significant portion of its nontransplant expenses.

Assuming, as I think we must, our client would not risk fudging the bottom line—that is, each affiliate accurately reports total revenues and total expenditures—my calculations show the PEIs to skew a minimum of six percent in our client's favour. Put another way, all the C-21 affiliates I studied would be of marginal profitability, at best, minus their transplant centers.

The question occurs that perhaps the individual affiliates are responsible? I think not, for two reasons. Firstly, it seems improbable that five sets of books, cooked independently, would show precisely the same six-percent skew. Secondly, all financial software and updates are issued by Knoxville and no patching—absolutely none—is permitted. I fear the problem goes right up to Mr. Reifsnyder or Dr. Wilkes or Ms. Osteen.

All this will make more sense when you examine the data on which I base my analyses. That data are in the encrypted files "Teddy01" through "Teddy16" residing in my queue. You can gain access via my log-on [TQUERE], my password [03Z8KL9], and the decrypt code 71559. As a precaution, I sent backups on disk in the overnight pouch to Dawn Mambelli.

The encryption and the backup disks (totaling

seven) are owing to my fear that my personal queue at the South Gay Street building, and quite possibly those of our entire team, is being closely monitored by person or persons within C-21. Permit me to present evidence as to why our network is compromised, as well as my reasoning as to why it must be an inside job.

As you know, Maggie, the e-mail software we brought down from New York has many customizable options. One is, upon retrieving a message, do we want the original left in the mailbox for manual deletion (the default setting) or do we want it autodeleted upon reading? I am fully capable of deciding which messages to save and which not, so I set my software to autodelete.

Since late last week, Sterling has sent five e-mails I never received. The fact I am receiving much other e-mail suggests there is no systems glitch, so I tallied up other electronic communications that are overdue and then made inquiries. Our Ms. Casselman in MD&N research informs me replies to three of my four outstanding queries to her department were posted days ago. Similarly, I recently sent queries to PHS, HFCA, and Veterans Affairs in Washington, as well as to several state health boards. They all posted replies that never reached me. I correlated the transmission times of these missing messages and found they were all sent at the end of day, Knoxville time.

In the off-chance I have been leaving my machine on at night, and the cleaning personnel are having sport on it, last night I e-mailed myself at 9 p.m., then turned off the computer and unplugged it. This morning there was no sign of the message. Ergo, someone is reading my mail. Reluctant as I am to believe our hosts capable of such an act, who else has real-time access to our network?

Believe me, Maggie, I hesitated before writing

this, for you have enough on your plate without an additional alarm. But I must confess to you my concern. Do not e-mail me back for the reasons discussed above. I count the hours until your return so we may discuss, clarify, and tackle all the above, face-to-face.

Yrs,

T.Q.

Time seemed to stop, the wan light of a dying day to dim, the sounds in the apartment and from the street to vanish. Maggie found herself in the tunnel-visioned zone she entered when driving in competition. Instead of racing around a well-marked track, though, she felt trapped in a vehicle she could neither steer nor brake as it hurtled through zero-visibility fog.

The implications of the letter on-screen were monstrous. Forget the fiscal shenanigans, which were bad enough; Teddy had all but pointed a finger at his murderers. She thought of the Caduceus 21 cofounders sitting in seeming distress through the memorial service. If one or more of them hadn't ordered the electronic monitoring of the Marx Dillon team, if one or more of them hadn't panicked as Teddy delved ever nearer their ugly secret, if one or more of them hadn't hired a bunch of sadistic butchers —then who the hell had?

Disbelief had given way to fury by the time she dialed up the Caduceus 21 net, typed in Teddy's log-in and password, and switched to his personal queue.

There were no files named "Teddy01" through "Teddy16."

It took a while, but Maggie finally heard an insistent buzz coming from the kitchen. She went in and picked up the house phone; the front desk was calling to say a messenger had just delivered a letter for her. Noticing that she was still in her bathrobe, Maggie asked for a porter to be sent up with it.

Five minutes later there was a knock on her door.

The plain white business-letter-sized envelope bore her name but no return address.

Inside it were a pair of three-and-a-half-inch floppy disks, one marked "PC" and the other "Mac," and three sheets of curly thermal fax paper on which the sending and receiving numbers had been snipped off.

Maggie glanced at the opening paragraph and slumped against the wall. My God, she thought, has the whole world gone mad?

Ms. Sepulveda:

I write you because you were cited in the October 16 Wall Street Journal *as the Marx Dillon & Neil partner overseeing a private placement for Caduceus 21 of Knoxville, Tennessee. My associates and I believe the company's lucrative network of transplant centers depends on black-market organs. Further, we have evidence strongly implicating Caduceus 21's exclusive OPA, a firm called MedEx, in the murder of Third World men and women for their organs.*

We also believe the offices of Marx Dillon are under extensive electronic surveillance. Specifically, the keystrokes of its computer system are being recorded and transmitted off-site. Your home computer of course cannot be hacked as long as it remains offline, but my associates feel your Internet access service may be vulnerable. You can therefore appreciate why we chose to contact you via hardcopy. (We have followed the news stories about your colleague's murder and assumed you would be in New York for the funeral.)

By now you must be wondering about the person making these off-the-wall allegations.

My name is Nguyen-Anh Dupree and I have been a physician with Médecins Sans Frontières since 30 July 1990. Proving my identity, character, and sanity won't be easy, but I'll give it my best shot.

First, identity. Perhaps the easiest way to prove I'm me is if you call the bank issuing my Master-Card at (800) 555–0199 and ask to check account activity. The customer service rep will ask several questions to verify cardholder identity. The answers to all possible questions:

*Account No.: 5410–5640–5575–4185, expiration date 10/31/99

*Name as it appears on the card: Nguyen-Anh Dupree

*DOB: 13 January 1964

*Billing address: c/o Frederick Alston Esq. / Alston Bensley Robeck / 221 Main Street, Suite 205 / Yazoo City, MS

*Social Security No.: 123–64–5754 (also the digits of my MS driver's license, valid until 01/13/01)

*Other cardholders on the account: None

*Mother's maiden name: Thieu

*Most recent charge: American Airlines, $389, incurred 8 November, Guatemala City

You can confirm my professional bona fides with my MSF regional director, Dr. Theo Periguey. He can be reached at either MSF headquarters in Brussels or his home outside the city of Louvain, Belgium (that telephone number is listed). My posting since 1 August 1997 has been a small village outside San Cristóbal de las Casas in Chiapas state, Mexico, and I have been on emergency leave since last Sunday, 8 November.

If I check out to your satisfaction, I hope you'll give us a chance to present our evidence.

The app on either enclosed floppy will take you to a secure Net site as well as automatically encrypt/decrypt all traffic from the site. Because your office links are definitely monitored and your home

*link might be, it'd be best if you used a line you
know to be clean.*

*Feel free to contact us at any hour—we'll be
watching the site 24 × 7 the next four days.*
Sincerely yours,
Nguyen-Anh Dupree

Only once had Maggie suffered a textbook case of
shock. Back in seventh grade in Tacoma, at the peak of
her tomboyhood, some ninth-grade boys had needed a
twelfth for a six-on-six game of touch football. The pass
was almost in her hands when that snot Billy Booth had
slammed into her from the blind side. Struggling up
through darkness toward the light, regaining consciousness to find herself drenched in ice-cold sweat, the after-
taste of bile—all the nauseating sensations were now
flooding back.

Get your shit together, she told herself sternly. Be
strong.

Maggie looked at the fax in her hand. Had it arrived
three days earlier, before Teddy's murder, would she have
thought it a sick joke and pitched it in the wastebasket?
Maybe, but it had arrived today. And whoever this Dupree was—true prophet, raving paranoid, even an industry dirty-trickster out to sabotage the Caduceus 21
placement—he would have had no way of knowing how
neatly his allegations dovetailed with Teddy's.

The first step: Track down Theo Periguey in Belgium
and Frederick Alston in Yazoo City. Maggie was reaching
for the phone when she suddenly pulled back her hand.
The fax warned that her modem transmissions from
home might be monitored. If someone could do that,
couldn't they also tap her phone? And then she thought
of the time she returned to the apartment to find the
notes secured by one of her refrigerator magnets scattered
on the kitchen floor. It was the night of the Toilet Bowl—
at which either Larry Marx or Rob Dillon had complained
about a mysterious crash of the firm's computer system.

Could the team of outside techies performing the reboot also have set up the keystroke surveillance mentioned in the fax?

Maggie wryly shook her head; she was starting to sound like Chicken Little.

Still, it would be safer to run her checks on this Dupree character from a pay phone. But there was another precaution she could take while home, an online search no one clickstreaming her would think out of the ordinary.

Changing quickly into sweater and jeans, Maggie went to her laptop and dialed up CompuServe. She clicked to the shareware forum, downloaded the latest update of the antivirus program F-PROT, and installed it on her hard drive. Maggie slotted the PC floppy from Dupree and scanned it. Only after F-PROT pronounced it clean did she drop the disk into her knapsack, along with two virgin floppies.

DETOURING around unplowed drifts was in Duane Strand's opinion a damn sight better than dodging suburban moms racing a minivanful of brats to meet Dad at the train station. The streets he briskly jogged had been emptied of traffic by the storm. Strand savored the Rice Krispies crunch of fresh snow compacting beneath his shoes, the sweat cascading down his torso, the view of Long Island at twilight across the darkening waters of the Sound. He had religiously logged eight miles a day for the past quarter-century, even when posted to the sweltering lowlands of Namibia in August or the snow-whipped mountains of Peshawar in February. Compared to those hellholes, this was a milk run.

In addition to controlling his weight, jogging afforded Strand a time-efficient way to stay current on several fields of interest. He once passed the miles with his Walkman pumping music. On returning Stateside to launch MedEx, though, he had come across a nonprofit organization that helped blind professionals by audiotaping for them articles from current technical and trade journals. Strand learned that enrolling MedEx as a corporate donor entitled him to borrowing privileges. Every week now, he received cassettes containing fresh news of the medical, aviation, and computer-security industries.

He had rounded the farthest point of his run, the cannons by the beach, and was on the homeward leg when he heard a beep above the voice on his earphones reading from *Aviation Week*. Strand pulled out his pager, checked the number displayed, and reversed his course for the pay phone a half-mile back.

Morris Tomczack picked up on the first ring.

"Yes, M.T.," Strand said.

"Duane, something's going down with the Sepulveda woman. She heads straight home after the memorial service. Next four hours, no calls in, one call out to an online service. Suddenly she leaves her apartment, ducks into a low-rent bar, and makes a beeline to the pay phone. Uses quarters instead of her calling card to make five calls, two of them ten, fifteen minutes each, and then she's on a subway downtown. We follow her to one of those Internet coffeehouses where twenty bucks an hour gets you online, the cappuccino's extra."

"She ever pull anything like this before?"

"Negative. The bitch has computers everywhere, even the summerhouse out on the Island. She needs a cyber-café like I need another notch on my belt."

Strand jogged in place to keep his legs warm, his breath frosting in thick white plumes. Finally he said, "What do you make of it?"

"It's never good when they break pattern."

"Agreed. How many men you got watching her?"

"Two shifts of three," Tomczack said.

"Tell 'em to look lively. Your guys manning the Marx Dillon node too. Especially those assholes—they pay attention, maybe Quereshi's not dead."

"We had no choice, Duane."

"You think I give a fuck you iced that Paki queen? What I do care about is the disruption it's caused. Look at C-Twenty-One—cops dropping by to ask questions, the funeral in New York. No one's done squat since Wednesday. They don't work, Marx Dillon makes no progress on their due diligence. We did not need this delay."

"I hear you, Duane."

Strand's legs were beginning to tighten in the cold so he hung up and retook to the road.

TWO hours after pushing through the doors of the Log Inn on Waverly Place, Maggie Sepulveda typed BYE, logged off, and slumped back in her chair. The sudden mental deceleration—from total engagement with Nguyen-Anh Dupree and his friends, Duchess and Data, to blank screen—had her reeling. Fragments of thoughts skittered across her brain like droplets of mercury, luminous but impossible to pin down. In her days as a computer-industry analyst Maggie had participated in her share of extended online sessions. None ever left her as wiped as this marathon on an outlaw board called NUROMNCR. Either Dupree & Co. were beyond the help of BuSpar, or the deal of her career was definitely about to go down the tubes.

"Hi. Had enough?"

"*No más*," Maggie agreed, looking up at the waitress.

"Wow, like you were awesomely into it," said the waitress, a bone-thin teenager with magenta-streaked hair, two rings through her right eyebrow, and a tastefully ripped Hole T-shirt. "Most people online that long, they're wanking on one of those role-playing games the poindexters play. You know—'Endor's praetorians have you surrounded, puny mortal,' and they're like, 'Whoa, do we use the Crystal Sword now or go into Changeling mode?' Hello? Like, talk to the hand?"

Maggie felt as if she had accidentally zapped to MTV after three martinis, but was willing to accept comic relief wherever she could find it. "Sounds more entertaining than my session," she said ruefully. "You guys serve food?"

The waitress pointed up to a board titled "Choice Bytes."

"How's the chili?"

"I'd go with the burger or the fish and chips."

"Fish and chips," Maggie said. "By the way, you do the Net?"

The waitress grinned. "More fun than a barrel o' funkies. Got my own home page. Here, visit sometime," she said, handing Maggie a business card:

HTTP://WWW.BRNXHISCI.EDU/
GRRRL__O'__MY__DREAMS

Maggie ejected the floppy on which she had captured the entire session with Dupree & Co. The line-by-line review would come later tonight, at home; for now, she just wanted to sort out her impressions of her correspondents, one of whom was no longer faceless.

Dupree had piped her a digitized passport photo of himself. If the grave-faced Asian-American wasn't who he said he was, the hoax was pretty cosmic; Maggie had gone through more than twenty dollars in quarters tracking down references in Belgium and Mississippi. No, Dupree seemed genuine. And his syntax, his vocabulary, even his pop-cultural references seemed consistent with that of a thirtysomething doctor who had been practicing outside the country since midway through the Bush Administration.

There were no photos of Duchess and Data, but Maggie had nevertheless gained a sense of them from their messages. They were younger than she and quite possibly not Caucasian, judging by certain of their locutions and phrases. They were also highly security-conscious; the first thing Duchess asked was whether Maggie had her back to a wall. She had typed NO, whereupon Duchess ordered her to log off and find a screen that couldn't be spied on before redialing them.

Finally, Duchess and Data were frighteningly skilled at manipulating the telecommunications universe. Data had constructed from scratch an ingenious telephonic version of a dead drop, a number in area code (212) that bounced to a voicemail box in Los Angeles without a trace. If circumstances compelled Maggie to use her easily monitored calling card, she could nonetheless leave a fifty-second message in the voicemail box from anywhere in the world without raising suspicion.

If she was trying to tease concrete images of Dupree, Duchess, and Data from the binary realm of cyberspace, Maggie thought, they must also be playing Sherlock on her. How had she come across to them?

When the waitress returned with the fish and chips, Maggie dug into her first meal since breakfast. As she ate, she reviewed the main charges laid out by Dupree & Co. Most of them concerned MedEx, and she was reserving judgment until she could see the files herself.

The most shocking revelation about Caduceus 21, though, seemed inarguable. Duchess and Data had hacked four C-21 affiliates with transplant centers and downloaded the past year's files. With these they had constructed a timeline showing the dates on which patients initially went on the waiting list for a new organ, as well as the dates on which they received them. There seemed to be a sinister pattern: When the number of waiting patients reached some kind of critical mass, lo and behold, a batch of harvested organs would providentially appear.

Dupree's friends had then laboriously cross-referenced these C-21 windfalls with CAB records of MedEx flights. In the hours preceding every such surge of transplants, the MedEx transshipment center at Dallas/Fort Worth Airport received flights that could ultimately be backtracked to places like Presidio, Texas; Prague, Czechoslovakia; Recife, Brazil; and Baguio, the Philippines. As

Duchess had tartly messaged, "Yo, like where did Bob from Brazil and Peter from the Philippines get the bright idea they should donate organs to Casper and his pals?"

Maggie had been sorely tempted to share Teddy's glyphgram with Dupree & Co., but in the end decided she should first check out the disks Teddy had pouched up from Knoxville.

Odd, she thought, how alone she felt at this moment. But in whom could she confide? Certainly not any of her firm's senior partners, not until she knew more details of a scandal that could cost Marx Dillon millions. Not Jill Unger, when the junior analyst was so distraught. Not someone from outside the industry, which ruled out her mom and her girlfriends. If she were still with Paul, would she use him as a sounding board? Probably not. Ironically, the one person she would trust in this situation was *el buscapleitos*, but she had divorced him, hadn't she?

Maggie checked her watch. The stores in Greenwich Village were still open, which meant she could get a start on the shopping list Dupree had given her. For some strange reason, he wanted her to arrive in Los Angeles in the guise of a snow bunny who had forgotten to deplane in Aspen.

S U N D A Y
N O V E M B E R   1 5

IN his home in Englewood Cliffs, New Jersey, Morris Tomczack kept the secure phone reserved for MedEx business in the den, which was off-limits to his family. This was to shield the kids from his temper. The one time he had lost it in front of them, after finding two car tires deflated by Halloween pranksters, his five-year-old daughter had burst into tears, shrieking, "Daddy's making Freddy Krueger eyes." After that, her nine-year-old brother was no longer allowed to rent *Nightmare on Elm Street* videos. This morning both kids would be scared witless just watching their father on the phone with the team keeping tabs on the Sepulveda woman; their report was twisting Tomczack's normally benign countenance into the mask of an angry stranger.

"What do you mean, she's getting in a cab with a suitcase?" he demanded. Sepulveda was ticketed to fly back to Knoxville with the rest of her team at dawn the following day, and nothing gleaned from the Marx Dillon nodes indicated any change in plans.

"She's getting in a cab with a suitcase, M.T. Looks like she's going skiing."

"Orange parka? And the suitcase with wheels—real big, comes up to her waist? The stuff she bought last night?"

"Affirmative. Plus a laptop."

"Okay. Stay on her. Her kind doesn't go Greyhound so it's an airport or a train station. Whatever the fuck she gets on, wherever the fuck she goes, one of you is aboard. You need a backup, get Feeney's ass out of bed."

"I roger that, M.T."

This was not good, Tomczack thought as he hung up. The Sepulveda woman had been acting strangely the last eighteen hours, and a career's worth of experience had taught him that humans were creatures of unbreakable habit, even under stress.

Back in the good old days of the Cold War, for instance, Tomczack had once found himself part of a team tagging the Soviet military attaché in Paris. Word was, Syrian strongman Hafez al-Assad badly needed arms to replace those lost to a Mossad strike that never made the news. It had been a complicated and at times comical assignment, for the attaché's KGB minders were also in the field. One day the target unexpectedly bolted into Galeries Lafayette, a Right Bank department store as chaotic, and as multi-entranced, as Bloomingdale's in Manhattan. Tomczack was about to join the others in haring through the store when he suddenly realized what day of the week it was and hurried to a café seven blocks away. Ten minutes later he was sitting at an outdoor table, pretending to read *Le Monde*, when the attaché strolled past and entered the apartment house where he visited his mistress every other Tuesday.

In the last five weeks, the Sepulveda woman had never gone near a cybercafé—why had she spent two hours in one last night? And the shopping expedition that followed—why had she suddenly needed a new ski outfit and an oversized suitcase? Sepulveda had taken her purchases home and stayed put the rest of the night. If the past was any guide, she should've spent it yakking with various girlfriends about her crappy love life. Instead, her only call was to a Famiglia Pizza to order a small bianco pie, extra ricotta. Equally out of character, she had let her machine answer all calls, not even picking up when one of her bosses and her mother were on the line. And now she was on the move without warning, apparently off on a trip for which she held no known reservation.

Something didn't compute, and Tomczack knew all too well that what didn't compute had a way of cleaning your clock.

Should he notify Duane Strand? Not yet; as he had been so forcibly reminded the previous day, Strand took unpleasant news better when it was sugar-coated with something positive, like a fully articulated response plan.

Tomczack returned to his computer and punched up the latest batch of reports from the Marx Dillon nodes in case there was something in them he had missed. There were two sets of reports. Transcripts of the phone taps, which had been given top priority, were running only four hours behind, a remarkable achievement by his motley squad of freelancers. Transcripts of the much more voluminous clickstreams from New York and Knoxville were running five days behind, not nearly up to Jefferson Leong's standards but still sufficient to have tipped them to that Quereshi guy. With the Sepulveda woman beginning to act squirrelly, Tomczack thought, it wouldn't hurt to turn around the clickstreams faster, at least until she fell back into line. He could put on more bodies—or summon up from Texas the best four-eyes that MedEx had.

Fifteen minutes later, the secure phone rang. Tomczack grabbed it and said, "Where are you now."

"Fifth and Fifty-second, outside her office. The cab's waiting, so I don't think she's going to be inside long."

"She use the revolving door or the night door on the left?"

"Revolving door, M.T."

The fact that the revolving door was unlocked meant many of the building's tenants came in on Sundays, which meant the security force would be at near-normal strength, which meant sending in one of his men would be dicey. Get a grip, Tomczack told himself; here he was, toying with extreme measures, and the Sepulveda woman hadn't even done anything yet. But the bitch sure was getting under his skin, and fast.

Thirty minutes after Sepulveda emerged from the building and got back in the cab, it became clear that she was headed for Kennedy International Airport.

Shortly after 10 A.M., Tomczack's secure phone rang again: "M.T., we're at American. There was a ticket waiting for her at the counter—she's on the ten-thirty to L.A."

"We have someone on that flight?" asked Tomczack.

"Affirmative. Stevie. There's still seats left. You want two of us should go?"

"Negative," Tomczack replied. "I'll set up something out there. Tell Stevie to call me half an hour before he lands so I can arrange his RV with the locals."

Tomczack punched his electronic Rolodex up on-screen and autodialed Jefferson Leong.

Four rings, and then a sleep-thickened voice murmured, "Hello?"

"Jefferson, this is M.T. One, there's a Marx Dillon banker name of Marguerite Sepulveda. Search her personal files in Knoxville and New York. I want a list of all friends, acquaintances, and associates in metro L.A.— names, addresses, phone numbers. You got two hours. Do I need to repeat myself?"

"No sir," replied Leong, who now sounded fully awake.

"Two, I want you here in New York by dinnertime. And Mrs. Leong's not to know her son's in town."

"But . . ."

Tomczack clicked HANG UP and punched up his list of specialists. Putting together a crew of six on five hours' notice, plus additional backups to check out the names Leong uncovered, meant a big hit on MedEx's slush fund. But hadn't Strand himself declared that to protect the Caduceus 21 placement, budget was not a consideration?

THE American Airlines 757 was over eastern Pennsylvania, slowly climbing to cruising altitude, when the pilot turned off the seat-belt sign. Maggie Sepulveda stood and walked toward the head of the cabin. Dupree had warned her that the people who had gotten inside Marx Dillon's net might also have the capability to scramble somebody aboard this flight. But no one followed her up the aisle so she went to the air-to-ground telephone, swiped her calling card through, and lifted the handset.

The number for the dead drop that Data had created, (212) 748-9454, was one digit away from that of the phone in her New York apartment.

Two rings, then the fingernail-down-a-blackboard squeal of a fax machine. The squeal would continue unless interrupted by the star-key button.

She counted to five and pressed *.

The squeal stopped. Speaking rapidly—she now had fifty-five seconds to complete her message—Maggie described her purchases of the previous evening. Then she pressed # for a fresh dial tone and punched her home number.

Two rings, and the sound of her own microchip-hollow voice: "Hi, this is Maggie. Wait for the beep and leave a message that may be as long as you wish." Three callers had: Rob Dillon and her mom last night, when she was home but under orders from Data to not pick up, and Dillon again an hour ago.

She waited through her boss's urgent plea to return his call, then slipped the handset back into its cradle.

Data had designed the dead drop to permit Maggie to use calling-card-only telephones like those found on commercial jets. Her long-distance carrier "rounded up" calls to the next full minute. As long as she disconnected from the dead drop within sixty seconds, anyone accessing her records and duplicating her calls would assume that in phoning home for messages, she had misdialed the first time and reached a dedicated fax line.

Maggie started back to her seat. She badly wanted to spend the long hours ahead poring over the disks in the packet she had grabbed that morning from Dawn Mambelli's desk. But as Duchess had rightly pointed out last night, computer screens were difficult to keep private in public. Maggie hadn't fitted her laptop with one of those snap-on privacy filters, so her seatmates would be able to easily read Teddy Quereshi's files, as would anyone walking up the aisle. Did she want to fly across the country scrunched up in one of the lavatories? Not really, so Maggie intercepted an attendant and said, "No lunch for me, okay? But please wake me half an hour before we land."

FROM the balcony of the Alamo Rent-a-Car depot on Aviation Way, Nguyen-Anh Dupree had a clear view through large plate-glass windows of the jitneys returning from their loops through Los Angeles International Airport, and of the travelers entering the building and joining the queue at the counter. Flights from New York were rarely early, but Dupree had been sipping bad vending-machine coffee since shortly after noon. His wait was almost over, for Esai Ayala, stationed at the American terminal, had just reported that Marguerite Sepulveda's flight was in.

Persuading Sepulveda to fly west had been a cinch compared to spiriting her away once she arrived.

For two reasons, the ticket had to be booked under her real name. Even before the destruction of TWA 800 in 1996, the threat of terrorism had caused the airlines to demand of passengers a photo ID. The Tres Equis document whiz could have whipped up a fake on the spot, but there hadn't been enough time to get it to her. More to the point, if she was in fact under surveillance in New York, and the bad guys trailed her to JFK, they would have six hours—the flying time to Los Angeles—to arrange a welcome wagon out here.

Dupree had apprised Sepulveda of that possibility during last night's epic online chat. This unseen woman of remarkable pluck and trust had merely messaged back, *I'm sure you'll figure out an escape from LAX.*

Which he and Duchess and Data had, though it took them half the night.

Dupree felt a vibration against his ribs and pulled out Data's flip-phone, which had been modified not to ring. He pressed ANSWER: "Yes, Esai."

"Yo, Doc, there be a sister wearing exactly what you say. Hurts my eyes just looking at her."

"Where are you?"

"Down in the baggage claim, waiting for my ride. You was also right about the other passengers. One of them, he waits by the carousel, pretending he don't be watching her. Grabbed a Polaroid of the chump without him knowing it. Anyway, he don't have no bags of his own, but soon as she gets her suitcase, he's following her out the door. And soon as she be inside the Alamo van, he's running over to a white Chevy that starts after the van."

"Thanks, Esai," Dupree said. "Did you get a make on the plates?"

"Only enough to see it be a rental or lease."

"Anyone else following her?"

"Nobody yet," Ayala replied. "But you tell me to set up this job, I put the backup out on Century, near the gas stations. Got to go past them to get out of LAX."

"I hear you, Esai."

"Yo, later, Doc, here's my ride. Call you when I get into position."

Dupree pocketed the phone and walked to the front of the building. Looking down at a white panel truck parked facing the depot, he ran both hands through his hair.

The panel truck's headlights flashed once, a signal all but invisible in the midday sun, and then its passenger-side door opened and a young woman climbed out.

Eight minutes later, an Alamo jitney pulled up. Esai was right; one of the women getting off wore an outfit gaudy enough to make Stevie Wonder wince. The lime-colored Gore-Tex baseball cap pulled low over her forehead, the fluorescent-orange parka, the rhinestone-studded leggings over white tights, and the black cowboy boots—all fit the descriptions left on Data's dead-drop tape, as did the oversized Samsonite with built-in wheels that she pulled into the depot.

While she stood in queue, Dupree received another call. Esai was now parked off Aviation, within sight of the Alamo lot—and the white Chevy that had tracked the jitney.

The woman finally reached the counter. Upon signing the rental agreement and accepting the keys, she headed not for the parking lot but for the escalator. As she rode up to the balcony, Dupree scanned the lobby below. No one was loitering by the doors, no one was suddenly breaking queue. Her tails had seen no need to follow their garishly dressed target inside, because her every move-ment was clearly visible through the building's large plate-glass windows.

Don't look around, Dupree thought, don't break script.

The woman didn't. Stepping off the escalator, she strode directly to the ladies' room, wheeling the suitcase behind her.

Four minutes later the ladies'-room door swung open again. The woman in the orange parka emerged, adjusted her lime-colored cap, and rode with her suitcase back down to the lobby. Dupree watched her continue out to the parking lot, wrestle the Samsonite into the trunk of a maroon Oldsmobile, and climb into the car. As she eased toward the exit, he took out the flip-phone and punched in Esai Ayala's number: "She's in a maroon Oldsmobile, Esai, turning south onto Aviation . . . right now."

"Got her, Doc. White Chevy be starting up . . . And yeah, some chump facing north on Aviation, he be making a U-ee. *Dos*, just like we figure."

"Thanks, Esai. Watch over her, now."

"No problem, Doc. Maybe tonight, she be wanting to show her 'preciation for how good we protected her, know what I mean? Not much happening upstairs with this one, but downstairs? *Ay caramba.*"

Dupree smiled. Just about every male in South-Central had evil designs on the young woman behind the wheel of the maroon Oldsmobile. Data had asked Lourdes to play decoy, confident she would agree; the actress was still trying to atone for introducing some industry creep to Javier.

After allowing Lourdes and her two tails—plus three carloads of Tres Equis muscle—ample time to reach the I-405, Dupree went over to the ladies' room and gently tapped on the door five times: shave-and-a-haircut.

Two-bits, came the instant response. The door inched open to reveal a woman dressed in a sweater, jeans, and steel-toed Doc Martens. She was gamely trying to hide her tension, but her eyes were as alert as a fighter pilot's.

"Nguyen-Anh Dupree," he said, caught off-guard by her unself-conscious good looks.

"Maggie Sepulveda," she replied, returning his handshake.

"Where are your bags?"

"You're looking at 'em," she said, hoisting her knapsack and laptop.

"And I thought I traveled light."

She shrugged. "Plenty of stores in L.A., in case I need something."

Maggie was surprised by Dupree's Deep South drawl;

the words in his letter, and on-screen at the cybercafé, had contained no telltale antebellum floridities. He was also decidedly less formal in person, she thought, as well as taller and more athletic than his passport mug shot had suggested. En route to the escalator she said, "Would you pronounce your first name for me again?"

"Nguyen. Think of it as spelled n-y-w-i-n, and slur the first three letters."

"Nguyen."

"You nailed it," he said.

"You prefer Nguyen or Nguyen-Anh?"

"Either's good. Or Dupree, or Doc, which is what Duchess and Data call me."

"Tell me, Nguyen-Anh, was this elaborate runaround necessary?"

He nodded. "One tail aboard your flight, two cars waiting here."

Maggie felt herself being swept back into that tunnel-vision zone. This was not some thriller writer's invention or a new virtual-reality game; persons unknown, perhaps the very ones who murdered Teddy Quereshi, now had her between the crosshairs. And then she thought to ask, "What's going to happen when they find out that's not me they're following? The nice young gal I switched clothes with back in there—isn't she in danger?"

Dupree shook his head. "Lourdes'll be fine. It's good of you to ask, but the escape route's solid. Drive to the Four Seasons, valet-park the car, check in as Marguerite Sepulveda. Up in the room she changes back into her own clothes. Leave the wig and suitcase behind, then it's back out front and into a cab. Those assholes watching her are in for a bad night. They say the temperature's dropping into the low forties."

Maggie allowed herself a small smile, buoyed by this undoctorly doctor's breezy confidence, by his refreshingly rude way of looking at things.

Dupree led her out of the depot to the white panel

truck. As he opened the door he said, "Maggie, meet Large Quintanilla. Large, Maggie Sepulveda."

"Pleasure, ma'am. Welcome to L.A."

"Thanks," Maggie said, nodding to the man-mountain behind the wheel.

Dupree climbed in behind her. "Mind if I smoke?"

She arched an eyebrow. "Go ahead. It's your life."

He rolled down the window and lit a cigarette.

Maggie shook her head in wonderment. "Strip poker in the ladies' room, wild-goose chases up and down the freeway, a doctor who's a nicotine fiend. Somehow, I don't think I'm in Kansas anymore."

"For sure," Dupree agreed. "And before we hit the yellow brick road, there's some things you ought to know about where we're going and about Data's brother, Javier."

NIGHT had fallen by the time Phillipa Walker turned into the driveway of the Tejada compound in South-Central. She was drained from ten hours at a MorpHaus workstation helping short-stroke the commercial for that new direct-TV service. The *2001* project—known to all as The Ad From Hell—was now passable, though just; to her eyes the hair on the digital apes still looked about as natural as Burt Reynolds's rug.

That morning Walker had been torn between spending the day at the office or here with Doc and Nacio and the newly arrived Marguerite Sepulveda. Dupree had solved that dilemma by saying the banker would need the afternoon to absorb the volumes of information she and Nacio had gathered on MedEx and Caduceus 21. He guessed the heavy lifting wouldn't start until after dinner.

Walker waved to the Tres Equis guards, waited for the gates to swing open, and parked her Miata.

Her nose led her directly to Nacio, who was tending a large Weber grill set up in the courtyard behind Javier's house.

"Yo, Nacio," she said, looking approvingly at the rows of salmon steaks sizzling over the charcoal. "Looks yummy. New dish for *la familia*, no?"

"Yup. Doc suggested it. Javier be dubious and asks *Abuela* Felicia. She says, '*¿Porqué no?*'"

Walker hesitated, then said, "Well? What's Sepulveda like?"

"You'll see," he replied enigmatically, flipping a steak. "Doc's in the kitchen. Tell him I got, like, another five minutes, tops."

Walker went into Javier's kitchen to find Dupree standing over a large pot.

"Yo, Doc, smells great. What is it?"

"Risotto with wild mushrooms."

"What's with all this Galloping Gourmet stuff?"

He laughed. "Ever sit around watching someone else work? They get antsy, you go nuts. Maggie wasn't ten minutes with the material when she evicted us."

"So what's she like besides pushy?"

"Real smart," he replied. "Anyway, Data and I killed an hour at a drugstore—damn near filled up that extra bag I brought—and then we went to the Farmer's Market. The salmon happened to look terrific. Speaking of which, did Data say how it's coming?"

"Five minutes, tops."

Dupree quickly emptied the last of a pot of chicken broth into the risotto, gave the mixture a thorough stir, then went to the intercom panel to summon three generations of Tejadas to dinner.

The sudden noise startled Maggie out of her deep concentration. She looked around Nacio's study for the source of the buzz, saw a wall-mounted speaker over the desk, and pressed LISTEN.

"Dupree here. Dinner's on."

"Oh," she said. "Okay."

"Downstairs, out the back, across the courtyard. Data'll be waiting for you."

Maggie happened to glance down at the snapshot on

Data's desk, a Polaroid taken hours earlier at LAX by a Tres Equis confederate, and was suddenly overcome by the unreality of the past four days. Could she ever have anticipated, standing in the OR of White River General Hospital, that she would receive a shocking call from Jill Unger? Or that she would soon be crisscrossing the continent in pursuit of Teddy Quereshi's killers? Or that she would be trailed from New York by the total stranger pictured in the Polaroid? Or that she would be spirited to the fortified compound of a South-Central ganglord? Or that she would be confronted by material that showed Caduceus 21 growing rich on fraud and MedEx on the murder of helpless Third Worlders?

Maggie looked at her worksheet. Caduceus 21's fiscal irregularities were laid out in damning detail in the files on Teddy Quereshi's disks.

MedEx's crimes, though, were not as self-evident in the files hacked by Duchess and Data. As Data explained the problem, it was only safe to log in with Jefferson Leong's password during the predawn hours, while the archnerd slept. Despite that serious handicap, he and Duchess had managed to begin copying files of obvious interest. There were many more to transfer, as well as several restricted sectors to crack and explore, but that would take time—unless Code Boy could be pushed in front of a bus or something.

Still, the MedEx data reviewed by Maggie meshed with Teddy's data in disturbing ways that cried out for further investigation. Yet should she share Teddy's findings with Dupree and his friends? Were an altruistic doctor and two young computer whizzes the right allies for the task that lay ahead? That was the question she had to resolve by the end of dinner.

Maggie considered arming her laptop's security software, decided against it, and headed downstairs.

Phillipa Walker was busy serving the risotto when she heard Nacio enter the dining room and say, "Everybody, this is Maggie Sepulveda."

She turned and felt her smile freeze, the blood drain from her face, the bowl of risotto start to slip through fingers grown suddenly cold. Walker clutched the bowl, hard. Online, Sepulveda had come across as the type of no-nonsense MBA who wore her hair in a steel bun and denied herself orgasms. Even dressed down, the off-the-hook girl in the doorway could suit up as a Lakerette.

Walker's eyes reflexively darted to Dupree. He glanced up to acknowledge the banker, then returned his attention to the salmon he was serving. Sepulveda had to be his type, Walker thought; she was every man's type. How had Doc described her? "Real smart"? Which was like singling out Denzel Washington for his penmanship.

Nacio gestured toward her: "Phillipa Walker, aka Leepi, aka Duchess."

"Hi, Duchess," Maggie said with a friendly little wave. Walker seemed far more stylish, far less brash than her on-screen persona. "So neat to finally meet you in person."

"Yeah, uh, likewise." Walker became aware of the peculiar look Javier was shooting her. Fighting back the swift sting of jealousy, she said, "Move aside, Juanito, this bowl be *muy caliente* and I don't want to burn you."

Nacio continued with the introductions—grandparents, brother Javier and his wife, in-laws, kids—and then everyone was seated around the immense table and Javier was raising a glass to salute the newcomer. "I no have to say this to Leepi and Doc, they be bros," he said. "You I don't meet until today. Maggie, your good fortunes, they are our good fortunes, and your troubles are our troubles. ¿*Comprende?*" When she nodded he added, "Okay, so how come a girl like you is a Sepulveda?"

As Javier had broken the social ice, so it fell to *Abuela* Felicia to crack the culinary tension. Most of the Tejada clan was still politely but suspiciously prodding Dupree's dishes with their forks when she sampled the mustard-coated salmon and the wild mushroom risotto and said, "*Este manjar es para el rey*"—fit for a king.

Maggie, who could follow most of the table conversation, suddenly felt as if she had been here before. Then she understood why: This dinner was a mirror image of the one in *Annie Hall*, where Woody Allen, portraying his usual Jewish nebbish, finds himself breaking bread with Diane Keaton's high Wasp family. Tonight Maggie was the fish out of water, the token Wasp.

After the flan and *café con leche*, Javier's kids began to clear the dishes.

Nacio hooked a bottle of wine and led the others back across the courtyard to his house. Up in the study Dupree cracked a window, took a seat next to it, and lit a cigarette. Walker, who had been uncharacteristically subdued over dinner, quietly curled herself up on one end of the couch. Nacio went around to refill the wineglasses, then set down his cane and slid behind his desk.

Maggie stared at her glass for a few moments, aware that the others were all watching her. Since there had been no talk at the table about the reason for her trip west, they had no idea whether she was willing to throw in with them. The downside of committing to Dupree and Duchess and Data? Despite the favorable impressions she had gained of them over dinner, they were still essentially strangers to her. The upside? Maggie knew that tackling Caduceus 21 and MedEx was not a solo mission; she would need capable allies.

She sipped her wine, then said, "You guys think we could work as a team?"

They exchanged glances, then nodded as one.

So she told them about Teddy's fatal discovery. She told them about Caduceus 21 and its three surviving cofounders. She told them about her meeting with the head of MedEx, Duane Strand. The process took time, for the others had to fit this new information with what they already knew.

And then Maggie remembered something that had been nagging her for weeks: "A while back, I accidentally saw a memo I wasn't meant to. It was from Reifsnyder and it described the progress of our background investigation. By 'our,' I mean Marx Dillon. That's proprietary information, but Reifsnyder was passing it to someone I'd never heard of, someone not on any C-Twenty-One personnel list. Could you guys scan the databases for a Century Chisholm?"

Tejada nodded and jotted down the name.

Finally, Maggie told them what she thought their next move should be.

Despite a half hour of spirited discussion, neither Dupree nor Walker nor Tejada could come up with a better plan, so they began to systematically weed the data currently in their possession. To persuade some law-enforcement agency to tackle MedEx and Caduceus 21, they needed to go in with a single folder of compelling documents, not an unfiltered core dump.

Shortly after 1 A.M. Maggie, her body clock still set to East Coast time, stifled a yawn. Then she turned to Walker and said, "By the way, Duchess, do you know someone who could do my hair first thing in the morning?"

Walker leaned back to inspect the pricey cut from Mr. Damian, still stylish after a month. "Sure, but what for? You look fine to me."

"Since bad guys are running around L.A. looking for me, might as well get myself a fresh look."

M O N D A Y
N O V E M B E R 1 6

THE sightseeing-bus guides who entertained tourists
with tales of the Hollywood institutions they were
passing—the studio gates Clark Gable once drove
through, the mansion Barbra Streisand called home, the
Wilshire Boulevard ziggurat built by a self-aggrandizing
agency—rarely mentioned Century City. Too bad, because this outcrop of sterile high-rises harbored many of
the backroomers who were the industry's true deal-
makers and -breakers.

As surely as the teenaged Julia Jean Mildred Frances
Turner had not been discovered sipping a Coke at
Schwab's by the talent scout who rechristened her
"Lana," so multimillion-dollar deals were not sealed over
salades niçoises and San Pellegrino at Le Dome and Mor-
ton's. Luncheon promises were just so much palaver, an
unsigned promissory note until the backroomers, the en-
tertainment lawyers and accountants, had renegotiated
every boilerplate clause and tacked on a piratical profit-
participation rider.

Nguyen-Anh Dupree, lacking an Armani suit and Porsche Carrera, ventured into Century City in another fashion that guaranteed anonymity: dressed in a courier's tan jumpsuit and riding in a white panel truck whose sides bore the freshly lettered logo CITY OF ANGELS RAPID DELIVERY.

Large Quintanilla wheeled the vehicle into the garage beneath 2001 Avenue of the Stars and parked in one of the short-term spaces set aside for messengers.

Dupree hopped out, slung a canvas pouch over one shoulder, and took the elevator up to the nineteenth floor.

The reception area of the law firm was white-rug plush yet curiously Spartan, as if its clients never had to wait long. Dupree handed an envelope to the haughty young woman behind the desk, explained that he had been instructed to wait for a reply, and took a seat.

Sebastian Sepulveda was in the midst of a four-way, two-continent call when he heard a soft tap on his door. He looked up in annoyance as his secretary slipped into the large corner office. She knew that he needed to iron out the last kinks in a three-picture deal before his eleven-o'clock with the studio out in the Valley. She also knew that when he was this hard up against a deadline, "no calls" meant no calls unless an A-list client had been booked on a felony or his own family hurt in an accident.

The voices on the speakerphone were debating whether to ask for an escalator tied to Southeast Asian gross receipts, so he motioned his secretary forward.

She handed him an envelope, along with a slip on which she had scribbled, *I recognized the handwriting.*

So did Sepulveda, instantly tearing open the envelope.

Buzzie—
I'm in L.A., way over my head in the kind of conspiracy I thought existed only in the fertile imagination of your screenwriter clients. I was followed out here from NY but am currently safe

and in urgent need of advice. If you're willing to
help, the man who delivered this note will bring
you to me. His name is Nguyen-Anh Dupree.
Thnx,
MKS

Sepulveda lowered the note, motioned his secretary to
stay, and stared out the windows for several moments.
Then he turned and leaned over the speakerphone:
"Guys, something's come up. I'm going to have to get
back to you." Punching OFF, he said to his secretary, "The
guy who brought this is out front?"

She nodded.

He picked up a zapper, flicked on his TV, and switched
to the feed from the securitycam in the lobby of Peterson
Sepulveda Watt. "Sure as hell doesn't look like a messenger, even with that jumpsuit," he said, studying an Asian
man in his mid-thirties.

"He doesn't talk like one either, Buzzie. When I saw
the note was from Maggie, I decided I'd better interrupt
you."

"You did right, Katie. Would you get the guy and bring
him in?"

Three minutes later Katie returned with Dupree, then
excused herself and closed the door behind her.

Dupree took in the luxurious office at a glance, then
focused on the man standing in front of his desk with
arms crossed, eyeing his visitor with undisguised suspicion. As Maggie had hinted, Buzzie was some piece of
work: rugged features, two-hundred-dollar haircut, wardrobe courtesy Savile Row rather than Rodeo Drive.

Finally Buzzie broke the silence: "What do you do in
real life?"

"I run a clinic in Mexico for Doctors Without Borders."

Buzzie digested that fact, which he found no more in-
congruous than Dupree's drawl, then said, "Okay, what's
this all about."

"Maggie should be the one to tell you," Dupree said.

"Look, friend, Mags isn't big on practical jokes, but something here's not sitting right. A guy in a Lawn Boy outfit who says he's a doctor shows up with a note out of a cheap mystery?" He unfolded the sheet of paper and read, " *'If you're willing to help, the man who delivered this note will bring you to me'*? Unh-unh. Not nearly good enough."

"Will talking to her help?" asked Dupree.

"It's a start." Buzzie reached for the phone. "What's her number?"

"No, let's use mine." Dupree took one of Data's portable scrambler phones from his pouch, turned his back to shield the number he was punching in, then handed over the unit.

One ring, a slight pause, followed by a guarded "Hello?"

"Hey, Mags," Buzzie said, relieved this wasn't a hoax, yet at the same time beginning to worry that his first wife's note might not be as outlandish as it seemed. "If we hadn't done marriage already, I'd call this a cute meet. Sounds like you're in Weird City."

"Tell me about it."

"What's with the bogus messenger and the James Bond phone? You could've just come over here yourself."

"I don't know that I could without drawing a crowd," Maggie replied. "Let me run it down real quick for you— my chief accountant on this placement I'm doing digs up an absolute deal-breaker and winds up dead. That's last Wednesday. My trip out here yesterday's booked at the last possible minute but there's one watcher on the flight and two carloads more waiting for me at the airport. Thanks to Nguyen-Anh and some friends, we lose them.

"Put yourself in the bad guys' shoes, Buzzie. If you wanted to find me again, wouldn't you be staking out the L.A. entries in my Rolodex? Starting with my ex-husband, the hotshot lawyer?"

"Okay okay, you've got my attention. Who's tailing you?"

"Good question," she said. "There's two sets of suspects. It's all in the material we want you to see."

"Whoa," he protested. "Last time I looked, I didn't own an LAPD badge."

"This thing is way beyond a nine-one-one call. We need sophisticated legal advice." Maggie hesitated, then added, "Remember what you wrote in that letter? After the divorce, after I moved to New York?"

Anyplace, anytime, anything, he recalled; a painless offer to make a woman who asked favors about as often as she botched a business deal. But here she was, asking. "Yes."

"If the offer still stands, I'm accepting."

Buzzie's eyes fell on the framed photograph atop his desk, of a sitcom star popular in the mid-1990s proudly posing with their infant daughter in front of Mangia Tower in Siena's Piazza del Campo. Those two were reason enough to give Maggie's troubles a wide berth.

And then he thought about the complex story behind the photograph. It had been taken on his family's most recent summer vacation. Though his wife ended up enjoying it immensely, the destination had perplexed her. Why did he know his way around Tuscany so well? Buzzie kept few secrets from Jen, but he never did get around to answering that question. After several more moments of indecision he sighed to himself and said to Maggie, "I'll come look at your material. If I see a course of action, I'll suggest it. That's all I'm promising."

"Understood, Buzzie. Thanks."

He handed the scrambler unit back to Dupree, then raised his secretary on the intercom: "Katie, call the guys I just hung up on, I'll get back to them. Call Mike, push my eleven o'clock to Wednesday, any time's good. Make nice for giving him short notice, some personal emergency's come up, yadda-yadda. I'm out of here until I don't know when, but anyone calls, I'm in conference and can't be disturbed."

Buzzie was shrugging into his jacket when he thought to ask Dupree, "How the hell does a pro bono doctor in Mexico hook up with Mags?"

Dupree smiled. "I saw her name in a newspaper and wrote."

THERE was no more secure meeting place in Los Angeles than the Tejada compound in South-Central, but taking Buzzie there would have inevitably led to questions that needn't be raised. So it was that Large Quintanilla drove due west from Century City, one eye glued to the rearview. Traffic was light, perfect for spotting tails. He saw none.

On reaching the Pacific, he turned south. Two Tres Equis members were stationed on Ocean Avenue at the foot of the bridge to the Santa Monica Pier. Shortly after 10 A.M. on a mid-November weekday, the pier's only visitors were the rare off-season tourists and elderly locals and inner-city Angelenos out for a morning of fishing. The lookouts would report by walkie-talkie if any cars filled with unfriendly looking strangers followed Quintanilla across the bridge.

The pier's parking lot was to the left, just before the start of the boardwalk. As the white panel truck entered it, one vehicle in a cluster at the far end started up and drove away. Quintanilla eased into the just-vacated slot.

"All the cars around us belong to friends," Nguyen-Anh Dupree said, sliding back the panel truck's side door.

At that moment the door of the Buick sedan parked alongside also opened.

Maggie, knapsack in hand, climbed out of Ignacio Tejada's geezermobile and into the truck.

"We've got to stop meeting like this," Buzzie muttered.

"Hi, stranger." Maggie laughed, returning his hug.

What was it Yogi Berra had said—it's déjà vu all over again? Funny how past paths had a way of recrossing, she thought, proving her mother's contention that it never hurt to remain civil, even after a divorce. When had she last seen Buzzie? It must have been the dinner in New York in 1996, when he told her of the birth of his daughter, because she remembered mailing out a teddy bear.

Buzzie made a show of studying his ex's fresh buzz cut. Finally he said, "You teeing it up at the Dinah Shore, Mags?"

She blushed and self-consciously ran a hand through the half-inch bristles that Duchess's haircutter had left behind.

"Yo, call when you be done," Large Quintanilla said as he opened the driver's door. "Want Nacio's thingamajig on?"

Dupree nodded.

Quintanilla reached over to a cylinder mounted on the dashboard, flipped a switch, then stepped out; the panel truck rocked as it resettled on its springs.

"What the hell's that?" asked Buzzie, gesturing at the cylinder. "Sharper Image's latest air freshener?"

"White-noise generator," Maggie said.

He skeptically cocked his eyebrows, then said, "How's Helen?"

"Very well, thank you. Your folks?"

"As ever. Know what Pop said when Rachel was born? 'You and Jen are going to have more kids, right?' The old goat wants us to keep going until we give him a grandson."

A smile tugged at the corners of Maggie's mouth. "I should send Manny an article I just read about what determines gender. It's not your fault you've got weak sperm."

"Ain't she a pistol?" said Buzzie to Dupree. "Okay, kids, so far this morning you've pissed on a forty-million-dollar deal, shanghaied me to the White Trash Riviera, locked me in a truck with Victor/Victoria here and a gizmo that's going to guarantee no male issue. Interesting? Sure. But am I having fun? Not exactly."

Maggie wordlessly took from her knapsack a folder containing printouts of selected files from the Caduceus 21 and MedEx nets and handed it to him.

Shortly before noon Buzzie excused himself from the panel truck and slowly strolled to the end of the pier. After studying the material, he knew that Maggie's note had it right: she was in way over her head. No question the gay accountant had been whacked, no question which company ordered it. The Hollywood types he dealt with were figurative sharks who liked to brag about spilling blood but fainted if they actually saw the stuff. The Caduceus 21 types lived higher up the food chain but were at best remora, the groupies that clung to sharks. Which left the MedEx types, who sounded like the genuine article.

His every instinct told him to walk away from Maggie's mess. But Buzzie Sepulveda, notorious in the industry for his lack of guilt buds, had never completely gotten over personally screwing up his first marriage. And yet Maggie had saved his life by sticking around, even after her love had soured, to hand-hold him through rehab. Out at the tip of Santa Monica Pier, where white-haired retirees and welfare recipients stood alongside one another casting for dinner, Buzzie headed for a pay phone, fishing his pockets for quarters.

LOS Angeles did not lack for luxe hotels: the Bel-Air, the Beverly Hills, the Four Seasons, the Peninsula, the Bonaventure downtown. The Chateau Marmont, an eccentric neo-Gothic heap atop a bluff overlooking Sunset Boulevard, lacked many amenities yet commanded a loyal celebrity following. That popularity was due in part to the unusual degree of privacy offered by its bungalows. Here trysted industry icons like Swanson and Joe Kennedy, Gable and Lombard, Bogie and Bacall; here ebbed away the life of an overdosed John Belushi. Set on the highest part of the property, each bungalow had a small front lawn screened by hedges and, better yet, a rear door to a private gate leading to Marmont Drive, a lightly trafficked road that curled up from Sunset.

On ascertaining that one of the bungalows was available, Buzzie had booked it under Dupree's name.

The two of them and Maggie had arrived an hour earlier. On the way from Santa Monica they had stopped at a deli for a platter of sandwiches and at a package store for beer and wine, one of Chateau Marmont's idiosyncrasies being its quaint notion of room service.

At 2:30 P.M. sharp there was a firm knock on the rear door by someone using the private Marmont Drive gate.

Buzzie answered it and returned to the living room accompanied by a man in his early forties whose bland countenance was dominated by eyes that were anything but.

"Anson," said Maggie, rising from the couch to hug the newcomer. "It's been too long."

"Sure has, Maggie," he replied. "Chic haircut. You've never looked better, which doesn't reflect well on old Buzzie here."

When Buzzie accepted the offer of the Los Angeles law firm recruiting him out of Harvard, Anson Horton was already an associate there. The two had grown close despite a pronounced difference in career goals. Buzzie went on to cofound his own firm and become a noted counselor to the stars; Horton went into public service. But their mutual respect must not have waned, thought Maggie, for Horton had agreed to this highly unorthodox meeting even though he was now an Assistant United States Attorney, Criminal Division, Central District, Los Angeles.

She turned and introduced him to Dupree.

"Quaint place," Horton said, glancing about; his knowledge of local hotels was confined to the ballrooms where political fund-raisers were staged. "And that's a nice cabernet you've got going there. Am I going to need some?"

Buzzie nodded and reached for the bottle.

Horton accepted the glass, rolled the tiniest of sips around in his mouth, and tilted his head in approval. Then, fixing his gaze on Dupree, the only person in the room he had not known for almost a decade, he said, "This meeting is not taking place. Agreed?"

Everyone nodded.

"Good. Now then, Buzzie said there are some things I should see."

Maggie studied Horton closely. Actually, Buzzie had said there were some things the prosecutor should know, not should see. Curious about the discrepancy, she said, "Would you like a heads-up on our material?"

"It's been my experience that the facts speak for themselves."

Surprised, Maggie looked at Buzzie, whose eyes flicked to the folder on the coffee table. She hesitated, then slid the folder toward Horton. "Okay, here are the facts. Feel free to ask us questions—Nguyen-Anh and I are pretty up to speed on the material."

"Thank you, Maggie, but that won't be necessary. Is there a bedroom down that corridor?"

"Actually, there's two back there," she replied, puzzled.

"If you'll excuse me?" Horton stood, hefted the folder in his hand, and said, "I shouldn't be more than forty-five minutes."

When the door to the master bedroom closed behind him, Maggie said, "Buzzie, what the hell's going on?"

"He's trying to inoculate himself."

"Against what?" asked Dupree.

"You don't just call up a federal prosecutor and say, 'Boy, do I have some choice shit you can nail some major crud with, let's meet,' " Buzzie replied. "Problem is provenance. Two of us are known to Anson, which helps, but none of us is a government agent, which doesn't. Think he needed a couple of hours to find his way here from downtown? He was busy trawling the Justice net for dirt on Caduceus Twenty-One, on MedEx, on Mags and me."

"I guess we passed," Maggie said. "But why didn't he want any preamble?"

"Who needs backstory when you can cut to the chase?"

Maggie stood, drifted over to the front door, and opened it. The sun was shining, the temperature in the low sixties. It was a far cry from New York, where that eyesore orange parka was necessary yesterday morning. A cold snap had left the city buried in last week's snow, and according to a radio report she'd heard on the drive over from Santa Monica, another major blizzard was fast approaching. Take advantage of the balmy weather while you can, she thought.

Dupree watched Maggie step out onto the small front lawn in front of the bungalow. He took out a cigarette, flicked his Zippo, then flicked it again; the flint was sparking but the wick refused to catch. Thinking ruefully of the new can of lighter fluid back at the Tejada compound, he went to the wet bar and found a pack of matches. Dupree lit his cigarette, saw that Buzzie's wineglass and his own were nearly empty, and carried the bottle back to refill both.

An hour later, Anson Horton emerged from the master bedroom, reclaimed his seat, placed the folder back on the coffee table, and squared its edges. He looked wistfully at the wine remaining in his glass, then said, "Maggie, Nguyen-Anh, I'm not going to pretend that what you've shown me isn't, how should I put it, isn't without interest. However, it would be inappropriate for me to comment further at this time. If you'll both agree to sit tight for several days, I promise to make some inquiries."

Maggie, unable to contain her dismay, said, "Anson, are you telling us we should call *60 Minutes*?"

Horton grimaced, as if he had been served a gamy oyster. "In America, the press is always an option. But I submit the sun has set on the kind of journalism that gave us the Pentagon Papers and Watergate. Wasn't it *60 Minutes* that self-censored a negative story on the tobacco industry? And ABC that settled a suit by retracting a true statement, namely that cigarette makers add nicotine during the manufacturing process? That's small potatoes next to what you're alleging. If the network newsrooms are now run by lawyers, as they seem to be, do you seriously believe they're going to take on a well-regarded health-care company?"

"Point taken," she said reluctantly. "How many days is 'several'?"

"No later than Friday."

Maggie exchanged glances with Dupree, then looked at Buzzie, who nodded with his eyes. She sighed. "Okay, Anson, we'll keep the lid on until then."

"How might I get in touch with you?"

Dupree said, "Through Mr. Sepulveda, if that's okay with him."

Buzzie looked none too thrilled but shrugged his assent.

"Fine," Horton said, standing. "We'll speak before the week's out."

Buzzie walked the prosecutor to the back door, closed it behind him, then turned. "You guys think you struck out, but I'd say you hit a gapper—two bases for sure, maybe more."

"So why isn't anybody out of their seats and cheering?" said Maggie.

"Because this isn't some stupid two-hour courtroom melodrama. Did Horton say your story sounds like Ralph Nader detoxing at Betty Ford? Did he say these documents are for shit?"

"No, but . . ."

"He's got three problems," Buzzie said. "Withdraw that, make it four.

"Yes, the Caduceus stuff shows they're cooking the books to gain a competitive advantage, but unless they're also cheating the IRS or defrauding the public, it isn't a federal case.

"Two, the MedEx stuff's pretty sketchy. I know I sure had to work hard to make the linkages back in that van. You go through the data and want to see a conspiracy, there it is. But where's the hard proof? And how do you go about getting it? If the feds do what you guys did, hack a private network, even I could get the case tossed—and I haven't done criminal work in ten years."

Buzzie gestured to the folder. "Three, nothing in there remotely suggests anything improper occurred within Horton's jurisdiction.

"Which leads me to his fourth concern—what's in it for him? Justice is as full of turf wars as the studios and the networks and, for that matter, any major corporation. Why should Horton knock himself out on something that can only bring credit to another office?

"Luckily, the guy isn't a glory dog. You really fucked his week, Mags. Horton didn't know it before he walked in here, but he's spending from here to Friday listening to the DOJ grapevine, making discreet calls to this district and that district. This isn't a case he himself can make, but he's going to find you a venue and a prosecutor who can."

"You mean I shouldn't have made that crack about *60 Minutes*?"

Buzzie grinned. "That little rise you needled out of him? Same as anyone else going ballistic. You could've been a contender in the courtroom, Mags. You could've been another Marcia Clark."

"Gee, thanks."

"No, really," Buzzie said. "Going eyeball-to-eyeball, exactly when you plop a pile of shit on the table is usually more important than the shit itself. You don't stick Anson, maybe this doesn't go to the tippy-top of his to-do list. You stick him, he's like, how about the end of the week? Look, all he's asking you to do is cool it for four days. Anybody have a problem with that?"

Dupree looked away and slowly shook his head.

"I do," Maggie said. "Two problems.

"The transplant timeline that Duch . . . that our associates drew up shows that when the C-Twenty-One wait-list gets deep enough, MedEx goes out and kills. In case you didn't notice, Buzzie, it's about time for another safari. The faster we put the hammer to C-Twenty-One, the faster we cancel Duane Strand's act.

"More selfishly, I got a small slice of Marx Dillon when I made partner. Gives me a share of the profits—and the risks. Parse this, Buzzie: The lead partner on a half-billion-dollar deal has been AWOL for six hours already. Say I continue to let this slide and say the C-Twenty-One placement blows sky-high because I knowingly failed to sound a warning. Are we talking major lawsuits or what? And it won't be just my ass on the line, it'll also be my assets."

"Fair enough," Buzzie said. "So call them. Though I'm not sure exactly how you're going to break the bad news —'Ooopsy, deal's off, guys, fill you in when I see you'?"

Maggie made herself set down her wineglass so she wouldn't hurl it at her ex-husband's head. Damn it, she thought, after all this time he could still infuriate her with a certain tone of voice, a few well-chosen words. And then she realized there was a purpose behind Buzzie's sarcasm: to provoke her into turning half-baked wish into attainable reality. She picked up the glass again and said, "No, they need to see these documents ASAP."

"Agreed," Buzzie said. "Last I heard, FedEx's still in business."

"Not good enough. Look, suppose you had the deal of the decade pending. Suppose something like this came sailing over the transom. Sufficient in and of itself to make you scrub the deal? I don't think so."

Buzzie scowled, intuitively sensing where this conversation was heading.

"The firm stands to make ten million on this placement," she continued. "Even more important, the account gives us the credibility we've never had. The financial press has quoted the senior partners more times this past month than in the last three years. Want to know how desperate the big funds are for a piece of C-Twenty-One? Managers who wouldn't return Rob Dillon's calls are standing in line to kiss his butt. My secretary says he's already gotten four invitations to the next Super Bowl and one to the Masters.

"Now add to this the fact that, like you said, the material we've dug up so far doesn't fit together in a neat package. We showed you and Anson the most provocative files, but they're only a small fraction of what we have. When Rob and Larry and Nigel get hit with the core dump, Buzzie, you're going to see a textbook definition of deep denial. I need to walk them through the material line by line. I need to convince them that if Teddy and Nguyen-Anh found the skeletons, so can others."

"And if they're still not buying?" asked Buzzie.

"Then I play my trump card."

"Which is?"

"I'm the firm's health-care specialist. With all due respect to my assistant, Jill Unger, if I don't sign off on the Caduceus Twenty-One report, Rob isn't going to find many takers for the paper. But you don't phone in that kind of ultimatum, you deliver it face-to-face."

"And then clean out your desk," Buzzie muttered. "Valid points, Mags, but I still don't like it. If this MedEx doesn't mind popping peasants for kidneys, they're going to love getting their mitts on you."

"I agree," Dupree said, breaking his long silence. "You flew out on zero notice, but they had you covered on the plane and at LAX. An outfit with resources that deep'll be hunting you on both coasts. Here, we have the manpower to shield you. Back in New York, you're on your own and vulnerable."

"Hey, guys, I appreciate the concern," Maggie said, "but it's not like I'm volunteering for a suicide mission. There are what, seven or eight airlines flying nonstops into three airports? Maybe fifty direct flights a day, plus all the cities I could connect through? Tell me how you can stake out every airline terminal in metropolitan New York without the National Guard. The only place they can spot me is Six-thirty-eight Fifth Avenue, and I don't plan on leaving that building before I drive a stake through the Caduceus placement."

Dupree turned to Buzzie with a silent appeal for help.

"Haven't known her long, have you, Dupree?" said Buzzie wearily. "Mags is one willful broad. She gets a notion in her head and she comes at you with one good argument after another. Eventually, it's like, *no más*."

"Why, Buzzie, that's one of the nicest things you've ever said about me."

Buzzie shook his head in disgust. "Another thing you should know is, she doesn't start in with that fuzzy-wuzzy, make-nice shit unless she senses victory."

"Buzzie, we've got to talk her out of it," Dupree said. "It's just too damned dangerous."

"Not if your pal's forgers are as good as you say," Maggie countered. "I'm talking about a one-day round-trip that has me back here tomorrow night. Then all we have to do is wait for Anson to call us to say DOJ's on the case."

Dupree stood and paced around the living room twice before bowing to the inevitable. "If you go," he said, "I'll go too, to ride shotgun."

Her face tightened: "You think I can't take care of myself?"

"For Christ's sake, Mags," Buzzie shouted, "don't pull that PMS crap on a buddy who's volunteering to watch your back."

"Sorry," she said to Dupree. "But can we get two sets of papers by dawn?"

"Why do I need bogus ID?" he replied, retrieving the secure phone from his pouch. "Whose enemy list am I on? Shucks, I'm just a country doctor taking in the bright lights of the big city."

TUESDAY
NOVEMBER 17

A T 2 A.M., the compound in South-Central Los Ange-les was dark except for the lights in the bedroom of Ignacio Tejada, who was grinding on his term paper for Greek Mythology 306. Having made dean's list each of his first three years at USC, it was pride that kept him at his laptop, trying to marshal his scattered thoughts on Agamemnon's unspeakable sacrifice into a coherent thesis. Perhaps signing up for a course so far removed from his core studies had been a mistake. Yet the epics on the reading list had been stirring and heroic and flat-out bloodthirsty; damn, those ancient Greeks were one bunch of vengeful mothers.

The paper wasn't due for eight days, but it was hard to focus when you were running on fumes. In addition to sleep dep, Tejada had been suffering leg and back spasms for the last week or so. He attributed them to the megahours he was spending online on behalf of Nguyen-Anh Dupree, who was at the moment sacked out on the couch in the study, Maggie Sepulveda having taken over the guest bedroom. Strong woman, that banker; not many sisters could turn Phillipa Walker into a shrinking violet.

Come first light, Doc and Maggie were off to New York so she could warn her company. It hadn't been easy setting up secure travel arrangements on such short notice. Before he and Leepi could go for airline seats, they had to wait for the Tres Equis document wizard to come up with a clean name for Maggie. By then all the early nonstops were sold out so they downloaded the passenger manifests and hit the phones, posing as airline reps. Leepi finally found two college kids willing to take a later plane in exchange for free tickets for a future flight. Then there was the problem of alerting Maggie's bosses. Midnight L.A. time was too late to be calling the East Coast, and e-mail was out because someone was clickstreaming the Marx Dillon net. In the end, they faxed a note to a Tres Equis *amigo* in the Bronx who would deliver it downtown.

Tejada blinked as the speaker of his laptop erupted with a quintet of plangent voices crooning, *"In the still . . . of . . . the . . . nigh-igh-ight . . ."*

It was one of Leepi's homemade alarms. All heavy users had their own technique for catnapping at the keyboard, for letting the gray matter take five. Get-a-lifers launched solitaire or Flight Simulator. He pulled threads on NUROMNCR. Leepi digitized sound bites from her Uncle Phillip's doo-wop collection into wake-up calls. Her snatch of the Five Satins was a reminder of the real reason for his all-nighter: It was his turn to hack MedEx using Jefferson Leong's password, and at this hour Code Boy should be fast asleep.

Tejada stored his partially written term paper, shifted mental gears, and punched his electronic inbox up onscreen.

There was a message from the Tres Equis documents wizard: As promised, one newly minted driver's license, one Visa card, and one ATM card, all bearing the name "Jennifer Lerario," would be at the gatehouse no later

than 6 A.M. In addition to serving as identification, the
plastic could actually be used by Maggie to make charges
and withdraw cash, because Leepi had hacked a bank and
created false accounts.

Two minutes later, Tejada was inside MedEx.

On previous sorties, he and Leepi had mapped out
three levels of sites.

The level accessible to all users contained the routine
nuts-and-bolts sites common to all corporations: customer accounts and proprietary databases, including organ requests from various Caduceus 21 transplant
centers.

The middle level was restricted to Leong and his
numb-nuts deputy, Rusty, plus two users in New York. It
contained payroll and personnel files, along with several
nasty surprises. One site, for instance, held data surreptitiously trapdoored from Caduceus 21 headquarters in
Knoxville; for some reason, MedEx was spying on its
business partner by way of clickstreams and voice taps.

The most tightly secured level remained a mystery because it required root access, which was denied even Jefferson Leong. It could only be accessed by the Big Willies
in New York—probably Duane Strand and Morris
Tomczack, according to Maggie—and their passwords
were not on file in Dallas.

Which is why he and Leepi had snuck some flypaper
onto the MedEx net. It was actually a little app, called a
wrapper log, that took up virtually no disk space, was
invisible to the host system, and performed but one task:
capturing passwords when users logged in. Based on Maggie's assumption that both Strand and Tomczack lived
within commuting range of Manhattan, they had coded
the wrapper log to respond only to dial-ups from the metropolitan New York area codes of (201), (203), (212), (516),
(718), (908), and (914).

Calling up the wrapper log, Tejada felt a galvanic rush,
as if he had just mainlined a liter of Jolt! Someone had

logged in from a remote terminal in area code (212) shortly after 8 P.M. Dallas time.

But the captured password——4E00AEB——was the very same one he and Leepi had been using to hack MedEx night after night. What the hell was Jefferson Leong doing in Manhattan?

Tejada quickly called up the system's activity log for Monday.

No sign of Code Boy in Dallas all day.

He scrolled back up the activity log to 7 A.M. Yes, Leong's No. 2, Rusty, had logged in at his usual time. Now he jumped down to 6 P.M., the sysop's normal quitting time. No logoff, so he continued scrolling down until he finally found it—at 2:56 A.M. If Rusty was just now headed home from a twenty-hour shift, Tejada thought, no way the nerd was going to be back in much before noon.

He reached for the phone. Leepi was surely going to ream his ass for waking her, but what the hell; with Code Boy and his caddy both on the sidelines, the two of them were free to roam MedEx for at least the next ten hours.

ROB Dillon's countenance was as threatening as the skies over New York as he got off the elevator and mag-carded open the glass door to the darkened Marx Dillon & Neil reception area. At 7:45 A.M., most of the staff was still in midcommute. He did notice lights on in the bullpen where the junior analysts sat. As he passed it, a young woman looked up from her desk and chirped, "Morning, Mr. Dillon. I put . . ."

He cut her off with a glance that could curdle skim milk. At the moment, nothing would cheer him short of some word from his point person on the most important deal in the firm's young history, the Caduceus 21 placement.

Maggie Sepulveda had been missing for three days. Dawn Mambelli last saw her boss striding up Amsterdam

Avenue right after the Quereshi memorial service, but had no idea where she might now be. Nor did Jill Unger. Nor did the front desk at Sepulveda's co-op, although the doormen who'd worked the weekend shifts wouldn't be back on duty until tomorrow. Nor did Paul Barry, whom, Dillon had been surprised to learn, she was no longer seeing. Nor did Sepulveda's mother, in Orlando, whom he had called in desperation before leaving home that morning.

Late the previous afternoon, Nigel Neil had suggested they check area hospitals, file a missing-person report with the NYPD, and issue a photograph of Sepulveda to the local TV stations. Nigel was an Australian and still clueless about the American press. As Larry Marx had scoffed, "Oh, great. Can't wait for the stories: 'Gal pal of murdered gay banker vanishes.' After that, who's going to buy a due diligence signed by her?" Marx's own theory, predicated on news of Sepulveda's breakup with Paul Barry, had her down in the islands, "screwing her brains out with a bunch of guys named Dexter." Typical sicko Marx fantasy, thought Dillon; but then, Larry's sex life was lousier than the Pope's.

There was a letter-sized envelope taped to his door.

The young analyst in the bullpen called out, "They gave that to me at the security desk downstairs. Some messenger left it with the overnight guards."

Dillon waved an acknowledgment, took down the envelope, and unlocked his office. He regarded the envelope as he hung up his coat. His name was typed on the front but there was no return address.

The single sheet inside was a fax of a handwritten note on which the sending and receiving numbers had been cropped:

Rob,
Urgent that I meet with you and Larry and Nigel
later today. Also urgent that you get our computer
network checked out ASAP. An intruder's penetrated

*it and is able to read everything we type, including
e-mail (which is why this note was hand-
delivered). I hope to make it in by late afternoon/
early evening but if I'm running late wait for me.
This really is critical.*

—Maggie

Dillon reread the sheet. It gave no hint of where
Sepulveda was, or where she had been. Nor was it like her
to be so over-the-top melodramatic. But on the other
hand, she appeared in full command of her wits; this was
not a note written with a gun to her head. He began feeling a bit better.

THE slate-gray clouds pressing down on New York
through the morning rush hour were finally unbur-
dening themselves. At first, the wet flakes had eddied
down like severe dandruff. Now the wind was whipping
them into horizontal sheets sufficiently opaque to blot
out Radio City Music Hall, a mere forty yards across
Sixth Avenue from Duane Strand's office.

In sharp contrast to the weather, thought Morris
Tomczack, Strand had become Mr. Sunshine himself
since Jefferson Leong's heads-up on the Sepulveda
woman. The L.A. teams had lost her the previous day.
When she failed to emerge from the hotel by lunchtime,
they tried calling her room—only to be told she had
checked out. But just minutes ago Leong faxed over a
Marx Dillon telephone intercept. One of the senior partners, Larry Marx, had called home to change his dinner
plans; Sepulveda had resurfaced with some lurid story
about the office computers being tapped, and would be
coming in at the end of the day to explain.

"Smart move pulling the Chink in from Dallas, M.T.,"
Strand said. "He doesn't clean up the backlog, we're playing catch-up ball again—just like Knoxville."

"We ended up getting to Quereshi in time, didn't we?"

Tomczack was irked; when would Strand stop busting his chops over the gay accountant?

"Any idea how Sepulveda tumbled onto our click-streams?"

"That's a negative, Duane. Jefferson checked the Marx Dillon activity log. She hasn't been on the network since late last week. He thinks it's just a lucky guess. Anyway, nobody knows we're inside their PBX too."

"Leong's uncoupling our node?"

Tomczack nodded. "He's going in through our trap-door and wiping all our software and partitions. By lunch-time, it'll be like we were never there."

"There's still the hardwiring."

"The techies Marx called in are going to find a clean system," Tomczack said. "No way they'll bother check-ing each of the several hundred lines coming out of those servers. False alarm, they'll tell him, just someone blow-ing a little smoke. Listen, Duane, the Orkin Man says you got no termites, you calling Terminix for a second opinion? To answer your question, I'm sending in a crew Saturday to yank the wires."

"Sepulveda won't be that easy."

"Jefferson's going over airline manifests," Tomczack said. "Less than a dozen flights out of LAX that get her back to New York before dinnertime."

Strand swiveled around to contemplate the snow. "You're still convinced she's coming from L.A. I'm not. She never contacted her ex-husband or the two college pals, right?"

"Affirmative. Granted, we didn't have time to put in taps. But my people are all over those three, wake-up to lights-out, and she doesn't go near any of them."

"So why the trip to L.A., the hide-and-seek at the ho-tel? To confirm the fact you have a special knack for recruiting incompetent assholes?"

Tomczack's eyes flared; lucky for Strand his back was turned. "I have no idea why she went out there, Duane. But I do know this. One, she isn't back in New York yet.

And two, wherever the fuck she's coming from, she's heading for Six-thirty-eight Fifth, which has been nailed tight since we got the intercept. Only thing is, I'd like to grab her before she goes through the revolving doors. Less fuss, less muss."

Sound reasoning, Strand thought. So why was he beating up on M.T. like this? For losing Sepulveda? Or because if they didn't find her real quick he himself would have to answer to Century Chisholm? He swiveled back around: "Okay, I'll buy that assessment. Just make sure you acquire her before she can see her bosses. We need to know for sure what, if anything, the Paki queer told her."

"That's a rog." Tomczack turned to leave the office.

"By the way, what's this costing us, M.T.?"

"Duane, you do not want to know."

THE Amtrak Metroliner from Washington, D.C., due to arrive New York City at 9:04 P.M. pulled into Pennsylvania Station almost an hour and a half late. The season's second blizzard had blown out to sea at last light, but not before paralyzing the Atlantic seaboard from Maryland to Maine. Among the casualties: Maggie Sepulveda and Nguyen-Anh Dupree.

Their flight out of Los Angeles, which took off before air-traffic controllers realized the severity of the storm, ended up diverted to Raleigh-Durham. The first airport on the East Coast to reopen had been Washington's National, which they finally reached at 5:15 P.M. Faced with wrestling a rented car up the snow-snarled turnpikes or taking the train, they dashed by subway to Union Station just in time to catch the standing-room-only 6 P.M. Metroliner. Bad choice. When Maggie tried to call Rob Dillon to advise him of her new ETA, she learned that a glitch in the microwave relay unit had knocked out all onboard telephones. On top of that, icy conditions had forced the train to limp north at two-thirds its usual speed.

Maggie, in a USC anorak on loan from Ignacio Tejada, stepped onto the platform shouldering a knapsack heavy with the documents she wanted to show her senior partners. Dupree, wearing a Raiders stadium jacket borrowed from a Tres Equis bodyguard, followed carrying his own small bag and her laptop. Their coats might have been heavy enough for November in Los Angeles but they were laughably inadequate for snowbound New York.

On the escalator up to the lobby she said, "How're you fixed for cash?"

"Forty bucks or so."

"Then let's see if Jennifer Lerario's credit is any good." Maggie strode over to the vestibule of a bank, slotted the bogus ATM card, and was rewarded by the buzz of the glass door unlocking. Inside, she swiped the card through a cash machine and was rewarded by the welcome screen:

ENTER YOUR PERSONAL IDENTIFICATION NUMBER.

She pressed 1, 0, 0, 2, 5, then GET CASH, then the $100 button.

A soft whir, and a sheaf of bills slid partway out the cash chute.

"When did Duchess and Data learn how to print money?" she asked, pocketing the bills.

Dupree smiled. "About three years ago. But they use their magic powers wisely."

Their next stop was a pay phone. Rob Dillon's line was on voicemail. As was Larry Marx's. As was Nigel Neil's. Damn, Maggie thought, had the troika gone home? Or could they be watching the large-screen TV in the conference room? But what the hell was the number of the extension in there? At this hour, there was no one at the office to tell her.

Dupree agreed they might as well go up to Marx Dillon, so she led him from Penn Station. The snow and the bitter wind had transformed Manhattan into Manhasset; Maggie couldn't remember seeing the sidewalks rolled up so tight at any hour of the day or night. They stood shivering on Eighth Avenue a full five minutes without spotting a single cab. Finally she led him down into the IND station, ascertained the E train was running, and bought two tokens.

THE van painted in the blue and gray of the utility New Yorkers loved to hate had been parked in a lot in the northeast corner of Central Park since 8 P.M. Crammed inside the vehicle was an array of electronic gear—satellite uplink, video monitor, secure phone—beyond the need of any Con Ed repairman but essential to a mobile command center. Morris Tomczack didn't need to be told that his men, huddled around an electric heater, were pissed; this was their third station on a long, cold, nasty day.

"Sir?"

Tomczack turned to the radioman, the youngest of his crew.

"Uh, how long you plan on maintaining surveillance tonight?"

Tomczack made a show of checking his watch. "Why, son? Parents expecting you home soon?"

The radioman lowered his head.

Not since the mid-1980s had a mission put Tomczack through such hell. He still fumed at the memory of the impossible conditions the Agency had placed on that operation: Use Filipino triggers but leave no tracks. Yet hadn't he pulled off the Manila airport hit? Just like he was going to succeed tonight, if he could keep everybody alert for the next several hours.

The blizzard might've knocked hell out of New York and the Sepulveda woman's schedule, but it ended up simplifying his task greatly. He hadn't thought so when they couldn't find her on any airline manifest; there weren't enough names in his Rolodex to stake out every terminal at the three airports. Once the worsening weather shut down the airports, though, he was able to concentrate his forces at her midtown office and at her apartment on the Upper West Side. The last potential hitch in his plan had disappeared shortly before 9:30 P.M., when her senior partners called it a day. Now, if his men had to resort to cowboy shit at 638 Fifth Avenue, who'd be there to witness it?

"Sir?" said the radioman. "There's some video they want you to see."

Tomczack hurried to the front of the van.

Flickering onto the monitor was a black-and-white view from the main securitycam in the lobby of 638 Fifth Avenue. A man in a stadium jacket and a woman in an anorak were entering through the night door. As they approached the security desk to sign in, the woman threw back her hood.

Tomczack grabbed the radio and shouted, "Go back and freeze on the woman's face!"

"Coming right up," replied the voice of Jefferson Leong.

"When was this shot?"

"Less than a minute ago."

Herky-jerky images as the tape rewound, then a single frame froze on-screen.

Tomczack couldn't suppress his smile. A hunter's most important weapon was patience, a maxim that had not let him down once in more than twenty-five years. Butch haircut notwithstanding, it was clearly the Sepulveda woman, accompanied by an unidentified bogie. Scramble in a team now, or let them come out? Why mess with the night guards? Since the senior partners were long gone, he reasoned, she had no reason to linger upstairs. And if she couldn't phone around in search of a hotel room, no question where she'd head. Let them come out. Tomczack had full confidence in the taxicab stunt, having pulled it off twice before, in Tokyo and Oslo.

"Take down their PBX," he commanded Leong. "Put

the wheelman on standby. Tell him it looks like two passengers. You can tap the feed real-time?"

"Piece of cake, M.T."

"The proper response is 'Affirmative,'" Tomczack snapped.

"Sorry," Leong said. "Affirmative."

"Okay, soon as they get off the elevator, give the wheelman a countdown until they're out the door."

"Affirmative. Who's the guy with her?"

"Won't know until we look in his wallet, will we?" said Tomczack. "Until then, he's just the wrong asshole in the wrong place."

A curse sprang to Maggie Sepulveda's lips when she stepped off the elevator and saw the darkened reception area of Marx Dillon & Neil; as she feared, the troika was gone. She slapped her mag card against the sensor in the wall and Nguyen-Anh Dupree pulled open the glass door. Had it been less than sixty hours since she was last here, to fetch Teddy's floppies? Unreal.

Maggie switched on the overheads and started through the funereal silence toward her office. She paused at the open conference-room door, reached in, and turned on the lights. The long rosewood table was littered with the residue of three deli takeouts. So the troika had hung around after the cleaning crew departed; why couldn't they have waited a little longer?

They continued down the corridor to her office. There was a yellow slip taped to the door:

Thanks for calling. Larry, Nigel and I will be back here 9 a.m. sharp. Your story better be fucking good.

Dillon / 9:20p

PS: Nobody's hacking our network. Nada, Zip, Nobody.

"Sounds like they left in a good mood," Dupree said.

"Yeah. And who did they get to check out the computers—Dan Quayle?"

Maggie unlocked her office and went in. Her desk was high with mail that Dawn Mambelli had sorted into piles.

Dupree looked around, his gaze pausing on a large studio portrait of an unusually handsome young man, then said, "Mind if I smoke?"

"It's against the law in New York, but feel free."

"You can't smoke in this city?"

"Not in restaurants and office buildings. School kids are shooting each other, some guy on Wall Street's pulling the next Boesky, sweatshop owners are still chaining immigrants to their sewing machines, and we've got nicotine Nazis hunting for secondhand smoke. Go figure." Maggie paused from tossing out junk mail to dig a coffee mug out of a drawer. "Here's an ashtray. Enjoy."

Dupree flicked his Zippo and scowled; why did he keep forgetting to refill it? As he rummaged through his knapsack in search of the lighter fluid, he said, "Okay, now what?"

"Larry's the only one who lives in the city. With these travel conditions, it'd be hard for Rob and Nigel to get back here by nine unless they're staying at some hotel. I'll find out which one and we'll go over there."

Dupree slid the Zippo's innards back into its metal shell and lit a cigarette.

Maggie went to speed-dial Dillon's home number in New Jersey, then frowned, picked up the receiver, and jiggled the hook. "Nguyen-Anh, would you try the phone outside, on the desk to your left? See if you get a dial tone?"

He left her office and picked up Dawn Mambelli's phone: "Dead."

"Great." On a night like this, their chance of finding a vacant room in Midtown was about as good as hailing a cab. Still, there was a row of hotels within easy walking distance up Fifth Avenue, from the Peninsula to the Pierre. Maybe one of them had a late cancellation.

Maggie led Dupree back to the elevator.

As they stepped from the building she saw a solitary yellow cab slowly cruising down the west side of Fifth Avenue. "Our luck ain't all bad today," she grinned, darting across the sidewalk and hoisting an arm.

As they clambered in Maggie said to Dupree, "We could go cruising for a hotel, which might take half the night, or we can be at my place in twelve minutes."

He frowned.

"I know what you're thinking, but we got in and out of here without running into a welcoming party, didn't we?"

"I guess you're right."

"Ninety-third and Amsterdam, please," Maggie said to the driver.

"You got it," he replied from the other side of the thick Plexiglas partition. "Mind if I take the Park?"

"Is it open tonight? Sure. That's usually the quickest way."

The driver punched on the meter and continued down the deserted avenue to 51st Street, which he took west. At Sixth Avenue, he made another right turn and headed uptown.

Maggie looked over at Dupree, who was slumped back in the seat, eyes closed. She patted his hand: "We'll get 'em tomorrow, kiddo."

"Promise?"

"Promise."

Across 59th Street and the cab entered Central Park. Though waist-high walls of frozen slush and compacted snow lined Park Drive, a lane and a half had been cleared for traffic. Lulled by the warmth of the cab and the familiarity of her surroundings, she let her thoughts drift.

It wasn't until they neared the 72nd Street transverse that Maggie felt a prickle of unease. Instead of slowing to take the transverse west, the driver was continuing north on Park Drive East, deeper into the deserted park.

"You missed our turn," she said.

No response.

She tapped on the Plexiglas partition.

The driver ignored her.

She leaned to one side to get a better look at the man and saw that he was a Caucasian in his forties. Her eyes darted past the meter to the hack license over the glove compartment. The face staring back was that of a young Nigerian.

Off to the right, Maggie saw the back of the Metropolitan Museum of Art, which meant the cab had gotten as far north as 81st Street. Where was the next exit off Park Drive East?

"Hey, take the Ninetieth Street exit," she yelled, banging on the partition.

"What's wrong?" said Dupree, opening his eyes.

"I think we're in deep shit. Hey, stop the car! Now!"

The driver continued past the 90th Street exit without a glance.

Maggie yanked on the door handle. The door wouldn't open. She pressed the power-window button. The window wouldn't go down.

Dupree found the controls on his side were also jammed, so he wrenched open the small change tray in the Plexiglas partition, but the gap was far too narrow to reach through.

The driver looked at them in the rearview and said, with a smirk, "Behave yourselves, kiddies."

Dupree hesitated, then grabbed his knapsack.

"Hey," the driver squawked, reacting to the icy liquid hitting the right side of his head. "Hey, what the fuck you doing?"

Dupree pushed Maggie back, positioned his Zippo under the hard stream of lighter fluid that he was squirting through the narrow change tray, and flicked.

A bright flare, a scream of pain beyond comprehension, and then the cab was veering hard left as the driver took both hands off the wheel to swat at the fiery halo wreathing his head and they were accelerating as he stomped the wrong pedal. Dupree glimpsed the tree dead ahead, beyond the snowdrift, and reflexively tucked Maggie's body into his as he turned his back against the impending crash.

It sounded like the end of the world: the loud *pop* of an airbag inflating followed a millisecond later by the bang of collapsing metal and then the wail of a horn that would not stop as it suddenly grew terribly cold inside the cab.

Maggie pried herself free of Dupree's slack grasp, scrambled to her knees, and looked through the Plexiglas partition onto a surrealistic scene.

The driver was slumped half on the steering wheel and half out the door, which had been sprung open by the force of the collision. Patches of his hair and shirt were on fire. Small gouts of flame also flickered on parts of the dashboard and in the change tray, where the lighter fluid had puddled. Over the partially deflated airbag, she could see that the cab had struck the tree a glancing blow; the engine was still running, the left headlight out, the right still working.

Maggie tried the door handle and power-window button again. Nothing.

She wrestled her laptop out of its padded case and bashed one corner against the window. The tempered glass cracked. She bashed again. The crack grew. Rolling onto the floor and bracing her shoulders against the transmission hump, she lashed out with the heels of her Doc Martens once, twice, and then the glass was falling away in a thousand tiny shards.

Panting like a miler, Maggie crawled headfirst through the opening.

A half-mile north of the crash site, a frigid wind blew into the ersatz Con Ed van as one of its back doors was yanked open: "M.T., something's wrong."

Morris Tomczack clambered out of the van and instantly heard the unceasing wail of a car horn that seemed to neither approach nor recede. In two strides he was at the door of his Saab. He swung inside, kicked the engine to life, and popped the glove box. Next to the pistol lay a thick metal cylinder. Tomczack much preferred the blade, the weapon on which he had trained so assiduously since the instructors at Fort Benning first identified his aptitude. It was easier to elicit information with a precisely gauged slice than with a coarse bullet hole. Sometimes, though, guns were necessary. He quickly threaded on the silencer and checked to see that a round was chambered. Setting the pistol on the passenger seat, he shifted the Saab into gear.

Maggie had slapped out the remaining flames on the unconscious driver. She had wrestled the man off the steering wheel, in the process finally silencing the horn, and lowered him to the ground. Now, kneeling over him, she saw that his burns were superficial but not his injuries. Better go see about Dupree, she thought, rising.

At that moment she spotted the rapidly approaching lights of a vehicle coming from the north, heading the wrong way down Park Drive East. The extraordinarily bright lights did not flash and there was no siren's bleat. She reached in and doused the cab's remaining headlight; if it turned out to be the police, she'd just switch it back on.

A dark Saab with flamethrower rally lamps cruised past at 25, the man at the wheel methodically quartering the terrain on both sides of the road.

Maggie lunged into the front seat of the cab and was pulling the door shut when she saw the Saab's brake lights suddenly wink in her rearview.

She slammed the transmission into reverse. The cab responded to the gas by lurching backward out of the underbrush and across the footpath, and then its rear wheels were gripping pavement.

In the rearview she could see the Saab had finally slithered to a stop perhaps a hundred yards down the drive and was now struggling to make a U-turn between the encroaching snowdrifts.

Maggie flicked the transmission into drive and accelerated steadily to maintain traction, the lessons learned all those years ago at the driving school in the Poconos automatically coming into play.

"Nguyen-Anh?" she yelled. "Dupree? Can you hear me?"

There was a soft groan in the back.

Onto the overpass above the 96th Street transverse, speed 45, still no sign in the rearview of the flamethrower rally lamps but she knew that wouldn't last long. The Saab was built for snowy roads, unlike this lame hunk of Detroit iron. She had to get out of the deserted park and onto the streets of the Upper East Side, where a patrolling police cruiser or even her own rusty driving skills would at least give them a fighting chance.

Suddenly the blackness to her left was stabbed by pairs of headlights springing on and as she passed a parking lot she counted two cars, no make that three, plus a van, and I'll bet not a Samaritan among them.

Up ahead now, the sign for the East 102nd Street exit. Maggie braked and made a tight right into the exit, the cumbersome cab sliding way outside the proper turn radius but then she had it back under control. One glimpse of the snow choking 102nd Street dead ahead—no matter who the mayor, East Harlem got plowed last—and she launched into another power slide, battling the cab until it was pointed due south on Fifth Avenue.

Only two of the avenue's five lanes were open. Lining both curbs were parked cars topped by shrouds of virgin snow that reminded her of corpses laid end to end. Damn, not a taillight in sight. Maggie fed the cab gas and played the wheel from side to side, trying to get a feel for the vehicle as she racked her memory for someplace, anyplace to the south that offered safety in numbers.

And then the looming bulk of Mt. Sinai Hospital

flashed by on her left but she was already up to 35, no way to brake fast on this treacherous surface and then suddenly an incandescent glare in the rearview: the Saab.

Maggie, having taken the cab's measure, floored the accelerator.

Crossing 95th Street and the avenue ahead growing as narrow as a bobsled run as the speedometer climbed past 50. Relax, she told herself; find the zone and settle into it. Her thumbs sought the horn ring and moments later lights began twinkling on in the posh high-rises overlooking Central Park, their tenants roused by the howling passage of a vehicle beneath their windows.

The speedometer continued surging rightward and the streetlamps, three pair to a block, flickered past so fast the cab seemed to be hurtling through a strobe-lit tunnel but Maggie couldn't slack off because the flamethrowers in the rearview kept growing and she was fast running out of time and wiggle room.

And green lights. The synchronized traffic signals that had been in her favor were turning against her, you were supposed to drive at 30 on Fifth Avenue and not 75, but she blasted through the yellows and then the reds and then suddenly up ahead an eastbound bus emerged from the 84th Street park transverse. The bus driver was looking straight ahead because he had the right of way and then he sensed the onrushing headlights and heard the approaching horn and he jammed on his brakes, worst decision possible because now the bus was skidding helplessly into the intersection.

Maggie instinctively flicked the wheel left and squeezed past its nose, just, at 80 miles per hour.

It took her almost three blocks to get the cab back under control. Damn, she couldn't shake the flamethrowers. The Saab had been fishtailing wildly as it came out of its desperate swerve around the rear of the bus but now the car was steadying and closing the gap on her oh, so effortlessly.

She thought of the hotels a mile farther down Fifth

Avenue. Even if all the cops were in the doughnut shop there'd be doormen at the Pierre and the Sherry-Netherland and the Plaza, at this speed she'd be there in less than a minute. . . .

A sharp *crack* and in the rearview now a whole posse of flamethrowers on her tail, but it was just an optical illusion caused by the bullet that had blown in the rear window and fractured the Plexiglas partition.

"Dupree?" she shouted. "Can you hear me?"

There was a muffled response from the passenger compartment.

"Stay down! We're under fire!"

Crossing 76th Street and another round thumping into the partition and then she remembered the transverse fast approaching on the right. Getting the speeding cab onto it called for a stomach-churning maneuver she hadn't tried since driving school. Yet from the 72nd Street transverse—the only one that didn't tunnel directly across Central Park—she could turn onto Park Drive East in either direction; shoot past Bethesda Fountain and turn onto Park Drive West in either direction; or continue straight across to the Upper West Side.

Decision-making window, none, so though her every instinct screamed to edge to the right, to cut down the Saab's firing angle, she angled the cab left until it was skimming past the row of parked cars with less than a yard clearance.

Crossing 75th Street, the Saab less than a half block behind: Now!

Maggie simultaneously stomped the brake pedal with her right foot and the parking brake with her left while cranking the steering wheel clockwise. Nothing much happened because the laws of physics held, as she knew they must from her practice runs on the skid pan in the Poconos. The cab was in a zero-traction skid and losing speed more from her foot being off the gas than from her braking. And though the vehicle's front wheels were now pointing dead right, it continued forward in an absolutely straight line.

Maggie sensed the flamethrowers surging alongside the cab's right wing but the bright beams were unsteady. She allowed herself a peek. Her full-flaps maneuver had caught the driver of the Saab off-guard. His left arm was still thrust out the window in firing position but his attention was on the road ahead as he engaged in a little panic braking of his own.

Crossing 73rd Street and her front wheels still pointing dead right and her speed down to 55, she'd pulled off this stunt going faster, but still it took an act of will for Maggie to pop the parking brake and lift her foot off the brake pedal.

Regaining traction, the cab continued to obey the laws of physics: Its nose jerked ninety degrees due right, a turn as impossibly abrupt as any made by Road Runner in dodging the coyote.

A *whump* as the cab muscled into the Saab's left rear fender and launched that car into a 360-degree spin.

On its first go-around the driver's face momentarily fell under the wash of a streetlight. He was struggling to bring his pistol to bear—a muzzle flash but the bullet flew wide—and then Morris Tomczack of MedEx disappeared from view as the Saab continued to waltz broadside down Fifth Avenue.

The cab had slightly overshot the entrance to the 72nd Street transverse and was sliding straight toward a streetlight stanchion. Maggie flicked the wheel, reflexes a split-second slow because there was another smack of metal on metal but then the cab was caroming off the stanchion and through the entrance.

How long would it take M.T. to recover and roar back up Fifth Avenue and into the transverse? Not long enough.

Suddenly thick clouds of steam spumed from beneath the hood of the cab; the repeated collisions must have cracked the radiator or snapped some hoses. A glance at the temperature gauge steadily climbing into the red told her the end was near.

And then Maggie thought of a stunt Tomczack could never anticipate. The escape route was high-risk—unless a big snowdrift was sitting in exactly the right place they'd be scraping up what was left of Dupree and her with teaspoons—but it still seemed safer than waiting for M.T. and his pistol.

She punched off the remaining headlight and ignored the blackness that swallowed the cab, relying on instinct and memory as she pressed into the park.

And then up ahead Maggie spotted her landmark, the traffic light halfway across the transverse. No flame-throwers in the rearview so she yelled "Hold on" to Dupree and tromped on the accelerator and turned the wheel hard right.

They mounted the frozen face of the waist-high snow-bank and slid down the back, one hard bounce off the sidewalk and then momentum was propelling them toward the easternmost staircase leading down to Bethesda Fountain.

As the nose of the cab dipped sickeningly Maggie stood on the brakes and tried to angle toward a wall in hopes the impact might slow their speed. It was like trying to turn an ocean liner with an oar. A terrible din now as they plunged in total blackness down the first flight of steps, gathering velocity with each spine-jarring jounce. Damn shame airbags don't work twice, she thought, div-ing for the floorboards. The cab slammed into the broad landing between flights of steps with enough force to send her head up into the bottom of the meter, and then they were rocketing down the second flight. Pain, noise, vibration, all accelerating, and then they were off the staircase and sliding toward a stone retaining wall and please let there be snow, lots of snow to cushion the im-pact, and then a violent but oddly sibilant crunch and she lapsed into merciful nothingness.

Up on the transverse, the Saab skidded to a stop at the

intersection of Park Drive East. Had the Sepulveda woman turned onto it? Morris Tomczack saw no telltale glow of taillights in any direction but he could hear police sirens in the distance so he shifted back into gear, hurried west past the mall and the steps down to Bethesda Fountain, and braked again at Park Drive West. Had she turned onto it or continued across to the Upper West Side? More important, had the bitch gotten a look at his face—had she recognized him?

Maggie forced open the door and rolled out of the driver's seat into a mound of snow. It was like waking up in that playground in Tacoma after being leveled by that little shit Billy Booth but this time there were no anxious faces peering down at her, only darkness. Her head felt as if it were stuffed with smoldering cotton. There was a dull pain in her left ribs. She struggled to her feet and lurched through thigh-deep snow to the rear door.

Dupree, sprawled on the floor of the cab, seemed to be stirring.

"You alive?" she said, her soft voice loud in the unearthly hush.

"Yeah, but I'm not sure I want to be."

"Anything broken?"

A pause, and then he said, "Don't think so. You?"

"I'm okay. Can you walk?"

"Yeah." Dupree pushed himself up and let Maggie help him from the cab.

It was too dark for either to see if there was blood on the other. The cold was intense; they needed shelter, and fast.

"Think we ought to wait for the cops?" she asked.

"Not if you can get us to a phone and I can get hold of Data."

"Can do."

Tomczack would probably concentrate his forces on the West Side, around her apartment, so she steered Dupree east. They were partway across the snow-drifted plaza when she realized they had forgotten their knapsacks, one of which contained the incriminating documents, and her laptop. She told him to push on, then retraced her steps to the cab. She had retrieved them, and was about to start after Dupree, when it struck her that perhaps they should leave something behind after all. Maggie fumbled open her knapsack and reached in for one of her business cards and a pen.

WEDNESDAY
NOVEMBER 18

DAWN Mambelli's face was as dark as an approaching thunderhead but her inquisitors were too preoccupied to heed the storm warning. Maggie Sepulveda's secretary had been summoned at 9 A.M. sharp to the office of Larry Marx, who was now safely barricaded behind his oversized desk. Mambelli sat opposite him, alongside Nigel Neil, while the third senior partner, Rob Dillon, prowled the room like a caged Gotti.

The troika had been peppering her with questions about Boss's personal life: Was Sepulveda despondent about her breakup with Paul Barry? Suffering from an unexpected financial reversal? Abusing a substance, either narcotics or alcohol? Most insulting of all: Marx's veiled suggestion that Boss might be down in the islands on some kind of nympho bender. That's when Mambelli had eyed the antique letter opener on his desk, just a short reach away, and wondered if it was sharp enough to inflict some serious hurt. Do the crime, do the time? In a

New York minute, she thought, if they kept this up much longer.

"You're saying you won't let us into Maggie's apartment?" demanded Rob Dillon.

"Right's right, Mr. Dillon. You don't have her permission to go in there."

Nigel Neil's face brightened. "Ah, well then, Dawn, what if we asked you to go visit the apartment? See that everything's in order?"

"What if it isn't?"

"Why, you'd tell us, surely," Neil said.

"My parents didn't raise a snitch."

"That is gross insolence and insubordination!" barked Marx, half rising from his chair. "I ought to fire you on the spot!"

"Make my day," she retorted. "I always wanted to be on Court TV."

Marx's intercom buzzed.

He stabbed TALK: "I said no interruptions!"

"Sir, it's, uh, it's the police."

Marx reared back as if stung. "The police? To see me?"

"Actually, no. They wish to speak to Ms. Mambelli."

The troika turned as one to stare at Mambelli.

"I paid the frigging parking ticket," she shrugged. "Honest."

"Sir?" continued the secretary. "They say it's urgent."

"Er, show them in," Marx said, reflexively straightening his tie.

Two men straight out of a Burlington Coat Factory commercial entered the room. The younger one seemed impressed by the posh office. The older one, who didn't, flashed a badge and said, "Detective Felipe Beltran. My partner here's Terry Fuller."

Marx came around from behind his desk, hand extended. "Larry Marx, senior partner. How can we help you?"

Detective Beltran ignored him and said, "You Dawn Mambelli?"

She nodded.

"You work for Marguerite K. Sepulveda?"

She nodded.

"Let's go somewhere we can talk."

"Wait a minute," Marx protested. "We're the senior partners of this firm . . ."

"Good for you."

"This is our firm, and it is our opinion that, er, absent a search warrant, you have no right to speak to our staff."

Beltran eyed the banker for several long moments, then said, "Know what a very wise man once told me? Opinions are like assholes—everybody's got one."

Marx turned beet red but pressed on: "Anything that involves one of our employees, we have the right to be present."

"In fact," Rob Dillon interjected, "if this is about Maggie Sepulveda, we want to hear what you know. No one's seen her since the weekend. That's why we were talking to Dawn."

"Anybody bother informing us of this fact?" asked Beltran. "That this Sepulveda is missing?"

Nigel Neil cleared his throat. "We were discussing just such a course of action when you arrived, Officer."

Mambelli lowered her head in disgust, her eyes darting back to the antique letter opener. Soooo tempting . . .

"Actually," Neil continued, "it wasn't apparent until this morning that Ms. Sepulveda is in fact missing. You see, she's been on assignment in Tennessee. She was back in town over the weekend for a funeral. . . ."

"Hold up," Beltran said. "Funeral? Tennessee? The gay banker they butchered in Nashville—he was one of you guys?"

"Er, yes," Larry Marx said. "Actually it was Knoxville, but . . ."

"Sweet Jesus." Beltran shook his head. "One dead, one missing. My Esme's thinking about business school. Wait till I tell her what safe lives bankers lead. Okay, you guys can stay. Fuller?"

The younger detective reached into his coat pocket for a sheaf of papers, unfolded a letter-sized sheet, and handed it to Mambelli. "Recognize the handwriting, ma'am?"

The page was blank except for a small rectangle the size of a business card. The photocopied words inside the rectangle read:

> <u>Gunman:</u> *Morris Tomczack, MedEx, 1273 6th Ave*
> <u>Car:</u> *Dark late-model Saab, rally lights, damaged*
>   *left rear fender, NJ plate 8L???4*

"Yeah, Boss wrote this," Mambelli said, her eyes widening. "Gunmen? Saabs from Jersey?"

Larry Marx grabbed for the sheet.

"Wait a minute," Beltran growled.

"Er, some of us live in New Jersey and we have friends who drive Saabs."

Beltran didn't bother to hide his sardonic grin. "Fair enough. Be sure to tell us if you know the owner of that vehicle."

Fuller handed Mambelli a second sheet and said, "This look genuine?"

She studied a photocopy of Boss's business card and nodded.

By now the troika had absorbed the words scribbled by Maggie on the back of the card. Rob Dillon looked up and said, "Where was this?"

"The backseat of that stolen cab we found in Central Park."

"Sepulveda stole a cab?" said Larry Marx, thoroughly flummoxed.

Beltran sighed. "Guess you guys don't read the tabs."

Mambelli, who did, exclaimed, "That cab in the *Daily News*? That's where this card was? Oh, wow."

Nigel Neil whispered something to Rob Dillon, then left the room.

Dillon turned to Beltran. "Detective, I assume your men have checked out this Tomczack and this Saab?"

"Why, golly, why didn't we think of that?" said Beltran, shooting Dillon a dark look. In fact, New Jersey DMV had confirmed that a Saab bearing license plate 8LW334 was registered to one Morris Tomczack. A unit from the Englewood Cliffs police department had arrived at the Tomczack residence shortly after 4 A.M. to find fresh tire tracks in the unplowed driveway but no Saab. Nor had Mrs. Tomczack been of much help; she claimed not to have spoken to her husband since he left for work early Tuesday. Efforts were under way to interview Tomczack's boss at a company named MedEx a block west on Sixth Avenue. Beltran saw nothing to be gained by sharing any of this information so he said, "When did you say you last saw this Sepulveda?"

"After the funeral Saturday," Dillon replied. "Must've been what, shortly after twelve noon?"

Nigel Neil slipped back into the room, having plucked a copy of the *Daily News* out of a secretary's wastebasket. He smoothed the front page and showed it to Marx and Dillon:

SLAY RIDE?

The large photograph below the headline was especially stark because it had been shot in the dead of night with a flash. Shortly before midnight police had found a yellow cab burrowed nose-first into a large snowdrift at the foot of one of the staircases leading down to Bethesda Fountain. It looked like a stunt vehicle sacrificed to make another *Die Hard* sequel. The cab's front fenders were scrunched up and several windows blown out; a cop was pointing to a bullet hole in one passenger-side door.

As the troika pored over the accompanying article, Dawn Mambelli gnawed her lower lip. She was thinking about the packet, sent by Teddy Quereshi from Knoxville, that had vanished from her desk over the weekend.

And then there was that note on Boss's door this morning. Might either be important to the police? Finally she looked up and quietly said to Detective Beltran, "I'm pretty sure Boss was in the office last night."

"Talk to me, Mambelli."

"Must've been pretty late."

"What makes you think that?"

"I found a message on her door first thing this morning," she said. "Rob—Mr. Dillon—taped it there about nine-thirty last night. Evidently, Boss was supposed to meet with him and Larry and Nigel."

"The other two clowns?"

Mambelli nodded. "Anyway, while she's been in Knoxville, I've been sorting her mail into piles—personal, business, junk, whatever. To make it easier when I packet it down, you know? Well, this morning, I see the junk mail's in her wastebasket. No way the cleaning lady did that."

Beltran exchanged glances with Fuller, then turned to the troika. "I think it's time you gave my partner and me some statements."

"Statements?" sputtered Larry Marx. "About what?"

"For openers, how come you guys stayed late last night waiting to meet someone you tell me is missing? Okay, Mr. Senior Partner, why don't we start with you."

CALL them back and say I flew to Europe on business," Duane Strand told the MedEx receptionist in New York. Ducking the NYPD was not a great idea but he needed to buy time, and this was an alibi that could be established with a few quick calls to friends who owed him favors. "Poland, Czechoslovakia, you're not sure which, the storm knocked hell out of my travel plans. Got that?"

"Yes, sir," she replied.

"Assure them you'll leave word at every stop on my itinerary. Tell them because of the time differences, though, I may not get the message until tomorrow." After the receptionist repeated his instructions, Strand hung up the phone and gazed from his bedroom down on the fresh snow carpeting his lawn. He was too numb from last night's fiasco to appreciate the postcard-pretty scene.

Ten hours earlier, Sepulveda had suddenly appeared at her office. And Morris Tomczack's trap had worked; she and an unidentified male companion were locked inside the ambush cab, just minutes from the welcoming party in Central Park—when the situation fell apart like Indonesian toilet paper.

First had come a garbled report of a high-speed pursuit. This was quickly followed by news that the cab's wheelman had been found by the side of the road in bad shape —a bizarre combination of burns about the head and shoulders and severe internal injuries. Twenty minutes later Tomczack himself called Strand to say Sepulveda had vanished off his radar in the middle of Central Park but that three teams were combing the Upper East and West Sides; in addition, Jefferson Leong was monitoring the police bands.

That was the last he heard from M.T.

At 12:07 A.M., Leong reported that the cops had found the ambush cab, empty, at the foot of Bethesda Fountain. Unable to raise a response on Tomczack's car phone, Strand had bowed to logic and called off the search for Sepulveda shortly after 1 A.M. She was on her home turf; shouldn't even take her an hour to get herself and her companion to a bolthole.

Strand was no stranger to operations blowing sky-high. In the past he just downed a couple of Scotches and went to bed. He might've felt like shit because a pal was dead or in enemy hands but the stakes during the Cold War were strangely impersonal: whatever advantage one side gained was only momentary. Here the stakes couldn't be more personal: If Sepulveda knew as much as he thought, it would mean scrutiny by the law and the dismantling of MedEx. Worse, it meant dealing with Century Chisholm, who had been closely monitoring developments since M.T.'s wet work in Knoxville the previous week.

Thus no Scotches, no bed. Strand had still been sitting at the desk in his den, weighing an unpalatable set of options, when the secure phone rang shortly before 5 A.M. Tomczack's wife was barely coherent, her story even less so. Rudely awakened by the local police, she had stonewalled their questions only to then discover that M.T. had in fact sneaked home during the night, packed a bag, and vanished again without leaving a note.

At that point, his fears confirmed, Strand had made himself e-mail a detailed action report to Chisholm.

The secure phone soon rang again. It was the old coot —when the hell did he ever sleep?—demanding to see the surveillance tape of Sepulveda and the unidentified male entering the lobby of 638 Fifth Avenue. Chisholm was apparently away from his Santa Fe lair and unwilling to reveal his whereabouts because instead of a modem-to-modem transfer, he wanted the tapes posted to a site on the Net.

Strand poured himself the dregs from the night's second pot of coffee, then checked his watch. It had taken Jefferson Leong much of the morning to digitize the relevant snippet of surveillance tape and to encrypt the file. Leong finally finished uploading the material, some six megabytes' worth, an hour ago. How long would it take Chisholm to download and review it?

As if in answer, the secure phone rang.

"Strand," said Chisholm without preamble. "Who was the feller with Ms. Sepulveda?"

"We're working on that."

There was a long pause. "I'm not happy, Strand. Not happy at all."

"I hear you, Century."

"You got a game plan?"

"I'm open to suggestions, sir."

"Let's start with Ms. Sepulveda," Chisholm said. "Assuming the gal's got half a brain, I don't reckon she plans on showing herself anytime soon. Only chance we got at damage control is if I can talk to her face-to-face."

"You think that's wise, Century?"

"Hell no, but it's damn well necessary. Wouldn't be if your people had done their job. But now we got us one seriously spooked gal who's had half a day to dream up something rash. Killing her's not the answer anymore. I need to reason with her, do some old-fashioned horse-swapping. Are you up to smoking her out, Strand? Finding me some leverage so she can't say no to a meeting? Can you do that for me?"

"Affirmative, sir."

"Good. Now the Tomczack matter. Any notion where he's hightailing it for?"

"Pretty much," Strand acknowledged.

"Know the escape routes he might use?"

"Affirmative. A bounty has been posted."

"That a problem for you, Strand? I know you two go back a ways."

"I don't like it, but no, Century, it's not a problem. M.T. failed to carry out his assignment. Mistakes, even major snafus, can be tolerated. Going AWOL cannot, not in my outfit."

"Fine. Keep me apprised," Chisholm said, hanging up.

Strand felt his gloom lifting. The conversation had gone more civilly than he dared hope. Better yet, Chisholm was offering him a chance at redemption. Sepulveda was an amateur; bringing her to the surface should be a cinch, he thought, creating a new file on his word processor and beginning to make notes.

Shortly after noon, he telephoned Jefferson Leong. Strand had passed on the new marching orders when he remembered something else: "Mr. Leong, please go into the system in Dallas and revoke M.T.'s access."

"No can do, sir."

"What do you mean, 'no can do.' "

"Like, only you and Mr. Tomczack own root access to our net?"

"So?"

"You have to own root access to deny it to another user," Leong explained. "You want me to zap M.T. from the system, first you have to pipe me your codes. Frankly, I'd just as soon not know them."

Strand thought for a moment, then said, "So how do I do it, Mr. Leong?"

"Got a pencil, sir? Or you want I should e-mail you instructions?"

"E-mail will be fine."

IGNACIO Tejada hadn't been so hungry since he couldn't remember when. Must've been the monster adrenaline hit the previous evening, he thought, followed by the scariest ten minutes of deck time he and Phillipa Walker had ever logged—cyberspace was no funpark when lives were at stake—followed by a deep and dreamless sleep. He mopped up the last of his *huevos rancheros* and said to Walker, seated across the breakfast nook in Javier's kitchen, "Girl, ever watch those *Max Headroom* reruns on the Sci Fi Channel?"

"Why for?" she replied. "It was dorky the first time round."

"But you know it, right?" he persisted, grabbing another tortilla. "Remember that fox who's Max's control, the one who always be pulling coordinates up on-screen and telling him which way to run?"

"Amanda What's-Her-Name," Walker said. "The one that married the horny Casper from *L.A. Law.*"

"Don't you feel we be living Amanda What's-Her-Name's role?"

"Amen, bro, amen."

The previous afternoon, after hacking US Airways to guarantee their friends seats on the first flight from Raleigh-Durham to Washington, D.C., Walker and Tejada had gone back to their everyday lives. Seven hours later she was at MorpHaus, one eye on the end of the Lakers game, and he was at home, working on his Greek Mythology term paper, when Tejada's pager went off.

The dial-back number was in area code (212).

His call was answered on the first ring by Nguyen-Anh Dupree, who was hiding with Maggie Sepulveda at the bar of a restaurant on Manhattan's Madison Avenue. Someone from MedEx had just tried to kill them. Her apartment was off-limits; they needed a safe house, fast.

Tejada called Walker and conferenced her into the conversation.

She had immediately pulled down an online list of dial-ups for hotels in Manhattan. Vacancies were hard to come by in the aftermath of a storm that had trapped many commuters in town but she finally spotted a late cancellation at a pricey Midtown establishment. Though the suite had only a single king-sized bed, she fought back her jealousy and nailed it by guaranteeing the reservation on the credit card of the fictitious Jennifer Lerario.

Meanwhile Tejada began hacking limo services in search of one offering corporate customers the convenience of electronic, rather than paper, vouchers. As soon as Walker booked a room, he filled out an electronic voucher billable to a Wall Street firm and had a car dispatched to the restaurant on Madison Avenue.

Thirty minutes later their friends were safely checked in and giving them a play-by-play of their wild night. During the chase Maggie had caught a glimpse of their would-be assassin and made a connection worth pursuing if only she could access Caduceus 21's disbursing records. Unfortunately, her laptop wouldn't boot up. The removable hard drive looked undamaged but she must have wrecked the box itself smashing out the cab window.

By midnight Los Angeles time, Tejada had arranged for an (800) computer store to overnight a replacement laptop, same make and model, to the hotel. And Walker had found what Maggie wanted on the Caduceus 21 net. It was now too late to call New York so she posted the data on NUROMNCR. Even if Maggie's hard drive was bent, the girl still had the floppy they'd sent her, the one containing the homebrewed app she ran at the cybercafé to access the outlaw board last weekend.

Walker glanced at the clock on the kitchen wall: 10:27. Doc and Maggie planned to spend the day recuperating, but would be checking in at 2 P.M. New York time. She put on a kettle of water and began clearing the breakfast dishes.

The morning haze was alive with chirping songbirds when Walker stepped from Javier's house carrying a carafe of fresh coffee and a two-liter bottle of Jolt! She walked Tejada across the courtyard to his house and up to the second floor. The study now contained two machines, Walker having brought over her PowerBook and jury-rigged it to his desktop.

"The new box must've arrived," Tejada said, settling into his chair. "They posted something on NUROMNCR."

While he retrieved the message she went to her PowerBook and called up a file, purloined from MedEx, listing the passwords of all the lower-ranking techies. It wouldn't do to log in as Jefferson Leong during the hours Code Boy himself might be online.

"Everything be A-OK in New York," Tejada reported. "Even Maggie's old hard drive."

Walker quickly spotted a part-time techie who only came in on weekends, jotted down his password, and dialed up MedEx.

"That dope you dug out of C-Twenty-One?" Tejada said. "Must be hot, 'cause they be detouring to Chicago on the way back here. We need to book them flights in the morning, plus a rental car. Also, they want us to hit some databases, see if we can scope out some dude name of Braunstein at One-five-eight-eight Sheridan Road, Evanston."

Walker waited as the modem breath gave way to the password prompt. She typed in the part-timer's access code, then called up the wrapper log they had planted in hopes of capturing the passwords of the New York users with root access to the MedEx net. Her mouth curled into a huge grin: "Yo, Nacio."

"Wassup, Leepi?"

"Check out what just landed in our sniffer."

Tejada minimized Maggie's e-mail and punched the MedEx feed up on his own screen.

It showed a password neither of them had seen before.

"One of the Big Willies," Walker said. "Dialing from Connecticut through the MedEx office in New York."

"Damn."

"And Code Boy's still in New York—which means that lame-o, Rusty, be at the stick in Dallas."

"Pinch me, girl," Tejada said. "I think we died and went to hacker heaven."

ROOM-service prices were usually higher than the quality of hotel food. The trick, Maggie Sepulveda knew from long experience, lay in ordering dishes that traveled well. Entrees like grilled meats and pastas continued to steam under the metal serving domes and tended to arrive overcooked. But stews, like the coq au vin she and Nguyen-Anh Dupree had just polished off for dinner, were the same up in a room as in the restaurant downstairs.

In the innocents-on-the-lam thrillers Maggie liked to read, the good guys were always going to ground in a dockside hotel in Marseilles or a grungy motel in New Mexico. The hideout arranged by Duchess and Data turned out to be a five-hundred-dollar-a-night suite with twenty-four-hour kitchen service, plush terry-cloth bathrobes, and the best-stocked minibar she had ever seen.

The DO NOT DISTURB sign had hung on the door of the suite since they checked in some twenty-two hours earlier. After phoning Los Angeles, Dupree had turned his attention to their battered and bruised bodies. Luckily, the most serious of the injuries were a nasty bump on her head from cracking it on the taxi meter and his slight concussion, probably sustained when the cab rammed the tree. His prescription: hot baths and immediate bed rest.

Dupree's fitful sleep on the sitting-room couch was broken around noon by a call from the concierge that a package for Ms. Lerario had just been delivered to the hotel. As soon as a bellboy brought up the new laptop Dupree slapped in Maggie's removable hard drive. It was undamaged so he used Duchess and Data's app to visit NUROMNCR and retrieve a message with the information Maggie had requested. Then he took a long shower and phoned down a brunch order before waking her.

Outside of a call to reassure Los Angeles that everything was fine, the two of them had spent the afternoon analyzing the events of the previous evening and preparing for tomorrow. Now, sated with good food and good wine, they were in the sitting room, chatting about not much in particular.

"When I think of Médecins Sans Frontières," Maggie mused, "I think of doctors and nurses so beyond us mere mortals. Men and women who are committed, selfless, free of material wants."

"Many are," Dupree said. "Others see it as the French Foreign Legion of medicine, a place to do penance."

"Which are you?"

He sipped his wine. "I'll let you know when I figure it out."

It was not the answer she expected. "How did you come to join them?"

"Blame it on Arthur, my mentor."

She waited a few moments, then said, "Tell me about it."

"This story doesn't tell short."

"So if I fall asleep," Maggie said, "throw a blanket over me."

Dupree smiled, shook out a cigarette, and lit it. "One night during my second year of residency," he began, "Arthur and his wife, Emma, had Liz and me over for dinner. I was under a lot of pressure at the time. Liz and I had been together about a year, and both of us were wondering where it was headed. The hospital recruiters had begun calling, offering to fly me out, show me around. Same treatment Large Quintanilla got, and I wasn't even a potential All-American lineman—just a passable affirmative-action candidate. So with all that going for me, why was I depressed all the time? Hey, any more wine left?"

Maggie emptied the last of the bottle into his glass.

"Arthur has a terrific private practice in L.A.," Dupree continued. "Teaches part-time just to keep his hand in. For all I know, the dinner was his low-pressure way of recruiting.

"Anyway, before Arthur and Emma had kids, they spent all their free time traveling. You know, just take off with a duffel bag each and no pre-planned itinerary. Our dinner must've been shortly after Ayatollah Khomeini died, because they began reminiscing about a trip to Iran in the early Seventies. They described one experience that was like, like . . . You know the French term *coup de foudre?*"

Maggie nodded. It meant "struck by lightning."

"That's what it was," Dupree said. "*Un coup de foudre.* Changed my life utterly.

"Arthur and Emma are in Shiraz when they hear about a mosque whose minarets sway. The mosque is on a highway twenty, twenty-five klicks outside of town. It's a gorgeous spring afternoon, so they decide to go see for themselves. Remember, this was when the Shah was still in power, before America became 'The Great Satan.' The taxi drivers want thirty dollars U.S. for the trip, the bus is about a buck round-trip for the two of them. They take the bus.

"A couple of cabloads of tourists are already at the mosque. The building is kind of disappointing. It's so small that it can't hold more than about a dozen of the faithful. The minarets are less than two stories high and so skinny that an adult would be hard put to squeeze inside.

"That's why when tourists show up, so do the local kids. The tourists give a boy of about ten some change to make the towers quake. He scampers up inside one of the minarets and begins leaning first one way, then the other. Damn if it doesn't begin to sway. A minute or so later, so does the other one—some kind of harmonic vibration. Soon as the kid has both minarets syncopated, he stops. Show's over, so the tourists pile into their cabs and roar back to Shiraz.

"Arthur and Emma learn the next bus isn't for another two hours. Sodas? The nearest shop is a three-klick walk there, another three klicks back.

"Then they see a dirt road leading from the highway toward what looks like a little forest. With nothing better to do, they decide to take a walk.

"Not more than a quarter-mile down the dirt road, they suddenly find themselves in a maze formed by high mud walls. Behind the walls, which are neatly laid out in a grid, stand lush apricot orchards. The land slopes noticeably so they keep working their way downhill.

"Eventually they come to a river. It's the dry season, and there's a big sandbar lying high and dry in midriver. A man is on the sandbar with two donkeys. The donkeys are carrying huge canvas bags that he's filling with pebbles."

Maggie found herself leaning forward, riveted as much by the way the story was being told as the tale itself. In the time she had known this polite and reserved doctor—God, was it really only three days?—she never suspected that Dupree might be an accomplished raconteur.

"The man looks up and sees Arthur and Emma," he continued. "They wave. The man's a bit taken aback—this spot doesn't draw a lot of tourists, especially foreign women wearing culottes, like Emma. After the longest pause, he waves back and motions for them to meet him on the bank at a spot to their right. The man leaves the donkeys on the sandbar and begins wading in.

"Arthur and Emma head downriver. They round a bend and see a teenaged boy sitting by a fire, boiling a pot of water. The kid turns pale at the sight of two foreigners, one a woman, walking toward him.

"Just then they're joined by the man from the sandbar, most likely the kid's father. Arthur and Emma introduce themselves. The man responds with his own name, Shahpur, and his son's name, which they no longer remember. That's about as far as the conversation gets because Shahpur speaks only Farsi, of which Arthur and Emma have but a few guidebook phrases.

"Shahpur says something to his son, waits for the kid to spread a coarse woolen blanket on the ground, then motions Arthur and Emma to sit. We think of culottes as being pretty modest, but both Iranians are working overtime to avoid glancing at Emma's bare legs. Evidently Iran was a pretty conservative society even before the mullahs took over. Shahpur squats to pour boiling water into a dented kettle. While the tea's steeping, he produces four thick glasses that are scratched and chipped with age.

"Emma had long since learned a great trick for breaking the ice in foreign countries—carry a supply of the local sweets. She takes out a bag of nougats and offers them around.

"The kid's flabbergasted, having never seen such generosity. He holds back until his father nods. One bite, and he's in heaven. Shahpur pretends to wave Emma off but finally accepts a piece and enjoys it hugely. She sets down the nougats with the bag open toward them, gesturing that they should help themselves.

"By now the tea's ready. Emma is of course the last to be served. Shahpur hesitates, then reaches into a leather bag and comes up with an old handkerchief. Inside it is a chunk of sugar the size of a child's fist. He treats it like it's extremely precious, which in Iran it probably was. He has no problem offering the sugar to Arthur. Emma's another story, but he finally wills himself to do it. She selects the smallest fragment she can find and drops it in her tea.

"Then the four of them turn to look out over the river. The water is low, the donkeys are standing patiently on the sandbar. There is not another human being in sight, there is not a man-made sound to be heard. The tea is incredibly musky, incredibly good. They sit and sip it without a word, having grown comfortable in each other's presence."

Dupree drained his glass and smiled. "I'll never forget something else Emma said that night: 'Nature abhors a vacuum, Americans abhor a silence.' Too true. Nobody gabbier than us except the French—unless it's Nguyen-Anh Dupree half-bagged on wine."

After a few moments, Maggie protested, "Hey, don't just leave me sitting on the bank of that river with Emma and Arthur."

"Not much more to tell, Maggie. When the tea was finished, Shahpur offered them some more. They politely declined and rose. Emma knew it would be bad form to leave the bag of nougats—it was a gift the Iranians could not repay—but she insisted both take large handfuls. Then Arthur and Emma said 'thank you' in Farsi and Shahpur replied with something that probably meant 'you're welcome.' They shook hands all around, and Arthur and Emma begin the long trek back, through the apricot orchards and up to the highway.

"It was a secondhand tale," Dupree said, "but so vivid it made me feel I was there at the river with them. Know what I mean?"

Maggie nodded. "Have you thought of going to that mosque?"

"All the time. But even if I could get into Iran—dubious, because American passports still aren't real popular there—I probably wouldn't. Arthur and Emma experienced a moment that cannot be recaptured."

"You mentioned earlier the story changed your life," she said. "Why?"

"Partly because it was so romantic," Dupree replied, "partly because it drove home a truth. I'm from a little place in Mississippi, Yazoo City, but I've had more chances than most to see America firsthand. I did my undergraduate work at Chapel Hill. One of my roommates there was from New York, so I got to know that city pretty well. I went to med school and did my internship in Baltimore and now I was in L.A. on my residency. Point is, America wasn't exactly an unknown territory, yet I'd found no place where I felt truly at home, where I longed to settle.

"By this time my mother and *Grand-mère* Lulu May, the two women who raised me, were both dead. I also knew Liz was not the person I wanted to spend the rest of my life with. So I flew to Brussels and volunteered for Médecins Sans Frontières."

"What was she like?"

"Lizzie? Smart. Funny. Ambitious." He stared at his empty wineglass. "But she had a careless streak. She wasn't always mindful of little details, or little people and their feelings. Know her reaction to Arthur and Emma's story? She was disappointed they hadn't taken snapshots. By the way, small-world department—Buzzie probably knows her."

"Oh?"

Dupree grinned. "She's now a producer. Four pictures, including one box-office monster."

"Duchess doesn't strike me as careless," Maggie said.

"She's not." He frowned. "What segue did I just miss?"

"Did you catch her reaction in Javier's dining room the other night?"

Dupree shook his head.

"When I came into the room with Data, Duchess looked like someone who was just betrayed by a lover. Her eyes shot from me to you, then back to me. I think she wanted the earth to open up and swallow her."

"She had a crush on me once," Dupree admitted, "but that was a long time ago. We met when I used to go to the compound to check up on Data. Duchess was an impressionable high-school kid then, and I probably seemed like the original brother from another planet. She's outgrown it."

"You know, you men really can be clueless," Maggie said. "That girl's still deeply in love with you."

He busied himself lighting another cigarette. "So's Buzzie, with you."

"Wow," she exclaimed. "That rates a ten for avoiding the issue."

Dupree smiled. "*Grand-mère* Lulu May used to brag on how Faulkner must've known some kinfolk of ours. Speaking of ducking the issue, it might interest you that Buzzie's a completely different man in his office than when he's around you. Fact is, I can see the two of you together."

"Maybe," Maggie said. "He's changed a lot in the last five, six years, all for the better. Maybe if I had stuck it out . . . But it seemed the right choice at the time. What about Doctors Without Borders? The right choice for you?"

He shrugged.

"Let me put it another way," she said. "Has it made you happy?"

"Ever read V. S. Naipaul?" he asked.

"Some of his essays, back in college."

"That's when I discovered him too," Dupree said. "I wanted to know more about the man, so I went to the library. Turns out one of the newsweeklies ran a cover story on him in the early Eighties. Found the bound volume, found the article. It contained a quote that was so powerful, I Xeroxed it and taped it over my computer screen.

"Naipaul said, 'Happiness is a kind of passive, animal state, isn't it? Whereas joy is a positive sensation of delight in a particular thing—a joke, another person, a meal —and you can have it in the middle of deep gloom.' "

"What's your favorite band?" Maggie asked.

No longer surprised by her jump-cut questions, he scratched an earlobe, then said, "Probably U2. At least their stuff through *Joshua Tree*."

"Figures."

"How's that?"

"They also see the glass as half-empty."

He pondered her observation for a few moments, then took a final drag on his cigarette, stubbed it out, and started for the bedroom. "Hey, we've got an early call and a big day tomorrow. I think we'd better hit the sack."

"Guess you're right." Maggie was surprised at how let down she felt by the ending of their conversation.

Dupree returned carrying spare sheets, a blanket, and a pillow, and began making up the couch again. "How's the body?"

She shrugged. "Achy-breaky, but I'll live. It's our clothes that give me the creeps. Hey, I know, take off your underwear."

He arched an eyebrow.

"Relax, Dupree," Maggie said acerbically. "I was only going to wash yours along with mine. If near-death experiences turned me on, I'd've jumped your bones last night."

T H U R S D A Y
N O V E M B E R 1 9

JEFFERSON Leong's keyboard felt gritty to the touch, as if coated with a fine layer of sand. The off-white substance was actually granules of Lipton's instant iced tea, the stimulant of choice for hackers deep in a marathon session they couldn't afford to mess up by popping bennies. Like many of his peers, Leong mainlined the powder straight from the packet rather than dilute it in water; the kick was stronger, the need to visit the head less. Stuff tasted like a petrochemical by-product but unlike uppers, it never clouded your mind or left you twitching the morning after.

The room in which he sat was part of a tiny suite on the second floor of 638 Fifth Avenue. Surrounding him were servers idle since he'd yanked the clickstreams and seines from the Marx Dillon & Neil network forty-one floors above.

The air was ripe with the moldering residue of half-eaten junk food and his own stale sweat. Since being summoned up from Dallas by Morris Tomczack nearly a hundred hours earlier, Leong had gotten less than one full night's sleep. His last shower had come on Tuesday morning, before M.T.'s ambush backfired. Small wonder his crimson-rimmed eyes burned from fatigue-induced dehydration and the lugies he coughed up were Crayola-colored.

Under normal circumstances Leong would have taken pride in what he had single-handedly accomplished in the past twenty hours, but at the moment all he could think of was staying awake. Duane Strand had ruled out bringing aboard an assistant, making a series of tedious jobs almost unbearable.

Strand's first task: identify the person closest to the Sepulveda woman.

Leong had trapdoored Caduceus 21 for the call log from her extension and accessed the last two local and long-distance bills from both her Knoxville and New York apartments. God, she spent a lot of time yakking. His frequency analysis went slowly because he had to sift out all her professional calls, but in the end his patience produced a lead. Sepulveda phoned Orlando, Florida, at least four times a week without fail: one number during the day, another at night. A reverse-directory check showed the first was a business called the Rec Room, the second a private residence occupied by one Helen Wagner. Florida's online business directory listed the Rec Room as a sporting-goods store managed by one Helen Wagner. Finally, a hack of the Social Security Administration database revealed the same Helen Wagner to be Sepulveda's mother.

Duane Strand had seized on this information like a Doberman a bone, then handed Leong a knottier assignment: "The person for whom you posted the digitized surveillance tape expects to hear from Sepulveda in the near future. However, he insists on concealing his current location. You are to devise some sort of communications channel that accomplishes three things. One, verify the incoming call is from Sepulveda. Two, alert him that she's calling. Three, guarantee that his privacy is shielded, even if she has tracing capabilities."

"Sir, are we talking voice-call or some kind of online-chat situation?"

"Good question. Set up both capabilities."

Great, thought Leong, just the challenge me and my vast army of techies need. In his fatigue he wasted several hours trying to construct an elegant solution before deciding to do it down and dirty. He could have completed the necessary hacks and hardware and software reconfigs in a few hours with the help of the lowliest Mushroom Farm serf. Working solo, it had taken most of the night.

Leong caught himself nodding off in his chair. The on-screen clock was coming up on 7 A.M.; Strand would be calling soon. He flooded his eyes with Visine again, too tired to mop up the excess flowing down his cheeks, then tore open another Lipton's packet. The granules stung his tongue, which felt like an open wound from the repeated hits of the last few days. He was still trying to generate enough saliva to gag down the powder when the phone rang.

"Good morning, Mr. Leong." Strand sounded chipper, Leong thought morosely, as if he'd gotten some sleep. "How are we holding up?"

"Like, I've been better? But I got your sites rigged." Leong began with the digital channel, which had been easier to set up. He had created a low-rent Website with chat-room capabilities on one of the idle servers in his office. If Sepulveda logged in and typed the correct answer at the prompt, she would get a message—DATA BEING PROCESSED. PLEASE WAIT—while Strand's pal was being alerted by e-mail. As soon as the pal logged in, he and Sepulveda could swap messages in real time.

Strand took down the Website address, then said, "What did you program in as the authenticator?"

"Her Social Security number."

"Make it something less obvious."

"Yes, sir. I'll do that on the voice-link too."

Leong then filled Strand in on the analog channel. He had created a miniature telephone switching station on another of the servers in the office. If Sepulveda dialed a number in Wyoming that was officially "not in service," call-forwarding would bounce her through similar unused numbers in three other area codes before ringing in New York. After punching in the correct authenticator with the buttons of her phone, she would be placed on hold while Strand's pal was being alerted by e-mail. To preserve his privacy, the pal would dial into another untraceable daisy chain of "not in service" numbers and, on reaching New York, be patched to Sepulveda.

"Outstanding, Mr. Leong," Strand said. "I'll only keep you a few more minutes while I field-test your handiwork."

Leong cradled the handset and began searching through Sepulveda's telephone logs for the home number of her former boyfriend.

The Lipton's was starting to impact his nervous system but instead of perking him up, it was stoking his jitters. Since becoming a master of cyberspace, Leong had often skirted society's laws. Some of his transgressions had even been performed with impunity, under the auspices of his first employer, NSA. And since 1993 he had harbored few reservations about his duties at MedEx. Hacking sorties, setting up covert clickstreams and seines? Everyone did it. The various dark-core sites he knew to be on the system? As they now said in the military, "Don't ask, don't tell."

Over the last four days, though, his assignments had escalated from easily rationalized white-collar mischief to attempted murder. For Tuesday night's radio traffic had been crystal-clear: Morris Tomczack meant to do more than merely question that woman. Events had subsequently spun even further out of control. When Sepulveda escaped the ambush, Tomczack also disappeared. Leong had noticed a frantic surge of dark-core e-mail several hours later and managed to hack some of

Duane Strand's outgoing messages. The head of MedEx was so stung by the desertion of his deputy and longtime friend that he had posted a hundred-thousand-dollar extreme-prejudice bounty on Tomczack.

Meanwhile, the local press was going gaga over the abandoned cab in Central Park. Cops weren't exactly Einsteins, Leong thought, but it would be fatal to underestimate their sheer numbers and their persistence. And when the hammer finally fell, he didn't plan to be under it. As soon as he caught up on his sleep, he was going to remote-access Dallas and begin combing the system for incriminating files that mentioned his name. Damn, he wished he owned root access; without it, there was no way to delete data on the sites now open only to Strand. Maybe he should plant a wrapper log . . .

The phone rang again: "All systems go, Mr. Leong. Grab some sleep. But stay near a phone, understood?"

Leong opened up his firewalls and coded in a new authenticator, the former boyfriend's home number, then dimmed the lights. Though his hotel was only four blocks away, he just laid his parka on the carpeted floor of the office and crawled onto it.

B Y the time the mall on Golf Road in the Chicago suburb of Glenview unlocked its doors, Maggie Sepulveda and Nguyen-Anh Dupree were stiff from sitting in the parking lot and bored from listening to the radio of their rented car. Their Central Park adventure had been colorful enough to rate a passing mention on the local all-news station: "In New York, authorities are searching for a thirty-four-year-old investment banker reported to be missing. They say she may have been a passenger in a stolen taxicab found abandoned in Central Park Tuesday night, following the big blizzard. Foul play has not been ruled out." Fortunately, the local media were more fascinated by a North Side alderman caught in flagrante delicto with his teenaged daughter's best girl-friend.

Maggie and Dupree had flown to Chicago to see a woman who lived in fashionable Evanston. Since they planned to show up unannounced at her door, it wouldn't do to look like fugitives from the fashion police; hence this pit stop.

The mall was filled with the usual dreary gauntlet of clothing chains catering to clients who wanted to dress like overage graduate students or loud-jacketed country-clubbers. After finally assembling passable outfits, Maggie and Dupree threw the bags containing their old garments into the car and continued east.

Reaching Evanston, Maggie crossed under the El into the heart of the Northwestern University campus and turned south onto Sheridan Road. Tiny whitecaps dotted Lake Michigan to their left. When Dupree spotted an imposing house that bore the number 1588, she made the next right and pulled into a space by a small park.

They got out of the car and started for the house. Upscale American neighborhoods shared a certain hush at all hours of the day, Maggie thought; it was as if money filtered out not only the kind of undesirable louts who filled their driveways with junkers up on cinder blocks, but also noise itself.

A suburban matron in her mid-forties answered the bell, her expression frosty at the sight of two strangers on the other side of the storm door.

"Mrs. Braunstein? Hi, my name is Maggie Sepulveda, and I'm a partner with the banking firm that's doing the private placement for Caduceus Twenty-One."

The mention of the health-care company and the pending private placement proved disarming, as Maggie had hoped it would. Susan Haas Braunstein received not only annual profit-sharing checks from Caduceus 21 but also periodic updates on the company cofounded by her late first husband, Carl.

"Actually, I'm overseeing the due diligence," Maggie

continued. "I apologize for not calling in advance, but we found ourselves in Chicago and Aurelia and Len and Mary said I could never really understand the company without talking to you. May we have a few minutes of your time?"

The name-dropping seemed to erase any lingering suspicion; Braunstein smiled and unlatched the storm door. "How are my old friends? How's K-town?"

"They're fine, and Knoxville is as ever," Maggie replied as she and Dupree entered the house. "Mrs. Braunstein . . ."

"Susan."

"Susan, this is my associate, Peter Lee."

Dupree, who had earlier suggested to Maggie that he use a pseudonym—why leave unnecessary tracks?—extended his hand.

"May I offer you coffee? Tea? No? Then let's go in the living room."

On the mantelpiece of the tastefully furnished room was a wedding portrait of Susan and Richard Braunstein. According to Duchess and Data's research, he was a pediatric surgeon. Next to it stood a small photograph in an antique silver frame of Carl Haas and his first son by Susan. Dr. Braunstein was obviously a better man than Barney Wagner, thought Maggie, remembering how pictures of her dad, Jeff Kragen, had been banned from her stepfather's house.

It took Maggie ten minutes to lead Braunstein to the spring of 1993 and to the hunch that had brought Dupree and her to this house. "The day I saw the tape of the survivors' group," she said, "Mary told me the police still haven't come up with a suspect."

Braunstein lowered her gaze. "They will. I last spoke to the detective in charge in late September. He promised me Carl's case is still active."

The finesse was working, Maggie thought; Braunstein seemed willing to discuss her first husband's death. "Did Mr. Haas go to New York often?"

"C-Twenty-One was negotiating a contract up there with a new company called MedEx," Braunstein replied. "They procure and transport organs. Carl had visited them several times to make sure he fully understood their business plan. I believe they were just on the verge of closing the deal."

"Do you remember if Mr. Haas went to New York that day?"

"No, the previous morning. He thought it would be a fast up-and-back. Something came up, though, and he had to stay over for one last meeting. He was supposed to . . ." Braunstein blinked rapidly, to hold back the sudden tears, but made herself continue: "You see, he was supposed to be home in time to take me out to dinner. It was my birthday that day. It's ironic, but the police think he's dead because of the gift he bought for me. They think the mugger saw the shopping bag from Gucci and marked Carl for a rich tourist."

Maggie waited for the woman to compose herself before asking, "Does the name Morris Tomczack mean anything to you?"

Braunstein's forehead furrowed. "Vaguely, but . . ."

"Director of operations for MedEx," Maggie said. "Everyone calls him 'M.T.' "

Susan Braunstein grew extremely still. "It was empty," she whispered. "Carl's last words—*I swear it was empty. Empty, M.T.* Oh, my God. Why?"

"We don't know, Susan," Maggie replied. "If we did, believe me, we would've gone straight to the police instead of putting you through this pain."

Braunstein rose from her chair a bit unsteadily. "Would you mind if we continued this in the kitchen? You may not want coffee, but I sure as hell do."

After putting on a kettle of water and grinding the beans in silence, she finally said, "Why did you two come here today?"

Maggie had anticipated that if Braunstein made the Tomczack connection, this question would come up. She and Dupree had decided to answer it truthfully: "Susan, we're trying to find out why MedEx wanted Mr. Haas dead. You said he was in New York to study their business plan. Could he have learned something he shouldn't have? Obviously you told the police everything you knew, but looking back now, does anything unusual stick out in your mind? A phrase, a word? Perhaps some letter or package that arrived days or weeks later?"

Braunstein fell silent again, then excused herself and returned shortly with a cardboard carton. "I haven't looked inside this since I sealed it nine months after the murder. Help yourself. Everything connected to that damned trip is in here except the clothes Carl wore. The police kept those for evidence."

Dupree borrowed a kitchen knife and slit the tape.

He and Maggie began taking out the sad artifacts of a sudden death: condolence notes, newspaper clips, a videocassette labeled TV NEWS STORIES, Haas's Filofax, even his last hotel bill. It was as if Braunstein had decided to literally compartmentalize her grief. At the bottom of the carton sat a box that bore the distinctive double-G insignia of Gucci.

"The police released it that summer," Braunstein said softly. "I could never find it in my heart to use it."

"May we?" asked Maggie.

Braunstein nodded.

Maggie removed the lid and said, "It's beautiful." As she lifted out a classic tan zippered shoulder bag, two slips of paper fluttered to the floor.

Dupree leaned to retrieve them.

"Don't trouble yourself," Braunstein said. "It's only the receipts."

Maggie looked at the slips. One was from Gucci, in the amount of $448.98, for the silk-lined shoulder bag. The second was from a leather repair shop not more than a block away, in the amount of $70.36.

She saw that a small leather panel just under the zipper was engraved with the initials SVH in plain block letters. Odd; why had Haas gone to a no-name store for monogramming instead of just asking Gucci to do it? Odder still, why would a no-name store charge an exorbitant $70.36 for five minutes' work? Unless it had performed another service as well. . . .

Maggie examined the bag's interior. Empty. Then on a hunch she examined the stitching binding the silk lining to the sides. Was it her imagination, or was the thread on the side with the monogrammed panel a slightly different color? She grasped that side of the bag and kneaded it.

They all heard something crinkling inside.

"Susan, may we open it up?"

Braunstein bit her lip, then nodded. "What do you need?"

Dupree said, "Do you have an X-Acto knife or a single-edged razor blade?"

"I can do better than that. Richard's a doctor. I'll be right back."

Braunstein returned with several clear plastic bags of the size used by the airlines to package plastic cutlery. Each contained a disposable scalpel.

Dupree unwrapped one, moved to a window for better light, and expertly opened the seam. He reached in and slid out a letter-sized sheet that had been folded over once.

The memo from Morris Tomczack to Duane Strand, dated 18 February 1993, was headed "Possible recruits." Tomczack had listed twenty-two names in alphabetical order, each followed by a foreign city and the designation "R-3," "R-4," or "R-5."

Dupree passed the sheet to Braunstein and said, "Do these names mean anything to you, Susan?"

Braunstein angled it so Maggie could read along with her. Finally she said, "I've never heard of any of these men."

But Maggie and Dupree had. Twelve of the names were in a file downloaded by Duchess and Data during their hack of the bank in the Caymans. Every time MedEx completed another Third World organ harvest, one of these men would receive one of those electronic transfers, always in multiples of $4,000, from Wings of Mercy Ltd.

Dupree recognized something else that warranted a follow-up. He had often dealt with a bureaucracy that used the prefix "R" in conjunction with a number that signified grade level. The U.S. State Department classified its permanent employees FSO, for Foreign Service Officer. Non-State personnel working out of an embassy or consulate were classified R, for Reserve. These might include administrators for AID, the Agency for International Development; outside consultants on government contract; and, of course, political or economic attachés, the cover preferred by Central Intelligence Agency officers. In Dupree's experience spooks, no matter how senior or junior, never carried a designation higher than R-3 or lower than R-5.

He looked at Maggie, then said to Braunstein, "Susan, we have a tremendous favor to ask. Would you keep this memo to yourself for now?"

"What?" said Braunstein, her face knotting in rage. "And let Carl's killer walk around free another day?"

"The police are already searching for him," Maggie said quietly. "He tried to kill the two of us in New York Tuesday night. Believe me, Susan, we want the bastard caught too, but it's also important to nail his bosses. Most of the men on that sheet of paper live overseas. The NYPD has no jurisdiction—all they can do is spook them, make them go underground."

Braunstein slumped into one of the chairs around the kitchen table, the revelations of the past few minutes sinking in. Finally she said, "C-Twenty-One's been working in partnership with MedEx for all these years now. Mary, Aurelia, Len—tell me none of them could be party to something like this."

"I'd like to," Maggie replied gravely. "But we won't know for sure until we bring down MedEx."

• • •

JAVIER Tejada sent his bulletproof limo and a complement of Tres Equis muscle to Los Angeles International Airport to meet the flight from Chicago. When Maggie and Dupree arrived at the compound in South-Central, they found Phillipa Walker and Ignacio Tejada giddy from another all-nighter—and from having unearthed MedEx's most closely guarded secrets.

Up in Data's study, Dupree immediately noticed a brand-new Iomega Jaz drive hooked to Tejada's computer. The megastorage device had been bought, Walker explained, to cope with the flood of damning files unlocked by Duane Strand's intercepted password. Using the ISDN line at MorpHaus, they had over fifteen hours downloaded enough material to fill a stack of floppies more than eight feet high.

"Root access is usually just cheap thrills," she said. "Lets you peek at other people's salaries, what the Big Willies are thinking about, maybe some choice office-romance e-mail. The shit that's on MedEx's top-secret sites is . . . is something I can't find a word for."

"Try 'evil,' " Tejada said, settling in before his monitor. "Yo, girl, let's take them through it."

There were five queues in the MedEx system that required root access. It would take days to finish sampling the material, weeks for a thorough examination. But every other file pulled up at random seemed to contain a smoking gun.

For instance, the GOODTOGO queue held data on private clients from around the world willing to pay top dollar for a perfectly matched organ, no questions asked. Not all were aging tycoons and ailing heads of state; in fact, the list of desperate men and women undaunted by a seven-figure finder's fee contained some real shockers.

SEECUBED was reserved for MedEx's procurers.

"You were right, Doc," Walker said. "After you called, me and Nacio hit the Net. There's a bunch of sites that out spies—East, West, Third World, doesn't matter, they name names. We even found one that's posted the internal CIA directory the Shiites found when they took over the embassy in Tehran. The names you gave us are all ex-CIA. So are Strand and Tomczack."

"It all ties together," Dupree said. "You usually hear rumors about black-market organs in countries with repressive regimes and government-sponsored death squads. Want to 'disappear' a victim with a desirable medical profile? A hit team's already in place. And who knows those thugs better than the CIA guys who used to liaise with them? Talk about an old-boys' network—the Cold War's over, Langley's downsizing, and then Strand calls to say, 'Your contacts are still worth money to me.' "

It appeared that SEECUBED served as a two-way channel for the procurers. They were automatically e-mailed the changes each time the "Priority List" of outstanding private-client orders was updated. The procurers also sent to this queue blood- and tissue-type data on Third Worlders they had targeted. MedEx matched these specs against the needs of the various Caduceus 21 transplant centers to order a harvest of those unfortunates whose body parts fit the bill.

Maggie said, "Does C-Twenty-One know that some of the organs they're getting from MedEx are black-market?"

"Me and Nacio don't think so," Walker replied. "We didn't see anything. Besides, remember it's MedEx running clickstreams and taps inside Knoxville, not the other way round."

Maggie nodded; that was the conclusion she and Dupree had reached on the plane.

The PAYMASTR queue documented the company's off-the-books finances, some thirty million dollars per year laundered through Miami and the Caymans. Unlike the records Walker and Tejada had downloaded from the Georgetown bank, these contained a full list of payees.

Among them: the holders of the two numbered Swiss accounts, Lester Haidak and Frankie Krapayoon, presumably the doctors who performed the illegal harvests.

DEEPSIX archived backups of incriminating internal MedEx communications like e-mail and video-conferences. Walker checked her notes, then called up a videocon: "Recognize him, Maggie?"

"Yes. Duane Strand."

Walker fast-forwarded to a boyish Chinese face. "This is Code Boy."

"Code Boy?" asked Maggie.

"Jefferson Y. T. Leong," Tejada explained, "ace MedEx sysop."

"Someday, somewhere, somehow, I'm going to teach this little geek what hurt is," Walker said, fast-forwarding again. "This the guy who tried to kill you?"

Maggie looked at the bland face of Morris Tomczack and nodded.

The final queue, BODYBAGS, was worthy of Hitler's meticulous record-keepers. It contained nothing but digital tombstones: vital statistics on the several hundred victims whom MedEx had already eviscerated. Searching by date, Walker had found the file on Guillermo Chacon.

Dupree studied it impassively for a few moments, then turned away.

"Okay," Walker said, "we got names, we got dates, we got figures. We can cross-ref all of that to tie specific murders with specific MedEx flights with specific C-Twenty-One transplants with specific payments. What more's that U.S. Attorney going to want?"

"Hard proof of a crime committed somewhere in the U.S.," Maggie said glumly. "We have records of Guillermo being killed, but not where."

Walker and Tejada looked at Dupree, who reluctantly nodded his agreement. "Damn," he said, "we're so close. There's got to be some work-around."

The cookies that came with the Chinese takeout they had for dinner yielded fortunes but no solutions.

"Look, it's getting late and we're just spinning our wheels," Maggie said. "Why don't we see what a night's sleep can do."

"Amen, sister," Tejada said.

Dupree glanced at his overflowing ashtray and made a face.

Maggie stood, then said, "Data, can you fix me up a secure line? I haven't checked for e-mail since Teddy's funeral."

Tejada swiveled back to his keyboard and rendered calls from the phone in the guest bedroom untraceable.

Five minutes later Maggie returned to the study, her face drained of all color, her open laptop in hand: "The empire's striking back."

The others clustered around to read the e-mail on-screen:

> *To guarantee Helen Wagner's safety call (307) 645-3041 or check www.mindmeld.com—ASAP.*

"Who's Helen Wagner?" asked Dupree.

"My mom."

"Where'd you retrieve this?"

"Marx Dillon. There's also a copy at C-Twenty-One and the same message was left on all four of my answering machines by some man whose voice I don't recognize." Maggie started for the telephone.

"Unh-unh, girl, not yet," Walker warned.

"Why not?" said Maggie, annoyed. "You and Data can fix the lines so nobody can trace the call."

"This is true. But tracing and listening in are two different things. And if your mom's in real danger, what are you going to tell her? Call nine-one-one? Run?"

Dupree thought for a moment. "Where does your mother live?"

"Orlando."

"House? Apartment building? Gated community?"

"A town house in a development southwest of the

city," Maggie said, feeling the knot in her stomach tighten. "It's about as secure as Central Park."

Dupree turned to Tejada: "Does Tres Equis have *amigos* in Florida?"

"*Nada*, Doc. Like, we never had much business to do with the Cubanos." He took the laptop from Maggie and began to examine the e-mail for clues.

"Nguyen-Anh, can I bum a smoke?"

Dupree couldn't have been more astonished if Maggie had sucker-punched him, but fished out his pack.

She accepted one and a light. The first drag made her cough; the second one didn't. "My kid brother was in and out of intensive care near the end," Maggie said. "I wanted to spend every last minute with him. Thought if I could kick the habit under that pressure, I'd never smoke again. Guess I was wrong."

Dupree watched her turn and walk over to a window. He tried to think of something encouraging or comforting to say, but came up empty.

"Yo, Doc."

Tejada was standing, laptop in hand, next to Walker, who was busy on her PowerBook.

Dupree glanced at Maggie again, then went to join them.

Tejada showed him the first dozen lines of the e-mail. "No way to track this, it be sent through a string of remailer boards. But that Website they want Maggie to visit's the giveaway. 'Mindmeld'? So *Star Trek*, so Code Boy."

Walker looked up from her screen and scowled. "Code Boy also phreaked the phone company in Wyoming. That area-three-oh-seven number is officially not in use. Since he sure as hell didn't fly his geek ass to Cheyenne, I'm guessing it's the top of a daisy chain."

"Translation, please?" said Dupree.

"The same stunt me and Nacio sometimes pull. You call-forward through a bunch of unused numbers all around the country, nobody can trace you."

Over by the window, Maggie continued to stare down at the darkened courtyard in the middle of the compound. The deep draughts of fresh air she had been taking weren't helping. Butchering Teddy wasn't enough; trying to kill her and Dupree wasn't enough; now they were after her mother. Maybe she should borrow a street-sweeper from Javier, fly back to New York, and blow all those MedEx fuckers away. But Maggie knew her rage was hollow; in truth, she felt almost paralyzed by the image of her mother sleeping soundly at this hour, oblivious of any danger. The strength she had been able to summon when Petey lay dying, when Tomczack sprang his ambush, was gone now. Because one wrong move, and she could be condemning the woman she loved.

Her decision made, Maggie finally turned to face the others. "Listen, guys, I'm the one Tomczack and his people are after, so I'm going to cut. This isn't your fight."

"Says who?" retorted Walker. "Girl, stick to things you know."

"Leepi speaks truth," Tejada said. "Doc told you about Guillermo? Then you know it's also his fight, which means it's Leepi's and mine too. Now you ain't got no choice but to answer 'cause those pricks be holding a blade to your throat. Only question is, you like to talk or you like to type? Either way, you got to play it out, see where it leads. And other than them telling you to off yourself, and you agreeing to do it, know that we're here for you."

Maggie was overcome by the show of support and by the logic she knew to be sound. Barely trusting her voice, she said, "Sometimes words are inadequate, so . . . thank you. In terms of contacting them, your call. Which way's safer?"

"Same difference," Walker said. "Calls that leave this compound can't be traced back. You might want to factor this in, though. We talk at maybe a hundred words per minute, faster if we're revved. Online means chat room or forum or modem-to-modem—maybe forty words per minute, eighty max unless you've got a Ph.D. from some typing school."

Maggie grinned. "Good point. Let's go digital. Something tells me that tonight, the more reaction time the better."

Tejada began linking her laptop to the other two boxes in the room so the session would simultaneously display on all three screens.

Five minutes later Maggie was on the Net, typing http://www.mindmeld.com.

After a slight pause a welcome screen appeared:

NAME OF VISITOR:

She typed "Marguerite Sepulveda."

ENTER HOME PHONE OF PAUL BARRY:

"Weird password prompt," Walker said, reading the words on her own screen. "Who's Paul Barry?"

"Guy I broke up with a while back," Maggie muttered, typing Paul's number. "What don't those bastards know about me?"

DATA BEING PROCESSED. PLEASE WAIT.

Five long minutes later Dupree stubbed out a cigarette and said, "Is this a stall? So Leong can attempt a trace?"

"Hope so," Tejada replied. "That'll keep the dork busy until Christmas."

Suddenly all three of their screens split into the familiar two-column chat-room configuration. The narrow left-hand column displayed the sender's log-in, the wide right-hand column the message itself. In the early days of computing, when online sessions tended to be modem-to-modem, words popped up on-screen a letter at a time, at the speed at which they were typed. Chat-room messages were composed offline, then posted in their entirety.

The first message popped up on-screen:

CENTURY   YOU AND ME NEED TO TALK
                           PRONTO. WHERE DO I SEND
                           PLANE FOR PICKUP?

Maggie was stunned. So much for their assumption that MedEx had left the summonses in her mailboxes and on her answering machines. But who the hell was "Century"? Then she remembered the memo glimpsed when she accidentally overrode Len Reifsnyder's screensaver. Could this be the same person who was receiving unauthorized copies of her green sheets? If so, then Caduceus 21 must be a party to Tomczack's murderous activities after all. Something wasn't adding up, Maggie thought; time to regroup. "Duchess, Data," she said, "you ever turn up anything on that name I gave you? Century Chisholm?"

"Not much," Walker replied. "Only one database reference. The guy wrote an article for some flower magazine back in the Eighties. The author's note says he lives in Santa Fe but there's no Chisholms in the directory there."

"Can you hack the telephone company?"

"Done," Tejada said, attacking his keyboard.

Maggie sensed from the brusque and condescending message that its author wasn't the type who expected his orders to be challenged. Perhaps she could use that to her advantage. She framed a reply that was meek and confused—not much of a stretch, really—and bounced it up on-screen:

MARGUERITE SEPULVEDA   *Don't understand what*
                        business we have. Who
                        are you? Do we know
                        each other?

CENTURY   NOT YET. WILL EXPLAIN
                           FACE-TO-FACE.

MARGUERITE SEPULVEDA   *I don't do blind dates.*

As the ensuing lag stretched on, Maggie guessed a
lengthy reply was being composed. She was right:

CENTURY   LAST NIGHT HELEN WAGNER
                           CELEBRATED FRIENDS B'DAY
                           @ RUTHS CHRIS STEAK N.
                           ORLANDO. ONE GLASS
                           CHAMPAGNE NOT FINISHED.
                           STEAK MED RARE. SPUD
                           BAKED NO BUTTER. SALAD W
                           HOUSE DRESSING. NO
                           DESSERT. DECAF W
                           SWEET+LOW. ARRIVED HOME
                           9:44 PM UP TODAY 6:52
                           AM. WATCHED GOOD
                           MORNING AMERICA. OJ. REAL
                           COFFEE. ENG MUFFIN W
                           MARMALADE. LEFT FOR REC
                           ROOM 8:12 AM. SPARE ME
                           MORE TYPING. PICK AIRPORT.

Maggie felt sick; the description of her mother's tastes
and habits was too dead-on to dismiss as invention.

"Yo," Tejada called out. "Found an L. C. Chisholm
with an unlisted phone. Address is a county road outside
of Santa Fe. Think it be the same person?"

"Duchess," Maggie said, "was that writer named Century or L. C.?"

"Century. First name like that sticks with you, know
what I mean? But I downloaded the article, so let me
double-check."

Maggie decided to table that issue for now, and instead
typed:

MARGUERITE SEPULVEDA	*Someone tried to kill me in NYC Tuesday night. How do I know you won't too?*

CENTURY	I HAVE NO CAUSE TO HARM YOU. ONLY WANT TO TALK. PERSONALLY GUARANTEE YOUR SAFE ROUNDTRIP RPT ROUNDTRIP.

MARGUERITE SEPULVEDA	*What about my mother?*

The response again took several minutes:

CENTURY	SHE IS SAFE AS LONG AS MY INTERESTS ARE. TO PROVE GOOD FAITH MAN BEHIND UNFORTUNATE NYC INCIDENT IS FORMER RPT FORMER MEDEX EMPLOYEE MORRIS TOMCZACK. WILL REVEAL MORE AND GIVE YOU PROOF WHEN WE MEET.

Maggie felt some of her confusion lifting. Whatever this Century's ties with Caduceus 21, he was also obviously in bed with MedEx. More significant, something had made him trade his stick for a carrot—instead of escalating the threats against her mother, he was suddenly dangling the promise of incriminating evidence against Tomczack. An interesting change of game plans; perhaps she should play dumb a bit longer:

MARGUERITE SEPULVEDA	*Who is Morris Tomczack?*

CENTURY	YOU MET HIM AT MEDEX WHEN YOU VISITED CEO

	DUANE STRAND. TOMCZACK NO LONGER EMPLOYED THERE. CALL STRAND WHO WILL CONFIRM.
MARGUERITE SEPULVEDA	*Back in five minutes. Bye bye*

She clicked QUIT and broke the connection.

Dupree, perplexed, looked up quickly: "You okay?"

"Actually, better than when we began. There's no question that this Century has his nose inside MedEx's tent. Oh, you mean signing off on him? Negotiating trick I learned from Rob Dillon—do whatever it takes to throw the other side off-balance."

"Negotiating trick?" said Tejada. "Girl, you got *cojones* we don't know about? What if this Century don't feel like playing?"

"He already is," Maggie replied. "Read only his words, it looks like he's ordering me around. But study the sub-text, and what he's really doing is opening negotiations. He tipped his hand the moment he mentioned Tomczack."

"Damn," Tejada said, "a classic 'prisoner's dilemma.'"

"What's that?"

"Game theory. I got a book about it somewhere. Basically, it's like you and a pal get busted and put in separate cells. The Man says, we got enough to send you up for one year on a lesser charge. Rat your pal, though, you walk, he does three. You dummy up but your pal rats, he walks and you do three. One more thing: If you rat each other, you both do two years. Everything depends on how good you read your pal—he be the kind that holds 'em or folds 'em?"

"Sorry, Data, I'm missing the connection," Dupree said.

Walker answered for her friend: "The connection is, what Maggie picked up on is true. It's like they're playing

Nacio's game—Century's treating her like an equal who can do him damage. Why?"

"He's as scared of me as I am of him," Maggie said, comprehension dawning. "And that's got to be because he has no idea how much we know."

"Not 'we,'" Tejada corrected. "He thinks you be in this by yourself."

"Right again," she said. "Someone may have spotted Nguyen-Anh in New York, but Century's clueless about you and Duchess. Which gives me an idea. Duchess, can you find me the article from that flower magazine?"

Two minutes later Maggie relogged into MINDMELD.COM:

MARGUERITE SEPULVEDA	*I'm back. Are you there!*
CENTURY	YES.
MARGUERITE SEPULVEDA	*Needed the break to give my associates time to establish your identity. A 1982 issue of "International Bonsai Arboretum Journal" ran a piece on repotting techniques by a Century Chisholm. Are you that author!*

"Atta girl," Walker said. "Take it to him!"

After a pause—they could almost hear the sound of Century's jaw hitting his keyboard—a reply popped up on-screen:

| CENTURY | I AM. |
| MARGUERITE SEPULVEDA | *Is your real name L. C. Chisholm, with a* |

*residence 14 miles north
of Santa Fe NM?*

This time there was a longer pause, during which they could almost feel Chisholm's anger boil across the Net and into Tejada's study.

CENTURY   YES.

Dupree, from his vantage point behind Maggie, read her next message as she was typing it and said in alarm, "Wait up. We've found out who he is and where he lives. Why take this risk?"

"Wouldn't you, if it was your mother?" she replied softly as she bounced the message up on-screen:

MARGUERITE SEPULVEDA   *I agree to meet you under
two conditions. 1) Specify
rendezvous point, will get
there myself. 2) Require
Tomczack proof *prior*
to departing. My mother
is your insurance policy. I
want one too.*

Chisholm was in no hurry to respond, so Tejada started calling up the schedules of the airlines that serviced Santa Fe.

Ten minutes later, a reply finally popped up on-screen:

CENTURY   CHECK THIS SITE 1400 GMT
FRI FOR AUDIOTAPE. EXPECT
YOU SAO PAULO SAT. ADVISE
FLT # SO DRIVER CAN MEET.

"Brazil?" said Walker in bafflement.
"Why not?" replied Maggie, by now beyond surprise.

"Anyway, I've done Santa Fe. Nice place if you have a thing for adobe."

MARGUERITE SEPULVEDA   *Pending quality of tape, will arrive Sao Paulo Saturday. My associates will message this site with flight number and ETA after I'm in the air. Bye bye*

S A T U R D A Y
N O V E M B E R   2 1

IN the strong, slanting light of early morning, the tropical landscape scrolling by thirty-five thousand feet below Maggie Sepulveda seemed lush and virginal. She knew her romantic images of Brazil, formed by such revival-house movies as *Black Orpheus* and *That Man from Rio*, were hopelessly outdated. The country of 190 million citizens had moved up to fifth place in world population following the disintegration of the Soviet Union and was the undisputed industrial giant of South America. It was also vilified by eco-warriors opposed to the government's attempts to develop the vast interior. If Brazil's mighty jungles and plains were indeed being bulldozed and asphalted into extinction, Maggie thought as she looked out the window, someone was doing a mighty slow job of it.

She was on the plane despite the digitized recording posted by Century Chisholm. After Buzzie Sepulveda listened to the tape—it was of radio transmissions that captured Morris Tomczack orchestrating the ambush in

Central Park—he pronounced it hearsay evidence and thus inadmissible in a criminal trial. Her ex had also relayed the news from Anson Horton that a nationwide APB had been issued for Marguerite K. Sepulveda, who was wanted for questioning in New York City. But when a Cuban gang in Florida did Tres Equis a favor and confirmed that Helen Wagner was under airtight twenty-four-hour surveillance, Maggie knew she could not ignore the summons to São Paulo.

She was traveling light, opting to leave her laptop behind in case Chisholm's people searched her. And to conceal the fact that her confederates were in Los Angeles, she had first flown to Dallas as Jennifer Lerario, then flushed the phony papers down a toilet before continuing on with another fake ID minted by Data's people.

Maggie was the only passenger up and about on the red-eye flight, having asked to be awakened at 0900 Greenwich Mean Time. Now, nursing a container of coffee, she was deep in an air-to-ground conversation.

The initial telephone channel set up by Ignacio Tejada —on which she could override a fax squeal by pressing * —had been adequate for dead-dropping messages. He had created a far more sophisticated channel to accommodate the critical signal she was to send the moment she departed São Paulo. Anyone scrutinizing Maggie's records would conclude that she was currently speaking to her own cell phone, which sat idle on the hallway table in her apartment in New York. In fact her call was being daisy-chained to Los Angeles, where Nguyen-Anh Dupree and Phillipa Walker were reviewing what few facts they had been able to unearth since she left the compound in South-Central.

Century Chisholm remained a cipher despite a full day of hacking. To leave so few electronic tracks, Walker declared, he was either one of America's disenfranchised or powerful enough to buy his privacy—and he clearly wasn't poor.

Social Security records listed a Luke Cantwell

Chisholm of Santa Fe whom city records identified as the owner of a thirty-acre spread and whom the state of New Mexico identified as the owner of several motor vehicles, including a Land Rover. Chisholm had not turned up on any of the databases that contained newspaper and magazine articles published since the mid-1980s. The major credit agencies reported that Chisholm carried no mortgage, had no outstanding loans, held no charge cards, and maintained a single bank account (average balance: $15,000). Chisholm's phone bills showed he made few local calls and none to Brazil; nor did the São Paulo phone directory list any subscribers with his surname. Most curious of all, Chisholm held no U.S. passport.

"I'm going to ring off so you guys can get some sleep," Maggie finally said. As reassuring as it was to talk to Dupree and Duchess, she realized they were exhausted, having stayed up past 2 A.M. to take this call; Los Angeles lay four time zones west of her current position. "Oh, I almost forgot—how's Data?"

"Him and Large landed safely," Walker said. "Listen up—be strong, girl."

"Everything's going to be all right," Dupree added. "Just trust yourself, and trust us."

"Will do. Thanks, guys. Speak to you as soon as I'm in the air and heading home." She cradled the handset, returned to her seat, and drifted back into an uneasy sleep that lasted another two hours, until the cabin crew began serving breakfast.

According to a guidebook Maggie found at the airport in Dallas, only Mexico City and Tokyo boasted larger populations than São Paulo. She had spent time in both but neither looked nearly as intimidating as the city they were now circling. If a photographer were to superimpose Manhattan's endless parade of high-rises onto Los Angeles's cloverleafed sprawl, surely the result would look like the smog-shrouded behemoth below her. Who needed *Blade Runner*'s noirish megalopolis of the future when it already existed?

The immigration officer at Cumbica International Airport accepted the U.S. passport issued to Marguerite Kragen Sepulveda—had the Tres Equis experts ever before forged a document that bore its user's true name?—and stamped it without a second glance. Carrying only a knapsack containing a toothbrush, a change of clothes, and several books, it took her less than a minute to clear Customs.

Maggie pushed into the lobby and spotted a dark-complexioned man in his mid-thirties holding a placard hand-lettered with her name.

The man was not expecting a woman rudely dressed in a baggy Butthole Surfers T-shirt, old jeans worn through at the knees and frayed at the bottom, and ungainly shoes like those that soldiers wore. But he recovered quickly and said, "Ms. Sepulveda? I am Pedro. *Tío* Century welcomes you. You have bags?"

She shook her head.

As Pedro led her from the terminal he said, "You are in São Paulo before?"

"No, it's my first time here."

"*Tío* Century say maybe you want to see zoo, or museums, or many, many fine stores. I will take you as you wish."

"Thank you," Maggie said, "but I came to see Mr. Chisholm."

"He is happy to see you too," Pedro replied, opening the door of a pearl-gray stretch Cadillac. "Maybe later. Now, he is most busy."

THE long rosewood conference table around which the Marx Dillon & Neil partners held their top-of-the-weeks was strewn with papers. The offices were deserted on a Saturday but the troika had come in to examine the stack of documents FedExed the previous day to Rob Dillon's home in New Jersey. Normally he would have been notified of the package's arrival and arranged for it to be messengered to the office, but his wife Deirdre had been at a charity luncheon and the au pair had taken the kids to the pediatrician.

Whoever sent the packet from La Guardia Airport shortly after dawn Thursday morning had left his or her name off the waybill and failed to include any explanatory note. Yet the source was obvious: Maggie Sepulveda.

Dillon, who had read the documents the previous night, was waiting for Larry Marx and Nigel Neil to finish. It was slow going. Teddy Quereshi had generated a series of complex charts and tables to support his contention that Caduceus 21's Provider Efficiency Index was based on fraud. Even more unsettling was the printout of Quereshi's last letter, his glyphed fax to Maggie.

Nigel Neil finally placed the printout back on the table and said, "Might I suggest we fly Ms. Unger up from Knoxville and have her look these over? They could be clever forgeries meant to harm our client. Or, Mr. Quereshi might have been cracking under stress . . . I mean, his daft allegation that someone from Caduceus Twenty-One was reading his e-mail? Now, really."

"I'm with you on that one, Nigel," said Larry Marx. "Christ, must be something in the water down there. Sepulveda said the same thing about our system. Know what it cost us to have those techies come in and sweep it? Twelve thou, just because she suspects ghosts in the machine. I vote we dock her year-end bonus twelve thou."

"Shall I call Ms. Unger?" asked Neil.

"I vote no," Marx said. "Too many people see this stuff, word's bound to leak out."

Rob Dillon looked up. "What are you saying, Larry? We sit on this?"

"Er, we have no idea of the provenance of this material," Marx replied. "A box of papers from some anonymous sender?"

"Shit," Dillon said, "I don't believe I'm hearing this."

Marx flushed. "I don't exactly see you walking in the door with another deal that nets us ten million."

Dillon squeezed the Bic in his hand so hard that it cracked. "We got one murder, one attempted murder, one missing partner. Our people, Larry."

"Since when is crap like this proof?" protested Marx, gesturing at the documents. "What do you propose we do, give it to that fucking cop Beltran? So he can give us the third degree again? This is guaranteed to hit the front page within twenty-four hours, and I'm not talking about those fucking tabloids. Unh-unh, Dillon, it's got the *Times* and the *Journal* written all over it. Suppose Nigel's right, suppose this is some kind of hoax. What happens to Marx Dillon? And what's our defense when Reifsnyder hits us with a libel-and-slander suit?"

"Larry's right, Rob," Neil said.

"Fair enough," Dillon said. "First we hear Caduceus's side of the story. Then we go to the cops."

"Wait a minute," Larry Marx said, planting a quavering hand atop the papers nearest him. "Er, we have a quorum present, and I vote against that course of action."

Nigel Neil studiously avoided the gazes of both his partners, wishing this moment would go away; there was no neutral ground available to occupy.

Rob Dillon spared him the decision by getting up, retrieving the large FedEx envelope, and reaching for the nearest document.

"God damn you, Dillon!" shouted Larry Marx, using both outstretched arms to frantically sweep papers toward the other end of the table.

Rob Dillon looked at him and said, "Who was the king that ordered the tide to stop?"

"What?" said Marx. "What are you, nuts? You're going to tear down all that we built, and you're asking about some fuck . . ."

"Canute," Nigel Neil said softly. "King of Norway, Denmark, and England. Tenth century. Rob's right, Larry.

We can't dig a hole and bury this material. These are printouts. Whoever sent them has the original files."

Marx froze, his face pale as parchment. He looked as if he were about to burst into tears. Instead, he bolted from the room.

Rob Dillon reached for the phone and punched 1-423-555-1212.

"Shall I go down with you?" asked Neil.

Dillon shook his head. "Information? Knoxville, please. The home number for a Leonard Reifsnyder."

THE courtyard of the Tejada compound was somnolent under the high morning sun. Nguyen-Anh Dupree sat against the trunk of a shade tree, a wineglass in one hand, a cigarette in the other, and a stack of newly purchased hardcovers and paperbacks by his side. On waking he had tried to distract himself by borrowing the geezermobile and driving over to one of the mammoth bookstores near the USC campus. To someone who usually depended on the kindness of friends for hand-me-down volumes, it was like being set loose in the proverbial candy store. Yet since returning to the compound with three hundred dollars' worth of books, he had done little more than glance at the cover blurbs and flap copy.

His immediate concern was for Maggie Sepulveda, who wouldn't be calling until she was safely en route back home. The wait reminded him of the most excruciating part of NASA's old Apollo program. Like most kids growing up in the late 1960s, Dupree had avidly followed the lunar missions on television. There was a period during each orbit when the spacecraft passed behind the moon and out of radio contact with Houston. The scientific term for this phenomenon now escaped him, but the communications blackout lasted about seven minutes. Maggie's stood at nine hours and counting.

Dupree felt as though he himself was also on a perilous journey, from darkness to light. For the past few days, he had been buffeted by emotions held in check since he joined Médecins Sans Frontières.

The organization's toughest requirement was that its volunteers suspend moral judgments; there was simply no place in a doctor's bag for outrage. Those who couldn't steel themselves against the miseries and cruelties and injustices they witnessed daily were soon history. Yet those who could were left pondering a terrible question: Was the soul like a muscle—something that withered unless exercised? If so, veterans like him were doomed. For each of them had learned to look the other way, to turn the other cheek, to affect studied neutrality as a survival mechanism.

In hindsight, the daylong talk with Maggie in the New York hotel suite had been like vigorously shaking a can of soda. And the tab-popper that released a maelstrom of pent-up feelings was her simple question about why he'd joined MSF. For instance, when had he last told the story of Arthur and Emma's adventure in Iran? Or thought of the Naipaul quote, much less shared it with another person? Why this unexpected breach in his defenses?

Or had the change within him actually begun the moment Don Joaquin informed him of the disappearance of Guillermo Chacon? Something had snapped for sure that night; suddenly, Dupree could no longer view the plight of the world's dispossessed from afar. And the more he had learned about Guillermo's fate, the more personal it got. So strong had his anger grown that less than four days earlier, he had without hesitation set another human on fire. Dupree knew firsthand that vengeance was an ugly and dangerous desire, having worked so hard to keep it at bay for more than two decades, since the incident in Lintonia Park.

Dusk had been falling on Yazoo City that long-ago spring day as Nguyen-Anh, then in seventh grade, hurried home from some after-school activity. The shortest way was through the park, a modest field with a playground at its southern end and a few trees along its northern border.

He had almost made it across when three high-school boys stepped out from behind the trees. He knew them to be members of the football team: the quarterback; his best friend, the fullback, who was shouldering a Louisville Slugger; and a benchwarmer who carried water for the two stars.

Gook-boy, the quarterback had said, we plain don't like you. Your kind've killed too many of our people. And when we're done whipping your little yellow ass, we're gonna go look up that mama of yours. See, we want to know if what they say about gook women is true, that their cunts go sideways?

Realizing that flight was not an option, Nguyen-Anh had found himself growing extremely still. The first blow of the baseball bat fractured his collarbone and the second broke a rib. The pain and nausea were sufficient to scramble his circuits—he still had no memory of the next five minutes—but somehow the bat ended up in his hands. Somehow two of his tormenters lay writhing on the cold ground. Somehow he had made it halfway across the park in pursuit of the third before passing out.

When his mother and *Grand-mère* Lulu May brought him home from the hospital, they found Chief Eddy Joe waiting in the living room. The man who headed up Yazoo City's police department had been welcome in the house since he was five and a kindergartenmate of Lance Dupree. The two went through school together, enlisted on the same day, and served side by side in Vietnam, where Eddy Joe was best man at Lance's wedding to Thieu Mei-lan.

But on this night his call wasn't social; the parents of the high-schoolers were demanding to press charges. The benchwarmer had escaped with no more than a bloody nose. The star quarterback, though, had a right wrist as severely shattered as his dreams of taking snaps for the Rebels of Ole Miss. And the fullback had been so severely kneecapped that he would limp for the rest of his life.

Chief Eddy Joe had taken him aside and asked two

questions. First, did Nguyen-Anh own a Louisville Slugger, Jake Gibbs model? He hadn't thought so. Second, what triggered the fight? As the boy reluctantly repeated the obscene threat against his mother, the policeman's face had hardened.

After a few moments Chief Eddy Joe said, "Nguyen-Anh, don't you worry about a thing except healing yourself. You did right to stand up for yourself. Fact is, your papa would've been damn proud of you.

"Now there's something else I mean to say. This town's basically pretty decent. That might not make much sense to you right now 'cause I've seen the tough times you and your mama have had. But understand the reason why not everyone's cottoned to you—it's ignorance, not meanness. Those mongrels you whupped, they'd be bad seeds anywhere, and I hope you come to realize that somewhere down the line."

No charges were filed in the wake of the fight in Lintonia Park. Nor did anyone in Yazoo City ever again hassle him; word spread that young Nguyen-Anh was a kung-fu black belt or some such thing. Nor did Dupree ever again consider himself just another American; it was a luxury he could not afford in a culture so tilted toward whiteness.

Dupree cocked an ear at the sound of a car entering the Tejada compound. The engine died, and then he heard the hollow *chunk* of a door shutting.

"Yo, Doc."

"Wassup, Duchess," he called out, peering around the tree trunk.

The bounce was missing from Phillipa Walker's stride and her haggard face was pale in the bright sunlight. A short night's rest had failed to repair the ferocious physical toll of the last few days. She flopped down on the grass next to him and raised her mirrorshades, revealing dark circles under her eyes.

"You need more sack time," Dupree observed.

"This is true, but tell that to my brain. It woke me up

when my alarm wasn't set to go off for two hours yet."
She looked at the half-empty bottle of Merlot and the
mound of butts in the ashtray. "Keep that up, Doc, you'll
be calling MedEx yourself to order some new kidneys and
lungs."

"You always think you'll get used to waiting, but you
never do," he said, passing her the wineglass.

Walker took a sip, then said, "You got Maggie on your
mind."

"Actually, I was thinking about my grandmother and
something that happened the spring they dedicated the
Vietnam wall." Dupree lit a fresh cigarette and leaned
back against the tree. "The American Legion post in
Yazoo City decided to have a special ceremony too, seeing that a lot of boys from the area were casualties of the
war. Including my daddy, of course. The officers came by
the house to ask us to participate.

"Mom was willing—bygones be bygones and all that.
Grand-mère Lulu May wouldn't hear of it. 'After what
you all put my daughter-in-law and grandson through?
Get out! Now!' Since moving to Yazoo City she had
never missed a Memorial Day observance. Her father, her
husband, her son, all bore this country's arms. But that
day the three of us were elsewhere. Took us and Chief
Eddy Joe's family four days to drive up to Washington—
Grand-mère was not well at the time—but damned if we
weren't on the Mall, praying and crying with all the other
survivors."

Walker was at a loss for words. In the decade she had
known Dupree, this most secure and self-confident of
men had never once hinted at a childhood scarred by prej-
udice. Finally she said, "What happened in Yazoo City?
What did they do to you and your mom?"

"Sorry, Duchess. Maybe some other time, okay?"

Realization dawning, she said, "We all thought you
joined MSF to get over Lizzie. But it was really something
that happened a long time ago, wasn't it?"

Dupree remained silent.

"Have all these years away made you happier, Doc?"

"Let's say I've experienced moments of great joy."

She contemplated the enigmatic response, then took a deep breath and said, "Does Maggie give you joy? That why you're in love with her?"

Dupree looked up, startled. "What makes you say that?"

"The way you act around her," Walker replied, her voice dull with resignation. "I knew it that first day at Javier's. You've always been a world-class listener, but when she talks you hang on every word, like you're committing them to memory. Yet you rarely look at her—it's like you're afraid she might look back and make eye contact."

"Duchess, I barely know the woman," he said defensively. "I will concede that at the moment I'm real concerned about her. Suppose the tightrope snaps. If what Buzzie says is true and that the tape is useless against Tomczack, it's sure as hell useless against this Chisholm character."

"Remember what you used to tell Javier?" she said. "When Nacio was learning how to walk again? Don't hover, you kept saying. The boy's going to fall down in front of his friends and embarrass himself. He's even going to hurt himself. It's the only way—you can't follow him around like a safety net."

Dupree nodded. "You're right. Maggie can take care of herself."

"That girl can take care of a whole lot more than herself." Walker hesitated, then said, "I never had a chance with you, did I?"

"Back when I was in L.A.? No one did. Not even Lizzie."

"That was then, this is now. I'm not the bratty little teenager you first knew."

"No, you're a fascinating woman who has yet to make peace with herself," he said, recalling Maggie's description of how Duchess had reacted in Javier's dining room. "And won't for another five or six years."

"Oh?"

"Some people peak early, Duchess. Others, like you, bloom late. Kids who get out of the blocks fast, the ones with eleven photographs in the high-school yearbook, they start to lose traction. One day you'll go to some class reunion and find yourself chatting with some very together strangers. Suddenly you'll realize you've known them since forever—it's just that back then, they were standing in the shadows, trying to figure it all out."

"Which group is Maggie?" asked Walker. "Yeah yeah yeah, you hardly know the woman, but give it your best guess."

"She's probably still peaking," Dupree replied.

"What about you?"

"I'm an outsider, watchful, suspicious. Same as you, same as her."

"How come you know these things, Doc?"

"I'm older than you, Phillipa. Age is supposed to make you wiser."

Walker looked away. "You know, that's the first time in five years you've called me by my first name."

"It's a distancing device," Dupree said lightly. "Just like you've called me 'Doc' since the night you burned dinner."

She blushed. "Believe me, I did not set out to make Chicken Chernobyl, but I was so wired I forgot to set the timer. Know what I can't get out of my mind? What if I wasn't so damn kitchen-challenged? What if that night I had gotten you to play lover instead of fire chief?"

"Our lives would have been different from that moment on," he said. "But things happen when they're meant to happen. Actually, the demographers say couples like us are going to be the rule in the Twenty-first Century."

"Medicine Boys hooking up with Code Girls? Some brave new world."

Dupree laughed. "*Life* had this article eight, ten years ago speculating about the future. Did you know that by 2025, more than half the U.S. population will be like us, people of color? Maybe that's when the madness ends."

"Don't bet on it. Casper's got Rush Limbaugh, we got Louis Farrakhan." Walker sighed. "You know, sometimes I think my life's like the title of one of Uncle Phillip's sappy songs."

" 'Big Girls Don't Cry'?" he said teasingly.

"No, 'Born Too Late.' "

The smile on Dupree's face turned quizzical as a half-forgotten refrain began to run through his mind. After a few moments he found himself chanting, almost under his breath, "*Toomba too-guh, toomba too-guh, toomba too-guh* . . ."

She looked up questioningly.

"Uncle Phillip wasn't the only one into sappy songs," he said. "My daddy was doing his training down in Texas when he heard this record by a local boy. It went on to become Number One all across the country so he made it his good-luck charm. Even took a copy to Nam instead of a rabbit's foot and it worked, too, at least his first tour, because that's when he met Mom.

"First time she invited him home for dinner, he insisted on playing it for her folks. They hadn't had such a good laugh in years. Mom told me Granddaddy Thieu said, 'The first thing the Americans must save us from is their music.' "

Dupree took another puff, exhaled, and followed the smoke upward until it became one with the air. "Every July twelfth, which was my daddy's birthday, Mom'd go to the cabinet in the living room and she'd take out this worn piece of brown paper. That's how they used to package forty-fives, plain brown paper with a big hole in the middle so you could read the label. 'Running Bear' by Johnny Preston, this one said, Mercury seven-one-four-seven-four. She'd play it once, then carefully slip it back in its sleeve. Not that it mattered—as *Grand-mère* Lulu

May used to say, 'Honey, that record's scratchier than Lady Godiva riding through a briar patch.' "

Walker, seeking to extend this moment of rare intimacy, this moment on a warm day under a high sky, said, "What reminded you of that song?"

"Trite as it was, it's about destiny. Running Bear and Little White Dove were an Indian Romeo and Juliet, meant for each other but kept apart by fate." After a few moments Dupree began to sing, in a voice as gentle as a kitten's breath, *"He couldn't swim / The raging river / 'Cause the river / Was too wide / He couldn't reach / Little White Dove / Waiting on / The other side . . ."*

"Life's not fair," Phillipa Walker said, melting into sobs.

"No, it's not," he said, folding her into his arms and clutching her tight.

THE neoclassical mansion off Avenida Paulista was built as the centerpiece of a sprawling *fazenda de café,* or coffee plantation, in 1852, when São Paulo was a sleepy tropical backwater. By the time the current owner acquired it, most of the original land had been sold off. What remained could still command a king's ransom: The grand house, restored to its former glory and surrounded by five acres of lush gardens, was a walled oasis in the heart of the city.

It was late spring in the Southern Hemisphere and as twilight approached the temperature still hovered in the low seventies. Yet the lord of the manor wore a down vest as he stood on the balcony of his second-story study; the battle to stay warm was not going well. For the past two minutes he had been studying his reluctant visitor from afar. Most men would have felt safer remaining inside and peeking through the blinds, but that wasn't Century Chisholm's style.

The young gal reading a book at poolside was certainly some piece of work. Marguerite Sepulveda damn well knew he was giving her the once-over but didn't seem to care. And if her nerves were jumpy from having to cool her heels all day, her body language didn't say so.

He hadn't meant to put off seeing her, but his priorities had been reshuffled by Haidak's e-mail of the previous day. Not that Sepulveda and her pals were any more threat to him than a pack of hounds. The dogs would sniff and track and eventually tree the coon, but then what? All they could do was mill around and bay.

Chisholm assumed the gal knew from the gay accountant that Caduceus 21's books were squirrelly. Didn't matter; no way to tie that company to him, and it was time to cut his losses on Knoxville anyway. She knew MedEx was a party to the ambush only because he himself had put her on Tomczack's trail. Didn't matter; no way to tie that company to him either even if she could get at its darkest secrets, which Strand's Chinaman swore was impossible. The one thing Sepulveda knew that irked Chisholm was his surname. How'd she come by that? Didn't matter; now that she was flushed from cover, Strand's people would cling to her like a cheap perfume. And even if she gave 'em the slip again, he still had himself an ace in the hole: Helen Wagner.

A pair of aces, actually. Sepulveda was a threat for only three or four more days, until MedEx delivered him a new heart. According to Haidak's e-mail, a prime candidate had been identified in Thailand. The ticker wasn't perfect, but compatible enough to schedule the transplant while Chisholm remained on the Priority List for a more positive match. He was returning to Santa Fe Monday. With that deadline looming, he had spent the day on a passel of business decisions that needed to be made between now and the end of the year. Strand, of course, was in on the pending surgery, but no reason for the managers of his other enterprises to know about it.

Chisholm checked his watch. Once he'd learned what flight Sepulveda was taking down, it was a simple matter for Strand's Chinaman to dig her itinerary out of the airline's database. She was booked on a flight back to Dallas late that evening. Plenty of time for Strand's people to properly stake out DFW, but would keeping her overnight in São Paulo soak some of that starch out of the gal? Why bother? He needn't pulverize her, just make sure she toed the line for another week. Might as well get it over with, he thought, turning and stepping back into his study.

Presently a young houseboy arrived at poolside to tell Maggie Sepulveda, in earnest but broken English, that *Tío* Century was ready to receive her. She looked to the house. The white-haired man in down vest, faded chambray workshirt, and chinos was no longer studying her from the balcony. Opening her knapsack, she slipped in the book she had been reading, a fascinating volume on the prisoner's dilemma borrowed from Ignacio Tejada, and rose from the chaise.

"Maggie, Maggie!" yelled one of the seven-year-olds who had been splashing in the pool for the past hour. "*Não vai,* Maggie!"

She smiled. The kids were like a canary in a mineshaft, a clear signal that she was in no immediate danger. For some reason Chisholm had given her the run of his lavishly furnished house. As a spy, Maggie felt about as competent as Maxwell Smart; the only intelligence she had been able to glean was the number of a telephone in a first-floor waiting room. Yet in her wanderings she had encountered a spectrum of people, like the youngsters in the pool, who seemed to use the estate as a country club. She had no idea of their relationship to Chisholm, but if the man intended to harm her within these walls, she reasoned, would he have permitted so many potential witnesses to see her here?

Maggie waved to the kids, then followed the houseboy into the mansion.

He led her up a formal staircase worthy of Tara to the second floor, then turned left down a corridor as wide as a five-star hotel's.

In the day and a half since her online session with

Chisholm, Maggie had game-planned a number of approaches to the pending meeting—and rejected them all. Strategy was for structured contests in which victory could be defined: rout the other army, cross the finish line first, score more points. This game was rigged; Chisholm's home-field advantage seemed insurmountable.

Which had left her pondering Muhammad Ali's eloquent philosophy, "Float like a butterfly, sting like a bee." The concept of aggressive opportunism that had guided guerrilla warriors since the dawn of history was also in vogue with late-twentieth-century American businessmen. Get Rob Dillon started on the subject of hardball negotiating tactics and he could sound like a disciple of Ho Chi Minh. Dictate the agenda, Dillon was fond of preaching, so your opponent can't. Rile the other guy, force him into an error. Outwitting is better than outhitting, but take a punch if it affords you a clean shot at his chops.

Such in-your-face bromides had always struck Maggie as needlessly macho. Driving school had taught her that nerve and willpower were anatomy-blind. At speed and in the zone, there was no room for social niceties like politeness or deference, no distinction between masculine or feminine.

Her only chance against Chisholm would be to rely on gut reactions. Unless she could pinpoint some vulnerability and exploit it, as he had by threatening Helen Wagner, this was going to be a slam dunk—with her the dunkee. And she needed to do it quickly; the daylong wait had severely jeopardized the plans that hinged on her catching a specific flight from São Paulo that night.

The houseboy knocked twice on the massive hardwood door at the end of the corridor, then turned the knob.

The high-ceilinged room had a more melancholy tone than the rest of the house. Its spare furnishings, mostly elegant antiques, were echoed by an oversized print hanging on one wall, a moody black-and-white photograph of an empty farmhouse standing on a bleak prairie. The room was also oppressively hot from a large fire crackling in the hearth.

By the fireplace sat the white-haired man from the balcony. Without rising from his tan Eames wingchair he said, in a reedy voice, "Howdy, Ms. Sepulveda. I'm Century Chisholm, and I do thank you for coming."

"Thanks for giving me so many options," she replied.

Chisholm seemed amused, rather than ruffled, by her hostility. He made a show of eyeing her outfit, calculated to be discourteous, and said, "That what fashionable bankers wear in New York these days?"

"Ever try outrunning a killer in a skirt and heels?"

His chuckle reminded her of a puppy's bark. "Ain't you the feisty one. That poor-little-me thing you did online the other night, that was just playacting, wasn't it? Good. I like to know young folks that aren't above tricking their elders, means you're going far in life. Come on over and set yourself down."

So much for riling Chisholm.

He was obviously American, Maggie decided as she crossed the room, even though he was the master of this grand house in São Paulo. In his mid-seventies, as indicated by the Social Security records; more diminutive than she'd imagined; extremely pale but in apparent good health. And probably a fan of Richard Nixon, who always kept a fire burning in the Oval Office, even in the heat of summer. She slid onto the sofa and plopped her knapsack on the coffee table that separated her from Chisholm.

"What can I get you?" he said. "Coffee? A drink . . ."

"I want your goons to leave my mother alone, Mr. Chisholm."

"Most everybody calls me Century and I hope you will too," he said mildly, motioning the houseboy from the room. "We'll discuss your mother shortly, Ms. Sepulveda. First, why don't you tell me a little about yourself."

"What is this, a job interview?"

He chuckled again. "Why am I getting the distinct impression you don't like me? You think the two of us are on opposite sides? Nothing could be further from the truth. Fact is, we both want many of the same things."

"Sure. That's why you sicced Tomczack on me."

"You think I was a party to that?" He shook his head ruefully. "If I wanted you dead, ma'am, doubt you'd be sitting here right now. And I'd danged sure be off doing something more profitable. First I heard of the incident was from Strand, who came across the tape by accident. He's sick, just sick about it, along with the boy Tomczack killed in Knoxville."

"Teddy Quereshi?" she said, injecting a note of scorn into her voice. "How convenient. Next you're going to tell me Tomczack also snatched the Lindbergh baby and helped McVeigh plant the bomb in Oklahoma City."

Chisholm's eyes narrowed almost imperceptibly before he could affect a pose of avuncular exasperation.

She had finally gotten under his skin; but why had one sarcastic crack worked and not others?

"Didn't know I was put on this earth to amuse you," he said a bit testily. "You want to be like that, missy, go right ahead. I got all night. What I'm trying to get you to understand is why Tomczack bushwhacked you. Had to after murdering the boy, to cover his tracks."

"You lost me," she said. "Teddy was looking into the finances of Caduceus Twenty-One. Tomczack works for . . ."

"Worked, I keep telling you. Past tense. Come Monday, the original of the tape I sent you's going to be in the hands of the New York police."

"But he was employed by them at the time he killed Teddy," she persisted, curious that Chisholm was working so hard to dissociate Tomczack from MedEx. "Why should he care about Caduceus's finances?"

"Short answer is, he's a goddamned embezzler as well as a murderer," he growled. "The account he was looting is where C-Twenty-One affiliates settle up with MedEx.

Tomczack wasn't figuring on a bunch of bankers nosing through the books in Knoxville, and he got to worrying that your accountant feller would pick up the discrepancies. Now we could follow that trail a spell, I got documents to convince you. But let's save you and me some time. Let me tell you a couple things you don't know."

"It's your bat and your ball," Maggie said with a shrug.

"Damn white of you to finally acknowledge that, ma'am." Chisholm leaned forward. "Question you're asking yourself is, how come this old cuss knows so much about C-Twenty-One and MedEx? 'Cause I own 'em both. Actually that's not technically true, the controlling interests are in the name of a nonprofit in Delaware called the A.L.B. Foundation, but that's mine too. You get the point. You're also starting to see why Dr. Wilkes and Ms. Osteen and Reifsnyder couldn't afford to do an IPO."

"The due diligence," she said. "We turn up a silent partner, the deal goes south."

"Bingo. Now here's something else you don't know. I'm shutting down C-Twenty-One."

Maggie's eyes widened.

"That's right, Ms. Sepulveda. Don't worry, we'll find a way to make your firm whole, but I can't let the placement go through. Soon as Strand told me Tomczack was fiddling the accounts, see, I had my people go in and assess the damage. Know what? That PEI index Knoxville brags about, the one that shows C-Twenty-One to be such efficient health-care providers? Based on bad numbers. Lord knows I'm no angel. I also don't steal, and in my book selling damaged goods is the same as stealing."

Maggie managed to maintain her poker face, but her mind was racing. Chisholm had no way of knowing about the glyphed memo from Teddy Quereshi spelling out the fraud. So why was he volunteering this information? She hesitated, then said, "How were the numbers cooked?"

"Gist of it is, they been underbilling some services, overbilling others," he said, waving his hand dismissively. "Didn't concern myself with the particulars, the bottom line was all I needed to know."

"Who's responsible?"

"Rather not say, ma'am. We're dealing with it internally."

Maggie screwed up her face in concentration. "Let me guess," she said. "You're going to pin this one on Morris Tomczack too?"

Tiny spots of color surfaced on Chisholm's pale cheeks. He plucked at his upper lip, then said, "All right. If you must know, it's Dr. Wilkes."

The response surprised her. The evidence clearly pointed to complicity at the very top of Caduceus 21, but Aurelia seemed the least likely candidate. Was Chisholm lying? And why was he so generously airing the health-care company's dirty linen while trying to lead her away from MedEx? Not wanting to let on how much she knew about Duane Strand's organ-snatchers, Maggie made her next question neutral: "What happens to MedEx?"

"Don't know that they can survive without C-Twenty-One," Chisholm replied. "The name of their game is volume, and no other health-care chain does that many transplants. Be a crying shame to see 'em fold, they've bailed out a lot of folks in need. Fine bunch of people—excepting Tomczack, of course."

"If you say so," Maggie said.

He frowned. "That look on your pretty little face says I'm not making much headway. Why's that, Ms. Sepulveda?"

"You could've told me these things online the other night. You didn't need to involve my mother, and I didn't need to pile up more frequent-flyer miles."

"The good Lord gave us five senses, some'd say six," Chisholm said. "The computer filters out all but one. I needed to see you face-to-face, hear your voice, sniff your scent. Reason is, I reckon you to be one spooked little lady after what Tomczack tried to do, and I don't want you acting rashly. I said I was aiming to disband

C-Twenty-One, not pull its plug. How many people they got signed up in their health-care plans? Three million?"

"Closer to three-point-five," she said.

"There you go, three-point-five million. Can't just throw all those good folks overboard without a peep. I don't want you accidentally fouling my rescue lines, so I thought it best that we have this little chat. That's why I had to get your undivided attention."

"Well, you got it. So cut the Mother Teresa crap and get to the point."

Chisholm heaved an avuncular sigh. "Here I am, trying to set you straight on lots of things you don't know about. What thanks do I get except a lot of lip? They tell me you're a smart gal. I was expecting better from you."

"And I was expecting better from you," Maggie fired back. "Are you a congenital liar, or just not very bright?"

Chisholm's face tightened.

"I'll give you a B-minus for effort, though," she continued, finally seeing the pattern: Chisholm did not take kindly to any suggestion that he was an unschooled hick. "Had me fooled for a while with how much you seem to know about the players at C-Twenty-One and MedEx. Then I realized any idiot with a modem can go online and search out things like corporate histories and officers. My job for the past seven years has been following the health-care industry. I've never come across the name Luke Cantwell Chisholm."

Rather than bristling, he surprised her by visibly relaxing and sinking back into his wingchair. "That so?" he said in a voice that was caginess itself. "What else you think you know about me, Ms. Sepulveda?"

"Born May sixteenth, 1924," she replied, "to the Reverend Richard and Mary Chisholm in Sapporo, Japan. Current residence, Santa Fe, New Mexico—and, by the looks of it, São Paulo, Brazil. Connection to the health-care industry, none."

Chisholm studied her a few moments, his patronizing smile grown almost to a smirk, then gestured to the oversized black-and-white print of the farmhouse hanging on one wall. "That look like Sapporo to you, Ms. Sepulveda? Try Benjamin, Oklahoma. Town shriveled up and died after World War Two, but things were real bad way before then. Left when I was fourteen. Made my way to Frisco, lied about my age, shipped out as an able-bodied seaman. Fetched up down here a couple years later.

"Now, I reckon you know as much Brazilian history as most Americans, which ain't much. Back then this country was like our Old West. Everything was wide open to anyone with a grubstake or an idea or a strong back. Didn't matter if you was white, black, yellow—we had us all colors here, working side by side.

"There was this feller from Hakodate, Sasaki, building cheap houses for other Jap immigrants. Started out digging foundations for him but I always had a head for finances, which he finds out about after a while. Pretty soon I'm doing his books. I'm also picking up the local lingo pretty good, so he begins sending me out to drum up business from the Brazilians. That's how I made the acquaintance of a feller named Getulio Vargas. Ever hear of him?"

Maggie shook her head.

"Took over the government early on in the Great Depression. Lots of things been said about him, not all of them kind, but Vargas kept the economy strong during a bad time by encouraging construction. I manage to get my company more than its fair share of projects in São Paulo. Sasaki-*san* shows his gratitude by giving me first option on buying the business when he retired, which I do. You with me so far?"

"Frankly, no," she said. "What I'm hearing isn't exactly the résumé of someone claiming to be a major force in the health-care industry. More to the point, I'm sure this Vargas character accepted bribes—but from a seven-year-old? I don't think so."

Chisholm's eyes fairly sparkled with mischief. "Always a pleasure to know a gal with a head for sums, not enough of you got that knack. You're correct, of course. If I was born when the records say, couldn't be doing business down here in the early Thirties, now could I?

"Anyway, everything's fine until Vargas outwears his welcome in 'Forty-five. Things get a bit tight for me here, so I leave the business in the hands of people I can trust and head back north.

"America was an interesting place to be at that time, Ms. Sepulveda. The situation was mighty fluid. Contractors were trading in their old heavy equipment, things like cranes and earthmovers and graders, to buy the postwar models. I began buying the used rigs and shipping 'em down here. Gave my people a hell of an edge over them other Brazilian companies. Plus you had millions of men back from overseas, not all of them wanting to return to their old hometowns. Taking on a new identity was not a bothersome chore."

"Is that your clever way of telling me your name's not really Chisholm?" she said.

"It is now," he replied with a self-satisfied nod.

Maggie realized that her attempts to rattle Chisholm had been at best laughable. Might as well go for broke, she thought, getting to her feet and reaching for her knapsack.

"Just where do you think you're going, missy?" he barked.

"Out for some fresh air. Your story's as overbaked as this room."

"Sit down!"

"Why, so you can bore me to death some more? Listen, Chisholm, maybe it's the onset of Alzheimer's, maybe it's just a chemical imbalance. Whichever, I really think you ought to save your wacko fantasies for some doctor who might be able to help you."

He glared at her, visibly struggling to regain control of his temper. Finally he said, "Gal, I try to show you every courtesy, but you insist on being a jackass about it. Fine. I reckon it's time to fish or cut bait. Let me spell out exactly what I want and exactly why you're going to give it to me. . . ."

Two soft knocks, and the door to the study inched open.

The houseboy stuck his head in and said, "*Tío* Century, Elspeth *em casa.*"

"*Deixa ela entrar,*" Chisholm replied, his anger instantly dissolving as he scrambled out of his wingchair.

As a woman in her early twenties entered the room, Maggie couldn't help but think of that most famous of all sambas: "*Tall and tan and young and lovely / The girl from Ipanema goes walking / And when she passes each one she passes goes A-A-H. . . .*" She was an exemplar of Brazil's interracial heritage, the genes of her Caucasian, African, mestizo, and Asian forebears having combined to create an arresting face dominated by almond-shaped eyes the color of jade. Her frame was that of a swimmer, her dress an austere off-white Prada that Maggie had window-shopped in Manhattan but could never justify buying.

The young woman glided over to Chisholm, who barely came up to her shoulders, kissed him on both cheeks, then smothered him in an embrace.

"Elspeth, say howdy to Maggie Sepulveda from New York," he said, a proud arm around her waist. "Ms. Sepulveda, Elspeth de Carvalho Freixas."

"It is so nice to make your acquaintance, Maggie," Elspeth said in a husky tropical voice, extending her hand. She noticed the Butthole Surfers T-shirt and grinned. "Their CDs are impossible to find here, it is still all *macarena*. Do you remember what store sells your shirt? It is too fantastic."

"Actually, it's from out of a friend's closet."

She laughed. "That is always the best store of all."

"Elspeth is fresh from her honeymoon," Chisholm said.

Maggie said, "My best wishes for a happy and long marriage."

"Thank you very much, Maggie. *Tio,* you must take some time to go back to Paris soon. It is as beautiful as ever."

"Then ten days wasn't enough."

"Yes it was, because France is still filled with the French." Elspeth giggled. "I am so happy to be in São Paulo again."

"You go back to work Monday?"

She nodded.

"This gal's a São Paulo correspondent for Globo's primetime newscast," Chisholm said, beaming. "She'll be a co-anchor before she's thirty."

Elspeth blushed. "*Tio* Century, *voce me enfeiticou!* The reason I am so rude as to interrupt you is, Django and I are making a little dinner party tonight. You are free to come? At perhaps nine-thirty? Of course, Maggie, we are delighted to have you join us also."

Chisholm said to Maggie, "I'd accept, Ms. Sepulveda. Elspeth and Django have the best damn chef in Brazil. Course, they stole him from me."

"Thank you, Elspeth, but I really must fly back to the States tonight."

"I hope you have had a chance to see São Paulo at least?"

"Not really," Maggie replied. "This trip is strictly work."

"You are in the construction business?"

"Actually, Ms. Sepulveda's an investment banker," Chisholm said with a puckish grin. "She came down to learn more about Caduceus Twenty-One."

The offhand remark floored Maggie; it seemed impossible for this young woman to be mixed up in Chisholm's machinations.

"The people who take such good care of me in America?" asked Elspeth.

Chisholm nodded, then said to Maggie, "This gal spent her junior year up north, studying broadcasting. I joined her up with a C-Twenty-One HMO."

"And I am so grateful that you do," Elspeth said. "I love the college but not the weather. I remember how sick I am almost every other week. I am afraid São Paulo is not very good practice for winter in Boston."

Maggie smiled, remembering the nor'easters that howled down from Canada. "I survived two of them myself in Cambridge, mostly in a little basement coffee-house that served the best *café con leche* and homemade soups."

"Not the Café Pamplona!"

"Where else?"

"Fantastic! You really must come back soon, Maggie. I will tell my station manager he must give me time off to show São Paulo to a good friend from the Café Pamplona." Elspeth turned to Chisholm. "So *Tío*, we see you later, yes?"

Chisholm checked his watch. "I'll do my darnedest to make it. Why don't I ring the house in an hour."

Maggie knew her reprieve was drawing to an end. Elspeth's providential visit had delayed, not canceled, the boom Chisholm was set to lower—no doubt accompanied by one of his revolting little chuckles. Though she'd pushed some of his buttons, he had never once relinquished his iron grip on the meeting. In fact he was openly toying with her. Why else arbitrarily inject C-Twenty-One into the conversation, why else urge her to accept the dinner invitation?

Watching Chisholm embrace the young woman again, Maggie was suddenly struck by the genuine affection he had for Elspeth. Was she his vulnerability?

The last-ditch counterattack beginning to form in Maggie's mind was vile beyond words; but then, all's fair in love and guerrilla war.

Chisholm walked Elspeth to the door. As he started back across the room, the pleasure of her visit was fast fading from his face: "Now, where were we?"

Maggie flopped onto the sofa and casually kicked her

Doc Martens up on the coffee table. "Aren't you kind of old to be her sugar daddy?"

"Come again?" he said, stopping short at both the outrageous question and the sight of her clunky shoes on his expensive antique furniture.

"Am I going too fast for you, Chisholm? My question is, when did you start fucking Elspeth? When she was thirteen? Twelve?"

"I'll thank you to watch your mouth, woman!" he roared, seeming to grow in size in direct proportion to his anger.

"Come off it," Maggie said, her voice as insolent as she could make it. "All day I've been hearing people refer to you as Tío. You're as much their uncle as I'm their aunt."

Chisholm continued to regard her in a cold fury. Then he smiled thinly and said, "Know how long a person's body's built to last, Ms. Sepulveda? Barring major injury or illness?"

"In theory, a hundred twenty-five years," she replied. "That your goal?"

"You bet."

Without another word he pulled free his shirttails and began undoing the buttons.

Maggie sat transfixed, as if she were being sucked into an alternate universe.

Chisholm slipped off his faded chambray workshirt to reveal a torso pale as an albino's and puckered with neat ridges of shiny white scar tissue.

Maggie instantly felt her gorge rise; the distinctive geometric incisions told her exactly which procedures had been performed. The vertical cut bisecting his chest from just below the Adam's apple to the sternum had been made to give surgeons access to Chisholm's heart. The horizontal cut that arced along the bottom of the rib cage, as well as a second vertical cut that descended to almost the navel, had been made to give surgeons access to his liver.

Chisholm, clearly enjoying the queasy look on Maggie's face, twisted around to display his back.

The pair of cuts just above the beltline, slanting downward and outward from the spine, had been made to give surgeons access to his kidneys.

He slipped his shirt on, then fastidiously buttoned it and tucked in the tails before turning to face her again. His eyes were hard as flint and his voice cold as ice as he said, "You know my last name's not really Chisholm but I failed to mention earlier that my first name really is Century. My folks thought it fitting, seeing as how I was born on the first of January, 1900. Yes, I aim to make it to a hundred twenty-five, and damn well ought to with all the fresh parts I got inside me. That explain my interest in health care? Good, thought it would.

"Another thing I failed to mention is, first year I was down here, met and married a wonderful gal. Cholera took Marpessa before I was able to afford this here *fazenda*, but not before she blessed me with five young 'uns. One of the pleasures of a long life is getting to know your grandchildren—and their children and their children's children. Did you know 'great-great-grandfather' happens to be more than a mouthful in any language? That explain why Elspeth and all the others call me *Tío*? Good, thought it would.

"Now, much as I hate to end our little chat, Ms. Sepulveda, I got someplace to be in just a spell. How long you think it's going to take for an orderly liquidation of C-Twenty-One? Transfer its affiliations, its HMO clients, to other health-care chains?"

"Four to six months," she replied.

"That's what I'm figuring too. To show you I'm not an unreasonable old cuss, let's call it four months. That's what I want from you and your 'associates'—mind your own business between now and mid-March. After that, you do anything you damn well please. Fuck with me before then, the biggest bunch of flowers at Helen Wagner's funeral's going to be mine. Any questions?"

Maggie shook her head.

"Sorry, Ms. Sepulveda, don't think I heard your reply."

"No, sir. No questions."

"Good," snapped Chisholm, who sank back into his wingchair and dismissed her by swiveling around to face the roaring fire.

WITH fifteen seconds to go in the first half, a one-touchdown lead, and the football on their own thirty-one-yard line, the UCLA Bruins elected to run out the clock. Phillipa Walker looked from the large-screen TV in Ignacio Tejada's downstairs den over to the easy chair in which Dupree dozed. With Maggie in Brazil, and Nacio in Florida, she and Doc had been reduced to couch potatoes; but then, they also serve who only sit and wait.

The two teams began to trot off the field.

Walker would rather watch coral grow than sit through a college halftime show, so she reached for the remote tuner.

A solid minute of channel surfing had her thinking that marching bands might not be so bad after all. Nacio subscribed to one of the satellite services that beamed down more than 125 stations. But the tube on Saturday afternoon brought to mind the axiom GIGO. Unless you were a sports freak blissing out on a menu of ten football games, a couple of late-season golf tournaments, an ice-skating exhibition, a stock-car race, and soccer from Mexico, the programming was indeed garbage. Walker restlessly began clicking through the lineup a second time, past syndicated reruns and rap videos and cooking shows and all-news channels and cartoons and slice-and-dice movies and infomercials and all-weather channels and home-shopping shows.

Now the forty-five-inch screen filled with a close-up of a tearstained Casper sporting a soaring bouffant, gaudy suit, and enough gold jewelry to make Deion Sanders jealous. "And the Lord sayeth, 'Confess your sins,'" sobbed the televangelist in a voice that reminded her of Jim Nabors talking with his mouth full.

Zap: ". . . be sure you clamp that chair leg securely while the glue sets . . ."

Zap: ". . . in my opinion, biotech stocks are still a good value . . ."

Zap: ". . . Kristin, give us your analysis of this surprising verdict . . ."

Walker suddenly backtracked to the televangelist and sat through the remainder of his sermon on the healing power of owning up to your sins. Then she pressed MUTE and shook Dupree awake: "Doc, mind calling Buzzie Sepulveda? I think I just figured out a work-around that'll nail MedEx but good."

S U N D A Y
N O V E M B E R · 2 2

A long row of Tampa PD cruisers sat idling along the curb, their turret lights filling the night with pulsating flashes that hurt Ignacio Tejada's eyes. The cops who had cordoned off Hillsborough Avenue were keeping a wary vigil over the three dozen low-riders that had begun rendezvousing at a deserted shopping mall around 2:30 A.M. Seventy yards away, the gangbangers in the low-riders stared back. The early-morning stillness was broken by sporadic bursts of radio traffic too faint and staticky to decipher except on a police-band radio like the one in the chopped and channeled '52 Mercury in which Tejada sat.

It had been forty minutes since he got the green light from Phillipa Walker: Maggie Sepulveda was in the air and en route home. Tejada turned to the driver of the Merc. "Not to be dissing your judgment, bro, but we need all these wheels? Like, the Man be ready to piss his pants."

"Only need three, Nacio," said Eduardo Mirabal,

leader of the Cuban gang known as Los Cuervos. "But you don't want nobody hurt, right?"

"Right," replied Tejada. Cubans were almost as bloodthirsty as the ancient Greeks, he thought; Eduardo's original proposal called for enough firepower to win an NRA life-achievement award.

Eduardo cocked an ear to the latest radio transmission and groaned. "You get to meet Chick Santiago. But thass okay. We be on the road in five, ten minutes, soon as he hauls his fat Twinkie ass down here."

Until yesterday Nacio had never heard of Los Cuervos of Tampa, Florida, or Eduardo of Tres Equis of Los Angeles, California. But Javier Tejada had arranged this alliance through the armorer known to Hispanic gangs across the country as Señor Uzi, an Israeli so successful he now lived on a private island off the coast of Georgia.

Thank God his brother wasn't here to see this scene, thought Nacio. Javier had wanted to send Esai Ayala because, as he explained it, if something goes bad Esai can run, you can't. Wrong thing to say. Nacio was sick of being coddled like some charity case incapable of pulling his own weight. Only after a stormy half-hour argument —the first time Javier had raised his voice at him in more than a decade, since the shooting—did Nacio prevail.

Eduardo suddenly leaned forward.

Tejada followed his gaze and blinked. At the entrance to the parking lot, the driver of a pizza-delivery truck was trying to talk his way past the police blockade. He leaned out his window and said, "Yo, Large."

"Wassup, Data?" replied Large Quintanilla from behind the wheel of a Lincoln Town Car rented from Hertz, the only unmodified vehicle in the group.

"You call for a pizza?"

Quintanilla nodded. "All the food places on the way here be closed. Want a slice? Pepperoni-and-mushroom, with double cheese."

Tejada laughed so hard he had to wipe his eyes. That screenwriter Erik might be able to invent a standoff as bizarro as this one, but no way could a *gabacho* dream up an appetite like Large's.

One of the police cruisers backed up to let the pizza truck through.

Quintanilla got out of the Lincoln to greet the teen-aged delivery boy, whose eyes were as big as golf balls and whose Adam's apple plunged up and down faster than Oprah's weight.

"Keep the change," Quintanilla said, accepting the box and passing back a fifty-dollar bill.

"Thankyouverymuchsir," the boy gulped, gunning the pizza truck into such a sudden U-turn that he almost collided with a Blazer coming the other way.

"Chick Santiago, Tampa PD gang liaison," Eduardo said scornfully, reaching to mute the police-band radio. "Fuckin' world-class wannabe. Watch this."

The Blazer stopped in front of Eduardo's car. A stocky man in an orange-and-white Tampa Bay Bucs wind-breaker got out, hitched his pants, and sauntered over to the Mercury.

"Yo, wassup, Officer Chick?" said Eduardo, flashing a set of hand signs that told the cop to perpetrate an unspeakable act on his own mother.

Santiago grinned and returned a big thumbs-up. "You tell me wassup, Eddie. Phone rings, and my night watch commander, he say to me, 'Chick, we got riders getting together like it's Ernesto Cepeda's funeral all over again. Some be coming over the Frankland from Saint Pete, some be coming out of Los Cuervos turf, and they all be heading for East Gate Mall.' I tell him everything be cool, but he say, 'Chick, go check it out.'"

Eduardo eyed the cop's windbreaker, which was zipped to the neck on a warm night, and said, "No disrespect, Officer Chick, but don't your night watch commander know this be the United States of America? That dick-brain ever read the Constitution? Like, freedom of assembly, you know? Or he be too busy giving blow jobs to drug dealers?"

Santiago turned pale and began to shift uneasily from foot to foot. "Hey, just doing my job, okay? So what's going down?"

Eduardo smirked. "You wearing a wire under that jacket, Officer Chick, or is your woman feeding you too good?"

Santiago looked like a man suddenly stricken with diarrhea. "Wire? No way, Eddie."

"Too bad," Eduardo replied. " 'Cause if you was, you don't be needing to remember what I'm going to tell you. Nothing's going down. *Nada.*"

"Then why all the cars?"

"We got a sick friend to see."

"All of you? At this time of night?"

"Thass right."

Santiago didn't believe Eduardo for one minute. On the other hand, if Los Cuervos was planning to bust heads or pick up a drug shipment, would they go in a convoy of almost forty cars?

"Listen, we want Smokey to chill," Eduardo said, "so maybe you can pass word we be taking the I-Four all the way up to Orlando? No one be speeding, no one be dropping trash out the window, so Smokey got no cause to hassle us. Just to make sure, some of us bros be packing these."

Santiago's eyes widened when he saw the object in Eduardo's hand. Then, remembering the miniaturized mike under his collar, he said, "A videocam?"

"Saved Rodney King's ass, didn't it? Yo, Officer Chick, this be a nice chat and all, but like can we hit the road before your buddies bust us for loitering?"

Santiago hesitated, then returned to his Blazer and reached for the radio.

A few seconds later, the lights atop the cruisers on Hillsborough went dark.

Eduardo turned the ignition key and said to Tejada, "The Man be such *putas* out in L.A. too?"

"All over, Eduardo. All over."

The low-riders and Large Quintanilla followed Eduardo out of the parking lot and down Hillsborough. They ramped onto Interstate 4 north, forming up in a single file that stretched more than three-quarters of a mile. Eduardo thereupon relinquished the point to settle into the Number Nine slot, with Quintanilla directly behind him. They were cruising at the posted speed limit of 65 when a pair of Florida Highway Patrol cars joined the parade, one at the head and the other bringing up the rear.

An hour later, the convoy courteously flashed turn signals and slowed to exit I-4 onto the Greenway. Begun during the go-go Eighties as part of a six-lane bypass around Orlando, the "Road to Nowhere," as locals called it, was the one section completed before the economy soured. The only people now using it lived in the handful of bedroom communities that developers had managed to finish before the real-estate market collapsed.

Eduardo turned up the volume on the police-band. Unless Smokeys were engaged in an active pursuit, they had to stick to highways and pass off suspicious vehicles to local units. How long would it take the two Highway Patrol assholes shadowing them to notice twenty low-riders peeling off and how long would it take Orlando PD to respond? More than ten minutes, and they miss all the action.

A few miles down the Greenway Eduardo spotted the road sign he had been looking for and said, "Make your call, Nacio."

Tejada took out his flip-phone and called home: "Yo, Leepi. Maggie on the line?"

"Sure is," Phillipa Walker replied.

"Great." Tejada looked over to Eduardo, who was holding up three fingers. "Give us three minutes, then do it and patch Maggie through."

"Three minutes," Walker repeated. "Yo, Nacio—good luck."

The lead Smokey and the first eight low-riders were already past the exit when Eduardo suddenly veered the

Mercury onto it without slowing or signaling. Large Quintanilla and the next twenty cars followed him up the ramp but the last eight low-riders stayed on the Greenway, followed by the second Smokey.

In the sideview Tejada saw that Large, as planned, was breaking off from the convoy and turning the Lincoln into a park-and-ride lot just off the interchange.

The Mercury and twenty low-riders had progressed deep into a residential neighborhood before the Smokeys tumbled to their great escape and all hell broke loose on the police-band radio.

A continent away Phillipa Walker, wearing a headset with a swingaway mouthpiece, kept an eye on the on-screen clock as she typed a command. Earlier in the day she had hacked the cellular-phone network servicing Orlando and pulled up a schematic identifying all the relay sites. Now she was back inside the network prepping her final move. "Fifteen seconds," she said into the mouthpiece. "You ready, girl?"

"Ready," replied Maggie Sepulveda.

"Okay, I'm going to put you on hold." Walker clicked HOLD in her telephone app, reactivated the window in which her hack was running, and hit ENTER. In Orlando the relay site that provided coverage to a particular southside residential neighborhood went dead. Now she zoomed the cursor back to her telephone app and clicked DIAL.

The ringing phone startled Helen Wagner awake. She groggily glanced at the illuminated dial of her alarm clock—4:12—then snapped on a light and picked up. "Hello?"

"Mrs. Helen Wagner?" said a young woman.

"Yes? Who is this . . ."

"Hold tight a sec, please."

A *click* and then Helen heard what sounded like distant thunder, over which a familiar voice was saying, "Hi, Mom."

"Maggie? Where are you calling from, a factory?"

"I'm on a plane, Mom. I . . ."

"I've been trying to get you for days," Helen said.

"I'm okay, Mom. But you're not. Listen, here's what I want you to do. . . ."

Outside Helen Wagner's town house, the street was empty except for a panel truck parked against one curb and a sedan parked against the other.

The man in the driver's seat of the panel truck was cursing softly as he continued to punch numbers into his cell phone. What a time for the fucker to cut out; a light had just come on in the subject's bedroom, abnormal behavior for this time of night, and he needed to coordinate contingency plans with the surveillance team in the sedan across the street.

"What's happening?" his partner asked sleepily from the back of the truck.

And then they heard an odd, throaty rumble washing toward them.

Several moments later they could finally make out the dark shapes that were the source of the sound: a column of low-riders, headlights off. The man in the driver's seat blinked in astonishment as he checked his sideview and saw an identical column approaching from the other end of the block.

The lead car of each column veered to the curb and stopped inches from his front and rear bumpers. Across the street, the other surveillance car was being similarly blocked.

The man in the driver's seat was reaching for the door handle when a third low-rider pulled alongside the truck, effectively trapping him inside.

A young Cuban cranked down his window, leaned out, and said, "Be cool, man. ¿Comprende?"

The man in the driver's seat nodded while his partner frantically punched numbers into a cell phone that still refused to work.

When Helen Wagner was pulling on a jogging suit she had heard a sound from her adolescence; now, opening her front door, she caught herself smiling at the familiar sight of wall-to-wall low-riders. Her neighbors probably weren't amused, though; lights were winking on all up and down the block.

A low, dark sedan pulled to a stop directly in front of her town house. Its passenger-side door swung open and a slender young Hispanic man with a cane got out and started up the walkway.

"Data?" she said.

"At your service, ma'am."

Helen locked the door and took his free arm. "Maggie says you'll explain what's going on?"

"Yes, ma'am. By the time we get where we're going, you be knowing as much as we do," Tejada replied, escorting Helen toward Eduardo's car.

"'Fifty-two Merc," she murmured as they drew nearer, her brief years with Jeff Kragen having taught her a thing or two about vintage cars. "She's a beauty."

The idling low-riders continued to hold their positions, pinioning in the two surveillance vehicles, as Helen and Nacio got in the Mercury. Then Eduardo flipped the driver of the panel truck a sardonic salute, turned on his headlights, and accelerated into the night.

Six minutes later two units of the Orlando PD converged on Helen Wagner's block in response to an advisory from the Highway Patrol about possible gang activity, as well as to 911 complaints about hot rods invading a residential neighborhood. By then, there was not a vehicle in sight. By then, Phillipa Walker had restored cell-phone service to the area. By then, Eduardo and his convoy were headed back south on I-4 toward Tampa. And by then, Ignacio Tejada and Helen Wagner were in Large Quintanilla's rented Lincoln, speeding north on I-4 toward Jacksonville.

·   ·   ·

THE sky to the east was pink with the new dawn as the jetliner from São Paulo taxied toward the American terminal at Miami International Airport. Maggie Sepulveda's watch read 6:22. If Data's scheme to pry her mother free of Century Chisholm's grasp had worked, he and she and Large Quintanilla were now airborne en route from Jacksonville through Atlanta to Los Angeles.

Would she have similar luck? Her flight had landed on schedule but it was still going to be a near thing. There was no other choice. Back in Los Angeles they had drawn up plans assuming she would be under surveillance aboard this plane; here in Miami, where she had two hours to kill before transferring to a connecting flight; and in Dallas, the final destination on her ticket.

The Muzak flooding the cabin gave way to one of the attendants droning out gate numbers for connecting flights. Maggie made a show of jotting down the information for Dallas.

The plane finally came to a stop. Getting off fast was hopeless; passengers had jammed the aisles long before the captain dimmed the seat-belt sign. Maggie reached into the overhead bin for her knapsack and took from it a green bandanna that she knotted around her neck. Acutely aware of the seconds ticking by—her leeway was now down to less than twenty-five minutes—she made herself resist the urge to begin climbing over seats.

The line eventually started to shuffle forward.

Up the jetway now, edging past slower passengers, hurrying through the gate area, and then she spotted a man in an orange baggage-handler's jumpsuit who sported a green Tres Equis bandanna just like hers. He was standing next to a metal door posted AUTHORIZED PERSONNEL ONLY.

Maggie headed straight for him.

As she neared, the man opened the door, then followed her through and locked it behind them.

They were in a windowless cinder-block corridor. Lying on the concrete floor was an orange jumpsuit, thoughtfully unzipped, and an upturned hard hat containing an envelope.

Someone began rattling the door handle.

She pulled two garments from her knapsack and stuffed in the envelope.

"*Ándale*," the man said, loping off down the corridor.

Behind her now, loud thumps on the locked metal door.

Maggie ripped off her T-shirt and jeans, stuffed them into her knapsack, then struggled into white hiking shorts and a black polo shirt. The man had already disappeared through the door at the end of the corridor. She climbed into the jumpsuit, jammed on the hard hat, shouldered her knapsack, and took off after him, struggling like a contestant on some cheapjack cable game show to zip up the jumpsuit as she ran.

Barging through the door and onto the tarmac, she saw the man ten feet away, sitting at the wheel of an idling baggage-cart tractor.

Maggie vaulted into the passenger seat and held on tight as the man popped the clutch and roared away from the American terminal.

At this hour, the first wave of early-morning departures were pushing back from their gates. The man never slowed as he weaved his way through the thicket.

Eight minutes later Maggie spotted a United Airlines 757 whose cargo-hold doors were pivoting shut as the baggage carts began trundling away. She tapped the man's shoulder and gestured questioningly at the plane.

He nodded, then flashed her a thumbs-up and a big smile.

She started unzipping the jumpsuit.

The man slalomed around the 757, braked to a halt alongside the United terminal, and hopped off to unlock a restricted-access door.

Maggie followed him into another windowless corridor and quickly peeled off the jumpsuit: "*Gracias.*"

"De nada," he replied, making rapid shooing motions. *"Ándale, ándale!"*

She sprinted up the corridor, stopping at the door to take several deep breaths, button her polo shirt, and dig out the envelope the man had given her. Inside were a ticket and a boarding pass issued to Jennifer Lerario, along with the requisite bogus ID cards. Her heartbeat back under two hundred, though barely, Maggie turned the handle and stepped into the gate area just in time to hear the final call for United's nonstop service to Los Angeles.

UNLESS there's something I'm missing," Rob Dillon said, his eyes swinging from Aurelia Wilkes to Leonard Reifsnyder to Mary Osteen, "Marx Dillon and Neil has no option but to resign the account."

Each of the surviving cofounders of Caduceus 21 looked as if she or he had been gut-shot. Either everyone's in it together, Dillon thought, or one of them deserves an Oscar. The officers of the health-care firm, two of whom had spent the previous day flying back to Knoxville for this emergency session, were staring with unseeing eyes at the documents covering the conference table. It had taken them several hours to wade through the material, breaking the profound silence only to query one another on technical matters. When the last person had finished the last page, there had been no discussion. After all, what was left to say?

"Our lawyers'll fax you something before the weekend's out," Dillon said. "Expect hardcopy with actual signatures Tuesday morning. You should also know that when I get back to New York, I'm making copies of these documents available to the police."

"They contain proprietary information," Osteen protested wearily.

"Not after our lawyers get done redacting them. What the cops get is Marx Dillon work product."

"I appreciate where you're coming from, Dillon," Reifsnyder said. "MedEx needs to go down, like yesterday. From what you've shown us, we deserve to be put out of our misery too. But can't you give us a little time to make the funeral arrangements? Have you considered what this is going to do to the health-care system? Millions of subscribers left without coverage, our affiliates suddenly losing all our centralized services? It's going to be chaos."

"It's no messier than if Teddy had lived," replied Dillon, who had in fact pondered just that problem with Nigel Neil. "Soon as we see his findings, it's *adiós*, placement. Without fresh money, you guys are in the toilet. All this does is flush the bowl faster. And if anybody in this company had anything to do with Teddy's death . . ."

Aurelia Wilkes's eyes flared: "You're out of line, Mr. Dillon."

"If anybody in C-Twenty-One had anything to do with Teddy's death or Maggie's disappearance—you will answer for it. To the law and to me, personally." Dillon stood, grabbed his overcoat, and stalked from the room.

The three cofounders of Caduceus 21 remained seated.

Mary Osteen gnawed on a fingernail.

Len Reifsnyder continued to stare at the printouts on the table, at the ashes of his dream.

Aurelia Wilkes scribbled a few notes before declaring, in a firm voice, "I feel I know you both well enough that we don't need to discuss MedEx beyond observing that perhaps we were all remiss for not looking a gift horse in the mouth. Our books are another matter. I most certainly had no idea they were being fudged."

Reifsnyder studied her for a few moments, then turned to Osteen: "Why, Mare?"

Osteen lowered her hand and examined the fingernail. "You're both bright. Figure it out yourself."

"Like Teddy did?" said Wilkes. "What do you know about his death?"

"Nothing. Don't be an asshole, Aurelia. Tweaking software is one thing, but I don't do murder."

"I'm not understanding why the PEI had to be tweaked," Reifsnyder said. "When we were developing it, the numbers worked."

"They don't in the real world."

"The numbers don't work," Wilkes said, "or we didn't try hard enough to make them work?"

Osteen sighed heavily and swiveled her chair around to look out the window. "We talked the talk but we wouldn't walk the walk. No heroic intervention on preemies weighing less than a thousand grams, right? An autistic eight-year-old needs a liver? Sorry, not at C-Twenty-One. Patient signs a 'do not resuscitate' and some second cousin objects, we go with the patient. Grandma has terminal cancer but chemotherapy can give her another painful eight months? No way.

"Does all that sound familiar? It should, because that's why we started this company, to rationalize health care. But then we started signing up affiliates and they all wanted a mechanism for case-by-case appeals. So we caved."

Osteen swung around to face Wilkes. "How many exemptions did you personally sign off on, Aurelia? Three a week? Four? There's fifteen million a year.

"And Len—remember in 'Ninety-five when you came to us and said the other chains were raiding our best physicians? How you needed a war chest to make counteroffers? There's twenty-five million a year, conservatively speaking.

"Meanwhile, every market we're in, there's some schlockmeister ready to underbid us. What the hell was I supposed to do, buy an engraving plant and start printing counterfeits?"

Wilkes's eyes misted. "Jesus Christ! I did not help start C-Twenty-One to participate in a Ponzi scheme."

"Maybe I'm being dense, Mare," Reifsnyder said, "but

how long did you think you could pull off this high-wire act?''

"Five years. Until we had the country's best damn transplant network in place, and swine organs started coming online."

"And then the numbers would have worked?" he asked incredulously.

Osteen nodded.

"You bet the farm on pigs?" said Wilkes, her voice rising.

"Aurelia, if I hadn't done what I did, there wouldn't have been a farm to bet. The regressive analysis Teddy performed was right on the money. C-Twenty-One would've gone under no later than first quarter, 'Ninety-six."

Silence descended on the conference room again, broken only by Wilkes blowing her nose.

IT wasn't like Nacio to be so tight-lipped, thought Phillipa Walker as she watched her pal attacking his keyboard. The gray of dusk had long since given way to the black velvet of a Los Angeles evening. Inside Ignacio Tejada's study, a platter of cold cuts lay mostly unnibbled as Walker and the others—Nguyen-Anh Dupree, Maggie Sepulveda, and Helen Wagner—communed with their thoughts, seeking an answer that probably didn't exist. Only Nacio seemed to have a sense of purpose; for more than an hour now, he had been grimly launching one hacking sortie after another against who knew whom.

This most peculiar day was certainly drawing to a most frustrating end.

In midmorning she and Doc had ridden out in Javier Tejada's limo to Los Angeles International Airport. Maggie staggered off the plane from Miami clutching a sheaf of airline stationery on which she had composed a meticulous play-by-play of her round-trip to Brazil. Shortly thereafter Nacio, Helen, and Large Quintanilla arrived.

The reunion between Maggie and her mother had been emotional—though it was hard to tell if Helen was more shaken by her daughter's adventures or her buzz cut. Yet the four travelers were understandably listless and fatigued, the rush of escaping Chisholm's clutches dulled by their journey across multiple time zones. Doc had quickly prescribed naps for all.

Walker whiled away part of the afternoon typing up Maggie's handwritten notes and printing them out. The encounter with Century Chisholm read like the script for a trashy B-flick—except it wasn't fiction.

The mother had been the first to wake. Resilient lady, Walker thought. Plus a quick study; since leaving her town house, Helen had elicited enough information from Nacio to bring herself up to speed on Caduceus 21 and MedEx. Once Maggie and Nacio rejoined the living, the five of them had repaired to the study.

The council of war had three issues to decide.

The first, Caduceus 21, had been a no-brainer. If the senior partners of Marx Dillon failed to act promptly on the contents of the packet sent them by Maggie, she herself would make public the information that cost Teddy Quereshi his life. Either way, the health-care firm's vaunted PEI would be discredited and Wilkes, Osteen, and Reifsnyder driven from the industry.

MedEx had also required minimal discussion thanks to Walker's brainstorm. Buzzie Sepulveda had pronounced her ingenious plan workable and gotten from Anson Horton two pieces of information: a Net address for the Department of Justice's ultrafast T1 port and a valid visitor's password.

It was the third issue—Century Chisholm—that buffaloed them. She and Doc had spent much of their long vigil searching the files siphoned from Dallas for evidence implicating him in MedEx's murderous activities. Some of the e-mail traffic between Chisholm and Strand was suggestive, but they'd found no smoking gun.

"Maybe we settle for nailing MedEx and C-Twenty-

One," Doc had reluctantly concluded. "Maybe two out of three is good enough." As hard as Maggie fought that point, in the end she had been forced to accept it: "I don't see how Anson can touch him. I think the son of a bitch is beyond the law."

It was then that Nacio had quietly taken a printout of Maggie's trip notes to his box, jacked in earphones, and gone to work.

Walker heard a final burst of typing, the purr of a laser printer, then silence. She looked up to see her pal remove his earphones, fetch several sheets from the printer, and swivel his chair around to face the others.

Tejada needed a few moments to collect his thoughts; in the past eighty minutes he had roamed the Net from MedEx and Caduceus 21 to three sites in Brazil. Finally he announced, "Yo, I know who the old geezer really be. Haven't figured out how to gift-wrap him for the Man, but I got a way to pay the motherfucker back big-time. Sorry about my language, Mrs. Wagner."

Helen waved a dismissive hand.

"Thing about Chisholm is his hubris," Tejada began, "which be what them ancient Greeks called too much pride. He don't even bother lying to Maggie or trying to hide things from her. Like, that phone number she sees at his house? I go São Paulo white pages and run it. Belongs to a 'C. Bengstrom.' That story about buying the construction company from his boss, Sasaki? I go yellow pages and yo, there be a construction company called 'Sasaki and Bengstrom.' That story about the nonprofit foundation? I go Delaware and damn if I don't find a site listing all nonprofits registered in the state. The initials of that A.L.B. Foundation stand for Ada and Louis Bengstrom.

"Knowing all this lets me work out how the old geezer be making trips to São Paulo without a passport. He don't need a U.S. passport 'cause he got one from Brazil, under the name Bengstrom."

Tejada paused to sip some Jolt! "Now Bengstrom don't

be a name like Jones, so how come I seen it lately? I try GOODTOGO—the MedEx queue with all them Big Willies wanting new body parts?—and bingo, there be a file called CBENGSTROM. Funny thing is, the fields for routine data—address, phone number, age, doctor's name? All blank. Not the medical history. C. Bengstrom be needing a new heart 'cause of something called 'endocarditis.' "

"Of course," Dupree interjected. "If his endocarditis is sufficiently advanced to indicate a transplant, his circulation would be severely impeded. That explains the vest and the roaring fire—he'd feel almost numb with cold."

"Next I go SEECUBED," Tejada continued, "to check out that list of organs they want ASAP? Old geezer's on it, and looks like they found him a new heart."

The others in the room stiffened.

"Ain't perfect, only the best available. There be a tag on the Priority List, 'Triple bonus for better match. Offer expires seventeen hundred hours GMT, twenty-three November.' "

"Which is when?" asked Walker.

" 'Nother eleven hours," he replied. "Know how we figure MedEx got two guys doing the organs? Thirteen, fourteen hours from now, that Haidak dude be on call in Santa Fe and that Thai guy be ripping out a heart. Hers."

Tejada passed around one of the sheets fresh from his printer. The black-and-white photograph, as grainy as a newswire mug shot and as stiff as a yearbook picture, was of a shy, bespectacled young Asian woman. "Downloaded this from MedEx. Suttatip Variporn, age twenty-three, grew up in Chanthaburi, Thailand. Now she be teaching nursery school in Bangkok. Single, so maybe nobody misses her too soon."

"Where is Chisholm at this moment?" asked Maggie.

Tejada shrugged. "Brazil, Santa Fe, somewhere in between—does it matter? We can't get at him, if that's what you be thinking."

Maggie reached for the phone: "Then we've got to alert Anson Horton."

"Why for?" said Tejada. "Like, the Man's gonna send FBI agents to Bangkok?"

Maggie was so distraught she helped herself to one of Dupree's cigarettes. "Nguyen-Anh, any idea who MedEx uses to snatch people in Thailand?"

He nodded glumly. "According to the disbursement records, they bought themselves an army general. Basically he's in business to protect the opium traffic out of the Golden Triangle but no one cares as long as his men keep beating up student protesters. The guy's more powerful than the king."

"But we can't just do nothing," Helen Wagner said.

Of those in the room, Phillipa Walker alone caught the telltale glimmer in Ignacio Tejada's eyes. "Yo, Nacio, you said you had an idea."

"Yeah. Nothing I'm proud of but like they say, desperate times, desperate measures." He picked up a slim paperback and showed them the cover. It was *Iphigenia in Aulis,* a tragedy by Euripides. "Iphigenia be the daughter of Agamemnon, this king who could teach Bengstrom some things about hubris. Agamemnon puts together an army to sail against his enemy, see, only some time back, he pisses off a god. Does he say sorry? Like, right. So now the gods don't be filling his sails with wind unless he does something way harsh.

"What I cooked up also be way harsh—maybe worse. But worse than MedEx? That's something we all have to decide. Anyway, I know how to take the old geezer's toy, this killing machine he built, and turn it back on him. We got to vote on it, though. One 'no,' one abstention, I leave it alone. Fair enough?"

The others nodded.

Tejada spelled out his plan to save Suttatip Variporn of Bangkok by substituting another involuntary donor.

No one jumped up with congratulatory high fives but to his surprise, no one tossed their cookies either. Instead, after a long pause, they began dissecting his plan like a jury who had convicted the defendant and moved on to the penalty phase: life imprisonment or death?

Dupree's immediate concern was practical. It didn't matter what Data did inside the MedEx servers, he observed; the company would verify donor-recipient compatibility before unleashing its death squads and harvesting teams.

Tejada passed him printouts of two documents he had hacked.

Dupree studied the tissue-typing data, then said, "Close. A much more positive match than the teacher."

Helen Wagner wanted assurance that Chisholm/Bengstrom possessed full knowledge of MedEx's murderous trade.

Tejada took a printout of a private-client file from GOODTOGO, circled the medical history field, and passed it to her. In 1993 C. Bengstrom had ordered a new liver that MedEx delivered after tearing it from a young Romanian man.

Phillipa Walker was concerned that Nacio's plan meant a delay in pulling the plug on MedEx, putting additional victims at risk.

"No way, Leepi," Tejada replied. "According to their e-mail, this Haidak be putting off a trip to Eastern Europe to go to Santa Fe. The Thai dude, Krapayoon, he got nothing scheduled after doing the teacher. Long as we act the moment they zip a new heart in the old geezer, everything be cool."

"I'm sorry, everything won't be cool." Maggie had remained silent up to now, struggling to comprehend how the others—including her own mother—could callously ignore the ramifications of Data's plan. "What gives us the right to sentence an innocent bystander to death? Did you try the legitimate channels? They may have a heart somewhere that's compatible, and we could . . ."

"Same zero-sum game, girl," Tejada replied softly. "Say there be one. The old geezer gets it, someone else don't. Like I said, my plan ain't nothing to be proud of.

Give us an extra day, maybe we come up with something better. But right now, we got as much wiggle room as Lourdes got brains. By the way, Maggie, I did log into UNOS. *Nada.*"

Maggie looked beseechingly at her mother. "Can't we sit this one out? Isn't one life-or-death decision enough? God knows we paid our dues with Petey."

"Actually, sweetie, Petey was about death with dignity," Helen Wagner replied, looking old beyond her years. "This is tougher because it really does involve life or death."

"This isn't easy for any of us, Maggie," said Walker. "We know it's even harder for you because you're the one who's been to Brazil. I'm asking you to think about this, though. No matter what we do, someone dies to give Chisholm a new heart. If we adopt Nacio's suggestion, yes, it's an innocent bystander. If we do nothing it's that girl in Thailand. Isn't she an innocent bystander too?"

Maggie turned to Dupree. "How can you sit there so calmly? How can you even consider such a course of action? You took an oath when you became a doctor. This violates it."

"Don't assume I'm necessarily voting 'yes,'" he replied. "Second, voting 'yes' wouldn't violate my oath. Duchess's take is dead-on, which means we're facing a classic case of triage. In theory, the decisions on who lives and who dies should be based solely on survival probability. You go to a crash and find Einstein with a ten-percent chance and Jack the Ripper with a twelve-percent chance, the book says you go to work on Jack the Ripper. In the real world, the calls are gut-wrenching and messy, about the hardest we can be asked to make. Like now. All I can say, Maggie, is follow your conscience."

Maggie slumped back, drained.

As the silence in the room lengthened, Walker looked at her watch. Finally she began handing around pencils and paper. "Maybe we should take a vote. That girl's down to ten hours and counting."

Two minutes later, the others reflexively passed their folded slips to Helen Wagner. She opened them one by one, laying each faceup on the table.

All five were "yea"s.

"Anyone be changing their mind?" asked Tejada. "Last call."

Receiving no response, he swiveled back around to his box. It took less than a minute to log into MedEx, switch to the SEECUBED queue, and call up the Priority File. It took less than thirty seconds to scroll to private client "C. Bengstrom" and add a single line. As soon as Tejada stored the file, the new data was automatically e-mailed to MedEx procurers on four continents.

Maggie said, to no one in particular, "May God have mercy on us all."

T H U R S D A Y
N O V E M B E R 2 6

PHILLIPA Walker studied her reflection in the bathroom mirror and saw why her boss, Glen Piscatelli, had called her into his office yesterday, on the eve of the four-day holiday weekend. He was frankly worried. She had visibly lost weight over the past month, he said, and had seemed especially unfocused and withdrawn the last three days. Was the *2001* project burning her out? If so, would she accept a two-week vacation anywhere in the world, courtesy of MorpHaus?

Walker was touched by the offer but declined it. Time off might renew her body, but how did you steam-clean a soul?

Her depression and guilt had come to a head at lunchtime the previous day. That was when CNN issued its first bulletin on a story that traced directly to the irrevocable decision made in Ignacio Tejada's study. The stunning broad-daylight kidnapping, captured in part on videotape, suggested that the five of them had acted in time; that young Ms. Suttatip Variporn was still teaching nursery school in Bangkok, unaware how close the MedEx scythe had passed. Yet after hearing the news Walker locked her office door and wept for ten minutes. Small wonder her boss had been concerned.

It was nearly time to leave for Thanksgiving dinner so she went to her work alcove and booted up the PowerBook. With Nacio still short-stroking his term paper, she had volunteered to monitor the MedEx net.

Dial-up, modem breath, connection, prompt.

Walker typed in Duane Strand's password and began scanning the overnight e-mail. There was a message posted to Strand's personal mailbox, with cc's to GOOD-TOGO and SEECUBED:

> *Operation a success. Patient stable and recuperating. Delete Bengstrom request from priority list.*
> —*Haidak*

Confirmation that rough justice had been served, she thought. What had Maggie said the other night—may God have mercy on us all? Amen.

Walker quickly showered and dressed, then packed up the PowerBook and headed for the Tejada compound. She had been there only once since Sunday night because everyone else was also behaving like a poster child for Prozac.

Heady aromas greeted her as she entered Javier Tejada's kitchen; Javier's wife was preparing the holiday feast with help from Nguyen-Anh Dupree and Helen Wagner.

"Wassup, Duchess," Dupree said.

"The fat lady sang."

Dupree and Helen exchanged glances, then wiped their hands and followed Walker across the courtyard.

Nacio was hard at work on his paper and Maggie was sprawled on the couch, typing on her laptop.

Walker unzipped the PowerBook and popped Haidak's e-mail up on-screen.

When everybody finished reading it Tejada said, in a quiet voice, "Yo, girl, you ready to do Code Boy?"

Walker nodded. She seated herself at Nacio's desk, jacked a telephone cord into the PowerBook, and auto-dialed MedEx. Upon logging in, she called up the system's activity log. Jefferson Leong was still dialing up from Queens; good, Code Boy must be carving the turkey with his family. She switched over to the box he kept running around the clock in his Las Colinas condo.

It took fifteen seconds to copy onto Leong's hard drive a macro she had written the previous night.

The macro held three sequences of commands that would take twenty to thirty minutes to execute.

The first would replace Leong's BIOS, or Basic Input/Output System. This little app, launched at every PC boot-up, performed routine initialization diagnostics like checking memory and identifying attached devices. Only if everything was in order could the user go on to launch an operating system such as Windows. That was the job of a conventional BIOS; Walker's did something alto-gether different.

The second command sequence would methodically wipe Leong's box, as well as all attached backup drives, so thoroughly that not even Code Boy could reconstruct the data.

The third command sequence would instruct Leong's hard drive to grind itself to death as its head-arm tried to access a cylinder that did not exist. Writing it was a cinch; all she had to do was drag-and-drop the Pit Bull code.

"You know, this is sad," Walker said as she typed a command. "Hackers have pretty much the same philoso-phy as doctors: 'Do no harm.' Harshest thing I've ever done online is flame someone—you know, beam 'em some vile e-mail. Leong deserves this, and more, but it still doesn't feel good."

With a shrug, she hit ENTER and started the macro run-ning.

Jefferson Leong would return home to a crashed box. There'd be no way for him to know its data was erased, its hard drive smashed, so he would reboot. Instead of performing routine initialization diagnostics, Walker's custom BIOS would flash on-screen the machine's last message:

> *Yo, Code Boy—This be no accident.*
> *Keep acting like a Klingon, we'll fry you again.*

Walker broke the remote link and said, "Your turn, Nacio."

Tejada looked at Dupree. "Doc, you started this, you finish it. I'll ground-control you through it."

Dupree hesitated, then sat down at Tejada's machine.

Tejada's first sequence of instructions hacked Dupree into the company that provided long-distance service to the Connecticut home of Duane Strand. The next sequence tricked the company's billing software into thinking that it was Strand, and not Dupree, now dialing up a Manhattan number.

Two rings, modem breath, and then the server in the MedEx office on Sixth Avenue answered with a prompt.

Tejada read off Strand's login and password.

Dupree typed them and hit ENTER.

Strand's personalized desktop popped up on-screen.

Surveying a dozen quick-launch icons, Dupree clicked MEDEX NET.

A message popped up on-screen:

WELCOME, DUANE STRAND

Dupree popped the MedEx file-transfer app up on-screen and, under Tejada's tutelage, began filling in the command fields. He entered the Net address for the Department of Justice's T1 port that Assistant U.S. Attorney Anson Horton had provided. Then he entered a valid

DOJ visitor's password that was also courtesy of Horton. Finally, by typing a lengthy string of characters supplied by Tejada, he specified exactly what data was to be sent.

"Do it, Doc," said Nacio.

Dupree spotted the cursor on SEND and clicked.

Down in Dallas, the MedEx servers began to transmit all files in five restricted-access queues—BODYBAGS, DEEP-SIX, GOODTOGO, PAYMASTR, and SEECUBED—to the Department of Justice. When DOJ sysops went to check out this unsolicited core dump, they would find evidence of a murderous conspiracy. MedEx was sure to claim that its proprietary data had been improperly obtained but the frame-up conceived by Duchess was flawless: There existed an irrefutable electronic audit trail that showed the firm's own CEO had personally initiated the transfer from his home in Connecticut.

"Poetic justice," Dupree said softly as he logged off. "MedEx 'volunteers' people to donate organs, we 'volunteer' their secrets."

"How long will it take for the information to go from one computer to the other?" asked Helen Wagner.

"On a T1 connect," said Tejada, "maybe twenty minutes."

"I hope they're not all taking a long holiday weekend in Washington," Helen fretted.

"There'll be a team of experts on duty," Maggie said. "Anson made sure of that. By noon tomorrow, those bastards at MedEx are going to know how it feels to have your guts ripped out."

A S twilight fell Helen Wagner paused by a window to look out at two silhouettes sitting in the courtyard of the Tejada compound. The daughter she had raised never made it easy on herself when it came to men. Nguyen-Anh Dupree was okay, though, even if he was smoking himself to an early grave.

Maggie saw her mother's shadow move away from the

window and for some reason felt as relieved as a teenager successfully sneaking home after curfew. Trying to keep her voice casual, she said to Dupree, "I overheard you on the phone after dinner tonight. You've booked a ticket to Mexico."

He nodded.

"When?"

"Tomorrow," Dupree said. "I arranged coverage of the clinic for two weeks, and I've already been gone eighteen days."

"How much longer does your tour there run?"

"I don't know. MSF likes to rotate us, and I've been in Chiapas a long time by their standards."

"Any idea where you go next?"

"Haven't a clue. You?"

Maggie sighed. "Hard to say. It depends partly on when Mom and I can leave here. Anson's offering witness protection but neither of us is really up for joining the undead, so we have to wait for them to roll up Chisholm and Strand.

"Remember seeing me typing this morning up in Data's study, before we dropped the hammer on MedEx and Leong? My letter of resignation, which gets mailed the day we go home—assuming Marx Dillon survives that long. Evidently it's like the *Titanic* back there. Duchess snuck me onto the system on Tuesday with sysop privileges, so I could read everyone's e-mail. The partners are taking turns suing and firing each other. Associates and secretaries, including mine, are quitting right and left. One thing I've got to do is help some of them land on their feet.

"Know what's interesting, Nguyen-Anh? Everybody's figured out this crisis is linked to that abandoned cab and my disappearance. Some people have surprised me, like Rob Dillon, who has a lot more honor than I gave him credit for. Others don't seem to give a damn whether I'm alive or not."

"Tough way to find out who your friends are." Dupree fished out his cigarettes and offered her one.

"No thanks," she said. "Have you thought about quitting?"

"MSF?"

"No, silly. Cigarettes."

"Sure. All the time. But if I'd given up smoking, we'd have died in Central Park."

"Touché," Maggie laughed.

"So whether or not there's a Marx Dillon, you're not part of it. Then what?"

She shrugged. "Mom's making noises about me moving to Orlando. If I wanted a lobotomy I'd see a brain surgeon, but it's tempting, at least for the next several months. New York winters can be harsh."

After a lengthy silence Dupree said, "Would you consider coming down to Chiapas? There's something I'd like very much to share with you."

"Again?" she replied with a knowing chuckle.

"That, too," he said, grateful she couldn't see his blush in the darkness. "Actually, I was thinking of some Calvados I've been saving."

"For what?"

When Dupree spoke again, his voice was unexpectedly thick: "The night Don Joaquin told me Guillermo was missing, I swore I wouldn't finish that bottle until I'd nailed the fuckers who did it."

Maggie reached up and laid a soft hand on his cheek. It was moist.

He snuffled twice, then cleared his throat. "What we've done isn't right. But damn it, it isn't wrong, either."

She started to say something, but didn't.

They heard a vehicle enter the compound and park by the gatehouse.

A minute later Ignacio Tejada and Phillipa Walker rounded the corner. Their trip to a store that specialized in out-of-town newspapers seemed to have been a success, judging by the stack she was carrying.

"Yo, guys," Tejada said. "Time to send that evil geezer a message."

Maggie and Dupree rose and followed them inside.

SATURDAY
NOVEMBER 28

WHEN Century Chisholm planned his dream house in Santa Fe, he made certain his bedroom would be a pleasant place to convalesce. It was situated in the northeast corner of the building, its large windows overlooking a majestic mountainscape dominated by distant Baldy Peak. And, of course, the room was large enough to easily accommodate a regulation hospital bed and an array of medical equipment.

One of the devices, a pulse monitor, chirped languidly in counterpoint to the soft samba filling the room. Chisholm had been permitted to install a CD player programmed with soothing vintage discs by Getz and Gilberto, Nasciemento, and Gil. However, Lester Haidak was denying him access to both a television and a computer for another four days. It was disconcerting for Chisholm to be out of touch with the world and with his empire for so long, yet he didn't really mind. Recuperating from a transplant wasn't getting any easier.

Tomorrow, the fourth day after the operation, they

were switching him from intravenous feeding to bland solids. At the same time he could begin getting out of bed and shuffling to the bathroom, a godsend because Chisholm hated using bedpans and pisspots. Dare he hope of returning to São Paulo for the annual party at the *fazenda* that celebrated both the New Year and his birthday?

Haidak hadn't ruled out the possibility. Thanks to the eleventh-hour availability of an unusually compatible heart, the procedure seemed an unqualified success: no sign of rejection, no infection, no fever, no side effects from the immunosuppressant cocktail. In fact, Haidak would be leaving Santa Fe on Monday, flying back once a week for the next month. Chisholm's recovery would be supervised on a day-to-day basis by Marta, the extremely pleasant and capable operating-room nurse who had accompanied Haidak here, and two highly regarded local RNs.

A short while later, the sound of vehicles coming up the driveway woke Chisholm from a light drowse. There was some kind of brief fuss, then the cars drove away. He sighed, sipped some water, and fell back to sleep.

It was early afternoon when he became aware of the bedroom door opening.

Natalie, the housekeeper, was peering into the room.

"It's okay," he said. *"Eu estou acordado."*

Natalie put on a brave smile but she was at her wit's end from the events of the last few days. On the heels of *Tío*'s surgery there was news from home so tragic even the American television was covering it. Then, just hours ago, four carloads of men had come to the ranch and taken away Dr. Lester and his nice nurse, Marta, in handcuffs. But these calamities must be kept from *Tío* until he regained his strength. Natalie entered the room, an overnight-delivery packet in her hand. As she gave it to him she noticed that the water carafe by his bed was almost empty so she went off to refill it.

Chisholm checked the waybill for a return address.

There was none. Odd, he thought, Federal Express didn't usually slip up like that. But when he unsealed the packet and withdrew its contents, his face crinkled with pleasure.

It was a recent front page of a major São Paulo tabloid, mounted on cardboard backing. Elspeth had never looked lovelier. Why had *Gazeta Mercantil* run a large four-color photograph of the gal? Did she win some sort of award? The anonymous sender was playing it coy, having covered up the headline with a rectangular panel of opaque paper.

As Chisholm lifted the panel the pulse monitor began chirping in doubletime.

> *¡ESTRELA DE GLOBO*
> *SEQUESTRADO!*

Elspeth kidnapped? How could that be? Like all Brazilians of wealth and fame, the gal traveled with a complement of bodyguards. Had they gotten to her while she was out covering a story and protected by only those pantywaist technicians in the crew? And when did this foul crime happen? The paper carried the date of Wednesday, November 25, so it must have been on Tuesday—even as he was fasting for his surgery.

Chisholm willed his mind to more practical matters, like the size of the ransom the kidnappers would demand. That's what it was, all right; hell, snatching rich folks was a growth industry in Brazil. Ten million U.S.? Fifteen? No problem, he could arrange it. His concentration was broken when his fingers brushed a flap of loose paper on the reverse side of the cardboard backing.

At that moment one of the nurses burst into the room, breathless from her dash across the vast house in response to the alarming pulse monitor. Her eyes widened as the machine's chirps continued to quicken, but then that ominous warning was lost beneath the howl of an animal in mortal pain.

For the yellow Post-it on the reverse side carried a handwritten message that tore through Century Chisholm's wounded chest like shrapnel:

Say howdy to the donor of your new heart.
   —*The friends of Guillermo Chacon*

I am grateful to these friends and colleagues, some of whom patiently tried to clarify technical issues and some of whom patiently tried to clarify my story and prose:

Ron Arias
Marion Bachrach, Esq.
Sofiya Balta
Lev Fruchter
Jerry Goodwin
Sallie Gouverneur
Ann Harris
George Kappakas, M.D.
Frank Kendig
Terry McGarry
Patricia Roberts
David G. Sánchez
Rodger Searfoss, M.D.
Angela Thornton
Rob Wood, M.D.

ABOUT THE AUTHOR

TONY CHIU was born in Shanghai and graduated from the University of Michigan. He has worked in all areas of media, from being a writer and editor at *The New York Times* and *People* to desktop publishing and documentaries. Chiu, author of the recent book *CBS: The First 50 Years*, is completing his next novel, *Tombstones*.

PHILLIP MARGOLIN

The *New York Times* bestselling author

THE BURNING MAN
____57495-7 $6.99/$8.99 Canada

AFTER DARK
____56908-2 $6.99/$8.99 Canada

THE LAST INNOCENT MAN
____56979-1 $6.99/$8.99 Canada

HEARTSTONE
____56978-3 $6.99/$8.99 Canada

GONE, BUT NOT FORGOTTEN
____56903-1 $6.99/$8.99 Canada